Death
Pans Out

Death
Pans Out

Ashna Graves

Poisoned Pen Press

First U. S. Trade Paperback Edition 2007

10 9 8 7 6 5 4 3 2 1

Library of Congress Catalog Card Number: 2006933106

ISBN 13: 978-1-59058-475-0   Trade Paperback

Poisoned Pen Press
6962 E. First Ave., Ste. 103
Scottsdale, AZ 85251
www.poisonedpenpress.com
info@poisonedpenpress.com

Printed in the United States of America

For Duncan Thomas, who would rather find moonworts than gold but who never lost interest in the story.

And in memory of Allen Throop, who got me to the mine, and Bob Kroeger, who was already there and is the original Skipper Dooley.

Chapter One

September 1991

The opportunity Burtie had been waiting for came on a Saturday when his partner went into town and did not return for the night. Hoping they would come while he was alone at the cabin, Burtie sat up late, and sometime after midnight he heard them. He headed up the lane walking fast, boots crunching on the rocky ground. There was no reason to be quiet until he reached the canyon road, when the sounds ceased abruptly.

He also stopped, and listened with his head bent. Lying in bed on other nights, he had heard the same pattern of distant rumbling and banging, always ending with this sudden silence. By his calculations, they could not be far away, although there was nothing up the creek, no reason at all to go there in the middle of the night.

Moving slowly now, placing his feet with care, he followed the dirt road up the canyon. It wound in and out with the shape of the land, climbing gently, every curve familiar to his feet, just as the smells of cooling pine and sage were familiar. He listened hard but heard no sound that did not belong to the desert night.

He came to a spur road, a pale track of quartz gravel leading off to the left away from the creek, and hesitated, considering it. The spur was no more than a hundred yards long, most of its length visible in the light of the stars. No sound or movement broke the stillness, and the dimly illuminated outlines of rocks and trees were familiar and as they should be.

Walking on, he kept to the high center between the ruts where his boots were as quiet as slippers in the dust. There was another spur not far ahead. Although he hadn't been up it for years, he knew that it ran parallel to the canyon road for about a quarter of a mile, separated from it by a pine thicket.

The entrance was bright like the first spur, but the track soon entered dense shadow between the canyon wall on the left and the trees on the right. A few paces into the dark he stopped to let his eyes adjust. His right hand went to his hip and massaged it in a gesture that had become habitual. He was old. He could not keep up this mountain goat life forever—but what else was there for him to do, where could he go? He didn't want to be anywhere else on the planet.

I've already been.

The thought made him smile in the dark, grimly, but also with the satisfaction of having done what he had to, of making the best of a bad draw. If he'd expected luck to get him anywhere, he might as well have died the first time. His only worry was Orson. If something happened, what sort of life would Orson have at the mine? He wouldn't be able to keep it up alone, but he might find a new life, a better life. And Enid would help him. Dear Enid. And Frances…He would write to Frances tomorrow, without fail. The thought of his sister brought a rush of affection and regret; he had let the silence go on for far too long, but now he would go to her in person to make amends and tell the truth at last.

Pushing his hands into his jacket pockets he listened again to the night, but heard nothing, not even wind. They must have gone farther up the canyon road. Or they might be standing close by in the dark, listening just as he was, waiting for another sound of movement. Burtie felt a chill start along his spine but he stiffened and set his face in lines that did not admit fear. He had to know what was going on here late at night where there was no possible reason for anyone to be.

Feeling the way with his feet, he continued up the rough track, wishing he'd used the road recently enough to know its condition, but there had been no reason to go up a minor spur to nowhere. He was long past the days of exploration, of choosing new walking routes just to see what was there, although now and again he did still hike to the top of Billie Mountain—the top of the known world. Again he smiled in the dark.

The next moment he stopped to listen. Was that a click of stone on stone? The prickling ran its course this time, flashing up his back and neck before he could control it. Immobile, straining to see, he waited and soon heard it again, the faint slither of movement, then the scuff of a boot or maybe something dragging.

He studied the blackness ahead, identified a denser black shape, and said quietly, "Whoever's there, I mean no harm. I'm from the mine down the way."

Chapter Two

Jeneva Leopold leaned on the axe handle and bent her head to listen. A breeze stirred the pines, a bird called from upstream, a squirrel gnawed the antlers nailed around the roofline of the woodshed. The evening was perfect, just as she had come to expect, perfect, that is, except for a sound she did not want to hear. The low growl of an engine could mean only one thing. A vehicle was coming up Billie Creek Road. The engine, throaty like a truck, revved, stuttered, and revved again. It was climbing, dropping gears as the canyon grew steeper, the sound fading and swelling with the curves and dips in the road. Soon it would reach the turnoff to the cabin.

Jeneva spun toward the woodshed, but with only three walls it didn't offer much cover. She could lock herself in the cabin or go into the woods—how ridiculous to run away simply to avoid company. It was too late now in any case. The vehicle had turned down the cabin lane and would be here before she could grab a jacket and get out of sight.

With a quick, decisive swing, she raised the axe and let it drop so that the blade stuck in the chopping block. She stepped away from the woodshed to look up the lane, and as she ran her fingers through her hair a white truck topped the rise behind the cabin. Seconds later it eased into the packed earth dooryard and stopped beside her. An unsmiling man with pale blue eyes studied her through the open window. Blond hair streaked with gray hung long around a sunburned face netted with fine lines, the skin stretched tight over his jaw and cheekbones. His nose was crooked from an accident or maybe violence, a long-ago bar brawl where she easily pictured him throwing fast punches. The cut-off sleeves of his white T-shirt revealed biceps that clearly had been mighty but now were wiry with age.

The stranger returned her look with a flat stare. "In seventeen years coming out here," he said with slow, clear enunciation, "I didn't see one single woman, not one."

"This was my uncle's claim," Jeneva said calmly despite the hostility in his voice, and the rush of blood up her back. "If you've been coming out here for seventeen years, you must have known him. Matthew Burt?"

"The one that disappeared? You bet."

They looked away at the same instant, the stranger at the cabin, Neva at the trim camper on the back of the truck, and the small trailer hitched on behind. Like the truck, the camper was white and as clean as it could be after navigating Billie Creek Road.

"Are you a miner?" she said to end the silence.

"Hell, no, lady." He gunned the engine and dropped a hand onto the gear stick. "I aim to camp on this creek tonight. You have any problem with that?"

Neva looked down the rutted lane toward where it ended at Billie Creek. There was a rustic campsite there in a small stand of pine and aspen, with a fire ring and rough tables. The mining claim was on Forest Service land, so the camp was technically open to the public, but it had not occurred to her that someone might use it. "The mine belongs to my uncle's old partner, Orson Gale. Does he know you're here?"

"Orson's never coming back." He shoved the stick into reverse, started to roll, stopped, and thrust his hand out the window. "Skipper Dooley."

"Jeneva Leopold. Neva, generally."

Dooley gave her hand a quick, hard squeeze, then nodded at the passenger's seat, where a German shepherd sat regarding her. "This here's Cayuse. He doesn't like girls. Excuse me, women."

As daylight dissolved into night, Neva sat on the long porch on the downhill side of the cabin just as she had done on every one of her fourteen perfect evenings at the mine, but instead of owls, distant frogs, and the murmur of Billie Creek, she heard Skipper Dooley slamming in and out of his camper. Trees hid the camp from view but didn't blunt the sound of curses and a harsh smoker's cough.

Skipper Dooley had said he wasn't a miner, but no one would simply wander in here for the night by accident. Eight miles of winding, rocky road lay between the mine and the two-lane highway through the Dry River Valley, a highway used only by local ranchers and the few miners still working old claims in the hills. The highway didn't lead anywhere that couldn't be reached faster on some other road. A traveler with a good map and no need to hurry might find his way to the Dry River, but for a stranger to notice the rough track that turned off the highway through sagebrush and rocks toward Billie Creek Canyon was just about unimaginable. And for such a person to follow that track as it wound into the hills and then climbed through the canyon for eight slow miles, each mile worse than the last one, and then to turn down the faint sandy ruts that led to the cabin—but Skipper Dooley knew the mine. He had said so. He had known her uncle and his partner, and he had known there was a camp on the creek.

So he wasn't a stranger to the mine, but what business could he possibly have here? It wasn't hunting season, and there were no fish in Billie Creek or the mining pond. He didn't look sporty, like a hiker or birdwatcher. He had towed a small trailer with a four-wheeled scooter lashed onto it. Maybe he was simply an old codger who liked to prowl around the backcountry on his ATV.

Whatever his purpose, if he stayed at the mine she would have to leave.

Packing the car to come out here two weeks ago she had felt suddenly certain that she was just as crazy as everyone seemed to think. She had no business driving for ten hours across Oregon from the Willamette Valley nearly to the Idaho border to live on her own in an isolated mining cabin abandoned these fifteen years. She would suffer terrible loneliness even though it was solitude she craved. But once at the mine she had not felt lonely for a single minute. She had felt gloriously solitary and happy. She would not be able to stand sharing the gold mine, certainly not with Skipper Dooley.

Despite her immediate impulse to hide from visitors, she was not afraid of Dooley. She was not afraid of much at all, she realized as she listened to the quiet that had at last descended on the night, and those fears she did have were very personal. She was afraid of water with dark, invisible depths. She was afraid of sharp kitchen knives because, a hasty cook, she was likely to cut herself. She was afraid to call her son on his cell phone because it might catch him driving and cause a crash. But she was not afraid to stay out here alone, or to walk anywhere through the desert hills with their treacherous rocky slopes and rattlesnakes, and she was not afraid of strange men with scarred faces. She just wanted to be by herself, to get back her emotional balance, and most of all to heal.

Neva stood up, leaned on the porch railing to listen, then went down the plank steps and looked at the deeply layered stars. There was not one streetlight to compete with the Milky Way; in fact, there was no electric light for many miles. Here, she was surrounded by pure night. Breathing deeply, calm again, she unbuttoned her cotton shirt and dropped it on the step behind her.

Cool night air moved across her bare back and chest, touching the two scars where her breasts had been. She traced each scar with her fingers. The surgery had healed well, so well that she did not find her flat torso ugly or repulsive, as she had feared before the operation. Her new chest wasn't disturbing to look at or to feel. It just wasn't her. Boyish and corrugated with visible ribs, her new front couldn't really belong to Jeneva Leopold, forty-five, mother of Ethan, columnist for the *Willamette Current* newspaper. She had not been able to accept this new shape—not, that is, until she arrived at the mine and turned her body over to the healing desert air. Every day she swam in the mining pond and then lay nude in the full heat of the sun. Often she hiked with her shirt off, walking randomly over the empty land, glorying in the touch of warm light that turned her skin golden-brown, except for the two pale pink lines on her chest. Her body was becoming familiar again, a shape she could accept as belonging to her, and even a shape she could like. But she was not done yet, not ready to leave the mine, and certainly not ready to share it with a stranger. With Dooley at the camp she could not swim nude, she could not walk around free in the air. She would have to behave properly again, to follow society's polite rules, and this she simply would not do.

Chapter Three

In the morning, Neva carried her coffee outside as usual to watch the rising sun bathe the canyon in cool light. The local raven family, two adults and two fledglings, sent hollow cries back and forth across the creek, but the sounds she dreaded to hear were absent. Either Skipper Dooley was sleeping late or he was far more subdued at the beginning of the day than at the end. Despite the quiet she was acutely aware of not being alone at the mine.

Waiting for signs of life from the camp, she felt suspended, unable to go comfortably about her usual activities, but when early morning passed into midmorning with no detectable activity, she made herself split firewood, fill the oil lamps and prepare a new batch of bannock mix. Working with the old speckled enamel cookware from the pantry, she put three cups of whole-wheat flour into a bowl and added baking powder, powdered milk, brown sugar, salt, and raisins. A cup of this dry mix combined with a little water made enough dough to divide into three donut-size rounds, which she fried each morning in butter. One was enough for breakfast, and the other two she ate cold during the day, generally for lunch on her long walks.

Today she ate breakfast late, and was clearing away when she heard the camper door slam. A sharp bark was followed by the bellowed command, "Shut up!" and then an engine roared into life. Hope flared but then she realized that Skipper Dooley had started the scooter, not the truck. She hurried out the kitchen door and across the open ground to the woodshed, determined to catch him as he passed. She would ask outright what his plans were rather than waste more time worrying. But Dooley did not come up the road. The sound of the engine moved away from her, across the creek and up the slope on the other side, slowly, as though exploring.

Disappointed and puzzled, Neva sat down on the chopping block and tried to picture his progress through the dry, scrubby woods on the east side of the canyon. The old trails over there were even rougher than on this side of the creek, and only collapsed timbers remained of the shacks that had been scattered through the drainage during the heydays of gold mining. Skipper Dooley had not struck her as someone likely to explore for exploring's sake. Her many years as a journalist had trained her to get information from people fast, and to sum them up neatly, but she also had learned how wrong first impressions could be. Even so, she would have bet that Dooley was a man with a purpose.

The sound of the scooter ceased suddenly, leaving only the usual quiet of midmorning. Either Dooley had turned the scooter off or he'd gone over the top of the ridge and was headed down the other side into Jump Creek Canyon.

With sudden decision Neva returned indoors. It was later than she usually set off, but she couldn't let a stranger ruin her day. She would go ahead with the plan she'd made yesterday before he arrived. Today she would attempt the most ambitious hike yet. Today she would climb Billie Mountain, the highest point on the ridge at the head of Billie Creek Canyon. Working quickly, she damped down the stove, filled a water bottle, put cold bannock and dried fruit into the small bag she wore on her belt, took up her hat and binoculars, and left the cabin.

Her step was light and easy. Gradually, she was exploring all four branches of the creek that lay between the cabin and the upper springs, each with its own mini-canyon. Twice she had made it to the spring line where the creeks originated on the lower slopes of Billie Mountain. There, the seeping waters created a bright mossy necklace across the dry sage. Now she felt ready to climb out of the spring basin to the top, where the view would stretch for miles.

To reach the basin she was following the smallest branch of the creek for the first time, walking along an old mining road that now was little more than a game trail. The dusty track climbed gently through scattered trees, the canyon gradually narrowing until she could have hit either side with a tossed rock. After about two miles, the trail entered a dense stand of ponderosa pines, the needles soft and slippery underfoot and only glimpses of sky showing through the canopy. The strawberry smell of warm pitch was heavy and sweet.

She walked slower, savoring the ripe air, and was considering whether to stretch out for a rest on the spongy needles when she saw a cabin ahead. Solid and dark, it stood close on the right of the trail. It was the first standing ruin she'd found, and she hurried toward it hoping the packrats had not done their worst, but it turned out to be airy and better suited to squirrels than the dark-loving rats. Even before she circled to the front, which faced away from the trail, she could see that the whole structure had slumped. Like a leaning drunk, it had sagged sideways against a large ponderosa that grew close on the downstream end. The front had popped out like a wall from a card house, leaving three tipsy sides and a caved-in roof, the single room fully visible despite collapsed timbers and scattered shakes. Everything was deeply layered in pine needles, and the squirrels had left their picnic remains—gnawed bracts from the pinecones—all over the plank table, the double bunk and the exposed shelves of a kitchen hutch.

The furniture, handmade and unpainted, appeared sturdy under its brittle blanket, as though waiting to be swept and made useful again. A graniteware washbasin still hung from a whittled wall peg next to the hutch, though its bottom was rusted to lace. Next to the bed lay a heavily worn boot, a woman's boot about Neva's size, still contoured to the shape of a foot. Searching with her eyes for the mate, Neva imagined pulling the boot onto her bare foot, the old leather cool and scratchy. But it wasn't her own wide brown foot she saw going into the boot. The foot was slim and pale, the ankle delicate enough to be elegant even when the boot was laced.

Standing very still, her back suddenly warm as though someone had come up close behind her, Neva listened to the heavy air. Slowly she turned to face the creek that ran slow and shallow along the east side of the clearing. She scanned the opposite bank, the crowded trees, the small flat scattered with boards and rusting metal half buried in grass. Of course there was no one. She was alone, utterly and perfectly alone in the midday stillness, with nothing stirring except for the stream. No one had lived in the cabin for decades. Judging by the overgrown path, no one had even visited for a very long time.

Her heart beat noticeably as she turned back to the ruin, but she was not afraid. Of course, the cabin site was haunted—the entire drainage was haunted by history—but the spirits that lingered here weren't angry or threatening. The broken tools, old graniteware pots, rusted chunks of metal and weathered timbers scattered throughout the canyon were mysterious and somewhat sad, but not frightening.

Though now shut in by tall pines, the clearing would have been sunny during the mining years. The tree that supported the cabin must have been small then, but was now too big to encircle with her arms and the patchwork bark was deeply fissured. She went up to the tree, pressed her nose into a crack, and breathed in the ripe scent of vanilla. As she straightened she glanced to the left, at an object that was sticking out of the trunk at about the height of her shoulder. It was a small tobacco can, oval in shape and about five inches long, which had been nailed to the tree so many years ago the bark had shaped around it like a cup holder.

Velvet Pipe and Cigarette Tobacco, The Smoothest Smoke in America, Burns Cool and Sweet in Pipe or Cigarette.

The writing was just legible through patches of rust, and the narrow lid stuck at first, then opened with a squeak. Sitting inside on a layer of powdery rust was a glossy piece of obsidian about the size of a quarter. The canyon trails were littered with obsidian chunks, many with flake marks as though from ancient tool making. How had this piece come to be in the can? It wasn't dusty so it couldn't have been here for long—but what did "long" mean out in this territory? A month? A year? A decade?

Like the lone boot and the cabin itself, the can and its obsidian clearly had a story, but there was no one left to tell it.

The sun had dropped below the horizon by the time Neva came down from the ridge feeling shaky but jubilant. She had made it to the top where the view did go on forever, with mountains in every direction, the distant Wallowas and Elkhorns still snow-capped. Even more flowers bloomed on the bright ridge top than in the creek canyon, and butterflies danced over the flowers as though drunk on air. She, too, had felt drunk with new life as she strode along the ridge top with her T-shirt off, showing her scars to blue distance, her sweaty skin cooling in the breeze.

But coming down the steep side of the ridge where rocks rolled underfoot, she had stopped to rest several times. Her food and water were long gone, her legs were bleeding from wading through brittle sagebrush, and for the last mile she had been driven by the thought of cold oranges. The oranges were in her cooler, a plastic tub sunk in the creek and weighted down with rocks, where she also stored cheese, potatoes, onions, carrots and tomatoes. The cooler was just upstream from Skipper Dooley's camp but screened from sight by a stand of young aspens. Approaching carefully, she heard nothing but the stream and saw no sign of man or dog.

Today she allowed herself two oranges, which she tore apart in her eagerness. She sank her sticky face and hands into the creek, resisting the temptation to drink. It was difficult to believe that such clear water was not pure, but giardia was now every-where in the West. She sat back on her heels, dried her hands on her shirt, and considered the best way to get from here to the cabin without risking a meeting with her unwelcome neighbor. Ordinarily, she went downstream to cross the creek opposite the campsite and follow the road up, but now it seemed better to cross where she was and angle through the woods.

Her hope that Dooley had left Billie Creek was dashed by the sight of his dimly lit camper window. A moment later, a dark form rushed from the shadows barking furiously.

"Cayuse!" a voice roared. "You stupid son of a bitch, shut up and show some manners."

Though she knew instantly that it was the dog, Neva's heart pounded and she had to steady herself with a hand against a pine trunk as she searched for Skipper in the darkness under the trees.

"You're quiet as a spook going along there," he said from close by, then detached himself from the shadow of a tree trunk and came toward her. "Where you been?"

"Up on Billie Mountain."

"Whoa. That's a distance."

"Where did you go?" she said, noting the smell of whiskey.

"Over to Jump Creek. That's the next drainage to the east, not that there's anything in particular to see over there."

"But you're not a miner?" Neva eyed the dog, which now sat by Skipper's leg and returned her look with no appearance of threat.

"No, ma'am. I'm what they call an artifact hunter, the legal kind, of course. I've plowed through just about every kind of site you've got out here, and most of Arizona and New Mexico too, just seeing what I can see."

"What do you see? I mean, what are you looking for?"

"Just about anything historic. I've found everything from China cups as fine as frog hair to old wedding rings. You have tooth powder cans, hand-blown bottles, square nails, even the occasional nugget."

"How about old tobacco cans? I found one today, nailed to a tree."

"Is that so? I'm glad to hear it. The miners used to put their claim papers in those cans. Used to be you found them everywhere but now you have too many people running around helping themselves. I don't keep much myself. I just like to find it." He turned his head, spit expertly, then looked at her sidelong. "Now, what's your excuse? You're no miner yourself."

She should have been prepared for such a question, but she hadn't expected to meet anyone out here, let alone someone curious about her. She had no secrets and didn't much care one way or the other what people knew about her, but even so, Skipper Dooley was not a person she could talk to casually about breast cancer. She said, "I'm taking a break from my newspaper job over in the Willamette Valley. I just needed a rest. A long rest somewhere hot and quiet."

"You call hiking up Billie Mountain resting? Lady, most people when they want a break don't go to the back of nowhere to do it, where you don't even have a hot shower at the end of the day. Tell you what, if I was a judge and jury I wouldn't believe a word of it."

Startled—he was as suspicious of her as she was of him—Neva resisted the sudden urge to laugh. She tried to think of an answer that would be truthful while not too personal, but before she could speak he went on with sudden earnestness. "See these hands?" He held them up for inspection, palms turned inward, and even in the near dark she could see that they were scarred by hard use. "I made a living with these hands for forty-six years, a good living, too, raised four boys, survived marriages to three women that would still like to see my hide on the wall. Anyway, I've been lucky. I'm sixty-nine now, an old man that can't walk like I used to. So what? Well, it means something. But sometimes you just have to get away. You don't have to tell me about it. Sometimes you just have to hit the road."

One of the glorious things about being at the mine was the opulent sleep that came so easily every night, but tonight for the first time Neva felt restless in bed. The image of Skipper Dooley hovered in her thoughts, a more complicated image now, and when she heard his truck in what felt like the small hours of the morning, she nodded as though she had been expecting just this sound. Her neighbor was leaving the mine. She sat up and held her breath in the dark to hear more clearly, and then, puzzled, got out of bed and went through the kitchen to the back door. She opened it and listened with a sense of déjà vu to the uneven rumble that came from Billie Creek Road. For the second time in two days a stranger was invading her canyon. This wasn't Dooley pulling out, but some larger vehicle making its way up the road beyond the cabin cutoff despite the rocks and potholes.

Whoever it was would not get far. But where had they come from? There couldn't be more than fifty people in the entire Dry River Valley, even counting Angus with its lone café, part-time post office, and boarded-up schoolhouse. Ranch kids looking for a place to park could find plenty of privacy without coming this far, and surely a diesel truck wouldn't be anyone's first choice for a date. Maybe someone had started mining higher up Billie Creek? Driving in on her first day she had seen two mines farther down the road, the Sufferin' Smith Mine near the bottom of the canyon, and the Barlow Mine about halfway up. Both were active, although there had been nothing to see at the Sufferin' Smith Mine aside from two plywood cabins sitting across the creek from the road. The Barlow Mine was a huge pit in the creek bottom. The road went around it without ever giving a view of the equipment or people working down below, but there was freshly bulldozed ground, and two pickup trucks were parked by the cabins at the upper rim of the pit. Both mines were marked on the area map along with Billie Creek Mine, but there was nothing higher up the canyon that she knew of.

Maybe it was a rancher bringing in cows by truck. She had smelled the pungent manure odor of cows up the creek today although she had not seen any. But no rancher would haul cattle in the dead of night. Or would he? Maybe it would be cooler for the cows this way. She really didn't know. In fact, she didn't know much about this high desert world of mines and ranches, not much at all.

Quiet returned to the creek, but as she got back into bed, the familiar coyotes started their midnight serenade, the usual long, wavering calls punctuated with short yips that made her smile. Her uncle must have heard the same chorus hundreds of times while lying in this same room. Maybe he, too, had enjoyed picturing the coyote pups pointing their noses at the sky to howl with the grownups and instead letting out excited barks. Uncle Matthew…She had met him when she was nine and had never seen him again. On that one occasion, she had come to the mine with her father. Her mother had stayed behind at home even though Matthew had been her only sibling. Too young then to wonder why, or why there were no other visits with her uncle, Neva hadn't asked her mother for an explanation until many years later, after they were told that Matthew had disappeared from the mine leaving no clue to where he'd gone.

"It's an old story," Frances had said, putting off Neva's questions. "I don't want to think about it."

Her father had said only, "Families are peculiar things, Neva. Sometimes it's best just to let the past alone."

Now she wished she had pushed harder for information about the family's black sheep, as she had come to think of her uncle, but when he disappeared she had been married to Carlo, with a small son to raise. Then Carlo also had died, leaving her with five-year-old Ethan to bring up on her own. Digging for information about a wayward relative had been a long way from her thoughts back then, but with every day that passed at the mine her curiosity about Uncle Matthew Burt deepened along with her regret. The family was too small as it was, and could not afford to let a relative simply vanish, not only from the known world but from family memory as well. She had tried to say this when her mother also lay dying, tried to persuade her to talk about Matthew, but it had been too late.

"You tell him I'm sorry," Frances had said through tears. "He'll come home someday. Please tell him I'm sorry, truly sorry. I know I misjudged him, I just know it now."

And this was all she would say even when Neva pressed, unable to believe that her gentle mother could have done anything deserving such regret. "Sorry for what?"

"He'll know. He'll know."

No information regarding his whereabouts or fate had ever turned up, but because his body was never found, her mother refused to believe that Matthew had met a bad end at the mine. Until her own death two years ago, she had insisted that he had left by choice and would return someday. Neva had not tried to talk her mother out of what she herself considered to be a fantasy, but now she could not help wishing that Frances had been right. Living at his mine, cooking with his pots, sleeping in his bed, she felt a growing bond to her uncle, and half expected to step out onto the porch some evening to discover him sitting in the twilight. She pictured him striding alongside her on walks even though, if still alive, he would be over eighty by now and possibly feeble like his partner, Orson Gale.

Poor Orson. Her uncle's disappearance had been the end of him as well, at least the end of his meaningful life. He gave up mining within a year, suffered a stroke, and ended up in the nursing home where he still remained, unable to speak or communicate in any way. Her mother had sent him a Christmas card every year, and Neva had carried on the tradition even though there was never a response. And more for the sake of form than because she thought it was really necessary she had sent him a note saying she would be in the cabin all summer. She had said nothing about the surgery or the depression that followed, only that she needed a quiet place to be alone for a while.

Chapter Four

He first noticed her as a light speck zigzagging up the rocky slope above the head of the creek. Not a deer. Not a coyote. He took out his field glasses, scanned, focused, and made a wordless sound. It was a woman. She was naked. His arm twitched and he lost her.

He steadied his elbow against a juniper trunk and searched the slope, too fast at first, but then with self-control. There she was, not quite naked but she wore no shirt and the shorts were rolled high on her legs. Her bare back was dark from the sun…shoulder blades, grooved spine, muscles moving as her arms swung.

Where had she come from? What was she doing out here, alone and half nude?

She wasn't old but she wasn't young.

He wasn't young either. If he were young he could start over again, get away from all this before it was too late, have a different life, a real life. He would live in Hawaii or maybe Florida, go to the beach, swim in the ocean. He had never been in the ocean, never swum in translucent green water with white sand below, never sat under a palm tree with a cold drink. Were there palm trees in Florida? Yes, of course, but were they originally there or had they been brought in like the orange trees?

It didn't matter. Palm trees, ocean, orange trees, a new life…

His elbow slipped and he lost her again. He held his breath and scanned the hillside, moving his head with the glasses, sideways, up and down. She was gone, gone, vanished into the dry air, yet another mirage, never real in the first place—ah, but there she was.

She had stopped for a drink in the shade of a juniper, balanced on the slope with her head tilted back. She drank, drank again, attached the water bottle to her belt, cinched the belt. She bent to pick something up off the ground, aiming the dusty bottoms of her shorts straight into his eyes, the cloth stretched tight. She stood, bent her head over her hand, dropped whatever she had picked up, and went on.

Her back glistened in the sun. From sweat? She was too far away to tell. His own back was clammy. He was sweating, he was always sweating, he had spent his whole sorry life sweating, hot sweat and cold sweat, the sweat of labor and the sweat of fear.

She topped a rise, was silhouetted for a moment against the dark ridge beyond, and then vanished behind the hill. Patiently he waited, the glasses trained on the slope beyond the rise. She was heading up and would soon appear again. Long, hot minutes passed. His arms ached. A fly crawled on his sticky neck and he slapped it with one hand. He hated flies, hated when they landed on his plate, would not eat food a fly had walked on.

The dead fly stuck to his hand. He flung it away with disgust, wiped his palm on his pants, and searched again through the field glasses, but she did not come back into view. She was gone gone gone into the stony land and he was alone in the silent afternoon, alone as he had always been and always would be. He wrapped the cord around the glasses, slid them into the case, and turned back to his work. He might have imagined her but probably not, not with the rolled shorts and the scratched legs. Had he imagined her, she would have turned around, and she would have had red hair. He had always liked red hair.

Chapter Five

The instant she woke up, Neva thought of the truck and felt certain that it had been Dooley pulling out after all, the sound of the engine exaggerated by the stillness of night. But as she slipped her feet into the flip-flops next to the bed, she heard the whine of the quad and hurried out onto the porch to check where he was going today. It sounded as though he was heading upstream toward Billie Mountain the way she had walked yesterday. Although she had not asked how long he meant to stay on the creek, their conversation had taken the edge off her uneasiness. He was looking for artifacts, and once he'd explored the immediate area he'd move on. Over the years he had been just about everywhere in the drainage, he said, "just rammycackin' around," as he put it. "But you never can see everything. It's amazing what you miss. That's why I come back every year."

Today he was certain to be gone for hours, but still Neva was driven by a sense of new urgency as she put her soap and towel in the basket and took the short trail to the old mining pond to wash off yesterday's dust and sweat. The pond was downstream from Dooley's camp, and like the camp, it was hidden by trees. About half an acre in size, it was roughly triangle-shaped, with an earthen dam as the base and the creek flowing into the apex.

Even though she knew that placer mining required water, she had been surprised to find a real pool given the small size of the creek and the general dryness of the high desert country. On her first day at the mine she had stood on the bank for a long time gazing at the water. The still surface had mirrored a perfect blue sky but as she watched, images appeared as though in a crystal ball, revealing depths where dead trees stood, their drowned limbs trailing algae. At last she had stripped but continued to stand on the dam, naked and uncertain, her attraction to the water struggling against irrational fear. The plain fact of being hot had finally driven her down the bank into the silky cold water, which gave off a musty-sweet, secret perfume, an underground smell of clean earth and old leaves. She had stuck close to shore, avoiding the dark drop-off into the deep center, paddling up and down where her hands could touch bottom.

Before her second swim, she had constructed a proper bathing spot with materials scavenged from around the mine. Short eight-by-eight timbers wedged into the clay made three steps down the face of the little dam. At the top of the steps she laid down an old wooden door for a changing and sunbathing platform, and next to it she set a wooden bench. That she had not thought of bringing a swimsuit to the mine was due more to habit than her expectations about whether she would or would not find a swimming hole—she rarely swam where she couldn't go in nude. Like discovering fresh-roasted coffee or locally made bread, it's impossible to go back to a lower standard, and swimming in any sort of garment definitely rated low once you'd felt lovely water slipping over every bit of your skin. The craving for sun on her skin was different; that was for healing, for letting the clean, strong light into every cell in her body. Water was purely for pleasure.

The bottom of the pond was soft but she had learned to push off without stirring up the silt. Every day she paddled a little farther from shore, vowing that before her stay at the mine was done she would swim from one end of the pond to the other right above the dead trees. The water felt particularly sweet and fresh this morning after a day without bathing, but Neva didn't take time to float on her back or lie on the towel while her hair dried. Listening for the sound of Dooley's scooter, she dried briskly and returned to the cabin.

It was still early enough to be slightly cool in the shadows when she set out walking, heading for the ridge on the east side where Dooley had gone yesterday. She had walked on that side of the creek before, but had not climbed out of the canyon bottom. Now she chose any faint remnant of a road or game trail that led away from the creek. Where there was no trail, she picked her way among scattered pines, sagebrush and rocks.

As she zigzagged upward, the pines thinned and the ground grew rockier. In a small meadow, larkspur made a carpet about six inches tall, the flowers a concentrated blue. Everything glistened today, the fine spider webs strung between trees, the needles of young pines, the silvery lupine leaves, the smooth obsidian chunks embedded in the hillside, the brushy tops of new grasses, even the fine hairs on her own arm. Her leg muscles felt like springs, and warm air moved freely in the new space between the tops of her thighs.

It had not been like this when she arrived at the mine. Was it really just two weeks ago that she had come here, weak and exhausted? She had never been a heavy woman, but as she had started up the creek trail for the first time the weight of her unexercised body had felt like more than her bones could carry. That she had made it to the mine at all was a miracle born of desperation. How could she have been so blind to her own depression? She had been so cocky, so sure she would sail through breast cancer with ease because what are breasts, after all, except lumps of fatty tissue stuck on the chest? Losing her breasts was not like losing arms, legs, or a lung. Her breasts had nursed a child and served her well in a womanly way for more than thirty years, but they were no longer essential to her life or happiness. If she had to trade part of her body to stay alive, then surely breasts were the best offering. Without them she could still function well in every necessary way.

Immediately following the end of chemotherapy, which had been surprisingly tolerable, she had felt euphoric because it was over. But after a few weeks the euphoria had given way to a sense of loss that had deepened steadily through rainy winter and into spring. Not only was her familiar body gone, but other important losses in her life came sweeping back to haunt her: Carlo's drowning when their son was just about to start kindergarten, her father's fatal stroke, and her mother's death just two years ago. Losing her breasts had opened these old wounds as though they were new, bringing pervasive sorrow that touched everything.

Nothing mattered as it had before. Everything turned gray—her work, books, friends, garden, even the regular telephone calls from Ethan, who was working so hard at Berkeley. Her sense that the world offered endless possibilities had disappeared. All her life she had been a morning person, but now getting out of bed was hard work. Instead of springing up ready for the new day, she had to talk herself out of the warm comfort of her quilt, pretending not to dread the weary hours ahead. And her body, she had to admit at last, had become alien. This was not really her, this unfit, weary, sexless thing.

That she was depressed took a long time to accept, but when she finally faced the truth she went dutifully through the usual steps for treatment and self-care. She joined a support group, found a counselor, made herself available to help other women diagnosed with breast cancer, and invited friends to dinner more often. She took leisurely baths despite having preferred showers all her life, and wrapped herself in a new plush robe. She had her gold-brown hair cut from shoulder length to a chic unisex trim.

Every day she reminded herself that she was lucky to live in a beautiful Oregon town and to have a stimulating job as a newspaper columnist, a job that put her in the middle of whatever interesting was going on in Willamette...but pep-talks were useless. Counting her blessings came to seem a symptom in itself. As the relentless rain of a Willamette Valley winter pounded down, she had begun to dream about the desert. She imagined hot rocks, and ridges standing against a cloudless sky. She could smell sagebrush and warm dust. And then one night as she lay sleepless in bed an image of a cabin had floated into her fantasies. It sat on a sunny hillside among twinkling aspens, encircled by quartz-lined paths. She saw a girl sitting on a white rock by the door while two men talked on the nearby porch—she was the girl, the cabin was at her uncle's mine that she had visited so many years ago, and that was her uncle in the black vest leaning forward to listen to her father.

This image, so long forgotten, began to haunt her thoughts day and night. One morning she woke up knowing she would go to the mine. She had got out the old, yellowed map of Oregon that had been on the dining room wall when she was young, on which her father had marked every personal landmark in the state he considered the most favored in the nation. The mine was noted as "M.Burt/Gold M" in fine black ink, with a small "x" on a hand-drawn dotted line representing Billie Creek Road. The prospect of a summer at the mine had not given her sudden energy, had not cured the lethargy and sadness, but it had provided her with enough purpose to make the necessary arrangements. She requested a three-month leave from work, found a summer renter for her house, and assembled gear and groceries. The most wearying part of the preparations had been assuring friends that she was not insane and did not need—did not want—anyone to visit or check up on her. Ethan fussed at first but then became her staunchest supporter. "Go for it, Mom," he urged. "And don't spend all your time writing me letters."

Despite her yearning for a clear sky and hot rocks, the first walk was a shock. Struggling up the trail, she felt like a convict in leg irons. Every step was hard labor, sweat drenched her shirt, and she soon retired to the cabin. That evening she made herself go out again, and again first thing in the morning, and on each occasion she went a little farther, a little faster, her step a little more buoyant. The extra weight disappeared as though melted by the sun.

Now, striding up the rocky slope, she found it difficult to remember that sad and weary woman who had arrived at the mine so short a time ago. She had set out walking fast, but slowed down when the ground grew steeper, pacing herself as she had learned to do, saving her strength for the heat of afternoon. She had just calculated that she was about halfway to the ridge top when she came suddenly upon a road, a surprisingly good road of sandy clay that sparkled with quartz fragments. It had to be Billie Creek Road, which looped around the top of the drainage and headed back down the canyon on the east side, but it was nothing like the pitted, rocky track that continued past the cabin cutoff on the other side. She had often crossed the road at the head of the canyon, and though it was somewhat better there than lower down, it still was deeply rutted and littered with rocks. According to the Forest Service map she had bought in Sisters, this end should be worse.

Faint tire marks showed in the sand. Thinking of the night truck, Neva squatted and touched the shallow tracks. They were crusted hard, and clearly old. Whatever its business, the truck had not come this far. Standing again, she unhooked the water bottle from her belt and sipped, savoring each cool mouthful to make it last while she considered what to do next. The road curved attractively away in both directions, with a rocky bank on the uphill side and low pines and shrubs on the downhill side. She was tempted to follow it, either to the left and all the way around to the cabin turnoff, or to the right down the canyon to the point where, at least on the map, it crossed over the ridge into Jump Creek Canyon. It might be an easier way to get onto the ridge, though the crossover point wasn't likely to be very high, and might even be far down the canyon toward the foothills. She could not remember that part of the map very well.

As she stood wondering which way to go and whether sticking to the road would be a cowardly ploy to get out of the difficult climb to the top, she heard the ring of metal on stone. A horse came into sight around the bend from the downstream direction.

The rider wore a wide-brimmed hat tipped low over his face. He gave no sign of seeing Neva until he was so close she could smell the horse. The horse snorted and stepped sideways. Looking up, the rider reined sharply, swung to the ground and pulled off his hat in a single gesture. Although he had appeared large on the horse, he was only a bit taller than Neva's own five-foot-six—and he was a woman.

"Darla Steadman," she said, offering a firm hand.

With a bag over her head, Darla Steadman could have passed for a man, her legs long and straight in Levis that fit easily rather than snugging around hips, her button-up shirt tucked in and nearly as flat in front as Neva's own. Even the shaggy hair would have been unremarkable on a young man. Her face, however, was riveting, the sort that no amount of sunburn, dusty sweat, or indifferent grooming can make other than beautiful. Such a woman would not be convincing if placed by Hollywood on a horse in Billie Creek Canyon, and yet—Neva looked at the scarred cowboy boots, the strong hand holding the reins, the lean figure planted before her with equal weight in both feet—and yet, Darla Steadman belonged here in a way that she herself did not. The thought brought a flicker of envy that had nothing to do with glamour.

"I'm Neva, Jeneva Leopold," she said. "I'm staying down at the mine, Billie Creek Mine. It belonged to my uncle."

"You're not mining?" The tone was polite, and nothing more.

"No, no. I'm just getting away from town for a while. My uncle was Matthew Burt. Did you know him?"

"I knew him."

"We've always wondered what happened. The disappearance, I mean. Some people think he died."

"That's right."

Neva waited but Darla offered nothing more, as though all that could be said had been said. She must have ridden up from one of the ranches along the Dry River, where the narrowness of the valley left little room for cultivation or grazing between the river and the hills on either side. Thinking back to the evening when she had driven into the mine, Neva realized that she had seen no cows as she followed the empty two-lane highway up the valley. In summer, the cows must be in the high country grazing on Forest Service and Bureau of Land Management property, which included just about everything out here other than the bottomlands.

"Are you looking for cows?" she ventured. "I think there may be some up the creek."

"How many did you see?"

"I'm sorry, I didn't see them, I only smelled them when I was walking yesterday, or at least thought I did. I've got an unusually good nose."

"They're not supposed to be in here until August. They have to rotate, first to Jump Creek, then Coyote, then Billie last. They can't stay here."

Again there was silence, although Darla made no move to leave. She must have ridden a long way from the valley and would have many hours more to go before reaching home, yet she carried no water, lunch, or anything else that Neva could see. Her jeans and work shirt couldn't have harbored even a chocolate bar. Nothing was tied to the saddle. Since dismounting, she hadn't smiled once, although there was nothing especially serious in her manner. She was simply neutral, flat, uninflected, like an exquisite mannequin that had been left out carelessly to weather.

At that moment, Darla stepped to the edge of the road, put a finger against one nostril, and blew a sharp blast through the other, clearing it explosively. She did the second nostril, then wiped with a wadded bandanna from her back pocket.

Well, not so very much like a mannequin. Neva smiled and said in a conversational tone, "I heard a truck on the creek road late last night. I wondered if someone had driven their cows up."

"That's how we drive cows." Darla nodded toward the horse, which had begun grazing at the side of the road with a leisurely air as though simply passing time. "You sure it was a truck?"

"It sounded like it. I suppose it could have been kids from one of the ranches."

"You're out here on your own?"

"That's right. I needed a stretch of quiet all to myself."

"Plenty of that around here."

Had the rancher smiled, Neva would have laughed and the encounter would have looked different later as she thought it over, but Darla gave no sign of amusement. She drew her horse in by the lead that had remained loose in her hand, and swung lightly into the saddle. Looking down at Neva, her face again shadowed by the gray hat, she said, "Just a small piece of advice.

It's not always what it looks like out here, the ground, that is. You have old tunnels just about anywhere and I advise you to keep away from them."

◇◇◇

It was late afternoon when Jeneva came down from the ridge, exhilarated by hard walking and wide-open spaces. As she approached the creek upstream from her cooler, she heard a low moo and found herself face to face with a black and white calf. Darla Steadman, it appeared, had failed to round up her wandering stock.

The calf fled in panic, tearing through the shallow water as though it had met a cougar. Two cows and another calf blundered after it.

"Dumb shits," a voice said close by, and there was Skipper Dooley sitting on a rock with one boot off and his foot in the creek. "I never did like cows. Any animal that eats and shits at the same time ought to be shot." He raised his pale, dripping foot and stared dolefully at it. "I stepped on a nail. Probably have lockjaw by morning. Hand me that towel there."

He had gone over the top of Billie Mountain to Rattlesnake Gorge to look at some old Chinese mining cabins, he said as they returned to the camper, Skipper limping with the help of a stick and Neva carrying the towel. He had heard about the Chinese cabins from a logger when he stopped at the Angus Café on his way to Billie Creek the first day.

"He said the place was in pretty good shape when he was over there cruising timber a few weeks ago. I found it all right, but somebody must have got there ahead of me. It was torn up pretty bad, boards scattered everywhere. They took anything that was worth carrying away. All they left me was the nails." Skipper hopped one-legged onto the metal step to the camper door and paused with his hand on the latch. "You better have a drink. My ice maker quit on me but I've got club soda and plain old water."

A drink with Skipper Dooley in his camper? Neva glanced around at the late afternoon light slanting through the pines.

It was much nicer out here than it was likely to be in a camper, but she could think of no good reason to say no, and when she stepped in she was pleasantly surprised. The camper was as fresh and tidy as though it had just come off the sales lot, the white counters and tabletop bare except for a pile of books on the table. If she'd speculated at all about whether Skipper Dooley was a reader she would have guessed his taste ran to Westerns and crime novels, but the two titles she could make out at a glance were *Cod: The Biography of a Fish That Changed the World*, and *Pancho Villa, the Man and the Myth*.

Skipper turned away to retrieve a bottle of whiskey from a cabinet over the little refrigerator. Observing him with new interest, Neva slid onto a bench seat upholstered in dark green corduroy. Skipper set two glasses and a pitcher of water on the table, settled across from her with his leg up, then poured a shot for himself and Scotch and water for her.

"You're a serious reader," she said.

"I never was serious about anything in my life. Except drinking." He raised his glass in a salute. "You'll have to drink fast. I got a head start on you. Whiskey's the best painkiller there is, and I don't mean to say I poured it on my foot. Have you read this book about codfish? No? Well, it's damned good, not a boring word in it. As it happens, I have a little story of my own to tell, a sort of mystery you might say."

Because of his hurt foot, he said, he had ridden the quad with extra care coming back over the ridge. As usual, he stopped to enjoy the view before starting down. "I saw something big moving around down there on the slope so I pulled out the glasses. It was that rancher woman, that Darla Steadman, the one that owns half the Dry River Valley. She was riding along real slow and careful, looking at the ground, and all of a sudden she swung off her horse, walked a few feet, and disappeared. Just like that, she was gone. I waited about half an hour, never taking my eyes off where she was last, but my eyes got tired and I rubbed them. It couldn't have been more than a couple of seconds, but wouldn't you know it, when I looked up there she was on her horse again. Well, I was pretty curious as you can figure, and I came down off the mountain a sight faster than I'd planned, hurt foot or no hurt foot. But when I got down there I couldn't find the place. I thought I had it marked exactly in my mind, I'd looked at everything so close, but down on the slope nothing looked the same. And with my foot swelling up I couldn't scramble around good. It's steeper than a cow's face in there."

Skipper reached for the bottle and poured himself another shot without a break in his talk. "Know what I think? I think there's a mine tunnel up there and she went in it. They say these hills are riddled with them from back in the days when they had the Chinese to do the digging. Some are hundreds of feet long. I came across one over at Mormon Valley once, but it stunk of packrat so bad I couldn't get far into it."

"I know what you mean. They got into a shed by the cabin and it's no good for anything now except burning down. Actually, I think Darla was looking for cows. I met her up on the road this morning."

"Well, I didn't see that she had any cows, and I never heard of a cow yet that would go in a tunnel, not with the stink of coyotes or bear or what have you in there along with the packrat. Not that I know much about cows, but I can tell you one thing. I wouldn't be a rancher for a truckload of the hottest artifacts going, not these days. You can hardly give away a cow, from what I hear. I'd be a miner before I'd be a rancher, and that's saying a lot."

"She warned me about mining tunnels, that they can be more dangerous than they look."

"Did she now? That's very interesting considering she went into one herself."

"Do you know her?" Neva watched him curiously, remembering their first meeting when he claimed never to have seen a woman in the canyon before.

Skipper shook his head. "I've never run across her before, but her picture used to be on the wall down there at the Angus Café, some news clipping from way back, can't remember just what. Have you run into Gene Holland yet? He's got the Sufferin'

Smith Mine down at the bottom of the creek. Now there's a smart man. He can tell you anything you ever want to know about this country, or mining, or just about anything that comes up. You should get along. He's college educated, not a dumb brick longshoreman like me."

Neva raised an eyebrow. People who call themselves dumb generally are a long way from it. The truly dumb of this world are too dumb to know it, mercifully. Her first impressions of Skipper were undergoing rapid revision and not just because of the books. Sure he was tough, but he was also shrewd, observant, and funny. "Where is the Sufferin' Smith Mine? All I saw driving in was a pair of plywood shacks on the road. There was no sign of actual mining, no pit or equipment."

"The mine's up on top of the ridge. That's just his cabin you see there, and his laboratory. I don't know what he does in there, only that it's complicated. Gene Holland never did anything the easy way if he could help it." He eyed her glass, which was empty. "And now that you washed the trail dust down, you can have a real drink."

Neva let him pour an inch of whiskey, then covered the glass with her hand. "I should have had some water first, after the walk. I might fall down a mine shaft trying to get back to the cabin."

"Some people think that's what happened to your uncle, but I never did buy it. He knew this country too well. I wasn't around here at the time, but Orson told me about it after. He said he went into Elkhorn to sell their week's gold, and ended up staying the night. He came back to the mine next day and your uncle was gone, no sign of him anywhere. He hadn't taken anything but his hunting rifle."

Skipper was quiet for a moment, his expression somber. "If you'll excuse me saying so, for a time I felt kind of funny wandering around here. To tell you the truth, I kept expecting to find his remains, not that much would be left after the coyotes and buzzards got through. That's a funny thing about these old mines, too. Some you walk around and they feel fine, and others give you the creeps, you don't know why. I've had to pack up and move on a time or two when I just couldn't stand to be in a place. Call it bad vibes or whatever. I've never been bothered around here except for that stretch after your uncle disappeared, and it didn't last or I wouldn't be here today."

"Why was Orson so sure my uncle had given up the mine and gone away? That's what he told my mother."

"Well, would you tell anybody that their only brother most likely fell down a mine shaft or was supper for a cougar?"

"You knew my uncle pretty well, then?"

"Just to say howdy. I'd only been out here a time or two before he was gone."

"How did you know he was my mother's only brother?"

Skipper had raised his glass to his lips but paused and looked at her over the rim without sipping. "You don't miss a trick, do you?"

"Was that a trick?"

"Whoa, lady, let's not get too serious here. Orson talked to me a lot right after Burtie died, or disappeared, or whatever. I guess he was kind of lonely after having a partner all those years. Like being married, come to think of it. No wonder the old boy couldn't hack it and went as crazy as a wind-up duck."

"Crazy? I thought he had a stroke."

"Oh? Well, that must be it, then, I don't really know. Cheers." He drained the glass, set it precisely before him, and said, "Now let's have a little whiskey truth. What's your real excuse for being at Billie Creek Mine?"

"Two reasons," she said, this time without hesitation. "Number one, I'm trying to decide whether to bury my mother's ashes at the mine as a sort of reconciliation with her brother. They didn't talk for years before he disappeared, I don't know why, but she was very sad about it when she died. Number two, I'm trying to get my health back again after an operation. As you may have noticed, I had a little visit not too long ago from Acme Breast Removal. Both sides. See? Flat." Neva swiped her open hand down the front of her shirt. "I tried a breast cancer support group, but I'm just not the groupy type. My idea of therapy is to run around the hills until I get my body back. I think it's beginning to work."

"Well, Jesus. That leaves an old coot kind of speechless. You sure you couldn't eat a stuffed pepper? I've got two ready to go in the oven."

◇◇◇

It was full dark when Neva walked back to the cabin. Stumbling a bit, feeling the whiskey, she laughed up at the stars. Skipper had said he would be around for a few days yet, but she no longer minded. In fact, she rather liked the idea of having such a colorful neighbor as long as he didn't stay too long.

The screen door to the kitchen stuck but scraped open with the usual shove. She stepped into darkness that was slightly warmer than outdoors, the afternoon heat still lingering full of comfortable smells, the breakfast fire, split pine, the bouquet of grasses in a tall green bottle. She hesitated inside the door. There was something else in the air, a smell she didn't know.

The kitchen, dimly illuminated by moonlight, looked as she had left it. She crossed to the door of the big room where her two oil lamps sat on a table with a box of matches. The smell was stronger in this room. Perfumey like hand lotion or aftershave, it made her pause in the doorway to scan the shadows, but she saw nothing unexpected.

Edging sideways to the table, she felt for the matches, lit the nearest lamp, and looked around the room. Everything was as it should be, her books and papers stacked on the little desk, the clothes folded in a basket, her straw hat hanging by the door to the porch. Her gaze settled on the small box containing her mother's ashes, which sat on the sewing machine table by the bed. Hadn't she left it in the middle of the table? It was positioned now to the left of center and not quite square with the rectangular surface. She must have moved it, maybe when she reached for her cup of water during the night.

Neva bent forward to smell the brown paper in which the box of ashes was wrapped, the same paper provided by the funeral home. Unnerved that such a small box could weigh so much—shouldn't ashes be as light as snowflakes?—she had not known what to do with it, and had put it in the hall cupboard while she considered a permanent spot. For two years the box had sat among candles, lamp oil, household polishing agents, and bath supplies received as presents and never used. Now the brown paper gave off a faint floral smell. It must have absorbed the various fragrances concentrated in the cupboard, and in the hot cabin the scents were vaporizing, although the smell of the paper did not seem quite the same as the scent that lingered in the air.

Gently moving the box so that it again was square with the top of the sewing machine, Neva addressed it in a tone of wistful affection "Looks like you've been wandering a bit, Mom. I should take you on a tour of the mine."

Sudden sorrow swept through her again. Why had she and her mother never come here together? She could so easily picture Frances sitting on the porch as evening settled over the canyon, not lighting a lamp until full dark. Even in town her mother would often sit late in a room with no lights on, savoring the transition from day to night. To anyone who came in she would say gaily, "Draw up a rafter and join the bats."

That Jeneva still had the ashes was a matter of failure rather than sentiment. Raised without religion, lacking brothers or sisters to help with the decision, she had found herself unable to dispose of the ashes in a way that was loving but without ritual. Her mother would not have wanted anything other than practical disposal. When Neva's father died, Frances had done just as her husband requested—she had added him to the garden compost while singing the sassy theme song from a public television recycling ad: "...and when I die, yes when I die, please recycle these old bones of mine."

Although Neva had understood her parents' rejection of the funeral business, she could not be so playful with her mother's remains.

"Is the mine the right place to leave you?" she murmured, resting her hand on the warm box. "I just don't know yet, I really don't know."

Chapter Six

Bernice Pangle leaned big arms on the counter of the Angus post office window and looked Neva up and down.

"General delivery?" she said, as though it were a new concept.

"For Jeneva Leopold. I'm spending the summer out at Billie Creek Mine."

"So I heard." Bernice glanced around her cubicle, lifted papers, sighed, and slowly scratched a spot on her left side by reaching her right arm around her considerable bulk. "A package, you said?"

"No, just letters." Reveling in solitude, Neva had not visited the post office during her first two weeks, and now she was so eager for news from Ethan that she watched the postmistress' hands, willing them to find what must be there. "Mainly I'm hoping to hear from my son."

"You have children?"

"A boy, more or less grown up. Do you have kids?"

"Does a pig have pork?" Bernice's chuckle sent waves of movement through the flesh under her flowered dress. "There were seven at last count, of my own that is." Again the full-body laugh. "Three boys, and four girls. Six grandchildren, three great-grandchildren, and a great-great on the way. Hard to believe, isn't it? Nobody ever believes it. But God's been good to me, I've had a good life, and that keeps you young." As she talked her hands had located two envelopes, which she held loosely.

Raising her eyes in an effort not to stare greedily at the letters, Neva said, "How many still live with you?"

"More than enough. So you're all alone up there?"

"Yes, but it doesn't feel lonely. I like the quiet."

"I know what you mean." Bernice leaned closer and dropped her voice. "Me, I lock myself in the toilet when it gets too much. I have a tape deck in there and I just turn it up so I can't hear 'em pounding on the door." She handed Neva the letters with an air of having concluded a successful transaction.

"You grew up in Angus?"

"Bet your boots I did, and never wanted to be anywhere else."

"Then you must have known my uncle, Matthew Burt."

Bernice Pangle's mouth dropped open cartoon fashion, then snapped shut. She looked hard at Neva for the first time. "Burtie never mentioned any family."

"He was my mother's brother."

"I never saw any letters from any sister."

"They weren't on very good terms toward the end, I don't know why. You ran the post office that long ago?"

"Missy, I been at this window a sight more years than I care to count. Just don't expect me to tell tales. I work for the government, don't forget." The postmistress stood with crossed arms and stern face.

Neva smiled, thanked her and went out. To walk away from someone who had known her uncle for years, even in the routine role of letter sorter, did not come naturally, but Bernice Pangle clearly treasured her role and her knowledge of the territory. Best to let her get used to the idea that Matthew Burt had a family before angling for information. She was clearly a talker, and given time, was likely to volunteer whatever tidbits she had stashed away.

Standing on the little post office porch Neva could see all of Angus, including the café, the boarded-up school, and half a dozen wood frame houses. Driving eight miles along the narrow Dry River Highway from the bottom of Billie Creek Road she had steered around two rattlesnakes, counted nine ground squirrels standing next to their roadside burrows, stopped to watch sandhill cranes in an irrigated field, but she had not met a single car.

Only two pickups were parked in front of the café. This was promising. The café would be as empty as she was ever likely to find it, and if she went in for a cold drink she would not have to face a roomful of strangers who all knew each other. Squinting against the glare, she crossed the parking lot, hesitated at the prospect of two doors, then chose the one marked "Bar." On it was a sign: *No One Under 21 Allowed Inside These Premises.* This wouldn't have struck her except that the first person she saw on stepping inside was a small boy sitting at the near end of the counter drinking from a tall glass. A man at the other end of the bar was watching TV while the squat proprietor thumbed through a magazine.

Despite the separate entry doors there was just a single room, the café portion consisting of three tables against the wall. Neva slid onto a stool.

"Hot enough for you?" the proprietor said affably and put the magazine under the counter.

"Almost."

"Can I pull you a tall cold one?"

Neva glanced down the bar at the other customer's glass, which was half full of beer. "Sure," she said. It wasn't yet noon but if the local custom was to drink beer she would drink beer.

Her neighbor stared at a rapid-fire news program, his shoulders hunched, his face impassive. Clearly just come from heavy labor of some kind, he still wore the grime of the job on his skin and clothes. His hands cupping the glass mug were so thickened, calloused, and stained they looked more like tools than parts of a human body.

"Where you headed?" the barman said, taking a white towel from his back pocket.

"I'm here for the summer, up at Billie Creek Mine."

The customer turned his head to observe Neva.

"You prospecting?" said the bartender.

"I hadn't planned to. I'm just staying in the cabin, enjoying a bit of quiet time. It used to belong to my Uncle Matthew Burt. I guess he was known as Burtie out here."

The barman didn't react visibly but the other man made a word-less sound of surprise, then reached for his glass and drained its contents in one quick toss, as though about to leave in a hurry.

"Not the one that disappeared?" said the barman. "Well, I'm damned. I never knew him, that was before I bought this place, but it was Tony here that found his rifle. I do remember hearing that. Wasn't that right, Tony?"

The man nodded and said in a gravelly bass that seemed disconnected from his wiry body, "That's right, Al."

"I'm Jeneva Leopold. Burtie was my mother's brother."

"Al Fleck," the barman said and offered his hand. "This here's Tony. Tony Briggs. Tell the lady about finding that rifle, Tony."

Only two stools stood between Neva and Tony Briggs, but his eyes as he considered what to say seemed to regard her from a great distance.

"Did you know my uncle?" she said after a lengthy silence.

"Everybody knew him."

"Where did you find the rifle?"

"I didn't find it."

Puzzled, she waited while he took a cigarette from a pack of Camels lying on the bar, lit it, drew deeply, and looked at his glass. Skipper had mentioned a missing rifle, but said nothing about it being found. At last she prompted, "Is the rifle still around?"

"It's yours if you want it. By rights it's yours." Another pull on the cigarette, and then words came out with the smoke. "It was on my back porch. That's where it was, on my back porch. Can you figure it? I never could figure it. It's yours, just say the word."

"Thank you, but I don't want it, really. I have no use for a rifle. How did it end up on your porch, do you think?"

Looking squarely into her face he said with sudden passion, "I can't even make a goddamn living for my family anymore. You understand what I mean? I'm okay this month, I'm working a private job over by Lookout Rock, big stuff, you can do what you want like we always did before, not this low-impact bullshit the Forest Service makes you do, like we're criminals that want to destroy the forest. It's not public forest anymore, it's a goddamn country, the Forest Service's own country. My tax dollars pay for the locks and gates they're putting on roads I went on since I was born. You know what I mean? Do you work for the Forest Service?"

"I work for a newspaper."

"You writing about logging?"

"I'm not writing anything. I'm on vacation."

"I never had a vacation in my life except layoffs. But then I never wanted one, all I want's work. If ranching still paid I'd keep on ranching, but I had to go to logging and now that's going tits up, too. Those people in Washington believe anything. If they believe spotted owls and frogs are more important than people they'll believe the moon's made of green cheese. Hell, maybe it is for all I know."

Abruptly, he laughed, a cavernous, unhitched kind of laugh that made Al chuckle along as though to anchor the wild sound. "It must be tough," Neva said, feeling phony. She had voted for every environmental measure that ever came her way.

"A lot of people have it bad," Tony said, evidently relieved by his tirade. "Miners, for one."

"It's not all the government's fault," said Al. "I used to log before I got into the restaurant racket, and a lot of those guys cheated, they lied on their sick leave and got workers' comp when they shouldn't have. How can a small operator afford it? So they get fancier equipment to do the job with only a couple of loggers, which means less accident insurance as well as a smaller payroll. Logging isn't what it used to be. Nothing is what it used to be. Of course, some things are better." He looked at the TV with a thoughtful frown. "Off hand I can't think of any. Can I fill that up?"

Tony Briggs pushed his glass toward Neva's. "It's on me."

Neva had neglected Rule One for drinking when you don't want to: nurse it. Her appetite for a second beer was even less than for the first, but to refuse could ruin her chance of drawing Briggs into conversation about her uncle. "Did you grow up here?" Her attempt at an easy conversational tone sounded false in her own ears, but Tony didn't appear to notice or care.

"Who says I grew up? Listen, your uncle was a good man. Give you the shirt off his back. What happened was a goddamn shame."

"What did happen?"

"It's been a lot of years. What took you so long to get out here if you're so interested? I didn't know he had any family."

"I didn't get a chance to know my uncle. He and my mother had some kind of falling out so we didn't see him much. I didn't come here specifically to find out about him, I just needed to get away somewhere quiet. But now I'm here I've become really curious. He'd be about eighty, I think."

Briggs nodded, drank, trailed smoke, and was silent.

"Do you think he died at the mine?"

"Who told you that?"

"There don't seem to be a whole lot of possibilities. Either he died or just walked away and disappeared. He might even be alive somewhere, but I find that hard to believe after so many years."

"Mining's a hard life, a real hard life. A lot of these guys work a job to support their mine. Go figure."

"As far as I know my uncle didn't do anything except mine. He must have been successful. I mean, he must have found gold."

"I knew it." Tony's tone was triumphant and his expression as he looked at her was not flattering. Sliding stiffly off the stool, he said, "It always comes around to money, doesn't it? Well, you might as well quit looking and go on back where you came from. There's no stash of gold hid out there at Billie Creek and there never was."

When he was gone, Al Fleck shook his head. "Don't mind Tony. He's our official, bonafide, gold-medal sourpuss. If they were all like that I'd sell out and move back to Medford."

Neva managed to get away without finishing the second beer, but even so the warm drive back up the Dry River Valley seemed long, and by the time she reached the Sufferin' Smith Mine in the lower end of Billie Creek Canyon she was fighting to keep her eyes open. There had been no sign of Gene Holland on her way out, but now a pickup truck was parked beside the first of the two small cabins. This she took to be the house. A second building, a little larger but of the same casual construction, stood about thirty feet upstream. This must be the laboratory. Beyond it in a patch of sun a man sat on a kitchen chair with a washtub at his feet. His elbows were on his knees and his hands supported a shallow, bowl-shaped pan that he was examining with such focused care that he appeared not to notice Neva as she left her car on the road and crossed a plank laid over the creek.

She was just a few feet away, wondering if he might be deaf, when he looked up, said, "Grab a seat," and nodded toward some log rounds lying next to the laboratory shack. She rolled one close to the washtub, set it upright and sat down.

"I'm Jeneva Leopold from up at Billie Creek Mine," she said, observing him with puzzled curiosity. Skipper's glowing account of Holland's experience and knowledge of mining had led her to expect a grizzled old fellow as wiry as the sagebrush, his thin beard stained with tobacco juice. The real Gene Holland suggested a scientist engaged in absorbing fieldwork. Looking through tinted rimless glasses, he studied the contents of the shallow pan, then tipped and rotated it and looked again.

"I'm just cleaning up a bit of material," he said in a low and pleasant voice. He glanced up at her over the top of his glasses, then focused again on the pan, tilting it so she could see that it held about two cups of water and a handful of fine black sand. He swirled the contents and let some of the water run into the washtub, which was half full of liquid mud.

"Are you panning?"

"That's correct." Holland's cheeks were ruddy above a trimmed brown beard, his skull was visibly round under a buzz cut, and he wore a faded green T-shirt, baggy khaki shorts, and tennis shoes without socks. A greasy rag hung out of his shorts pocket. A knapsack next to his chair gaped open to show a water bottle, a lime green plastic sun visor, and a sheaf of rolled papers.

"I thought gold panning was done in creeks or rivers," she said, and stifled a yawn.

"True enough in some places, but we don't have enough water around here to count on, plus it's easier to pan in the comfort of home, so to speak."

"Do you mine here year-round?"

"Too cold. I spend winters down in Nevada. I have a mine down there, too. It's just as hopeless as this one."

Taking the comment as a joke, like downplaying a personal talent or skill, Neva laughed. She wanted to ask him what kind of take it was reasonable to expect in a week, but it was too much like asking the amount of his paycheck. He remained focused on the contents of the pan, which he continued to swirl without seeming to progress in any way she could recognize, the black sand remaining at about the same level and no gold appearing. Faced with his bent head, she felt heavy with beer and the unmoving heat of early afternoon. The creek murmured, cicadas buzzed, her eyelids sank irresistibly, and to get a conversation going seemed suddenly like hard work. All she wanted was to be back at the cabin reading Ethan's letters on the porch with a good cup of coffee to undo the beer. She would tackle Gene Holland another day.

She stood up, brushing wood chips off her shorts. "I drank two beers at Angus just to be polite and now I can't keep my eyes open. All I'm good for is a nap."

Holland stopped agitating the pan, and after a moment of reflection, said, "Thanks for stopping by."

"I hear you know all there is to know about Billie Creek," she said, roused somewhat by his apparent lack of interest in whether she stayed or went. "I'd planned to cross-examine you about local history but I guess it has to wait. I'd appreciate it particularly if you could tell me about my uncle, Matthew Burt."

Holland's nod was slow and thoughtful. Before replying he explored the black sand with one finger. "Your uncle. Yes, I see. Another time would be better. I'm in kind of a hurry to get through that lot." He nodded at a nearby bucket that was half full of sandy gravel. "It's kind of surprising to find out he had any family."

"Bernice Pangle down at the post office said the same thing, but you know, it's just as surprising for me to find people out here who knew him. I'd never heard of anyone connected with his life other than Orson. Why don't you come up to the house some evening? I generally walk during the day. I could have a meal ready in short order if you don't mind it canned or dried."

"I just might do that one of these evenings."

Settled on the porch with coffee, Neva read Ethan's letters, which were predictably brief but amusing, and affectionate enough to restore her spirits after the mildly disconcerting trip to Angus. She particularly enjoyed the final lines of the second letter: "I know I said not to spend the summer writing to me, but I didn't think you would just disappear into the desert. You know what I realized? This is the longest I've ever gone without talking to you or email or anything and it's a little weird. I'm not saying you should rush off to the nearest phone—are there phones anywhere out there?—but a few lines scratched on a rock would be nice. It doesn't even have to be gold."

He was right. Never before since his birth had they been out of touch for more than two or three days, though this hadn't felt to her like a two-week silence because she had added a paragraph or more to her own letter every day. As she prepared for a quick, late walk, she tried to picture him reading the letter in his cramped apartment, but her thoughts weren't ready to linger in that outside world, not even for Ethan. She left the cabin as the sun was dropping toward the western edge of the canyon. It was too late to aim for the high country, but there was plenty of daylight left to return to the leaning cabin where she had found the tobacco can. There might be other interesting things there that she hadn't noticed the first time, and now that she knew the function of the can it was worth another look. Sunlight slanting in from the west brought out apricot tones in the ponderosa trunks, and made strong shadows that gave the woods and rocks extra three-dimensionality. This was her favorite time of day, when light thickened and deepened in color. Easily falling into her trail stride, she covered the two miles to the ruin in what seemed like no time. As she approached the tobacco can she saw that the lid was open even though, fastidious about leaving things as she found them, she had made a point of closing it.

The can still held a small stone, but it was the wrong one. Instead of obsidian, there was now a rough yellow pebble that she pulled out with one finger. She'd never seen raw gold before but knew immediately that this was a nugget. Dull yellow, about the size of a pea, it was irregular in shape, even lacy, as though it had once been a soft string of gold that was dropped in a heap and then hardened.

Cupping the bit of precious metal in her hand she scanned the darkening woods. Who had exchanged the obsidian for gold since she was here two days ago? Her earlier sense that the cabin was haunted came back in a rush, but rather than hurry away she turned to face the ruin. Ghosts don't put rocks in cans. If she let herself be senselessly frightened by one site in the canyon, the uneasiness might spread and then what would become of her summer?

She moved to the center of the clearing where the light was better, and studied the little rock. Was this dirty yellow mineral really the cause of gold fever, of land rushes, claim jumps, even murders? Had her uncle really spent a lifetime pursuing such dull rocks? She shook her head. The pebble would not have caught her eye in a streambed. Other stones were prettier, the deep reds and turquoises, even the peachy orange of certain quartz appealed to her more than this oddly fake-looking gold. It stirred no avarice. What would it be worth? Very little, obviously, or it would not have been left in the can—by Skipper Dooley as a joke? Of course. He had driven up the creek after she told him about the tobacco can.

A few moments of hunting about turned up an ornamental hinge that had fallen off the old hutch in the cabin. She washed it in the creek, dried it on her shirt and pushed it into the tobacco can along with the nugget, then carefully closed the fragile lid.

Chapter Seven

Stars were showing when Skipper came bouncing down the road on the quad with Cayuse sitting tall on the seat behind him. He pulled into the dooryard where Neva sat on the chopping block drinking mint tea and looking at the blue-black sky.

"Hey, Walkie-Talkie," he boomed. Cayuse jumped down and ran to Neva.

"Walkie-Talkie?" Neva laid a tentative hand on the dog's head.

Skipper half sat against the quad seat and folded his arms across his chest. "You walk like a champ and talk like a champ, and there you have it. It's a compliment, in case you're wondering. Somebody was out here looking for you today."

"No one knows I'm here."

"Well, this Forest Service squimp was in no doubt about it."

"Did he say why he wanted to see me?"

"Not a clue, but you can bet it's bad news. He said he'd be back tomorrow. If I was you I'd take a long walk, starting at sun-up. What you don't know, they can't get you for."

"I'm sure there's no problem, Skipper."

"Don't count on it."

"They probably just have to keep tabs on people staying in the national forest. Could you eat some beans and rice?"

"I ate at Sumpter, and anyway Cayuse and me are pretty tired. I like to hit the sack by dark when I'm out here. I sleep like I'm dead. And that's an interesting thing—how come nobody wants to die but there's nothing better than sleeping like you're dead? Answer me that one."

All the following day Neva waited around the cabin for the ranger to return. She split wood, cleaned the lamp chimneys, wrote a letter to Ethan as well as an extra long entry in her journal, watched birds, read, heated water on the wood stove and washed her hair outside in the galvanized laundry tub. At last, restless and satisfied that he wouldn't show up today, she left the cabin in late afternoon following the trail along the main branch of the creek. When she reached the point where it crossed Billie Creek Road, the sun had already dropped below the ridge, throwing the canyon bottom into shadow. Rather than return through the woods, she turned left down the road. The distance was longer in miles because the road followed the contours of the canyon's sloping wall, but it would be lighter up here, with views of the other side of the canyon and the distant ridges to the south of the Dry River.

Late light bathed the upper reaches of the canyon's east side and overhead the sky deepened to evening blue and rose. The day's heat softened. Her bare arms and legs moved through the warm air as though through invisible balm, and she slowed to a dreamy pace, devouring the twilight with her eyes, nose and skin.

The road rounded a broad bend and widened slightly, and in the wide spot at the base of the canyon wall stood a water trough. A pipe that once connected it to the hillside, and presumably to a spring, had rusted through, and instead of brimming with clear water the trough now offered a foot-deep mat of yellow-green algae. The wide spot faced south, down the canyon. She stopped to watch the colors on the distant hills across the Dry River harden like an image developing on photo paper, the high spots gleaming with sunset polish while the hollows blackened with shadow.

The light was dazzling, and when she started down the road once more she dropped her gaze to the ground for relief. Directly in front of her was a bright blue patch in the sandy gravel. Kneeling, she dug out a baseball cap with *Wallowa Tractor and*

Irrigation emblazoned in white letters on the front. She shook the cap free of sand and raised it to her nose. Diesel, sweat, tobacco…a man's smell, fresh from someone's head. Wide tire tracks and boot prints had churned up the area around the hat, and in the bottom of a boot print a sliver of shiny metal gleamed. It was a clasp knife, and like the cap, it could not have been here long, certainly not through wet weather. It easily wiped clean, though the blades grated with sand. She opened an awl, tweezers, a serrated blade, and delicate pliers.

Solid and warm on her palm, it was an attractive tool, too nice to leave behind. She rolled it in the cap and pushed the roll into her shorts pocket, but it bumped against her thigh at every step and she soon turned back to the water trough. The rim was wide enough to hold both hat and knife in easy view of the road. If they were still here in a week or two, she would take the knife for Ethan.

◇◇◇

Though the sun was well down when she arrived back at the mine, there was still enough light to see the piece of paper sticking out from under a rock on the back step, and to read the message written in blue ink.

> *Dear Ms. Leopold,*
> *I meant to stop in earlier but unexpectedly I had to spend the day in town. This is an urgent message—you must vacate the cabin. This is national forest land and the cabin can be used only for active mining purposes. I don't know who gave you the idea that you could just live here. Believe me this is no laughing matter. The mining claim will be terminated if you don't move out immediately. Call me if you have questions about this matter. I am out of the office most of the day but I will return your call as soon as I can.*
> *Very Sincerely,*
> *Andy Sylvester*
> *U.S. Forest Service Mining Technician*

Neva was more puzzled than shocked. How could they "terminate" a claim when there was no active mining going on? Orson was the sole remaining owner now. He would never come back, and if she wanted to take up placer mining she'd have to file a claim in her own name because mineral rights aren't hereditary. True, it was Forest Service land, but the cabin had been in her family for nearly half a century. She didn't need anyone's permission to stay in it, and she certainly wasn't causing any problems. And how was she to call Andy Sylvester? He must know there wasn't a telephone for miles, and even cell phones didn't work out here. Clearly, there was some colossal error or misunderstanding.

Leaving her binoculars and water bottle on the porch, she hurried down to Skipper's camp. "Hey, Walkie-Talkie, you missed Smoky again," he called out from his seat under a pine tree. "No great loss, if you ask me."

Neva handed him the note without a word. Squinting, he said, "An owl couldn't read out here. Come on inside."

A glance was all he needed before his hand slammed onto the table and he exploded into cursing. When he paused for breath, Neva said, "They probably don't understand that I'm here just for the summer."

"Of course they do. I told him so today. I didn't know why he was asking or I wouldn't have told him a damn thing. I said you'd had some health problems and needed some rest and quiet and general rammycackin' around the hills. They've got no good reason to do this. What kind of people would kick a sick lady out of her cabin? It's true you don't look sick, but he didn't even see you. What's such a big deal about people living in old shacks on public land?"

"They can't let people live in the national forest, I understand that," Neva said more reasonably than she felt. "But I'm not really living here. And that's odd about terminating the claim if I don't move out."

"It's just dumb, that's all, the dumbest thing I ever heard. Don't go, W.T. Make them carry you out. You're not hurting anything, you're even cleaning it up. And who cares about the claim. As you said, Orson'll never be back and you aren't going into the mining business."

"I'll go to the ranger station in Elkhorn tomorrow and get it straightened out. They obviously don't understand what I'm doing."

"Don't be so goddamned reasonable. If I was you I'd be waiting on the porch when they got there in the morning, and I'd let them have it with such a tornado of two-fisted words they wouldn't know what hit. Don't you want to stay?"

"Of course I want to stay. But if I can't stay in the cabin I'll camp somewhere. You can camp in the national forest. That I do know."

"Only for two weeks, then you have to get a permit. That's why I move around all the time, to keep them off my back. Now, I'm due to shove off here soon, you could have this camp, but still I'd fight it if I was you. Hell, your uncle Burtie is local history. Don't they respect anything but the letter of the goddamn law?"

Suddenly Skipper threw his head back and laughed. "What a joke, though. You look at that outfit downstream there at the Barlow Mine, bulldozers chewing up the ground and messing up the creek. But they've got a permit. You, where's your permit to sit on the porch and read? Maybe if you paid them twenty bucks and filled in some forms in triplicate you could get a permit for R&R on government property!" Musing and shaking his head, he was briefly silent, then said, "I was down there today talking to Reese Cotter. He runs the Barlow Mine. He said his brother, Lance, got pissed off about something and took off yesterday, and didn't even take his truck. He asked if I'd seen a dumb-looking kid anywhere around. Meanwhile, there's just him and one other guy trying to run that whole operation."

Skipper shook his head in wonder. "What a joke. Maybe you better just get yourself a gold pan and go for it. Hell, W.T., you might strike it rich."

Chapter Eight

That night, Neva lay wide-eyed and worried, even though the eviction notice must be a mistake. She was so obviously harmless in every way that no sane official could seriously insist that she leave. When she explained the situation, Sylvester would most likely be embarrassed. Skipper had said he was young. He was probably new on the job and had never heard of her uncle. To leave Billie Creek Mine now, when she was still gaining strength every day, was unthinkable. She could not—would not—leave until she was ready. Despite what she'd said to Skipper about camping, she was too happy and healthy in the cabin to move out, and it was never comfortable to read or write outdoors without a good chair and table, and screens to keep off flies in the hot afternoons.

Having seen the cabin only once before moving in for the summer, Neva hadn't remembered much about it. She had expected it to be a mess after standing empty for fifteen years, and had planned to camp nearby on the first night, and to spend at least a day cleaning and making the place habitable again. What she had found, instead, was attractive order that had made her wonder in those first puzzled minutes whether someone had been living here recently.

The setup was not at all what anyone would expect to find in a sixty-year-old cabin inhabited for thirty years by a pair of bachelor miners and then locked up and left. Not only was there order, but the furniture was almost elegant, from the bent-arm rocker to the Victorian loveseat upholstered in leather, now finely cracked. The table by the bed turned out to be a treadle sewing machine with the top closed. There was a small writing desk under the window where she set out her books and journals, and a wicker settee on the porch where she sat with her morning coffee to watch the sun rise over the opposite ridge. Who had chosen this unlikely furniture, her uncle or Orson? And which one had been the gardener, for it was still easy to see that the hillside around the house had been terraced into flowerbeds marked out with chunks of quartz. A few jonquils and iris survived, along with a spindly lilac shrub.

The two faded Korean art prints above the bed had puzzled her at first, but then a long-forgotten memory surfaced; her uncle had fought in the Korean war. It was one of the few facts she had been told about him. Next to one of the prints hung a black and white photograph of a young Asian woman wearing a sundress and holding a parasol above her head. Her uncle's Korean girl friend? Why else would he keep the picture for thirty years? Although, Orson might also have served in Korea. Maybe this is how the two men had met, and the woman had been Orson's sweetheart.

The only thing that had needed serious attention in the cabin was the handsome St. Louis Majestic woodstove in the kitchen. After emptying the ash drawer and scrubbing rust and ancient grease off the wide cooking surface, she had opened the dampers and lit a lone twist of paper in the firebox, watching for backed-up smoke. The flame flickered and smoke drew up the flue just as it should, unhindered by ancient birds' nests and other debris that she had feared might have accumulated over the years. The slender sticks of kindling crackled with cheerful heat, transforming the old stove into the warm heart of the cabin.

By the second night she had felt completely at home, so at home that she also found herself feeling suddenly close to her uncle. This was just the sort of hideaway she had created many times in her fantasies, and therefore, surely, she would have got along with the man who had made it and lived in it for decades.

In the morning, instead of driving down to the Dry River Valley and then over the mountains to the Forest Service office in Elkhorn, Neva decided to avoid Sylvester for as long as possible. Until they met face-to-face she could not be expected to move. Sometimes, no action is the best action when dealing with bureaucracy, and this situation couldn't be high on the Forest Service's list of important business.

Without taking time for her morning dip, she hurried into the woods above the mine right after breakfast and chores. She didn't return to the cabin until late afternoon, and was relieved to find Skipper waiting for her rather than another note or even Sylvester himself. They settled on the porch with mugs of miso, Neva on the wicker settee and Skipper in the rocking chair she had dragged out to accommodate his long legs. Last night, upset by the note, she had forgotten to tell him about finding the hat and knife at the water trough, and now began relating the tale as he sniffed suspiciously at his cup.

"It's like drinking straight salt," he exclaimed after the first sip. "You don't realize how much you sweat out here until you taste something like this. Now, I don't know why you didn't keep the knife. It sounds like a Leatherman, a real spendy item, but I'd bet the owner isn't likely to reclaim it, now or any time soon. He was probably some old dude like me dinking around looking for interesting stuff, or more likely, hoping to trip over a boulder of pure gold. You have to remember that any old Tom, Dick, or Harry can go anywhere they want to out here. They read a book about mining and they still think they can get rich in a weekend. And of course, they don't want anybody to know they're here because it's not their claim, and if they find something, they sure as hell don't want anybody to know where they got it. They wouldn't come asking for something they left behind, that's for sure."

"If the knife is still there in a week or so, I'll take it. I'm sure my son would love it." Neva let a brief silence pass before saying, "Skipper, I just have to ask—did you put that gold nugget in the tobacco can?"

"Gold nugget in a tobacco can? Well, aren't you just the luckiest greenhorn going. I never found any fancy knife out here, and I never found a gold nugget in a tobacco can in my life. If I had a gold nugget worth the name I'd have me a gold tooth made. Let's have a look."

"I left it in the can," she said, continuing to look at him with suspicion. "I thought you were playing a joke."

"You left it! Well, damn. You leave a nugget, you leave a classy knife. I told you that I don't take much of what I find, but you're worse than me. Not that a little piece of gold is worth anything, except as a souvenir. Now, if you don't mind switching gears, I'm planning to pull out of here soon. I was thinking you could move down to the creek if Smoky runs you out of the cabin. You have a tent and all that? Well, then. It's a great spot to camp, and it's closer to your bathtub."

Never having mentioned her dips in the mining pond, Neva looked at him over the top of her mug but he was gazing with an air of thoughtful preoccupation at the distant ridgeline.

Chapter Nine

He had taken to watching for her whenever he worked out in the open. Twice he was fooled by calves far up on the ridge. Then he thought of turning the glasses down the canyon, scanning what little could be seen of the creek bottom. He started low and worked up, past the mine near the mouth, the Barlow Mine pit, the Billie Creek Mine pond—he stiffened, spun the focus knob, and bent forward as though to bring the image closer.

Something was in the pond, something was swimming around by the dam. There weren't beaver out here, or muskrat—it was a dog, it must be a dog. The fur glinted red against the dark water, and now there were pale lines on both sides...He let out a breath. Shoulders. Bare shoulders. It was the woman. She was in the pond, she was getting out of the pond, she was naked this time, naked all the way, naked but alive.

Holding the glasses steady, he felt with his foot for a rock and sat down slowly, watching her bend for the towel and rub all over, including her hair. She was a pale little form, without detail, stretching now with her arms toward the sky, the towel dropped around her feet. She was alive but still her skin would be cool from the water...He blew through his lips, lowered the glasses, and raised them again instantly. She shouldn't be out here, no place for a lone woman, not for anyone with sense, and soon he'd never have to come back here himself, thank God.

He frowned, became aware of pain and realized he was pressing the eyepieces hard against his face. Easing his grip, he propped his elbows on his knees. She was dressing now, one leg and then the other into shorts, the shirt pulled on over her head, bending over, shaking her hair, toweling it again.

She folded the towel, put it in a basket, pushed her feet into slippers or sandals, he couldn't tell which.

Motionless, holding his breath, he watched her stand for a long time looking at something. The water? Something in the water? She squatted, got onto her hands and knees, then sat up and threw her head back. She was laughing! What was this crazy woman up to? He would have to go down there and find out. The next time he saw her on the ridge, out of the way, he would go to Billie Creek Mine and—no, no, he couldn't do that, he could never do that.

With the basket on her arm she walked along the dam, reached the bank, and was gone, leaving him alone with rocks, heat, distance, silence. Such heavy, heavy silence.

Chapter Ten

In the morning Neva woke up knowing she couldn't leave the cabin question up in the air. Directly after breakfast, she left the mine, drove down Billie Creek Road, and at the bottom she turned left for the first time rather than right. It was another ten miles to the east end of the Dry River Valley. Here the road split, the left hand fork heading over the mountains to Elkhorn while the right continued into the Dry River Canyon. She turned left, and soon was into a long section of switchbacks which cut through high banks of cream-colored rock that appeared freshly scrubbed in the morning light. The turns took on a hypnotic rhythm. Swing left, swing right, swing left, swing right. Cruising at an easy speed, she fell into a dream and after a while even stopped rehearsing her arguments for staying in the cabin.

The road crossed a high ridge east of Billie Mountain, and dropped down the north side toward the Elkhorn Valley. Wetter over here than the south side, the slopes were more heavily forested, but when she reached the flat and pulled over at a picnic shelter to look back, Billie Mountain stood up against the sky in familiar outline. It appeared higher and steeper from this side, but she was viewing it from a considerably lower elevation than the mine. It would be a good challenge to walk from the cabin right over the top sometime and at least partway down the north side. It would be a long day, but not impossible.

Skipper had told her to watch for a three-story modern glass and concrete building on the edge of town as she approached Elkhorn, but she didn't notice it until too late to turn into the parking lot. Traffic was so light she made a quick U-turn and pulled in next to a line of Forest Service vans and trucks. The ground floor was the Elkhorn Post Office. She stopped to buy stamps before taking the stairs to the second floor, bypassing the elevators as she always did when there was a choice.

The Forest Service offices took up the entire second floor but a single receptionist at a desk in the main foyer served as the checkpoint for anyone coming or going. The cheerful young woman said that Andy Sylvester had gone out, and as far as she knew he would not be back that day, but she would be happy to give him a message.

"Thank you but I need to see him in person," Neva said, not attempting to hide her disappointment. He was probably at the mine right now looking for her, though she could not recall passing a Forest Service vehicle on the way into town.

Back outside in the clear light of midmorning, she stood near the double glass front doors and considered what to do next. Her day at the mine was already ruined, regardless of whether she rushed straight back. She should take a look at Elkhorn, buy gas, and pick up supplies while she was here, and certainly fill the water bottles she had loaded into the trunk. Maybe there was a handy outdoor spigot on this building. She went around to the parking lot on the north side and followed a sprinkler hose past a line of shrubbery to its source at a complex faucet that she was unable to turn on.

Back in the car, she headed toward the center of town but within three blocks she was stopped in a line of vehicles waiting their turn to get through the single narrow lane left while road repairs were underway. All four windows were down but the air in the car rapidly grew hot and heavy. The nearest street tree was half a block away. She could use the air conditioning—if it worked. Preferring fresh air, no matter how hot, and living most of the time in the cool Willamette Valley, she had never used the air conditioning in this car, and as she fiddled with various knobs it struck her that she didn't want to begin now.

Cars had lined up behind her, the nearest idling so close that she could not back up to turn around. A broad driveway on the other side of the street offered a lovely tunnel of shade. She pulled into it and found herself on a curving drive that circled past a large and elaborate Victorian house with multiple gables, porches, small balconies, and gingerbread, fronted by a perfect lawn and shrubs. A sign announced *Garden of Eternal Peace*. Why is that the best old houses in so many towns end up as funeral homes?

Emerald lawns require plenty of water. Neva's scrutiny switched from the house itself to what she could see of the foundation at the back of the flower border, and immediately she spotted a plain faucet with good clearance for filling jugs. As she was considering whether to venture onto the immaculate porch in search of someone to ask for permission, a man appeared from the back of the building, walking slowly up the walkway that ran along the flower border, his thin shoulders hunched. For a moment she wondered whether he might be drunk even though it was not yet noon, but then it struck her that his uncertain step suggested a recent illness or psychological or emotional setback. He looked up, returned her scrutiny for several seconds without a change of expression, and then approached the car.

"May I help you?" he said without real interest, though not in an unfriendly tone. His long-sleeved yellow shirt was buttoned to the collar despite the July heat, and his face and hands had the pale cast of an indoor worker, a denizen of air-conditioned rooms with shaded windows.

"Sorry to bother you," she said. "I was stuck in that line of cars and got too hot, so I pulled in here to turn around."

"No problem. The drive circles right back to the street." As he spoke he was already turning away.

"One more thing, please. I'm traveling, and I was heading into town to fill some water bottles, but it's very hot and slow waiting in line. Would you mind if I filled them from your faucet over there behind the oleander or whatever that shrub is with the pink flowers? I don't need much. And I'd be glad to pay for the water."

"Water?" He looked back at her with a frown, but his words were neighborly. "I don't see any problem with that. There's nobody here anyway."

"Thank you," she said, but he was walking away again. This really was a stroke of luck. She had lost interest in seeing Elkhorn today, and with full water bottles she could head straight back to the mine and possibly catch Andy Sylvester.

Squatting by the spigot, she was filling the last bottle when the man returned along the walkway. Looking up with a smile, she said, "I really appreciate this. It's much more pleasant than a gas station."

"Not everybody likes a funeral home," he said without slowing down.

"I don't care one way or the other. It's a beautiful old house, and the grounds are like a park. Do you happen to know whether this is a ladybug? It looks like a ladybug, but I've never seen one that was green with black spots. They're usually red."

The change in the man was instant. He stopped, turned, and regarded her with interest, as though really noticing her presence for the first time. Without having to look where she was pointing, he said, "*Diabrotica undecimpunctata undecimpunctata.* Western spotted cucumber beetle. Not a ladybug. Most people kill them but that's because their cousin, the striped cucumber beetle, is a serious agricultural pest in California. Up here they don't bother much except corn and peas. I don't mind them myself, not being a farmer."

"Say that again, please, the taxonomic name."

"*Diabrotica undecimpunctata undecimpunctata.*"

"What a wonderful name for such a humble little bug." Neva stood up, the full bottle hanging heavy in her left hand, and crossed the flower border to the walkway. "Are you an entomologist?"

He shook his head. "I guess you're new in Elkhorn."

"This is my first visit. I'm from the Willamette Valley."

"I'll just give you a hand with those so you can be on your way."

"Thank you again," she said when the bottles were in the trunk. "I'm Jeneva."

He met her proffered hand with his own thin hand without clasping hers. "Darrell," he said. "Have a nice trip."

Puzzled, she watched him go down the walk and out of sight around the rear corner of the house. A nice trip? Ah, she had said she was traveling. She should have asked whether she could fill the bottles at the Garden of Eternal Peace as needed in the future. She started the car and followed the drive around behind the house hoping to catch him, but Darrell was not to be seen.

It was a fine day, with one small white cloud floating high in an otherwise intense blue sky. As usual on the minor highways of the West, there were more hawks and ground squirrels than cars, though only one rattlesnake sunned itself today on the lower stretch of Billie Creek Road before it entered the canyon. About a mile beyond Gene's cabin, Neva rounded a bend and saw a green truck heading down the road. It rolled to within a few feet of her front bumper, stopped, and was engulfed in its own dust. A young man in a short-sleeved khaki shirt and jeans emerged from the cloud.

Skipper had referred to Andy Sylvester as a punk kid but still Neva was struck by his youth. She found it hard to believe that someone who looked younger than her own son had the power, or maybe gall was a better word, to order her to leave the mine. As she got out to meet him she didn't know whether to be cordial, indignant or motherly.

"Andy Sylvester," he said. "I've just been up at the mine looking for you."

His grip was firm and his manner businesslike despite the smooth cheeks that looked as though they had yet to see a razor. "You got my note?"

"I did. It was quite a shock. I was hoping we could talk over coffee."

"I'd intended to tell you in person. But that's the way the cookie crumbles."

"It's more than a cookie to me, a lot more," she snapped, and then took a breath and tried for a more diplomatic tone. "Are you in a hurry? I could have coffee ready in short order."

"I have to be somewhere this afternoon, but I don't see why we couldn't have a little talk right here." Sylvester half-sat against the hood of the truck, his arms folded. "So, what's up?"

"What's up?" Neva took an identical stance against her own hood, but with her hands in her shorts pockets. "You've told me to move out of a cabin that's been in my family for forty-five years, that's what's up. You may not have understood that I'm here for the summer recovering from surgery and doing a bit of writing. I plan to stay until the end of August."

"Sorry, can't do. Squatting isn't allowed on the national forest."

"Who's squatting?"

"Are you mining?"

"Nothing but ideas."

"Nice try, but no gold medal."

"How old are you?"

"Twenty-seven."

"Are you the ranger?"

"I'm the mining technician. I handle all the mine-related business for this forest."

"How long have you been on the job?"

"Two years." His self-confidence appearing only slightly ruffled, Sylvester straightened, opened the door of the truck, took out a small cooler, and offered her a Coke.

"No thanks. I picked up a quart of orange juice on the way out of Elkhorn and drank the whole thing."

"Elkhorn? You've just been to Elkhorn?" Andy peeled off the pop-top, dropped it into the cooler, returned the cooler to the cab, and again leaned on the hood.

"I went in to find you, as it happens."

"I wasn't there."

"So I noticed. Listen, Andy," she said with an effort at patience, "I've been here for just about three weeks and my health gets better every day. In fact, at this rate I'll soon feel better than I have since my twenties. I really can't go back to town yet. This is what I need. I'm not bothering anything, and I have no intention of staying beyond August. I've been cleaning up around the cabin."

"So I noticed. Looks great. But it can't be allowed. You'd be amazed at the people we get trying to live in the national forest. Anything with four walls, and they move right in like it was private property."

"It is public land."

"Public means for everybody, not individual squatters. Look, it's not up to me. I'm sure you're very nice and everything, but I'm just following orders."

"Whose orders?"

"It's federal policy."

"How did you know I was here?"

"It's no secret, if that's what you think." He grinned. "You aren't exactly inconspicuous in a place like this."

"Don't you see any irony in the fact that the Barlow Mine crew can tear up the creek with backhoes and road graders because they have a permit, while I'm not allowed to sit quietly writing a few miles upstream?"

"I don't make the rules. Believe me, if we didn't have rules this place would be torn to pieces. You talk about the Barlow Mine, well, that's a model project right now. We're working with them on a plan that will put the creek in better shape than when they started."

"I understand they moved the creek from one side of the canyon to the other."

"That's right."

"They can move a creek and I can't walk along it for the sake of my health?"

"You can walk along it until you're blue in the face, or whatever. You can even camp on it. You just can't occupy a permanent structure unless you're actively mining."

"I'm about to begin panning on a regular basis."

"Again, nice try, but you're no miner."

"Says who?"

He smiled and drank from the Coke.

"What happens if I refuse to leave?"

"The owner could lose the claim."

"The owner has been in a nursing home for years." As the words left her mouth, Neva was struck by a puzzling thought—how could Orson have kept the claim all these years without actively mining it, or paying the yearly fee of a hundred dollars per twenty-acre claim? As far as she knew, you couldn't keep mineral rights indefinitely, without any investment of time or money. Strange that she hadn't wondered about this before. There was no way her uncle's old partner could have continued to send in fees or arrange for improvements to the mine. "Orson is still the owner of the mine?"

"In part, yes."

"Who owns the other part?"

"That's not my area of responsibility."

"Do you know?"

"Look, this is all beside the point. I have to get back to Elkhorn. I'll be up in the next few days to see that you're out. I hate to put it that way, but that's the way it is. If you want to camp on the creek, that's fine, but I want the cabin shut up the way it was."

"You want?" Neva raised an eyebrow.

Appearing uncomfortable at last, he said, "That's just an expression. It's the law. Of course I can see you aren't hurting anything, but the government can't make exceptions."

That she had handled the meeting clumsily was only too apparent to Neva as she drove on, her blood racing with unaccustomed anger and frustration. Andy Sylvester was an over-zealous, inexperienced, rule-bound brat. The whole thing was ridiculous, and a tremendous nuisance. She would have to go over his head, which would mean another trip to Elkhorn and another day lost in her already too-brief life in the canyon.

As she approached the Barlow Mine she met yet another vehicle in the road, this one a great lumbering yellow beast of a bulldozer—lumbering, that is, had it been moving. Not only was it stopped, but it appeared to have blown apart, scattering bits of itself across the road so there was no way to pass. Wondering how Andy had got by, she opened the car door as a man came around the side of the bulldozer, wiping his hands on a rag. He wore no shirt under his grimy overalls, leaving his lean brown arms bare to the shoulders. Built more like an athlete than a laborer, he appeared strong without bulk, his movements simultaneously controlled and easy.

"Reese Cotter," he said, gripping her hand and smiling with white teeth.

"Jeneva Leopold." That Reese Cotter was a man rather than the boy she had expected made Neva suddenly aware of her flat chest under the T-shirt. It was not that he attracted her—for one thing, he was younger by a good ten years—but his confident maleness made her wish suddenly to look like a proper woman. Surprised at herself, she added crisply, "I'm generally known as Neva."

"Sorry about the roadblock," he said, releasing her hand after a good squeeze. "We'll have her moving in a couple minutes."

"There's no rush on my account. How's the mining business?"

"I wouldn't say great, but in the last week we've started paying expenses at least. It takes a lot of money to get an operation running."

"I thought this was an old mine. Hasn't it been running for years?"

"Yes and no. There's been mining here off and on since the first gold rush, but nothing like this size operation. It changed owners a while back, and they hired me to run the show, but I had to finish a job over at Mormon Basin. We've only been putting this together since the snow went. And just about everything that could break did break. In this business you get so you feel lucky if the sun comes up."

Neva listened with interest and also some perplexity. Skipper had gone on at length last night about the Cotter brothers' escapades, leading her to expect rowdies from the wrong side of the tracks. They were regulars in the Elkhorn county drunk tank, and had totaled enough pickups between them for a demolition derby. "They're the kind of characters that have real skinny girl friends," he'd summed up. "Like going to bed with a bicycle."

The description didn't seem to fit. Reese appeared more talkative and at ease with her than Darla, Tony Briggs, Bernice Pangle, Gene Holland, or even Skipper himself on first meeting. Reese's pleasant expression made it easy to say, "Would it be any problem for me to go down and look at the mine?"

He considered her quizzically for a moment with his arms crossed. "You want to see the operation?"

"If I'd be in the way, then never mind, but I am interested. You can't see down in there from the road."

"Well, hell, if I knew anybody was interested, I'd put up a sign and sell tickets."

Was he suggesting that she pay to tour the mine? Before Neva could think of a response that felt right, he grinned and said, "Don't look so serious. I'm kidding. It's just that nobody ever asked to see the place before, or any other mine I worked on. Most people couldn't care less about mines. In fact, most people hate us. Are you an environmentalist? You have any hidden cameras or anything?"

Again she found it difficult to tell whether he was in earnest or teasing, and decided to risk on the side of playfulness. "Actually, I'm a Greenpeace robot and I'm filming everything through my eyeballs."

His grin widened though he didn't laugh. "Well, I never saw a robot with such a good tan." He turned and called out to a young man who squatted by the front blade of the broken-down bulldozer with a box of tools open at his side. "Ho, Roy, I'm going to show this little lady around. I got that pump replaced, so you may as well put her back together and give her a try." And then to Neva, "I hope you don't get heat stroke easy. It's a cooker down there."

They descended into the pit by walking down a heavily graveled road as though into a huge, dry sauna. The excavation was deeper and longer than Neva had expected, the bottom an uninviting expanse of gravel mounds. To the right of the entry road a huge, cartoon-like apparatus stood against the earth wall below the road bank. It seemed a random jumble of conveyor belts, pipes, sieving tables, and sorting troughs, topped by a truck-size drum like a cement mixer full of holes, but the complexity took on visual logic as Reese explained. The ore is scooped out of the ground by backhoe and dumped into a giant funnel called a hopper. The hopper feeds into the rotating drum, or trommel, where the rocks get sorted by tumbling out through holes of graduated sizes. The big rocks fall onto a conveyor belt that dumps them in a heap to be replaced in the ground.

"If we don't put it back the Feds have a shit fit," he said cheerfully. The small rock gets sorted again and yet again, until only fine gravel and black sand remain. The sand and gravel are mixed with water that flows over a sorting table ridged to catch flakes and grains of the precious metal. They had to process tons of rock to produce ounces of gold, but still turned up enough nuggets to make it fun.

"We like to pick out the big stuff by hand," he concluded.

Reese led the way up a ladder to the sorting table, which was about fifteen feet above the ground and enclosed by a protective railing. Leaning over the table, he riffled a patch of fine black sand with his fingers and exposed a yellow bit. Reaching into his back pocket, he drew out a knife, opened a blade in the shape of tweezers, and plucked the small nugget. Neva noted the gold, but she was far more interested in the tool in his hand.

"Are those knives unusual?"

"You bet. I special ordered it from an outfit in Grays Harbor. It's a custom design. Most of them don't have this nifty little bugger." He held up the tweezers, but he was paying more attention to the yellow pebble in the palm of his hand. "See that? Jewelry grade. We're turning up a lot of these the last few days. They're too pretty to sell."

The reverence in his voice made her forget the knife for a moment and instead consider his bent head, which was covered with wavy black hair many women would envy and others would want to sink their hands into. As for the nugget, like the one in the tobacco can, it looked like nothing to her except a dull yellow blob with a bit of grit clinging to it.

"See that?" He tilted his hand so the stone rolled. "The gold on Billie Creek is famous for its color and purity. My mom's fillings are all Billie Creek gold. She wouldn't have any other and neither would her dentist. I wouldn't mind having gold teeth myself."

She held out her hand for the nugget. He tipped it onto her palm and turned to the table to look for more. After inspecting it for long enough to show proper appreciation, she handed it back and said, "I recently saw a knife just like that one. It even had the pliers."

Reese froze half bent over the table and said nothing for a moment, then straightened and turned slowly toward her, showing a face that had lost its flirtatious warmth. "Where was it?"

"Up the road past the turnoff to my place, by an old water trough." As Neva spoke the explanation came to her—the knife must belong to his missing brother Lance.

Reese gazed over her shoulder for several moments with an unseeing look. Then he glanced down at the tool in his right hand, folded it with a quick snap, and put it in his pocket, at the same time removing a rolled blue cap from the other pocket and jamming it onto his head. Neva didn't have to look to know it said "Wallowa Tractor and Irrigation."

"There was a cap just like that not too far away from the knife."

"Well for fuck's sake why didn't you tell me?"

Reese's sudden ferocity made her recoil backward on the catwalk. Her foot hit a support strut and she fell against the railing. His hands flashed out, grasped her shoulders, and pulled her upright again without a break in his outpouring. "Those belong to my brother and nobody else, hear me? He went missing. We didn't have a goddamn clue where he went. Not a goddamn clue."

She looked at him without speaking until he said with controlled calm, "Sorry. I didn't mean to get rough, it's just I'm worried about the little sonofabitch and you gave me a shock. He doesn't have all his marbles, if you know what I mean. He's not safe on his own. Where's the hat and knife now?"

"I left them where I found them, at the water trough. I had no idea they were Lance's."

"Let's get out of here."

She followed him down the ladder and up the slope, half running to keep pace with his stride. Roy was just closing his toolbox, and stood up when they reached him. Taller and less visibly muscular than Reese, he looked like an overgrown kid as he raised his hand in a mock salute and said, "Ready to sail, captain." Then he saw Reese's face and looked quizzically at Neva, but Reese spoke first. "She found Lance's knife. His hat, too. Move this turkey out of the way. I'll be back in a while."

"Wait a second," Roy said, but Reese strode by with a terse, "Can it, Roy. I'll be back."

"But I want—" he tried again.

"I said can it. I'll be back in a jiff."

Neva exchanged a sympathetic look with the young man, and was struck by his dark eyes, the irises precisely defined against the clear whites in the manner of a Byzantine painting. She said, "He's really worried."

Roy shrugged and smiled, the two conflicting gestures seeming to sum up frustrated good intentions.

"He'll be right back. Nice to meet you."

By the time they were seated in her car with the engine running, Roy had the bulldozer moving and they were able to pass, just clearing the sloped bank on the right where Neva noted a single set of tire tracks in the exposed earth. Sylvester's little truck must be four-wheel drive, she thought with the part of her brain that automatically took in such details.

"Stop at the house and I'll get my truck," Reese ordered. They said nothing during the short trip to the upper lip of the mine pit where the two cabins stood, but when she pulled up to the porch, he said, "Come on inside."

Feeling like a child who has misbehaved and has lost the right to question, Neva followed him into the nearest cabin, which was dark and reeked of grease and dirty socks. A small black and white dog leaped off a bunk and dashed around Reese's legs in happy greeting but he took no notice. "See there." He pointed at a guitar hanging on the wall above an unmade bed. "That there's Lance's guitar. He never went anywhere without his guitar in his life, even when I treated him like a useless turd. Which I did just about every day of his life. I'm his big brother, right? That's the way it works, isn't it, I push him around and he pushes around whoever he can? The weird thing is, we didn't even have a fight this time. Things were going good for a change."

Savagely, he kicked a boot that was in his path, yanked open a drawer, and pulled out a handgun. "Don't worry, I'm not planning to use it, but you never know in the mountains." Lifting a worn Army surplus knapsack down from a nail driven into the plywood wall, he began stuffing things into it, a shirt, box of matches, water, flashlight, and a bottle of whiskey.

Within minutes they were back out the door and he was climbing into the nearest of two pickups, a dusty red Ford with huge wheels like a Tonka toy. "You can leave the car at your cabin turnoff and ride with me."

Reese shot up the road. Following more slowly, Neva worked through an internal argument between the part of her that was fascinated by smart roughnecks like Reese and the part that wanted to keep plenty of distance. It might be fun racing up the ridge with Reese Cotter to claim his brother's lost possessions. On the other hand, he was overwrought and a known wild driver, and it had been a long and complicated day. The sensible course was to give him directions and let him find the hat and knife on his own. He couldn't miss the water trough.

Reese was waiting at the head of the cabin lane, his truck engine idling. She left the Honda in the lane and went up to his open window to make her excuses. He sat with his head bowed, his big hands gripping the steering wheel, and when she spoke, he didn't look at her.

"Reese, I'm really tired and need to go back to the cabin. You'll see the water trough, no problem. Just go up the road a mile or two and it will be on the left, right in plain sight. I'm sorry, I'm not very good at estimating distances."

He glanced at her then, and his eyes were unmistakably wet, although without actual tears. "Right," he said, looking away again. "Thanks." Rather than shove the truck into gear, he continued to sit with his hands on the steering wheel and his gaze fixed on the road beyond the dusty windshield.

What had she stumbled into? Had he bellowed like a wounded bull he couldn't have appeared more in pain—and it would have been far easier to know how to react to a raging bull than a tearful miner.

"I'm such a shit," he said. "There's just the two of us, kids that is, and I mostly raised him. You think you can keep a kid out of trouble by being there, but sometimes I wonder if I was his biggest trouble. Maybe he would have figured things out if I wasn't always there with the answers. Some kind of answers, anyway. Shit."

"I have a son," Neva said, relieved to be back on familiar territory. "Probably about Lance's age. When you come right down to it, people are who they are, and they're going to do what they do. You can only help so far. It's a cliché, but true."

"I never knew exactly what that means—cliché." Reese still kept his gaze forward but his voice was steadier. "I lost my dictionary about a hundred years ago."

"A cliché is something, a word or expression, that's overused and unoriginal, and loses some of its force or meaning because of being obvious or just too familiar."

"Are you a school teacher?"

Neva laughed. "Nope, not a teacher, a journalist. But if I use a word wrong in one of my columns, I hear from all the retired English teachers in town. It's pretty embarrassing so I check definitions all the time."

Reese looked directly at her now, not quite smiling but clearly amused. "You sure you don't want to come with me? It won't take long."

Though he appeared to have calmed down, he accelerated before she was fully seated. She grabbed for the armrest and half shouted above the engine roar, "The road's pretty bad. I don't think you can drive all the way to the trough."

"Watch me." His grin showed no trace of the earlier emotion. "That spring used to be the best water in the canyon."

"I thought you were new here, but you seem to know your way around."

"My grandparents lived over at Charity. I ran all over these hills when I was a boy, me and Lance together, and I've mined just about every major creek drainage between here and Malheur. Shit." He swerved around a large rock, skidded toward the edge on the canyon side, regained control and said coolly, "What are you doing fooling around old mines anyhow?"

"Exactly that, fooling around. I'm out here for my health. Really, it's true even though no one seems to believe it."

To walk to the trough from the cabin lane would have taken more than half an hour, but Reese got there in minutes, barely slowing down for washouts and boulders. He pulled into the wide spot and was out the door while the truck was still shuddering from the violent stop.

Neva got out slowly, staring at the empty rim of the trough where the hat and knife should have been. "They're gone, Reese. They were right here."

"You're sure it was here?"

"Absolutely. They were half-buried over there where it's all trampled up. I put them on the edge of the trough so they could be seen from the road." She peered in to be sure they had not fallen onto the algae somehow, but the mat lay thick and undisturbed. "Skipper said he was coming up for a look. Maybe he took them."

Reese wasn't satisfied until he'd searched the entire area and gone over the trampled bit on his hands and knees. Under a rock he found a silver dollar, which he clasped, then began to search even more furiously. Neva wandered about feeling weary, hungry, and uneasy, her sympathy overshadowed by Reese's alarming mood. It was getting late. She was ready for a bowl of something hot, and an evening alone on the porch.

At last he crossed to where she had settled on a rock and sat down with a groan. "He was here all right, he was here, so where the hell is he now? He wouldn't leave his knife behind if he had any choice, he does have that much sense. It's not so easy to disappear out here, you know. Maybe for rabbits, but not for people. Something happened to the dumb shit. It always does when he gets out of my sight, and one of these days it's going to be serious, real serious."

Chapter Eleven

Food was the main thing on Neva's mind as they climbed back into the truck. Tonight she would eat one of her two cans of China Lily curry sauce on rice, followed by something sweet. She hadn't stocked actual desserts, but she would make something with lots of brown sugar and cinnamon to eat on the porch, and then she would go to bed early. The sun had gone down behind the ridge and it would be dark soon.

But instead of wheeling around and heading back down the canyon, Reese sped up the road. Before she could protest, he cranked the steering wheel hard to the left. The truck slid sideways, sending up a spray of gravel and dust, and then tore uphill through low trees and sagebrush where there was no sign of a road.

"This used to go through to the top," he shouted with the air of a tour guide. "Maybe we'll see something from up there."

"Reese, stop!" The words came out in a shriek, but she didn't care how she sounded. She'd had enough. "I'm going home. I'll walk back."

"Can't stop, I'd never get going again." He gunned the engine and the truck bounced and kicked like a wild animal in flight.

"It's getting dark," she yelled, but it was impossible to stop this crazy man. And suddenly, looking at where he was going, Neva was intrigued. He was zigzagging up the nose of a low ridge, cutting in and out of small clumps of mountain mahogany and juniper trees, climbing fast. "Where does this end up?"

"It doesn't end up, that is, if you know your stuff you can get right over the mountain and down to Elkhorn. You can also get lost pretty bad. What bothers me is what the hell did Lance come up here for? We haven't been up this way since we were kids. There's nothing up here."

They pulled out on top just as the sun dropped below the mountains to the west. Reese brought the pickup to a lurching stop on a flat covered in knee-high plants with small, pale pink flowers, grabbed his knapsack, and strode away toward the canyon rim. Rather than hurry after him, Neva paused to smell the richly colored evening air. It carried a faint hint of peaches, which seemed to come from the little, mustard-type flowers. She hadn't been up here so late in the day before because she would not have been able to get back to the mine on foot by dark. Now she was glad that Reese had dragged her along.

When she caught up, she found him sitting on the ground with his back against a small outcrop of limestone, scanning the deeply shadowed creek basin through binoculars. It was a fine vantage point, but what he hoped to see she couldn't guess. She settled close by, also leaning against the rock. He lowered the glasses and turned to her with a face that was sad again despite the tough words.

"I don't know what I expected. It was probably a stupid idea, but I just have this feeling he's out here somewhere." He jammed the binoculars into the knapsack and pulled out the whiskey, his forearm flexing like an independent live thing as he twisted the cap off. He raised the bottle to his mouth, then lowered it without drinking and offered it to Neva. "Ladies first."

Was she to drink with everyone out here? First Skipper, then Tony, now Reese. In the months following the surgery, she had given up her daily glass of wine before dinner, not on doctor's orders but as an instinctual effort to help her body find its normal self again. The beer at Angus had nearly put her to sleep. The whiskey with Skipper had made her arms and legs rubbery, and she had laughed up at the stars on the walk back to the cabin. To swig straight whiskey with this complicated young miner could have an even more debilitating effect, but if he drank the whole bottle himself, he might kill them both trying to get down the ridge in the truck.

The bottle was there between them, suspended, waiting.

To refuse would be rude…and she needn't do more than sip. Maybe she could pour some out surreptitiously once it was full dark, if they stayed that long. She touched the bottle to her lips and allowed a small trickle to pass. It was enough to burn her throat and send warm currents into her arms and legs. She took another small sip, released a long breath, and leaned easier into the rock. The stars came out as they drank. The whiskey took away her hunger, and the flannel shirt Reese dug from his pack kept her warm. He insisted that he was fine in the overalls.

"I lost my jacket so many times when I was a kid they quit buying me any," he said. "I never notice hot or cold. Maybe that means I'm a primitive type of human, I don't know, but it beats being a candy-ass. Lance is a candy-ass and always was a candy-ass. He would have been beat to crap in school if I didn't protect him. Of course, I had my price. Who doesn't?

"You know what I figure? I figure I was born a hundred years too late. This is no kind of world for me, all this regulation and everybody looking over your shoulder. I'm a professional, you know what I mean? Just before the Mormon Basin job I headed up a job over in Colorado, an environmental cleanup. Ha! I thought that would surprise you. But it's the same thing. You take a bunch of dirt and you run it through a process, and in one operation you get gold and in the other you get some kind of poison chemicals. Then you take all the dirt and put it back in the ground and nobody can tell the difference. If you know what you're doing. Which I do. I went to college, you know, two years, geology, chemistry, mineralogy, you name it. I didn't get such shit-hot grades but I learned enough. My people aren't trash. My granddad was the mayor of Elkhorn back when I was a kid. He had a huge house, one of the best in town, but the dumb shit lost everything in a poker game. They turned it into a funeral home. Can you beat that? I could be living there.

I guess maybe this family isn't too big on what they call good judgment."

"Is that the one a few blocks up from the post office, the Garden of Eternal Peace?"

"That's the one. It's the only one."

"Well, that's funny. I filled my water bottles there this morning, from the outside tap."

"Lucky you. I never go near the place. It pisses me off too much. How much did they charge for the water?"

"Actually, the man seemed surprised that I didn't mind taking water from a funeral home. He knows a lot about bugs."

"That's Darrell. He used to run around with one of those stupid net things before his dad cheated in the poker game. Just kidding about that. He won the house fair and square. It was my grandfather who was the idiot, but it's water under the bridge now. I'm probably better off out here than anywhere, so no great loss."

The bottle was half gone, and sat between them for long intervals before one or the other would reach and swig. At first Neva drank only when Reese handed her the whiskey, but she got into the rhythm and soon kept pace with him as though they were playing a game involving serve and return. Her uneasiness about the drinking had vanished. She felt simultaneously at ease and extraordinarily alert, not only to the night but to Reese himself. He seemed to her like a peculiar sort of hero, tough and ready for anything life might dish up, but also tragic and potentially dangerous should circumstances call for it. Twenty years ago, she might have been attracted despite their differences. Now her response was almost maternal, maybe because of the tears he had not quite shed and the confusion and regret about his brother.

"What do you think made Lance run off this time? It sounds like your fights are business as usual, and anyway, I think you said there wasn't any fight," she ventured after a silence.

"I wish I knew. He's been worse than usual lately. He goes around like he has some kind of bag over his head, or like he's thinking so hard he can't see out of his eyes anymore. Then he does stupid things, like losing tools and leaving valves open, and starting in on the same job he just finished. I mean, you found his hat and knife out in the dirt. He never did take to mining like I did. He didn't ever know what he wanted, but it wasn't mining, no way doggies. I told him to go do something else then. Maybe he finally followed my advice."

Reese took an extra long swig, wiped his mouth on his open hand, and said, "Now, tell me what you're really doing out here."

"Why does everyone ask me that?"

"Because you don't fit, that's why. You said you're a journalist. I hope you're not writing about mining. There's so many lies about mining out there. They think we're murderers, earth murderers. Shit. We're just making a living. But I can tell you one thing." He turned toward her and his voice dropped. "If you do write some kind of crap about mining, you'll have me to answer to."

"Do you always threaten people you're having a friendly drink with?" Even as the words came out of her mouth, Neva marveled. Was this really her speaking? It was not at all her style, but it was just the right touch, playful while not weak, and it threw the ball nicely back in his court. She should drink whiskey more often.

"Well, shit, if you put it like that. It wasn't a threat. I'm just saying don't tell lies about us. People like you always write about us like we're a bunch of stupid Okies and dumb shits."

"Do I treat you like a dumb shit?"

"No, you don't. But I don't know what you're thinking."

"I don't know what you're thinking either, but I'm not insulting you over it." This was fun. Smiling in the dark, Neva reached for the bottle just as Reese did. Their hands collided and were snatched back at the same instant, with stereo "sorry, sorry about that, go ahead, you first" and then they both laughed.

"Go ahead and write whatever you want," said Reese. "Just send me a copy."

"I almost hate to say it, but I'm not writing anything about mining. I'm really and truly out here for a rest. I keep a daily journal, but that's it for writing."

"Then why do you ask so many questions?"

"It's just a habit from years of journalism. This is a new world out here. I don't know anything about mining or ranching, and the best way to find out is from the people who do it. Plus I've become really interested in finding out all I can about my uncle. Believe it or not it had never occurred to me there were people out here who knew him. We didn't know he was part of a community."

Reese gave a low grunt. "Since we're being so goddamned honest I might as well admit that you worry me. We mind our own business out here, and when you get somebody that doesn't, well, you wonder why. You wonder what they're up to. Down at the café they think you're after your uncle's gold."

"It never crossed my mind that he might have any."

"Then what'd he spend thirty years mining for?"

"Gene said he has two mines and both are worthless. Of course, I didn't believe him."

"Well, Gene's different. He's too smart to grub around in the dirt like the rest of us—" He leaned forward abruptly. "Who in Jesus name is coming up the creek this time of night?"

In the darkness below, headlights flickered through the trees, tiny and silent like fireflies. "It must be the truck I told you about, Reese, that comes up at night."

"What truck? You didn't tell me about any truck."

Confused, Neva tried to think back over the past few hours of rambling talk, but the whiskey won and she couldn't be sure what had been said by either of them. "I've heard it several times late at night. I have no idea where it goes. There's nowhere to go. Don't you ever hear it?"

"Don't be funny. When the sun goes down I sleep like road kill. Anyway, if I wasn't looking for Lance I wouldn't give a shit who comes and goes out here. It's a free country." He was standing now, feet planted wide, arms crossed on his chest, his head cocked as he listened and watched. They were silent, waiting, and at last the faint sound of an engine reached them.

"Let's go," he said. Kneeling, he reached for the bottle, knocked it over with a clatter and an oath, and snatched it up again. "Shit. We may as well kill it." He threw back his head and poured the whiskey down with a gurgle.

When it was her turn, Neva did the same without hesitating, and felt hot liquid spill from the corner of her mouth and run down her cheek to her ear, where it turned cold. Reese emptied the bottle on the next pull, then said in a schoolboy chant, "As a feather is wafted downward from an eagle in its flight." Cocking his arm back, he hurled the bottle out into black space. Neva listened for the crash of glass on rock, and when it didn't come she felt the world had shifted in some inexplicable way so that bottles could fly and swarthy miners quoted poetry and large trucks appeared and disappeared without reason. She stood up, swayed and caught herself against the rock. Reese had vanished but she didn't care. She could walk back to her cabin if need be, heck, she could roll, just tuck in her head and tumble down the slope through the sagebrush like a tumbling tumbleweed—

"Hey! Are you coming or what?"

"Yo-o-o-o-," she called. Smiling, walking with big steps, she made her way back through the tall mustard or whatever it was to the truck. "It doesn't smell like peaches anymore," she said as she climbed in.

"What about peaches? You really are crazy. Did you say you were old enough to be my mother? That's a damned lie. When we get down off here I'm going to give you a big kiss."

How they made it down Neva couldn't remember later, other than that there was a lot of bouncing and banging and whooping, and then they were on the mining road, and Reese was saying, "Which way, we don't know which fucking way he went."

He turned hard left toward the top of the canyon, which they reached without seeing any sign of a truck. About half a mile farther on they came to a trench cut across the road that even Reese wouldn't tackle.

"So he has to be behind us," he said, cranking the wheel over hard. "Maybe he's down at your place." With that he was racing back in the other direction, skidding on turns, and catching the quick glint of wild yellow eyes in the headlights. Neva simply held on and trusted to fate. Her head was large and her hands and feet numb, whether from cold or whiskey she had no idea. The thought of sleep had taken strong hold in her mind so that she no longer cared about dinner or even about finding the mystery truck. All she wanted was to be in her quiet, warm bed.

They reached her car without seeing anything unusual. Reese followed her down the lane to the cabin and when he saw that the truck wasn't there he bellowed out the window that he was goddamned if he was going to let anybody play such a trick on him, he was going back up the mountain and find the bastards if it took all night. With that he wheeled around the woodshed and was gone in a spray of rock and dust.

Crawling into bed without any of the usual preparation other than removing her clothes, the bed tilting strangely but not unpleasantly under her, Neva tried to think back over the day but it seemed very long and jumbled. Was it only this afternoon that she had met that troublesome puppy Andy Sylvester? She should have told Reese about that one, just for the fun of the fireworks.

Chapter Twelve

"I got the knife when I went up in the morning," Skipper said, handing Neva a large mug full of coffee. "I didn't mean to make trouble for anybody, but it didn't make any sense leaving a perfectly good knife out there. And I had sort of thought that I'd seen a hat like that sometime recently. Seems I was right."

Sitting in the shade under a pine tree outside Skipper's camper, Neva drank the strong coffee gratefully, hoping it would do for her aching head what her first cup had failed to accomplish. Half a bottle of whiskey…how could she have been so idiotic?

"You look peaky, W.T.," Skipper teased. "Beats me what you were doing drinking with that character. He looks to me like the kind of guy that likes the smell of his own farts. You know what he told me the other day? He said he always keeps more of the gold than he lets on to the mine owners. He calls it his 'percentage.' Now, I admit that would be a serious temptation even for a saint, but it's stealing just the same. I'd sure like to know what's going on around here. Nothing ever went on here before, not that I knew about, except for your uncle's disappearing trick. I'm tempted to stick around for a few more days, but once I've decided to move on I just have to go or I get real uncomfortable. You fixing to move down here on the creek soon?"

"I'm still thinking about how to handle the Forest Service. Andy Sylvester's so young it's hard to take him seriously, but I guess I should decide on some kind of action. On the other hand, I could go on playing deaf and see what they do next. I did hear a strange thing from Sylvester. He said Orson isn't the sole owner of the mine. Do you know anything about that?"

"Can't say I do. I've wondered a time or two why things keep in pretty good shape around the place. And I've thought now and then that somebody had been getting ready to mine again. That pile of pipe over behind the old outhouse turned up new last year. It never seemed worth bothering about, but now you ask I'm kind of curious myself."

"I should have thought of it before," Neva mused. "The law says you have to pay a fee every year or do a certain amount of work on the mine or you lose the claim. I don't know the details, but I do know that Orson hasn't set foot out here for an age, and he has no money. So why didn't the claim go back to the government?"

"That's a thought. If it had, you can bet your booties they'd have burned that cabin down like they did the old Johnson place and half a dozen others I could name. A damned shame." Skipper settled on a canvas chair and Cayuse moved from his spot at the base of a tree to lie at his feet. "As for that truck disappearing, it's no big deal. You have so many old roads around here it could go anywhere. Too bad Reese ran all over in that big rig of his or we might tell something from the tracks. What it's doing up here at night is the question."

They sat for a while in silence, Skipper visibly pondering while Neva nursed her head. At length he said, "What do you make of Reese Cotter?"

"Smart, with a dangerous temper and some sort of chip on his shoulder. He actually got a little tearful about Lance, and seemed to feel guilty for being tough on him. I have to say he was very good company. I remember laughing a lot, and it wasn't just the whiskey."

"I hear he knows mining as good as anybody so he always gets jobs even if he is quick to blow and skims off his percentage. You may as well know I'm not feeling too great about leaving today with all this happening, and you alone at the mine. It doesn't feel right in my bones, and my bones are about as trusty as Cayuse's nose."

"I really appreciate your concern, Skipper, but there's no reason to worry about me. Truly. My only problem is the possible eviction and there's nothing you could do about it other than help me carry stuff down to camp if I have to move. And that I can definitely handle."

"A man has disappeared, W.T. Kind of like your uncle, in case you hadn't noticed, and his cap and knife have turned up without him."

"We don't know that he really disappeared. He walked off the job in a huff and most likely lost things along the way."

"Still. My bones aren't happy. I'll be moving out of here in the next hour or so but I guess I'll head back this way in a few days, just to check things out. Meantime, keep your distance from that Cotter outfit. Are you sure you don't want a bit of the hair of the dog for that headache? And I don't mean Cayuse."

Standing in the camp watching the old artifact hunter pull out, Neva felt genuine regret that she could not have imagined just a few days ago, when the arrival of the white truck had seemed to signal the end of her happiness on the creek. She would miss Skipper, and was glad he'd decided to come back this way before too long.

Half an hour later she followed him down the canyon, the hat and knife beside her on the car seat. She slowed down when she passed the Barlow Mine cabins, where Reese's dog was tied to a porch post, but she didn't stop. Reese and Roy were undoubtedly working in the pit at this time of day and she preferred to put his brother's things directly into Reese's hands. Today no yellow bulldozer blocked the road, and when she got out of the car at the entrance to the mine she was met by perfect silence. When it was operating, the trommel could be heard for a mile up the road, the ore crashing into the funnel like thunder. Even when the equipment wasn't running there were generally voices shouting, and vehicles rumbling around. Now the excavation was as quiet as though it had been abandoned like most of the Billie Creek mines.

The steep track leading down into the mine was scored by deep wheel marks in the gravel. The young men must have driven down, but her little Honda would never make it back up even if it managed to get to the bottom. She didn't mind walking, though the air soon turned hot and heavy, the high banks blocking any movement of air. At the bottom of the road she stopped to study the scene, which appeared just as it had yesterday apart from a blue pickup that was now parked next to the trommel. Reese's red pickup was not in sight, though it could easily be somewhere up the pit among the mounds.

"Haaalloooooo!" she called. Her tiny voice disappeared without an echo.

Trudging toward the pickup through heaped gravel, she found it impossible to believe that this had been a healthy creek bed not so long ago. How could Andy Sylvester call the Barlow Mine a model project?

The pickup was pulled in close to the trommel, with the driver's side next to the ladder. She peered through the dusty window on the passenger's side and found the cab surprisingly tidy, with only a lunchbox on the seat. It must be an oven in there. Runny cheese, half-cooked apple, liquid chocolate bar. They should take a cue from Andy Sylvester and keep a cooler in the truck—but what was she thinking? They had no electricity at the mine cabins, no refrigerator and no way to make or keep ice. It was unlikely they even bothered with a cooler in the creek, although Reese might be driven to such a refinement by warm beer.

The dome light was on, which, she realized after further peering, must be due to the failure of the driver to close his door properly. She circled the truck, pushed the door shut, and turned to climb the ladder for a better view, but the metal rung burned her hand. Snatching it away, she moved out from between the truck and the trommel to where she could scan the entire excavation. A desert of rocky dunes, it felt empty, without life apart from her own small presence. No water trickled, no trees whispered, no birds called in the distance. To hear Reese talk, mining was a swashbuckling life, but to spend even a day in this pit would be hell.

She turned and began trudging back toward the entrance, but had gone only a few steps when she stopped and looked once more toward the opposite end of the pit. Ten minutes would get her there and back. She was unlikely to come down here again and it now seemed like a waste to have ventured this far a second time without seeing the whole Barlow operation.

Wheel tracks led away through the gravel, winding between mounds. Aiming for a mound that stood somewhat above the others, she followed the tracks to take advantage of the slightly packed gravel. Still, her feet sank at each step and sweat streaked her face. When she reached the base of the tall mound she started up without pausing, but soon slipped backward as though on a steep sand dune. She bent to dig in with her hands but recoiled from the hot, sharp little rocks. Balancing upright on the slope, ignoring the stones in her shoes, she scanned the stretch of pit behind her, the distant trommel, the pickup truck. Such still silence on a working day really was strange. Could Reese have had an accident last night after dropping her at the car? Could he be lying somewhere up the canyon, unconscious or dead in his truck? Could Roy have gone in search of his partner?

Neva shook her head thoughtfully. Someone had driven the blue truck down here. These young men didn't walk anywhere if they had a choice, she was certain, so where was Roy?

"Halloo," she called, and again her voice disappeared, a mere pebble in the petrified sea of stone.

Most likely Roy had gone somewhere with Reese, but still she had to walk on to the end of the pit or slog to the top of the mound or she would not feel comfortable leaving the mine. Her concern wasn't rational, but she had learned long ago not to ignore such feelings. The mound wasn't high and she could sit down on top while she scanned the territory.

Two steps upward, one step back...Like a bug trapped in an ant lion pit.

With a forced burst of energy, she flung herself uphill, scrambling on all fours despite the nasty gravel. She reached the top, collapsed on her stomach, and stared in shock at empty space. Had the bottom dropped out of the earth? Moving with slow care, she eased forward and peered down, far down. Instead of the other side of a sloping mound, as she expected, she faced a drop-off into a second pit with a floor a good thirty feet lower than the bottom of the main excavation. Had she managed to climb the mound standing upright, she might have tumbled right into the pit headfirst, in which case she would have left the mine a corpse.

Damn those crazy Cotters—anyone else would put up warning signs or flagging.

Angry and shaken, Neva eased back away from the edge and lay with her head on her arms until her heart slowed down. Then she hitched forward again to study the strange scene below and realized that she was looking at an old mining chamber. Unlike the rough, bulldozed excavation of the current mine, this pit was a neat rectangle, with dark pillars supporting the walls except along a caved-in stretch on the opposite side. Boards and other debris littered the rocky floor, and a dark opening in the right wall surely was a tunnel entrance. Maybe it was one of the original Chinese-dug mines, in which case it was of historic importance. Could Reese have gone to town to report the discovery?

No, impossible. Law or no law, Reese Cotter was not the sort to risk delaying work while officials decided what to do about artifacts. He was far more likely to bulldoze history out of sight. Thinking of the bulldozer, she focused on a bright yellow patch in the cascade of rock at the opposite side of the old chamber. Later, she would try to recall the next few minutes but never was satisfied that she remembered correctly. It seemed to her that she knew instantly the full dimensions of the disaster even though she could not have known that more than the bulldozer was buried over there. Still she ran, her feet slipping in the gravel with nightmare clumsiness. Drenched in sweat, her mouth dry, she reached the far side, got down on her knees and crawled to the sunken edge. Peering over she could see nothing of the bulldozer, but she was certain of the spot because it was the only caved-in section. To verify that it really was the bulldozer that lay buried in rock she would have to go down.

She should not go down there. She knew this in her very bones, as Skipper would say. She knew it—but she also knew that she could not walk away without looking closer, to be certain that nothing more than machinery had plunged into the pit.

The safest way down was backwards. She turned her back on space, eased one leg over, felt for solid footing, lowered the other leg. Reminding herself to breathe, pausing after each move to detect shifts in the tumbled rock, she made her way down step by step. The stones held as though gravity had jammed them into a new form that might last another century. At last, below her and to the right, she saw yellow metal and changed course. A large rock near the metal gave her a platform to stand on as she peered in among the stones. Glass glinted in the shadows. Her eyes clamped shut, refusing to look. Leaving them closed, she breathed slowly, willing her knees to hold.

Steady again, she cleared away the smaller rocks until a section of windshield showed. Although it had shattered into myriad tiny veins that gave it a milky cast, the glass had held together. More stones came away and then she saw the face behind the glass, blurred as though under ice. Her gaze locked on a pair of open dark eyes that seemed to observe her distress with complete composure. Despite the blood that covered the lower half of the face it was clearly Roy, the pleasant young man who had called Reese captain.

Chapter Thirteen

Jeneva parked in Elkhorn's old downtown, drew a long breath, and sagged against the car seat. Less than twenty-four hours had passed since she found the body of Roy DeRoos. She had sped down the canyon to Gene's cabin, certain he had no cell phone and that it wouldn't work if he did have one, but hoping she was wrong. He was not there. Furious, as though he had deliberately failed her, she had driven too fast to Angus, watched in stunned silence as Al called 911, then returned to the base of Billie Creek Road to wait for the ambulance and the sheriff. It was after dark by the time the body had been excavated and taken away without sirens.

She had returned alone to her cabin at last but there had been no sleep, no escape from Roy's young face, at one moment bloody and staring, and the next moment radiant with life as it had been on the day they met. And where was Reese? Sheriff Tug McCarty had sent a deputy up the road in search of the red pickup when he heard about their wild night on the ridge, but they had found no sign of the truck, no sign of an accident. When the sun had risen at last she knew she had to be among people, lots of people, people doing simple things like shopping, eating sandwiches, drinking coffee at sidewalk tables. Unable to manage breakfast, she had headed down Billie Creek Road with her morning coffee beside her, stopping to feed and water the little black dog that remained tied to the porch post at the

Barlow Mine. At the Angus post office, Bernice Pangle had been heavily mournful and sympathetic, her suspicion of Neva evidently forgotten or set aside.

"Hardly more than a boy," she said. "I can't help thinking it could have been one of mine. What a shock for you, dear."

The twisting, forty-mile drive over the mountains to Elkhorn had passed like a slow dream, as though she were suspended in a moving landscape rather than steering a car through curve after curve. Now, watching strangers go about their business in the clean morning light, Neva felt her internal landscape begin to shift into more familiar shape. She would sit here until she could get out of the car without yesterday's horror blazing from her face. The windows were down, letting in the sound of voices and traffic. The sun rose above the buildings on the east side of the street and shone full on the car. She moved to a shaded bench in the entryway of a pharmacy with etched glass windows.

As her eyes began to work, to see more clearly what was before them, she recognized that Elkhorn's solid old 19th-century downtown was the real thing, a genuine Western small city center from a hundred years ago. Elegant Old Western rather than cowboy, it had not been abandoned, not sacrificed to big box stores sprawled on the outskirts of town. The handsome two-story brick buildings offered real shops on the ground floor, shops full of things that people actually need. From the bench she could see women's wear, stationery, books, hardware, computers and software, a bank, even a soda fountain.

Hunger and the smell of roasting coffee drew her down the street at last, past the newly refurbished Grand Hotel and its Eldorado Bar & Grill, to the Daily Grind Café. Soon settled at a corner table with both hands around a mug, she sat very still between sips, her eyes closed, feeling herself breathe. The living breathe. The living sit in cafés drinking coffee. The living are left to think about the accidental dead, to try to grasp what it means to be vibrant at one moment and nothing in the next. She had seen Roy alive only once, on the day the bulldozer blocked her way. Healthy, playful—"She's ready to sail, Captain"—evidently a skilled mechanic, he had lived barely a quarter of a normal lifetime. He had died instantly from a blow to the head, the sheriff had told her as they watched the useless ambulance pull away. Driving too close to the edge of the old mine pit, he had plunged down along with an avalanche of rock that had buried him inside the bulldozer.

Neva reached into the bag hanging on the back of her chair, felt for the letter from Ethan that Bernice had produced without being asked, and read hungrily. Then she took out a notebook and started a reply.

With several pages covered in close script, she felt steady enough to order a toasted bagel and more coffee. Usually she wrote letters in installments, but now she wrote until she was finished, the six pages folded and ready to go. From her seat at the Daily Grind she could see Blue Mountain Books across the street, and headed straight there from the café. A pleasant bearded man behind the counter directed her to the mining section along the south wall, where a quick perusal turned up *Golden Days in Oregon*, by Morton T. Bellamy. As she waited for change, she asked for directions to the library and newspaper office, and was not surprised to learn that both were within easy walking distance.

"You're new here?" the proprietor said without real curiosity.

"I'm spending the summer over on Billie Creek."

His expression sharpened to positive interest. "Then you must be that lady that found the DeRoos boy." Barely waiting for her nod, he rushed on as though thoughts of Roy had been building in his mind all morning. "Now, that's a sad situation, real sad. He was well liked in this town, won cross-country trophies in high school, never in trouble. He must have read every Western I ever got in here. I don't know what he was doing working at a mine. He was set on being a cowboy, never mind that the real cowboy days are gone. Even most of the rodeo riders are professional rodeo now, not your actual working cowboys. I hear his mom is taking it hard, but who wouldn't."

As he talked, Neva's heart squeezed painfully again, and she realized with shame that she hadn't wanted to know details about the young man's life, hadn't wanted him to become even more real in her mind. Now she could see him in his numbered cross-country running shirt, his mother watching near the finish line with a bottle of water and an anxious look. *Roy, are you sure that knee's all right?* Please don't let him be an only child.

"The funeral's day after tomorrow but I hear there won't be any viewing because of the injuries," the man said. "Kind of makes you sick to think about it. I'd rather have any part smashed than my brain. I know it sounds crazy, but I've been thinking all morning about his brain full of Westerns. He never got the chance to put anything better in there."

Handing her the receipt with a sad shake of the head, he added, "If only he hadn't been working alone. It's hard to figure."

Walking on to the Elkhorn *Times-Standard* office, Neva felt heavy and tired again. Reese must have been told by now, most likely last night by Sheriff McCarty or the deputies who had been alerted to watch for him in town. He had not returned to the mine. It was unknown whether he had been there at all that day, or had headed for town the night before after leaving Neva. McCarty had put a note on the cabin door but it had still been there this morning when she stopped to feed the dog. With Lance gone and Roy dead, Reese could not continue mining. She couldn't imagine that he'd want to, but what would he do with himself, how direct his colossal energy?

Pausing in the lobby of the newspaper building, Neva let the familiar smells and sounds fill her senses. Telephones, jumbled voices, a police radio, burned coffee, newsprint, possibly cigar smoke. There would have been a death notice in today's paper, and now a longer story about the loss of a local youth would be in preparation. Interviews with family members, teachers, coaches, maybe a girl friend. It would run with a picture of him grinning at some moment of young triumph. She had written many such stories in her early years, before she became a columnist, and now she sent up silent thanks that she did not have to coax good quotes out of anguished family members.

Suddenly feeling conspicuous in the otherwise empty foyer, afraid she would be recognized as the one who had found Roy in the pit and cornered for an interview, Neva crossed to the reception desk. A cheerful young woman informed her that back issues were kept at the library on microfilm. Relieved, Neva hurried out again into the bright day.

At the Elkhorn library, which was still in the original Carnegie building, she scrolled through fifteen-year-old issues of the *Times-Standard* and soon found what she was looking for. There were just two items, including a news story, "Local mining veteran vanishes," and an editorial, "Evidence suggests bad end." There was nothing new or interesting, though she was struck by the old-fashioned language in the editorial given that Uncle Matthew had vanished in the 1990s, not the 1890s, particularly the conclusion.

"As most readers know, Mr. Orson Gale and Mr. Matthew Burt are among the few old-timers left who still pay for all their business in gold. Neither man has a bank account, which raises the interesting question of travel money: If Mr. Burt did not meet an accidental death, as many surmise, then he must be paying his way with gold, which surely would get attention and give away his current whereabouts. It seems most likely that this familiar and well-regarded member of our far-flung mining community met his fate through an untimely accident while working alone on Billie Mountain. May his soul rest in peace wherever it may be."

She had not necessarily intended to do more than look up the local news coverage of the disappearance, but the editorial reminded her of what Bernice Pangle had said that morning as she handed over Ethan's letter.

"I was thinking after you were in here the other day that you ought to look up Enid Gale. I guess she knows as much as anybody about your uncle Burtie." Enid, she explained, was Orson's sister, and at one time had stayed with the partners for several years before moving to Montana. "It was Kalispell, I believe. People who didn't know any better used to wonder about her and Burtie but there was nothing in it, of course. For obvious reasons, if you don't mind my putting it that way. But you know how they are—people! Sometimes I think they're the worst thing on earth, don't you?"

Neva sat down at a library computer and logged onto the Internet. A quick search of the Kalispell, Montana, telephone directory brought up no Enid Gale. A bit more hunting turned up the homepage of the local newspaper, the *Kalispell Daily Inter Lake*, but the electronic archives button brought up a page that said the site was under construction. She then found an email address for the Kalispell public library and typed the following message: "Dear Librarian, A friend of mine who's in a nursing home has a sister, Enid Gale, whose last known address was Kalispell. Would it be possible for someone at the library to search the newspaper records for any mention? I tried online but the archives aren't available yet. If she died, there should have been a published notice and possibly an obituary. I'm a columnist for the *Current* in Willamette, Oregon, but I'm on vacation right now near Elkhorn and only check email when I get into town. If you write back and don't get an immediate reply, please know that I will respond as soon as I can. Thank you for your help."

It was late afternoon when Neva finished buying groceries and gas. Heading out of town, she passed the Garden of Eternal Peace and pulled over to the curb, wondering whether she could summon the nerve to ask Darrell for water again. Then it struck her that Roy must be inside this gingerbread palace. She couldn't stop here. As she reached for the ignition, however, she noticed two figures standing on the funeral home porch, one familiar and one startling. The first was Sheriff McCarty. The second was an extraordinarily tall, thin man dressed in black that made his shock of white hair stand out like a signal lamp at night. This was clearly the mortician; Darrell must be an assistant.

Sheriff McCarty had questioned her at length last night, but now she could remember little of what had been said, by her or the sheriff. She had found him comfortable and as reassuring as anyone could be in such a situation, and she felt an urge to speak with him again, though she had nothing in particular to say. She wasn't eager to go back into details of her experience in the Barlow Mine pit, but it suddenly seemed important to connect again with someone else who had been there, who had shared the experience.

She got out of the car and was spotted instantly by McCarty. He waved, shook the other man's hand, and strode across the lawn toward the street, calling out, "You saved me a trip. You aren't in a hurry I hope?"

Stocky, affable, with dark red hair, McCarty leaned on her car hood, supporting his weight with a big meaty hand. "How're you doing? You were a bit stove in yesterday and can't say I blame you. To come on a scene like that all on your own." He shook his head. "Good kid, Roy DeRoos. A damn shame. Not pretty to look at right now. I had to agree with Lloyd, it's better to hold a chapel service and skip the viewing and graveside bit. But you don't want to hear about that. I'm worried you're going to see a rush of artifact hunters digging around in that pit and we might end up with another cave-in. I told Reese he better keep a good look-out."

"You found Reese?"

"It was as I figured. He'd come into town looking for Lance and ended up hitting the bars. I found him in the only cheap room at the Grand. He took the news hard. Along with everything else, he can't mine all by himself. Don't know just what he'll do."

"If you see him again could you remind him about the dog? I fed her, or maybe him, this morning."

"He said you'd take care of her for the time being, and he did say her."

"Well, yes, I certainly will." Pleased by Reese's confidence in her, Neva smiled for the first time since finding Roy. "That's some funeral palace."

"Lloyd's done all right for himself. Funny thing, when I was a kid that was where the mayor lived. He lost the place to Lloyd in a poker game, and Lloyd buried him a few years later."

"Oh, right, I heard about that from Reese, about the poker game. He seemed bitter about it."

"Is that so? Well, you can bet that side of the family would never have inherited the place, no matter what they may claim. Lloyd's buried a lot of folks around here. Sometimes I think I should have gone into the funeral business myself. Everybody dies sooner or later. Of course, there's no shortage of lawbreakers either. The difference is I don't get paid per client like he does." His laugh was easy but Neva was aware that he was watching her closely, and she waited without speaking until he said, "I know I gave you the third degree last night, but could you please tell me what you're doing out at the Billie Creek Mine? We didn't get around to that."

"At the moment I'm being kicked out by the Forest Service."

"Is that right? Kicked out why?"

"For reading and writing on federal property without a permit."

A split second of perplexity was followed by an explosion of laughter. "Hooo, that's good. I'll have to remember that one. But how'd you find your way to a mine at the backside of nowhere?"

"I needed a quiet hideaway for the summer, and since it used to belong to my Uncle Matthew, I knew it was there and empty."

"Matthew? Would that be Matthew Burt? Burtie was your uncle? Well, I'm damned. I never heard he had a family apart from Orson. I can tell you one thing, if I'd been sheriff back then, we would have done a lot more looking when he turned up missing. I'd like to buy you a drink later, after I take this thing off." He flicked the badge on his shirt. "Say, about six?"

"Thank you. I'd enjoy that any other day, but not tonight, I think. I want to get back to the mine early, before dark."

"That's understandable. But why don't you stay the night in town? Give yourself a well-deserved break. You'd love the Grand."

Neva pictured an evening with the sheriff at a lively bar full of locals, followed by a night in the lovely old hotel. At any other time in her life the prospect would have been irresistible.

In her regular life, it would have turned directly into a newspaper column, but now, thinking of her quiet cabin, the young man lying dead across the street, and the little dog waiting at the deserted Barlow Mine, she shook her head. "I'm not myself today, Sheriff. I'm better off going home."

"Then how about letting me know next time you're in town." He squashed her hand in his. "Just stop in at the jail. I'm easy to find."

Neva arrived back in the Dry River Valley when the sun was low in the west. Black Angus cattle, the first cows she had seen apart from Darla's, stood like ebony carvings on a bright green field bordering the river. In the next field, sandhill cranes stood immobile on long legs. She slowed to a creep, watching in vain for a head or wing to move. She also watched for mailboxes that stood at the head of the lanes leading away from the highway every half-mile or so. The lanes ended at farmhouses, most on this side of the river, but a few on the south side across narrow plank bridges. The mailboxes, all large, bore names in weathered paint or flat brass letters.

An especially decrepit box bore the name Anthony Briggs. Neva pulled over onto the gravel shoulder next to the mailbox and looked down the lane at a house set among cottonwood trees just across the river. Even from this distance it was easy to see that the house matched the mailbox. Tall and narrow, as though starved, it sat behind a picket fence missing half its posts, with a gate that was propped rather than hanging on hinges. Briggs hadn't been exaggerating when he complained about struggling ranches.

Recalling his rudeness, she knew she should drive on, should not expose herself to further distress on this of all days, but curiosity kept her sitting at the side of the road watching the house. It appeared abandoned apart from dogs. With luck, Briggs wouldn't be home and another family member could show her the rifle. In any case, she was prepared for unpleasantness so at least it wouldn't take her by surprise.

Her tires bumped over the loose boards of the bridge. The motley set of dogs, stiff-legged and silent, watched her park. Their eyes followed her up the walk to a weathered door showing chipped layers of paint. There was no bell or knocker so she rapped with her knuckles, and was relieved when the door was opened by an old man with white-grizzled cheeks, who regarded her with a moronic, though friendly, grin. His baggy trousers hung low on suspenders that had lost their elastic, while his hands hung passively as though they had been of little use for years.

"Eh?" he said, beaming. "Eh?"

A television roared behind him in a room that, cave-like, was heavily curtained against the rich evening light outside. Stepping aside he waved her in, then folded like a dropped marionette into a recliner, his eyes fixed on the television. Neva followed, and from just inside the door she examined the strange room. From the shag-carpeted floor to the walls hung with velvet paintings and woven throws depicting country scenes, every surface was shaggy. Ancient, overstuffed couches and chairs left no space for movement except for a narrow path to a bright doorway where a little woman appeared, her gray hair standing out against the light.

"Don't mind him, don't mind him. Lazy and crazy, aren't you now, Father?" The woman laughed and waved Neva forward.

The old man paid no attention to the woman or to Neva as she passed him to get to the kitchen, a first cousin to the living room. Heaped objects hid every surface, including an old wood range, which sat next to a gas range that had evidently usurped its function without actually driving it out of the house.

The woman wiped her hands on a pinafore-type apron and offered them to Neva. "Tillie Briggs, I'm so glad to meet you. Just have a seat there. I'm fixing his dinner. If he doesn't have his dinner on the dot he gets very upset."

"I'm Jeneva Leopold. I'm staying the summer up at Billlie Creek Mine."

"Sure you are," Tillie said, then disappeared into a small side room where Neva could see the corner of a freezer lid go up, followed by a rummaging sound. The lid dropped and Tillie emerged waving a bag of home-frozen peas.

"His favorite," she said, pouring peas into a pot steaming on the gas range. "I've been reading the *Capitol Press*," she continued as though she and Neva were comfortable acquaintances, and Neva would of course know that the *Capitol Press* was the state agricultural newspaper, which she certainly would not know if she worked in a field other than journalism or farming. "I can't afford the subscription any more but I pick it up when I can. I've just been reading where they're growing organic vegetables over there in the Willamette Valley. Don't I wish we could grow them here, but you can't grow anything here for profit. You can't hardly grow cows anymore, not so it pays. And sheep, well, it's not worth selling them with the imports from Australia. I just look at mine as pets. If we could grow organic vegetables we might get out of debt, but don't say that to him, he won't go for anything but cows. He says a ranch without cows is no kind of ranch at all. No, you can't talk to him. He doesn't even like for me to talk this way because of what people will think."

The old man had come shuffling into the kitchen during this speech, and was pawing among the medicine bottles in a plastic tub nestled into the debris that covered the table. Smiling, blinking in a thoughtful manner, he looked simultaneously simple and wise as he lifted one plastic bottle after another, shook it, and put it back.

"Need my pills," he mumbled.

"That's a lot of pills," Neva said.

"Oh, some are for the dog!" Tillie laughed merrily as she ladled peas from the pot, then followed her shuffling husband into the front room carrying the bowl of peas with both hands while talking over her shoulder. "You just wait one minute until I get this guy settled with his supper and then we'll have a good talk."

Outside, the low sun flooded the river valley with ripe evening light. Cows grazed, cranes stood in deep grass, herons flapped above the river, rattlesnakes stretched out on the pavement to soak up the last of the day's heat. But in here behind heavy curtains time was of no account. Whether it was late or early in the day, spring or fall, last year or next was not significant. Peas would boil and pills would be swallowed. Tillie would read the agricultural news in the kitchen while the old man faced the roaring TV in the front room. Tillie Briggs, she thought with sudden appreciation, was a woman who would never bother to fold fitted sheets. She would roll them into a quick wad when they came out of the dryer or off the clothesline and stuff them into a cupboard so she could get on with something more interesting.

"I suppose you're wanting to see your uncle's rifle," Tillie said without preamble when she returned. She stood before Neva with her hands folded over her apron front.

"Well, yes," Neva said. "But there's no hurry, and I don't care about keeping it. I'm just curious about anything that was part of my uncle's life. We didn't have much contact with him when I was a kid."

"Of course you'd be interested and perfectly right, as I told Tony myself. He's the only one of the boys who stayed on the ranch, and he means well, but it isn't an easy life. I do have to say that. He's out at the new house. I'll ring him." A search uncovered a cordless phone on a small table. "It's just me," she said into the telephone with no greeting. "You have that rifle? She's here to see it." Tillie clicked off, then addressed Neva with regret. "He says he'll come right out. I thought we'd have a little talk first, but you might as well see what you came for."

Neva followed her through the back door and across a lean-to porch even more crammed than the house, leaving just enough room for them to pass between high banks layered like geological formations with wooden boxes, tools, flowerpots, twine, gunnysacks, cans, stakes, wire rolls, soil-encrusted tubers with pale root fingers twining outward. The smell was rich and attractively organic. Neva would have enjoyed lingering but Tillie moved briskly out onto a ragged patch of lawn where Tony Briggs was waiting.

Turning just beyond the door, she again took Neva's hands. "I'll get back to the house, then. Come talk to me any time. I do enjoy a talk. And I was real sorry to hear about that poor boy's accident."

Beyond Tony stood a modular home with rust streaks below the windows and weeds around the small metal porch. A tricycle lay on its side in the weeds and on it was a red chicken that appeared to be sleeping. Without a word Tony handed her the rifle.

Not accustomed to firearms, Neva held the rifle gingerly and was surprised by its weight. The wood stock was scarred but well oiled. "Does it still work?"

"Why wouldn't it?"

"Looks like it's had good care."

"Damn straight it has." Tony was clean today, and rather than work boots he wore old moccasins on his feet, but still he scowled as though his head ached.

"You said it was on the porch?"

Without turning, Tony indicated the house behind him. "So it was you that found that kid, DeRoos. Head smashed in, they say. He was a little sissy, anyway. I wouldn't have him working for me."

Neva looked at him in silence until he said, "Well, just because he's dead doesn't mean I have to like him. Nobody's going to like me any better when I'm dead. Funny thing, you come out because of a dead man and you end up finding one, but it's the wrong one."

"You are a very unpleasant man." Neva dropped the rifle on the ground as though it had stung her, turned, and strode away around the corner of the house. The hen flew up from the tricycle squawking and a dog rushed at her from an open shed. Too angry to bother dodging the dog she marched on while it followed, making quick dashes at her legs but veering off without biting.

She slammed the car into gear and sped up the lane and across the little bridge without slowing down for the planks. Her grip on the steering wheel was hard and she talked furiously to herself all the way to Billie Creek Road. Forced to slow down as the road steepened, bumping along in the last glow of sunset, she felt her anger begin to dissolve. She didn't care what Tony Briggs said or thought, and recalling his gentle, eccentric mother and his failing father, and the impoverished look of things, she felt an involuntary rush of sympathy. They were clearly struggling. She would visit Tillie Briggs again soon, earlier in the day when Tony should be at work, and they would have that nice long chat the old woman had mentioned so wistfully. She did not need to see the rifle again, and she was glad to have left it behind.

Gene's truck was not at his cabin and there were no lights in the window or she would have stopped. He must have learned about Roy by now. She would have welcomed the chance to talk with someone who had known all three of the young miners, and drove regretfully on.

It was nearly dark when she approached the Barlow Mine. Going slowly, dreading the sight of the road into the pit, she wished she had accepted McCarty's suggestion and stayed at the Grand Hotel. Right now she would be sitting in a bar full of people, most likely half drunk herself, the noise level so ferocious it would chase everything else out of her mind. But someone had to feed the dog. Resolutely, she drove past the mine entrance without looking at it, followed the road around the pit, and pulled up at Reese's cabin.

The dog was gone.

The chain lay on the ground still attached at one end to the porch pole. At the other end was an empty collar. Neva got out of the car to whistle and call, but she did not walk far. The absence of the dog put the finishing touch on the bleak scene, and she wanted only to get away. She filled the empty water and food dishes from closed containers on the porch, got back in the car, rolled up the windows, and drove too fast up the creek.

Chapter Fourteen

In the morning, Neva sat on the porch with coffee to watch the day begin, as usual, but her thoughts were not on the scene before her. She was thinking of the absent Skipper, and wishing she could walk down to the camp to sit with him under the pines talking over the accident. Even at this distance, she could feel the emptiness of the Barlow Mine, the absence of a single soul between here and Gene's place. Her gaze was on the trees that surrounded the deserted camp, and as though in answer to her thoughts, there was movement between the pale trunks. A horse and rider appeared. It was Darla Steadman, she saw after a puzzled moment, and the rancher was leading a second horse with three dogs trotting behind.

Despite the lack of warmth on their first meeting, Neva went eagerly to wait for Darla by the woodshed, relieved to have human company of any sort. Without a word, Darla swung down from the saddle, dropped the reins for both horses, and removed her hat to reveal a mat of sweaty hair. She pulled a bandanna from her pocket, wiped her forehead, folded the bandanna, and said, "Bad luck about Roy."

Neva nodded and looked away.

"I'm going up for the cows. I brought Barbry Allen in case you felt like going along. Sometimes a ride's the best medicine there is."

The offer was so kind and unexpected that Neva looked at her visitor for a moment, nodded without speaking, then turned her gaze to the tidy little brown horse that stood on three legs, letting the fourth leg rest in a slightly cocked position with only the point of the hoof on the ground. The saddle was worn shiny where a thousand pairs of jeans had rubbed it. Neva hadn't ridden since her teens, but she could feel the creak of the leather as she imagined swinging into the saddle, which would be warm from the sun and the body heat of the little mare. Had she been asked five minutes ago what she would enjoy most in the world, riding a horse would not have made the list. Now, suddenly, she wanted to take the reins on the spot, grasp the saddle horn, swing into the saddle, and head for the high country.

"You can ride?" Darla said.

"Yes, that is, I can stay on. Thank you, Darla, thank you so much. I'd love to ride with you."

"Your feet look about right." Darla's tone was matter-of-fact, and she turned with businesslike briskness to untie the thongs that secured a bundle to the back of the saddle. "I only had size eight. They've seen better days, but who hasn't."

She handed Neva a pair of dark leather riding boots that truly did look as though they'd been worn from New Mexico up to British Columbia and back again. But they had been freshly oiled and though they were stiff to pull on, they were comfortable apart from a slight squeezing in the toes. Wearing the boots, Neva felt as though she'd undergone a subtle character change, had become more commanding and even a little dangerously sexy. "They're just fine," she said. "I feel tall."

Darla declined coffee, saying they had a long ride ahead and had best be going. Walking self-consciously in the wedge-heeled boots, Neva hurried inside, made her usual preparations for departure, and was back outdoors within minutes. Resisting the urge to affect nonchalance, she got her left foot into the stirrup, swung the right leg up and found herself perched alarmingly far from the ground.

"You got on, that's a good start," Darla said, handing her the reins. "She knows what to do."

The dogs leaped up from the shade of the woodshed where they'd flopped on arrival and took up positions behind the horses as they started down the road. Two were short-haired, spotted and looked like twins, while the third was small and had the long silky hair of a show dog, and long ears that fell over his eyes but didn't appear to slow him down. The twins trotted shoulder-to-shoulder, with the silky dog dashing around them like a small child who has just been allowed to play with the big kids for the first time.

Neva felt rather like a child herself as she tried to match her posture to the rancher's, which was relaxed and controlled at the same time.

"In heat like this the cows pretty much stay to the creek," Darla observed as they rode through Skipper's camp. "If we head up it we should get most of them."

"What if some are downstream?"

"I came all the way up the creek from Gene's place and didn't see any. They always did like the upper bowl. Like me, I guess, they prefer the high country."

From the camp they rode single file with Darla leading. Noting the way she reined through the trees, Neva did the same even though Barbry Allen seemed to need little direction. The docile horse responded to the slightest signal, stepping lightly over logs, navigating through scattered rocks, squeezing between close-set pines. The first time she jumped the creek Neva clutched the saddle horn, then let go as though stung, recalling that only greenhorns hang on. While she didn't mind confessing to being a greenhorn she didn't want to look like one. The land was not quite the same when viewed from the saddle though she could not easily identify the difference—a little less intimate, maybe? The crowns of the scattered pines and junipers felt closer, while the sagebrush and flowers were not so easy to see in detail.

Soon they picked up a group of cows. Bellowing and kicking up dust, the cows rolled their eyes in terror even though the two riders ambled along well behind, ignoring them unless one strayed, when Darla would spur ahead to outflank the runaway and, aided by the dogs, drive it back with a whoop and a slap of her hat against her lean thigh. Most of the time they rode side-by-side, and during one of these stretches, Darla said, "I can't figure out what Roy was up to. He knew better than to drive close to the edge like that. He wanted to work for me, to be a cowboy. He thought he'd be riding into the sunset every day. I asked how he'd like to mend fences, and move irrigation pipe, and drive around the hills checking salt licks. I wish now I'd talked up ranching instead of discouraging him."

"You couldn't foresee something like this." Neva studied the rancher from the side. Her tone was sincerely regretful, which shouldn't be surprising, but her habitual wooden expression seemed to deny emotion just as it denied her beauty. "Young men are their own worst enemies."

"When you're dealing with a Cotter, you better expect anything. Hey, cut that out!" Darla spurred after a young bull that had already tried three times to circle back down the creek.

Around noon, they rested on top of the ridge where two fences came together, trapping the cows. Settled against a large rock in the shade of a juniper, they could see Billie Creek Canyon spread out before them, with a stretch of Dry River Valley visible to the south.

"Is this all Forest Service land up here?" Neva was wondering about the fences.

"You have a few private bits here and there. I own part of the upper bowl and a few acres right down on the creek, but mostly I have to lease for the grazing. Look at a map sometime. It's like a patchwork quilt, with BLM and Forest Service and private property mixed together all which-a-way."

"Skipper Dooley told me he saw you go into a mining tunnel on that day we met on the road, or so he guessed."

"He guessed right."

"I've walked all over the basin and haven't found any tunnel entrance. Is it possible to see roughly where it is from here?"

Darla pointed to the opposite side of the canyon where turkey vultures often circled in an updraft. Today there were three, floating lazily in big loops. "See where that middle buzzard is right now? Run your eye straight down to the big rock you can just see the top of, there by that snag with what looks like a nest stuck on the side. Below the rock is the old Calypso Mine, the deepest mine around here, or used to be. It caved in years ago about thirty feet back, which is a good thing because there were pits in there you couldn't see until you were right on them. It didn't smell so bad then. Now it smells worse than pack rat, like a herd of cows went in there and died. I only went in about ten feet. I wouldn't bother to look at it if I was you."

"I'm too claustrophobic anyway. I just wanted to know where it is. Did you think a cow might have gone in there?"

"I went in for old time's sake. My cousin that died a few years back from leukemia used to go in there with me. He liked this country better than anywhere, same as me." After reflecting for a moment, Darla said, "Some folks thought your uncle went into a tunnel and fell in a pit, but he knew the rock around here like you know your own face. Anyway, that mine was already caved in and the only other big tunnel on Billie Creek runs under the Barlow Mine."

"Did you know about that one before the accident?"

"Everybody knew it. Reese was real careful working in there until they actually found the old mine and knew where it was safe to drive the equipment without falling through. I hate to say it about the dead, but Roy was real careless or real stupid or both."

Neva was only half listening. Looking through the binoculars, she tried to find the entrance to the old mine across the way but the hillside looked like the usual expanse of sagebrush, rock, mountain mahogany, and scattered junipers. At least now she had a better sense of where to search next time she was on that side of the canyon. Turning her glasses toward the south, she studied the hills on the far side of the Dry River Valley. About a third of the way down from the top of a ridge she saw a faint line, like the trace of an old road.

She pointed it out to Darla, who said with almost possessive pride, "Not a road, a ditch, the Eldorado Ditch. They built it in the 1860s to bring water down for mining in the dry months. Talk about range wars. You had the miners and ranchers out to kill each other. The miners took all the water from every creek the ditch crossed, or tried to. The ranchers had to fight for their water. Right across there, where you're looking, they floated dynamite down and blew the ditch wide open. The miners patched it and set up groups to patrol every night. The crazy thing is, I heard the ditch cost a hundred and sixty thousand dollars to build even with Chinese labor, and they never made a cent on it. It was shut down inside of two years, I don't know exactly why."

After a silence, Darla said as though answering Neva's unspoken questions, "When I was a kid I was bored. I wanted more than anything to get out of this place and really live. You wouldn't know this, I guess, but I was queen of the Pendleton Rodeo, and the next year I got the Miss Oregon title, oh whoopee. I tried the modeling bit, but I was hungry all the time because you can't eat, so then I did some itty bitty parts on TV, and life was okay, good enough anyway. I still thought I was pretty hot stuff, but then my Gran died. That was fifteen years ago. I came home the next day. That's a day late, in case I'm not making myself clear. At least I did one thing right. I made them bury her on the ranch. They wanted to put her in Elkhorn with Granddad, but I wasn't letting those weirdos get hold of Gran. We put her in the ground ourselves, our own ground, with our own hands."

Neva regarded Darla with surprise and admiration, but before she could tell about her mother's ashes, the rancher continued in a more cheerful tone despite the gloomy prediction, "You know what? The way it's going with the price of beef and the cost of ranching, there won't be any cowboys left in a few years except the rodeo variety. At least Gran didn't live to see that. That's one good thing. If she was still alive, she'd probably tell me to go organic."

"That's what Tillie Briggs said, though I think she mentioned vegetables."

"It's where the money is now, boutique beef, they call it. Well, I have been blabbing on. I don't often get to talk to women, not my age anyway, and especially not anybody that actually likes it out here. You ready to ride?"

Neva let out a silent inward groan and her leg muscles screamed as she got back into the saddle, but once she was settled and they were moving again, she loved it all—the bawling cows, the little mare moving under her with eager confidence, the view stretching forever. Then Darla headed the small herd steeply downhill, and the cows disappeared into a storm of churned dust. Without warning, Barbry Allen's head was way below her rear and Neva was flung forward, barely saving herself from being thrown to the ground by gripping the mane. She could just make out Darla off to the right. Instead of sitting upright on the saddle, the rancher was leaning back with her stirrups up by the horse's shoulders and her head on his rump. Struggling against gravity and the lurch of the horse, Neva managed to get her own head uphill and her feet downhill. Barbry Allen continued to stumble as though drunk and her hooves clattered against loose rocks, while Neva clutched the saddle blanket, her knuckles digging into hot, hairy belly. Darla had been doing this all her life—surely, she wouldn't risk horses or riders for the sake of a shortcut?

The ground leveled, the cows stopped bawling, the dust cleared. Neva sat up and met the rancher's eyes, which appeared amused for the first time. She said, "Sorry about that, but it's good to give the horses a little challenge now and then. Keeps them on their toes."

Chapter Fifteen

Neva was so stiff and sore that evening that she didn't try to do anything except sit on the porch reading the mining book she had bought in town. It said nothing about Billie Creek in particular, which was disappointing, though it gave a good account of the general territory stretching from La Grande along the Oregon/Idaho border to the southeast corner of the state. There was plenty of information about Elkhorn, which had been "named for the nearby Elkhorn Mountains. Nobody realized this little upstart village would become the financial center of a vast mining district." Elkhorn was incorporated in 1874; by 1879 the population was 1,193, which included only 143 women.

"Among the hotels was the famous Grand, one of the finest in the West, with seventy steam-heated rooms and a hydraulic elevator. Harvey Crisp, who claimed he hadn't taken a drink of water in thirty years, operated the brewery. He also ran the opera house next door."

Neva read until dark, holding the book close until she could no longer see the print. Putting it aside at last, she stood up and groaned aloud. Her leg muscles burned and the insides of her thighs were red and raw, but it had been a great day, worth twice the pain. Darla hadn't talked much once they left the ridge, and had begged off staying for dinner with the excuse that she had to feed the stock, but still Neva felt that she'd made a little progress in getting to know the rancher.

A wind started up as she brushed her teeth, and by the time she fell asleep the tarpaper was flapping violently on the roof. When she woke up sometime later, however, it was to absolute silence, as though there was no such thing as wind on this earth. Stiff and aching, she rearranged herself carefully in the bed and was floating into unconsciousness again when she heard a shuffle and thump. Next came a soft scraping of wood against wood.

The sound was close, on the porch. It came again, a drawn-out rasping such as chairs make when pushed back from the table.

Someone or something was out there.

Had she latched the screen door? Easing onto her side, she tried to see the latch but it was too dark to make out.

The scraping came again, like a chair being dragged across the weathered floorboards—the chair she had placed on the porch to serve as a table for her coffee and books. Full of sudden, superstitious dread, Neva watched the square of starry sky that showed through the top of the screen door, expecting it to be blotted out by a dark human form. No form appeared. The scraping ceased and quiet returned, but she could not possibly sleep without knowing what was out there.

The night air was cool on her hand and arm as she reached for the flashlight that sat on the bedside table. She rarely used the flashlight, preferring to light a lamp or rely on the stars, but now the cold metal cylinder was reassuring in her hand. Easing back the covers, she placed her left foot on the floor with care, and was swinging her right leg off the bed when something thumped against the outside wall. Another thump. And then came a low whimper and a puppyish whine.

Neva sagged back onto the bed, wanting to laugh but unable to summon the breath after the adrenaline rush. Reese's dog had found her. He must have crawled under the chair and dragged it along on trying to get out. When she felt steady enough to get up, she crossed the room and aimed the flashlight beam downward through the screen, onto a dark mound of short, curly hair pressed against the base of the door. A tail thumped once.

◇◇◇

In the morning, the dog sat on the back step regarding Neva with steady eyes, as though to say, "Well, I got myself here and the rest is up to you." A mixed dingo breed like most of the ranch dogs, she had a skinny, shifty look but also a certain dignity. Dogs out here were bred for work and didn't tend to bark or get excited unless they were chasing cows. Even Tony Briggs' dogs hadn't barked at her.

"What's your name, pooch?"

A slight cock of the head.

"You scared me ridiculously. I'll call you Juju for now."

Juju calmly cleaned out a dish of tuna and crumbled bannock, drank half a graniteware basin of water, then settled in the shade at the end of the porch to sleep while Neva drank coffee.

When she headed up the creek after splitting the day's wood, Juju was at her heels and trotted in that position without straying until they approached the spot where Neva had found Lance's hat and knife. She had come here on purpose, to see how Juju would react, but still she was surprised by the little dog's intensity. With her nose to the ground, Juju ran back and forth whining, stopping to dig, then rushing on. Rocks and sand flew out behind her, but she unearthed nothing apart from more rocks, and at last sprawled with an exhausted whimper at Neva's side.

The exposed rocks, pale below the surface layer of sand and earth, looked hard and barren. Today was Roy DeRoos' funeral. He would be lowered into the stony, indifferent ground, never to come out again. Neva's chest squeezed as though in a brace and she broke out in a fine sweat.

"Let's go, pup," she cried, and strode up the road swinging her arms and breathing deeply. Soon she angled downward along a game trail that led to the creek. Turning upstream, she found a small pool, and knelt to study the colored gravel that lay under clear water. According to the gold mining book, certain early peoples believed that metals grew in the ground like plants and changed color as they ripened. Before her lay a multitude of tiny half-ripened mineral fruits, green, blue, jet, white, rose, and yellow, forever glossy under the polishing lens of the water. She sank her hands into the feathery cold current and scooped up water and pebbles together.

"They're much nicer than gold," she said, offering the mineral fruits to the dog.

Juju lowered her muzzle to the proffered water and drank with lady-like care.

After a simple dinner of rice and hot mango pickle, Neva shut Juju in the cabin, carried a blanket to the pond, and settled at the end opposite the dam with a large comfortable pine root for a backrest. She had tried several times to get up early to be at the pond before daylight, but had failed to talk herself out of bed. Twilight might or might not be as good for catching a glimpse of elusive wildlife, but it was a lot easier than getting up before dawn.

Frogs began a slow chorus around the edge of the glossy, opaque water. A noisy clattering on the slope to the east of the pond turned out to be five elk, the first she had seen on Billie Creek. They lined up to drink, then rattled away downstream like a herd of clumsy domestic cows. With a satisfied sense of being in the right place at the right time, Neva settled deeper into her nest and let her head rest against the trunk so that she could look slightly upward with ease. She was expecting bats, and they soon appeared as live shadows darting overhead.

As it cooled the pond water released a ripe, fruity scent into the twilight, mixing with the earthy smell of sun-baked ground giving up the day's heat. Night was a good time in the canyon. She would make sure to take better advantage of it from now on, particularly when real heat struck in August. It would make sense to get up at daybreak, nap in the afternoon like the wild creatures, and be out and about again at night. On clear nights the stars were bright enough to light her way even when there was no moon.

A stone rattled, and then another. She dropped her gaze from bats and early stars to scan the dim shape of the dam at the other end of the pond, expecting to see elk or bear. Instead, she discovered an upright silhouette that was unmistakably human.

The silhouette moved to the left, then right, and then stood still for so long that Neva blinked hard, suddenly certain that it was an illusion. When it moved again at last, it went to the far left end of the dam where the creek flowed out of the pond and there were no trees between the figure and the last traces of daylight in the sky.

Gene Holland.

She had seen him only once, when she stopped to introduce herself but was too sleepy to talk. Even so she was certain. The buzz cut hair, the slight build, the glint of reflected light that must mean glasses.

What would bring Gene Holland to the pond at this hour, on foot?

Though she had studied the Sufferin' Smith mine through binoculars from up on Billie Mountain, she had never seen Holland actively mining like the Barlow crew. The mine covered several acres on top of one of the lower ridges that bounded the canyon, an extremely barren stretch even for this territory. There were two trommels, earth movers of various types, and heaps of pipes, barrels, and what appeared to be defunct machinery and parts of machines scattered everywhere. She had never seen a sign of activity, or of Gene himself, though his pickup was sometimes parked at the top of the road that zigzagged up the ridge from the creek.

What did Gene Holland do all day? What was he doing here now?

She took a breath to call out to him, but hesitated. If she gave herself away, she'd never know whether he intended to visit the cabin to make his presence known. On the other hand, if he disappeared into the night she would be left puzzled and uneasy about where he might have gone and why he had come to her pond so late, without a word.

As she tried to reason out what to do, he began walking around the shoreline in her direction. She lost sight of him against the dark bank but she could hear his progress. The absence of stealth in his movements, and the probability that he would walk right to her, settled the question.

"Gene," she called, getting to her feet and gathering the blanket around her shoulders like a shawl. "It's Neva. I'm over here."

"What? Neva? Good lord."

"Here," she called again. "I'm coming."

When they were about fifteen feet apart, he said, "I can't see you. How about I wait where I am and you find me?"

"Here I am."

"I didn't expect to see you here at this time of night," he said.

"I live here."

"Well, of course. I meant at the pond."

"What are you doing here is more the question? I didn't hear a car."

"Sorry to take you by surprise, but it never occurred to me you'd be sitting out here in the dark. I walked up the creek, checking my water line."

"What water line?"

"The pipe that runs down the creek. You must have seen it. I take water from this pond to fill my own little pond."

"You've got to be kidding, Gene. Even I know water doesn't run uphill."

"But it's not uphill from here to the mine. Think of how the road climbs. It's all gravity flow."

"Did it spring a leak?"

"I don't wait for a noticeable leak to check it. If a joint goes, we could lose thousands of gallons before anybody knows it. We can't afford that out here. Without the ponds we'd all run out of water by late June most years."

He leaned forward as though to look closely into her face even though there was not enough light to show more than general shapes. He said, "Sorry to have to mention the funeral, but I saw the sheriff there and he said to tell you he was thinking of dropping up in the morning for a chat. He seemed concerned about you, about finding Roy, I guess, the shock of it. They did okay on the service but every time I go to one of those things I swear they aren't getting hold of me when the end comes. At least it gives me a fresh motive to stay alive."

"I thought of going," Neva said as they started up the path to the cabin. "But I didn't know him, really, and I just couldn't face it."

"No reason you should go. You can't undo what's done."

They walked on in silence, their feet finding the way. Despite her inclination to believe Holland, Neva could not help wondering whether he would have come up to the house had she not discovered him. Why couldn't he wait until morning to check the water line?

But her doubts were settled when she lit the lamp and he produced a bottle of Cabernet from a canvas bag, followed by smoked trout, clearly meant for a social occasion. He wore clean jeans and a button-up blue shirt, and smelled faintly of floral scent that seemed familiar, though she couldn't place it.

While she got out glasses, he arranged fish and crackers on the lone China plate from the cupboard. She was hunting through drawers when he said, "The corkscrew's hanging on a nail just inside the pantry, if that's what you're looking for."

"You know this cabin better than I do, it appears," she said, flourishing the new-looking corkscrew.

"That's where I'd put it."

They carried everything out to the porch, which was softly lighted by the glow of a lamp burning in the main room.

"To Billie Creek gold," Neva said as they touched glasses. "That includes everything from the evening light to what comes out of the ground. This is really a lovely treat, Gene. Thank you."

"Thank you," he said. "If you weren't here I'd be falling asleep in my bunk over some technical article or other. This feels like a holiday. To be honest, I didn't feel like being alone after the funeral. I needed a good long walk with a friendly face at the end of it."

"I'm glad you came up."

"You've got the dog, I see."

Neva told the story of Juju's midnight arrival, which made Gene chuckle, easing the somber mood. Even so, conversation did not come readily, and after a particularly long silence, Neva gave in to her curiosity. "Do you have a family somewhere?"

"A stepson is all. I was married for six years. She didn't like the mine but it's hard to blame her. You have to be a little crazy to like this life."

"Does your stepson like it?"

"He's a real nice kid but afraid of everything that moves, snakes, mice, porcupines, even cows. All his life he was so afraid of getting shots he decided to go into acupuncture to get used to needles. That's what he's studying. He said he'd like to practice on me sometime but I said I preferred to take my chances with the rattlers, thank you."

Neva laughed, then waited for him to perform the usual social echo of asking about her family. He said nothing, so she volunteered, "My husband died kayaking when our son was little."

"That's a real shame. I'm sorry to hear it. Where's the boy now?"

"At Berkeley. Studying geology, as it happens."

"Not for mining, I hope?"

"If so I've never heard a hint of it. He's always liked rock, which I've been thinking must run in the family."

"You didn't get hitched again?"

"It seemed more important to focus on raising Ethan. Now, if you wouldn't mind, Gene, I'd like to talk about a different part of my family. Is this a good time to tell me what you know about Uncle Matthew? You must have known him far better than I did."

"Well, I didn't really know him all that well, I'm afraid. He was so quiet, and it was a lot of years ago that I last spent much time with him and Orson." After a moment of reflection, Gene said in a storyteller's voice, "To understand your uncle's life, you really need to know something about mining, about this mine in particular. I suppose the place to start is with Johnny Jorgerson who first staked the claim. That was in 1898, and as it happened, it was the very first mine out here. Jorgerson and his partner spent the first winter in an 8-by-8-foot shack they built in two days, believe it or not. That one burned down a few years later, not much of a loss, I'm sure. Anyway, they worked all winter cutting a serpentine through the pastry so they'd be ready with plenty of ore to sluice by spring."

"Wait," Neva said. "Could you please put that into English?"

"What's that? Oh, I see. I guess I've been around mining too long to know what I sound like." What he meant to say was that the partners had cut a zigzag trench through the surface soil of the slope to get at the gold-bearing gravel from the old riverbed. When spring came they constructed a trough of split logs to bring water from the creek to process their heaped ore through the sluice box. "You know sluice boxes?"

"Kind of like a big sieve?"

"Same idea, different design. It's basically a big flat box with ridges on the bottom. You wash the gravel over it and the heavy gold lodges against the ridges. It's like panning but you can process a lot more material mechanically than by hand. Out here we do placer mining, which is nothing like hard rock mining, where you blast and tunnel your way along veins of gold or whatever mineral you're after. Placer mining gets at the alluvial gold, that is, the stuff washed down by rivers and creeks. You understand that gold is heavy? So even in nature it settles out lower than anything else. Miners look for deposits that have settled out over eons. The gold gets left behind in rock fissures and the bottoms of pools in the creek bed after the lighter material is washed away by the river, but still you have to sort the material, getting it down to finer and finer grains. Gold even gets trapped in the roots of rushes and other plants that grow right along the bank. Does this all make sense?"

"Fine so far. I had a general idea from seeing Reese's operation."

"Good. Now to get back to Johnny, he and his partner soon began turning up some real nuggets and when the news reached town, it started a small gold rush on the creek." Back in those days, Elkhorn had been such a boomtown that the local banks minted their own money. Miners dug ditches to bring water for sluicing, and for spraying away the soil as they followed rich deposits, often deep into the hillsides, which is why there were a few tunnels still to be found. But it wasn't until the Depression that the creek's biggest rush hit. "You had whole families out here working the claims. Men, women, and children too. A claim is twenty acres, and the person that claims it is called the locator. You can put up to eight names together to get a hundred and sixty acres. By all accounts, things were lively out here until Roosevelt put the lid on it by capping the price of gold at thirty-seven dollars an ounce."

Gene shook his head with an air of regret. "I know it was a rough life but I can't help wishing I'd been around for the heydays, when everybody and his brother expected to strike it rich and at least some of them did." When he was a kid, he said, a few of the 1930s cabins were habitable, with homemade furniture, cooking pots, and jackets still hanging on the walls. Artifact hunters, packrats, and weather had done for most of it. By the 1950s when his dad began mining, there were only half a dozen active claims on the creek, and it stayed that way until the 1970s when President Nixon deregulated the price of gold.

"It shot up to eight hundred bucks an ounce, and you had miners prowling all over the place again, mostly digging where it'd been dug before, but still finding gold. Your uncle was in this place by then, along with Orson. I think they didn't do too bad, but you wouldn't know it from how they lived. That's why the stories started up. If they never bought anything, what was happening to the gold?"

Before Neva could ask what Gene thought they had done with it, he said, "Orson had a sister, Enid Gale. She was nothing like Orson. She was tall, with a big laugh. It seems to me she was around for a couple of years and then one day Orson said she'd moved to Whitefish or some such place in Montana and I never saw her after that."

"Bernice Pangle at the post office told me about Enid. She said she moved to Kalispell."

Gene nodded but did not reply for some time, and when he did it was in a thoughtful, almost sad tone. "Your uncle had a secret of some kind. Even when I was half-grown I knew there was something about him. Most people assumed that it had to do with gold. And maybe it did. But maybe it didn't. For whatever reason, I wasn't very curious back then, but after he died—or whatever happened—I really kicked myself then. Now I think the secret most likely did have to do with gold, either a new strike or a stash he kept all those years and was worried about. You couldn't get anything out of Orson. He was always close-mouthed, and losing Burtie made it worse. Burtie had done the talking for both of them, you see, even though he was no great talker himself. Forgive me if I'm being nosy, but do you know what might have been bothering him all those years? Or what he did with his gold?"

"Not at all, not even a hint. I think I mentioned this, but he and my mother had a falling out and didn't talk for years before he disappeared. Basically, I grew up without an uncle. What do you make of his rifle turning up on Tony Briggs' porch?"

"No big deal, I'd guess. Tony had probably borrowed it from Burtie sometime before and didn't want to admit he couldn't afford his own gun and just made up the story about finding it on the porch. You can't believe him, unless he's talking about ranching. He knows his business when it comes to ranching." Gene reached for her empty glass, refilled it, set the bottle back on the porch boards next to his foot and said, "Now I've told you everything I know, don't you think it's fair to tell me what really brought you out here?"

"It really is very simple. I hoped to get healthy again where there's lots of sun and no stress, where I could relax and rest and so on. Some people seem to think I was hoping to find Burtie's gold, but it had never occurred to me there might be any. I hadn't thought about this before, but looking back I can see that my family considered my uncle's mining a sort of eccentric survival activity, to the extent they thought about it at all, and certainly not something profitable."

"So what you're telling me is that you came to Billie Creek to get a good night's sleep, more or less?"

"Exactly. And it's so successful I'm thinking of giving up the newspaper business and turning the mine into a health retreat for the sad and bewildered. Those with money, of course. Now it's your turn. You don't quite fit the image of a miner, you know."

Summarizing the facts as though they could not be more boring, Gene said that he worked as a chemical engineer in Pocatello to support the mine, and had done so for more years than he was prepared to admit. He took frequent leaves from the job to work on the Oregon or Nevada mine, depending on the season and the state of his finances. "You've heard about the miner who won the lottery?" he said. "They asked what he planned to do with his new wealth and he said, 'Keep on mining till the money runs out.'"

A comfortable silence followed their laughter. The stars were thick and brilliant, and the air moved just enough to bring them the complex perfume of the dark canyon without creating a breeze. "I do love it out here," she said. "It may seem odd, but this feels like a family place."

"I've always liked this spot myself. I used to like visiting Burtie and Orson when I was a kid. I would have come more often but I wasn't supposed to hang around here."

"Didn't they like company?"

"It wasn't that. My being a young male, you know. My dad was uncomfortable about it."

"About what?"

"You really don't know? You weren't aware that your uncle and Orson were, shall we say, married?"

"My uncle? Gene, are you saying he was gay?"

"That's what I always understood, at least when I was old enough to figure it out. Before then, I didn't understand why my dad was always asking what I did up here. I thought he was hoping to hear some mining secrets, that they'd struck it rich or something. It was never said right out. Even now I wouldn't go asking about it in Angus, not straight out. I hope I didn't upset you. I assumed you knew."

"I'm not upset, just surprised. And also puzzled. If it was true, my mother should have known and so would the rest of us. It just wouldn't have been a problem in my family. I'll have to think about that one for a while." After another, longer, silence, Neva said, "I've been trying to understand the attraction to gold. I don't find it very pretty in its raw state, not like some of the other rocks out here, particularly the orange-tinted quartz."

"It may not be pretty when it comes out of the ground, but there's nothing like gold, and that's been known since the cavemen. They've found gold amulets dating back some forty thousand years in Spanish caves. And when Columbus landed in the West Indies he found the natives fishing with gold hooks. Gold isn't just a nice yellow rock. It doesn't rust, or corrode, or tarnish. It's chemically inactive and unbelievably workable. An ounce can be stretched into a wire a mile long or pounded into a sheet like a tissue a hundred feet square. Believe me, it grows on you. Reese Cotter really has a case of gold fever. It's the old Midas syndrome. He likes to look at it, not sell it. I hear he's had a few run-ins with mine owners who suspect he's hanging onto more than what he's due. I've seen some nice nuggets in his little box of goodies. I'm sure he'd be happy to show you, if he hasn't already."

"Was he at the funeral?"

"McCarty said he was too drunk to let in. He's taking it hard, worse than I expected, to be honest."

"He must wonder whether he could have saved Roy if he'd stayed on the job instead of going to town to look for Lance. You didn't happen to hear anything about Lance, did you?"

"Afraid not. He's a different kettle of fish from Reese, you know. Not quite up to rowing both sides of the boat at once, to put it politely. Now, I'd better get going before I curl up with your little friend there for the night."

"I'd be happy to drive you down."

"That's very nice, but I've been wandering around in the dark out here for so long it's like a second skin. The walk will be good for me, downhill all the way, and it's only to the Barlow Mine where I left my truck." He stood up, stretched with a crisp popping of joints, then said, "You haven't seen a monk wandering around up here, have you? No cassock, too hot he says, but he's a big man, always in one of those collars they wear."

"I certainly have not seen a monk. I thought this place was isolated but every time I turn around there's someone new popping up."

"Most don't stay long, not like you. But Father Bernard's something else again." Father Bernard Shore was a Benedictine monk who spent several months every year at Angus. Although his local home base was the tiny priest's house by St. Mary's Church ten miles up the Dry River Valley, he traveled every other week to perform services for congregations scattered over hundreds of miles. "He's been coming here for years. He says this is the only place he can work without interruptions. The funny part is that the rest of the time he lives at a monastery over in Montana. If there's anyplace you could get peace and quiet to translate old church writings you'd think it would be a monastery. But he says there's no place like the Dry River Valley for concentrating on antiquities. Sometimes I feel like an antiquity myself. If I could get a half decent offer, I'd sell out tomorrow."

"I'm not sure I believe that."

There was sufficient light to show Gene's serious expression as he regarded Neva, started to speak, then shrugged. Without another word, he picked up his glass and led the way indoors. She followed him through the cabin and out the kitchen door, where they stood for a moment looking up at the sky.

"Johnny's claim papers are in a pipe right up there behind the cabin," Gene said. "The old claim cans have mostly been replaced with plastic because people take the cans, and the law says you have to keep copies of the original papers at the site. You might find them interesting."

"I noticed the pipe but thought it was a survey marker. I'll check it out in the morning. Do you know anything about a vehicle, a large truck by the sound of it, that sometimes comes up here at night?"

"There've been active mines up-canyon from me ever since I've been out here, so there's always somebody coming and going. I've learned to sleep through it."

"But this truck comes all the way up, past my cutoff, and only at night as far as I can tell. It's been here at least twice."

"Most likely just ranch kids from the valley horsing around."

They were standing side by side in the dark, not far apart, giving Neva a particularly good taste of the floral scent she had found familiar. Now she knew why. "Gene, did you go into my cabin a week or so ago when I was out?"

"How in the hell did you know that?"

"I have an extraordinarily good nose. Your aftershave gave you away. I knew I'd smelled it somewhere before and it just came to me." Neva spoke lightly but she stepped away from him, casually, as though to get a different view of the stars.

"Sorry not to let you know, but I was curious about who was staying in the cabin. You can't blame me for wondering who was using the place after all these years. You must have the nose of a bloodhound—next time I'll take a purifying sauna first."

"Next time leave a note." This sounded so sharp after the nice evening that she added, "Thanks for the lovely wine and fish. And the history lesson. At least some of the ghosts around here will now have names."

When the crunch of his boots on the lane had dissolved into the night, Neva settled Juju on her porch bed, returned indoors, brushed her teeth hastily, and pulled the covers up high to keep out—what? She wasn't sure, only that the friendly warmth of Gene's visit had ended with a chill. Entering her cabin for a quick look around was one thing, but why had he moved the box containing her mother's ashes? As far as she could tell, he had disturbed nothing else, so maybe he was checking the address label that was still on the package, hoping to discover her name.

Whatever else Gene Holland was, he knew the creek, though he must be wrong about Matthew and Orson. The family would have known that Matthew was gay, and not cared one way or the other. Gossip, that's what it must be, just unverified gossip that lived on long after the subjects themselves were gone.

Chapter Sixteen

The sun was well over the ridge when Neva woke up and went out to wash in the graniteware basin on the kitchen porch. Her body felt slow, and the rumor of a wine headache was whispering somewhere above her eyes. Instead of the usual splash of cold water, she used a cloth, wringing it out and holding it over her face. If she were careful, if she did everything right, the headache would fade out rather than get loud.

She dried by patting her skin with the dark blue towel that hung on a nail above the basin, and then, rather than return inside to make coffee, she went around behind the cabin and walked the short distance up to the white plastic claim pipe. About four inches in diameter, it stood above the ground at waist level, with a smaller pipe wired to the top. With an easy twist, she removed the cap on the end of the smaller pipe and pulled out a plastic bag containing a single, rolled sheet of paper. It was a photocopy of a claim deed, handwritten on a lined notebook page.

"Jorgerson" it said at the top, and then, "That I the undersigned citizen of the United States over 21 years of age located one claim, the ground running down from this notice 1500 feet to Billie Creek in Elkhorn County, Oregon. Located this 13th day of August, 1898. Known as Billie Creek Mine, witness J. Parker and T.R. Davis. Filed for Record March 6, 1900 at 4 p.m., I.H. McCord, Recorder."

Neva rolled the paper, put it back in the bag, and returned it to its plastic canister. Continuing to stand next to the pipe for some time, she tried to imagine what the spot had looked like in 1898 when Johnny Jorgerson and his partner first sank a shovel into the ground, but the ghosts refused to be summoned in the bright morning.

Contemporary visitors were not so shy, however. As she started back to the cabin, she heard a vehicle approaching along the lane, and walked faster to beat it to the dooryard. An official-looking SUV pulled in beside the woodshed, and Sheriff Tug McCarty boomed out the open window, "You got my message? I brought doughnuts."

He climbed out, stretched his arms overhead with a groan, then reached back inside the cab for a white box, which he handed to Neva. "I'm a jelly-filled man myself but I threw in some old-fashioneds for you."

"I beg your pardon. I'm not even half a century yet, you know."

"I didn't mean it that way," the sheriff said, appearing genuinely abashed. "It's just, I mean you didn't look like you had much of a sweet tooth."

"Just teasing, Sheriff, just teasing. As it happens, you're right. An old-fashioned was definitely the best choice. I did get your message but to tell the truth I'd forgotten, so I'm afraid the coffee isn't ready."

Rather than follow Neva into the cabin, the sheriff wandered around outside while she put water on to boil, using her one-burner camp stove rather than the wood stove for greater speed. When the coffee was ready, she found him on the porch already settled in the white rocker.

"Only time I was up here before was when we were looking for your uncle," he said. "I was a deputy then. It hasn't changed all that much, except for the garden going wild. A real nice spot."

"Sometimes I feel like I must have been born here, it's so satisfying." Neva took a doughnut from the plate she had arranged with the jelly-filled on one side and the old-fashioneds on the other. "I've been thinking a lot about landscape, and why some people love the mountains, some the desert, and others the ocean."

"And some never go outdoors at all if they can help it." McCarty finished a doughnut in two bites and washed it down with coffee.

Neva watched him almost warily, and did not try to keep the conversation going. She liked this large, straightforward man, and thought he was curious about her, but curiosity was not enough to get him up at dawn to drive the long road from Elkhorn, bringing enough doughnuts to feed a large family. The sheriff had a reason to visit, and the less she talked the sooner he was likely to spill the beans.

The explanation came with the second round of coffee. Sitting straight and setting his cup on the railing, McCarty said, "I'm afraid I have bad news that's best told without fooling around. Roy didn't die in the accident. He was dead when he went over the top. Someone else sent the bulldozer over the edge of the pit after putting him inside. At least that's the theory. I've got some boys down there now checking it all over again."

Neva simply looked at the sheriff, waiting for his words to make sense, but they refused to arrange themselves in an acceptable order.

"I suspected from the first that something wasn't right, so I wasn't surprised when the report came back," he went on with matter-of-fact efficiency. "He died from a blow to the head that couldn't have been done by anything in the cab. The bloodstains were wrong too, but I won't impose the details on you. Now the thing we have to do is go back over everything that happened when you found him. Take your time. I can see you're taking it hard."

Taking it hard…she wasn't taking it at all. It made no sense, not one bit. The murder of a cheerful young miner simply did not fit the world of Billie Creek.

"I can wait," the sheriff said, selecting a third doughnut and gazing out at the ridge as he chewed.

"Does Reese know?" she managed at last.

"Reese was taken into custody last night. At the moment, he's at the top of my list."

"No, Sheriff! It wasn't Reese."

"How so?"

As a feather is wafted downward from an eagle in its flight... Reese's voice came back clearly and she could see him looking up at the stars as he recited the fragment of Longfellow before launching the whiskey bottle into space. But she could not tell McCarty that she was being guided by instinct and a line of poetry. "I don't know exactly, it's a feeling. I don't know him particularly but it doesn't feel right. That's all I can say."

"I trust feelings but only up to a point. Then you have to look at the evidence. People don't always do what you expect them to. That's one thing this business teaches you. I've had shocks both ways in my time, the good folks that turn to killing, the bad folks that risk their lives to help somebody. That's what makes it interesting. I've known Reese Cotter since he busted all the windows in the high school gym when they benched him for swearing at the coach. Some folks thought the coach needed more than cussing, but that's not here or there. Reese did community service for that one. He's going to do a lot more for this one, I'm afraid."

Murder, in Oregon, is a capital offense.

Neva could barely get the words out to ask, "Why did you arrest Reese? Is there some evidence?"

"Let's just say that when two and two add up to four it's time to pay attention. Now, if you don't mind, I'd like you to go down with me and walk through it again. The guys from the special investigations unit in Pendleton are down there now, this being federal land. But as the first officer on the scene, I'll remain involved. Before we head down I'd just like to ask a few questions, if you're up to it."

She nodded even as she felt her initial regard for McCarty plummet. He was taking the easy out. Didn't he know that the obvious person is never the one who did it? The thought of Reese's restless vitality penned inside bricks and bars made her feel sick—but this was crazy. Why was she anguishing over Reese's plight when it was Roy who had been murdered?

"You said you spent the previous afternoon with Reese and he was in a wild mood because of Lance," the sheriff pressed with sudden focus. "You drank a bottle of whiskey. Would you say he was drunk when he dropped you off?"

Two hours later, following an hour of questioning and a trip down to the Barlow Mine pit, McCarty delivered her back to the cabin exhausted, depressed and in the grip of a full-scale headache. As they stood in the dooryard, the sheriff assuring her that she was not in danger as far as he could tell, while she assured him wearily that she hadn't supposed she was, her second guest of the day arrived.

"Oh, lord," McCarty said as they watched Andy Sylvester pull his pickup in beside the sheriff's rig. "What's he want?"

"For me to move out of here," said Neva. "I think I told you I've been evicted."

Sylvester's manner was excited as he shook hands with McCarty. "I saw your people down there. What's up? More bodies? Homicide on Billie Creek?"

"Just routine," McCarty said. "How are things down your way?"

"Just routine," Sylvester said, then turned to Neva. "How's the moving going?"

"I'm still thinking about it."

"What's to think about? Frankly, I'm surprised to see you here. I thought you understood the situation."

"What is the situation?" McCarty inquired flatly. He listened without expression as Sylvester explained, then looked at the younger man in silence for a long, thoughtful minute before saying, "There was a law on the books in Oregon until not so long ago. It said black people couldn't get married inside state lines. Now, what do you suppose people did while they were getting around to changing that useless old law?"

"Beats me."

"I can tell you what they didn't do. They didn't go arresting anybody. Nobody at all."

"This isn't the same kind of situation, Sheriff. Nobody's trying to arrest Ms. Leopold. This isn't a state law, it's federal government policy, and not about to be changed any time soon. All she has to do is move down to the creek."

"Well, son. This may be federal property but as the sheriff of Elkhorn County, I am the chief law enforcement officer in the area. It happens to be very important to me right now to have this little lady staying right here in this house. I don't doubt you mean well, but you have to remember that things work different around here than out there in D.C. where they make these rules. I suggest you go on back to the office and stop troubling your mind over where she's putting her head down at night."

Sylvester stood up straight and silent, facing the sheriff.

Neva no longer cared whether she was in the cabin or camped on the creek. She loved the cabin but the weather was fine for camping and to be outdoors around the clock—and right on the creek—had its own appeal, although she was not about to say so until she was driven into a corner. If McCarty could put off her eviction for the time being, then this was fine and dandy.

Sylvester gave in first. Dropping his gaze, he said to Neva, "Just remember, if it wasn't for federal protection this creek would be torn to pieces by miners who don't give a rat's ass for the environment. I would have thought you could see that." He strode to his truck, revved the engine high, and shot up the road.

McCarty chuckled. "Well, I don't suppose that was very diplomatic but it should calm the waters for a while anyway. Not a bad kid, just a little big for his britches. Some of my deputies have the same problem once they get that badge on them. This new breed of forest rangers all seem to have bees in their bonnets of some kind or other. If it isn't spotted owls it's frogs or butterflies. He'll settle out in a few years and realize that folks have to live, too. Anyway, you should be okay in the cabin for now."

"Thanks for the defense but I don't really mind moving down."

"I don't want to alarm you, especially after making a point about no danger, but we don't know that for certain, do we? Just as well to have doors you can lock at night. And I'd keep that little dog close by."

As he drove away, Neva wondered what McCarty would say if he knew that she didn't close the doors at night, let alone lock them. Was there really a good reason for her to be more cautious? She shook her head. The day when she felt unsafe at the mine would be the day she'd pack her gear and leave. The killing of Roy DeRoos was a nightmare but it had nothing to do with her. Men had always killed for gold.

Chapter Seventeen

The day turned hot even for Billie Creek. Neva stayed longer than usual in the pond, floating on her back while trying to make sense of what the sheriff had told her. Miners are tough customers, everyone knows this. They fight, cheat, claim jump, tear up the landscape to get rich, and then lose everything on a roll of the dice at Diamond Lil's. Western myths, like most myths, must contain some truth, although Gene Holland was no brawler and surely her uncle had been a gentle soul by all accounts. The Cotter brothers were colorful and tough, but this didn't make them killers.

She looked toward the dam where Juju lay waiting on the changing platform, as calm as a dog could be. She didn't flinch if Neva made a sudden movement, she responded to subtle signals, and already she recognized when a walk or trip to the pond was about to happen. Dogs raised by violent owners are neurotic, not calmly observant. Reese had not been cruel to this little dog. Remembering his powerful, work-roughened hands gently cupping the nugget from the screening table, Neva could not imagine Reese killing for the sake of gold. The only thing that might trigger murderous violence in him would be discovering that someone had harmed his brother. Lance was his personal property to bully but let anyone else cock an eyebrow and Reese would be up in arms in an instant. Such is the weird world of families...Or could Reese have killed Lance in a drunken fury, then got rid of Roy out of fear that he knew the truth and would eventually spill the beans?

No, no, no. This was all wrong. Had Reese harmed Lance, he wouldn't cover it up, he'd most likely do himself in.

Lance was alive somewhere, she was sure of it, and until he returned the cabins would stand empty, inviting the curious and greedy to look for Reese's stash. Reese's habit of saving nuggets was clearly known and likely to have been exaggerated enough to attract greedy interest. McCarty had said nothing about finding gold when the investigators searched the cabins, but would they have confiscated it? They were hunting for clues to a killing, not to Reese's Midas tendencies. And an officer finding a collection of dull yellow rocks might well have reacted with as little interest as she had felt on seeing her first nugget.

There was nothing she could do about Reese being caged like a beast, but she could make an effort on behalf of his hoard. That a portion of it might not be legitimately his was only a rumor, and not really her concern.

She climbed out of the pond and stood in the air to dry without toweling off, gazing at the alluring top of Billie Mountain far up the canyon. Her lovely life on the creek was in serious danger of derailing, and to save it she must maintain a firm hold, which meant sticking to her routines and continuing to hike and do everything else that made the days here magical. She would carry out this one little errand on Reese's behalf, now, before her walk, and then avoid any other distractions and interference.

Neva put away her bathing things, drove down the mountain to the Barlow Mine cabins, and sat for a while with the windows rolled down, listening to silence. The quiet was not like the quiet of the woods. Here, where every sign pointed to a busy human presence, quiet was unnatural and uneasy.

The silence was broken by a whine from Juju. Neva leaned across to open the passenger's side door. The little dog leaped out and rushed up the porch steps, but Neva did not follow immediately. This morning when she had returned to the scene with McCarty they had gone back down into the pit, not into the cabins. She had seen no one here when they passed on their way up and down, but the investigators must have searched the young men's living quarters. Even so, she felt like a trespasser, a trespasser on what now struck her as a fool's errand.

And yet, here she was. To go back up the canyon without at least looking around would be foolish in a different way, a pure waste of time.

Although she knew that Reese's cabin was empty, she knocked and listened before trying the knob. It turned and the door swung open on a dark interior reeking even stronger than before of old grease, smoke and sweaty clothing. Juju pushed past her legs, circled the room sniffing and whining, then jumped up on Reese's bed, lay down, and pushed the tip of her nose under his pillow.

Neva stood just inside the door, suddenly repelled by the prospect of looking through the young men's possessions. Everything on the open shelves appeared furry with oily dust, and without having to touch anything, she knew that the kitchenware would be sticky. She moved to the middle of the room, using her eyes to search as she turned in a slow circle.

Juju had withdrawn her nose from the pillow and watched Neva with her head up.

"Okay, pal, where's the gold?"

The dog's tail flapped once on the tumbled bedding.

Under the mattress?

Neva squatted for a better view, but could see nothing under the bed apart from dust and wadded socks. Shelves at the head of the bed held shaving gear, toothbrush, playing cards, magazines…Her scrutiny shifted to a single shelf that ran along the wall about four feet above the bed. A row of paperbacks, a quartz rock bookend, a dusty radio, a cigar box. She considered the cigar box for a moment, approached close enough to see the label, and smiled.

Gold Tips. What a guy.

Minutes later, driving back up the creek with the box beside her, Neva considered what kind of man would keep gold on an open shelf in this obvious container. It was only a small amount but the large, jewelry-grade nuggets were handsome even to her eye, and Reese evidently valued them. He had not struck her as naive. He must have had perfect confidence in Lance and Roy and this was reassuring. Those who trust are most likely to be trustworthy...Well, it sounded good at any rate.

Back at the cabin she was faced with the question of what to do with the stash now that she had made herself its guardian without being asked. The sky was clear and bright. It was late morning already, and yet another day at the mine would slip away from her if she didn't get on with it. Wasting no more time on thought, she went into the woodshed, made her way to the back wall, moved some splits, set the gold in the space that was created, and rearranged the wood. If necessary, she could direct Reese to the stash without having to be at the mine herself.

Pleased to have taken care of this interesting errand efficiently, quite apart from whether it made sense, Neva filled her water bottle, laced the binoculars and lunch bag onto her belt, and set out walking, driving her body hard. She reached the highest point on the ridge in record time. Flowers were at their peak up here now. Mariposa lilies on slender stalks shimmying with every breeze, desert parsley, blue delphiniums, red paintbrush, and others she couldn't name. So many bees worked over the flowers that she could feel their humming on her skin. The land was full and busy even though empty of people other than herself. Full of fierce joy that welled up despite the tragedy at the Barlow Mine, she walked with her shirt off and her shorts rolled to the tops of her thighs. Striding along the ridge road, singing until her throat was dry, she did not start down until the sun was below the horizon and soft shadows smudged the foothills.

It was the latest she had stayed on the ridge apart from the involuntary evening with Reese, but she wanted to see the whole panorama washed in sunset gold as she descended. She was strong and fast enough now to get back to the cabin before it was fully dark. Confident and solid on her feet, she bounded downhill with Juju dashing ahead and even yelping with excitement at the unusual speed.

The air grew cooler as the evening advanced. Wearing her shirt again, Neva jogged the last mile out of pure pleasure in the energy that still drove her despite the rugged five-hour hike. She was following a different path than she'd used before, which brought her out of the woods a bit west of the cabin, onto the lane. She stepped out of the trees, glanced up the track toward Billie Creek Road, and stopped in astonishment.

"You're a goddamn nuisance, Walkie-Talkie!" Skipper roared, and brought his quad to a stop in front of her. "You're late. You always come down about seven o'clock and it's damn near nine. I've been out looking for you. It's a good thing you're not my kid or I'd tan your butt."

"It's a good thing I'm not your kid or you'd have a coronary worrying about me for no good reason."

They eyed each other in the twilight, fiercely, playfully, then whooped with laughter, triggering a barking duet by the dogs. Soon they were settled on the porch with mugs of miso and chocolate chip cookies that Skipper had baked in his little camper oven.

"Now, here's the deal, W.T.," he said, wasting no time on chitchat. "I've been thinking, and I've changed my mind. There's no point fighting the Forest Service. It's time you cleared out of here and went back to town like a good girl."

Just able to see him in the lantern light that shone through the window, Neva studied the craggy, cagey face. When he left the creek a few days ago, he had been ready to fight the Feds on her behalf, possibly even with fists, if necessary. Such an about-face could have been triggered only by news of the murder. Despite feeling grateful for his concern, she could not help teasing. "I suppose you're right. The government knows what it's doing, and it's not for people like us to question the rules. I'd hate to be a nuisance to those busy rangers."

The response was so satisfying it was difficult not to laugh but Neva managed to keep her expression serious as Skipper slammed his cup down on the porch railing and exploded, "Nuisance my

ass. You know damn well that's not what I'm saying. I just think
it's time to let the dust settle, you know what I mean?"

"No," she said with feigned innocence. "I don't know what
you mean."

"I thought you were an intelligent person. Do I have to spell
it out? Okay then, here it is. You have a man dead, you have a
man arrested for murder, you have a bad situation. It's no place
to be."

"Sheriff McCarty was here this morning. He didn't seem
to think there was any problem for me. He believes it was
personal."

"It usually is when you kill somebody. Doesn't mean that's
the end of it."

"I've rented out my house in Willamette for the summer so
I can't go home before September, Skipper. Anyway, I'm not
finished here, and I've never felt safer anywhere in my life. It's
incredibly sad and bizarre, but it doesn't involve me."

And so it went, back and forth, until Neva said she had to eat
something more substantial than miso and cookies, and could
he manage a bowl of canned black beans with hot sauce and
olives? No, he said, he'd eaten a steak at the Angus Café and it
was past his bedtime, but please to sleep on what he'd said and
they'd decide in the morning.

"Remember," he said as he stood up to leave, "today's the first
day of the rest of your life. I read it on a bumper sticker on an
old VW bus over at Sumpter, parked since I don't know when,
probably since the last hippie lived in it. Think about it. How
many days do you want the rest of your life to be?"

Chapter Eighteen

He sat on the usual rock and rested his elbows on his knees to steady the binoculars. She was moving fast today, almost bounding uphill like she was running away from something.

Well, he couldn't blame her. If she had any sense, she'd keep on walking and never come back to the canyon. He'd miss her for a few days and then it would all be over anyway.

The flowers were thick up there now. She stood in the middle of a bunch of white ones with her arms spread, her back to him. He focused on her shorts, which were rolled to the tops of her thighs.

She squatted, almost disappearing into the flowers. She wasn't going to pee! He flushed, lowered the glasses, raised them again and saw that she was moving out of the flowers. Strange woman, kind of like a kid. Did she expect to find her uncle's remains? That's what they were saying down at the café. And his gold, too.

Well, she wouldn't find any remains, and no gold either. The gold at Billie Creek didn't come out of the ground.

A sudden snort of laughter.

It really was comic, in a way…His hands trembled and he lowered the glasses, set them on the ground, wiped his face with a rag from his back pocket. He wasn't well these days, he was losing weight, but no one cared. They never had cared. And now there was the kid to worry about. They never should have bothered with the stupid kid. He said so at the time, but they didn't listen to him.

He grabbed up the binoculars, swept the side of the ridge, failed to find her, cursed under his breath, scanned the full expanse again, more slowly this time, and locked onto a figure silhouetted on top of a rock to the west of the summit—what was she doing?

Dancing!

The crazy woman was dancing up there, her arms flying and her feet kicking high.

Again he let out a single snort, then leaned forward involuntarily, as though to get closer, realized what he had done and sat up straight with a jerk that threw his cap off.

Holding the glasses with one hand, he groped on the ground behind him, feeling, leaning, keeping her in view, ah, he had the hat—she jumped from the rock out of sight and was gone, disappeared over the rim of the ridge.

He lowered the glasses, replaced his cap, breathed deeply with his hands gripping his thighs. Just a few more days, a week maybe, it's all they needed. He hadn't told on her yet but it wasn't looking good. Why had she come now, after all these years, a crazy woman walking everywhere, nosing into everything, causing trouble, half naked…He stood up, crammed the binoculars into the case without bothering about the dangling strap, and went back to work.

Chapter Nineteen

As promised, Skipper showed up for a summit conference in the morning and the upshot was that Neva refused to leave Billie Creek and therefore he said he was going to stick around to keep an eye on things. But first, he said, he had to go over to Idaho for two days to take care of some business and then he'd be back for the rest of the summer or until she had the sense to clear out.

"You can't change your plans because of me," she protested, and almost added that people simply don't do such things, particularly for someone they've known for less than two weeks, but his earnest expression checked her words.

"One thing about being retired, I can do whatever I damn well want with my time," he growled. "I suppose you can take care of yourself for two days? I'd leave Cayuse but he goes crazy if I take off without him. That little excuse for a dog you've got there won't be any help, so behave yourself, you hear me?"

Skipper's dust had barely settled on the road before Neva, too, headed down the mountain. Clouds had drifted in from the west and the air was heavy by the time she pulled into Elkhorn. She parked by the soda fountain and went in for two scoops of butter-brickle on a waffle cone. Licking ice cream, she drove one-handed to the library where she left the car windows down a few inches for Juju. She sat on a bench to finish the cone, then went into the library, requested a computer station, pulled up her email, and scrolled down to the reply from the Kalispell library.

"Dear Ms. Leopold, I'm sorry it has taken a few days to get the information you wanted, but it was a challenge to track down. Still, it kept us entertained for a while. The person of interest, Enid Gale, is still living but she moved away from Kalispell ten years ago. She is now in the town of Hatlee, Oregon, which, according to the map, isn't far from Elkhorn. I thought you might be interested in the following small news item that appeared in the *Kalispell Daily Inter Lake* a few months before she left for Hatlee. Under the headline 'Artist blames glue,' was this: During a tea reception for her latest show, long-time Kalispell collage artist Enid Gale fainted to unconsciousness but was luckily seated at the time and escaped serious injury. The unfortunate episode occurred Friday in the activity room of the Kalispell Senior Center, where the exhibition is on display through the remainder of the month. Gale was revived through the efforts of friends before the arrival of an ambulance summoned by Senior Center staff. Refusing to go in the ambulance, she was driven home by Dial-a-Bus and is reportedly doing well despite the episode. She told a reporter who called to enquire after her condition that this had never happened to her before and she didn't know why she passed out. 'Maybe it's that new glue I've been using,' she said, assuring this reporter that she would henceforth refrain from it.'"

Neva could not help smiling at the quaintness of the report, which shifted her mental image of Enid Gale away from the robust, striding figure that Gene had described to an elderly, fainting artist. No matter. She was a member of her uncle's generation, not a relative youngster like Gene, and if any living person could tell her what kind of person Matthew Burt had been, it would be Enid Gale. Her own suspicions of a romantic link between Enid and her uncle had, it seemed, been mistaken, but the two must have been good friends to share the cabin for several years. Maybe this was even better than sweethearts because it meant that no disappointment or bitterness would be likely to color Enid's memories.

Neva printed the message, sent a grateful reply, and then sought an atlas. Located on Interstate 84 south of Elkhorn, Hatlee looked like a mere crossroads rather than a town. The postmistress surely would know where to find Enid, and if the town lacked a post office, she would knock on doors.

Her plan to head for the jail next was sidetracked by Juju, who made it clear that she was tired of sitting in a hot car. Neva dug a length of laundry cord from the trunk, fixed one end around Juju's neck, and set off through the old residential neighborhood adjacent to downtown. The architecture was just the sort she liked, the houses close-set, each one different from the last, with porches, gables, and bay windows.

They had walked for about six blocks when large drops began splatting onto the sidewalk, filling the air with the dusty metallic smell of summer rain. Neva sheltered under a tree, debating whether to turn around, but a large open area at the end of the street drew her despite the shower, and by the time she reached what she had guessed correctly to be a cemetery, the little storm was spent. Seeing no one else about, she let Juju off the leash, and then located the old section of the graveyard, where darkly weathered angels, crosses and cherubs crowded together. It was easy, as usual, to find family plots with a patriarch and multiple wives, at least one of whom had died in her twenties and lay buried next to a tiny cross for the newborn who had died with her. Why she was drawn to these mournful testimonials to women's vulnerability Neva didn't know, but she sat for some time on a stone bench musing over the revolutionary power of easy birth control, sanitation, and antibiotics.

Juju had disappeared but the little dog was too sensible to get into trouble, and would turn up soon, no doubt. Sure enough, Neva soon found her in the newer section of the cemetery where headstones gave way to simple markers flush with the lawn. The little dog was scratching at the ground where a new grave was being dug, or had at least been marked out by the removal of grass sod that exposed what appeared to be solid rock, a good challenge even for the small backhoe that stood nearby. Juju gave up the fruitless attempt to dig through rock, and sat by Neva's feet, also contemplating the grave. As Neva bent to retie the rope, she heard a shout and looked up to see a stout little man barreling toward her across the grass.

"What are you doing there?" he shouted while he was still some distance away.

"Walking my dog," she said with determined friendliness. "I was just thinking it's a good thing graves aren't dug with shovels anymore or you wouldn't get far in this rock. It looks like hard work."

"What business is it of yours?"

Standing straight with the rope coiled around her hand, Neva eyed the little man warily. Wouldn't it be nice for a change to scowl back at him and snarl, "You are a stupid ass," rather than try to be pleasant? Why did she always make an effort to pacify rude people, to smooth things over and create a pleasant mood? *Just sling it back, Jeneva, just let him have it with both barrels like you did Reese that night on the ridge.* But already she was speaking as though the little man were the very soul of cordiality.

"I'd also like to find a young friend's grave, just recently buried. Roy DeRoos?"

The gravedigger continued to glare with his hands on his hips until it occurred to her that it might be due to a mental problem rather than temper. Maybe grave digging, like janitorial service, was now contracted out as a charitable enterprise to employ people incapable of more demanding work? Juju tugged on the leash. As Neva turned to go, the man climbed onto the backhoe with an air of such stiff self-importance that she had to restrain a smile. He wasn't a stupid ass, but only a backward character with a chip on his shoulder.

Even so, his rudeness had put her back up. Rather than head for the car as she had intended, she strolled about in search of Roy's grave. It proved difficult to spot because rather than the new mound she expected, the grave was as flat and tidy as all the others around it, the seams between the individual rectangles of turf barely showing.

Standing with her head bowed, she felt sudden resentment of the grave, of its colossal insufficiency. A young man had vanished from life mere days ago, yet the grave had closed over him like a calm sea, leaving almost no trace. The plain marker, like all the markers in the new section, was flush with the ground and bore only his name and the dates, with no ornamentation or further inscription. To a casual glance, the modern part of the cemetery seemed no more than a vast lawn, perfectly cultured and mowed like a golf green. How different it was from the old graveyards of New Orleans, or Père Lachaise in Paris, that extravagant city of the dead crowded with miniature mansions, chateaux and chapels like elaborate children's playhouses, the whole crisscrossed with small streets named for the famous figures interred there, each grave with its own street address. When she walked there years ago with Ethan it had stunned her with excess, but surely this was too little. Why bother at all? What kind of special feeling could family members find here when they returned to remember and mourn? The modern cemetery was a suburb for the dead, mass-produced and featureless.

And yet, what more would she do if she did bury Frances' ashes at the mine? A hole in the ground, some handsome local stone for a marker, and that would be it.

Juju whined and looked up with an anxious air.

"Okay, little pup," she said. "Let's get going."

As she turned away, Neva looked for the backhoe driver, suddenly aware that she had not heard the machine start up. He sat where she had left him, gesturing in her direction and talking to a man who stood next to the backhoe. The man looked around, spotted her, and started across the lawn.

Was this a private cemetery? She'd been a walker in graveyards all her life and not once had anyone paid her the slightest attention, yet these two men clearly were bothered. If it was Juju that worried them, at least she was now on the leash.

Neva walked to meet the newcomer, noted his long-sleeved shirt buttoned to the collar, and recognized Darrell from the

Garden of Eternal Peace. "Hello," she said. "I haven't found any cucumber beetles out here, but there are a few butterflies."

"You don't get so many interesting ones in these places." His vague gesture indicated the cemetery around them. "I never collected here." He considered Juju for a moment, and then inquired with an air of formal politeness, "Are you particularly interested in the funeral business?"

"Funeral business? I—oh, I see what you mean. First I turn up at the mortuary and then here. No, actually quite the opposite, I've never even been to a funeral. But I find graveyards inter-esting, particularly the old parts like your pioneer corner over there. I came here to walk the dog. My family doesn't believe in funerals. I'm sorry. I don't mean to be rude."

He shrugged his narrow shoulders. "Fine by me. It's a family business."

His apparent indifference felt like permission to continue her thoughts out loud. She said, "Why is it all so flat?"

"Excuse me?"

The sudden flush of color in his face made it plain that he was not indifferent after all. Clearly, she had committed a funeral business faux pas, but before she could explain, he protested, "We use the most modern burial procedures. The material is placed back in the hole precisely, leaving no unsightly mounds. Our gravedigger is a certified expert with twenty years' experience."

"I'm sorry, I didn't make myself clear. I meant the markers, you know, they're so different from the usual headstones, just the flat plaque in the ground, no crosses or angels or anything."

"The markers? You're asking about the markers?" He scrutinized the area around them with a quizzical air, as though he'd never noticed the absence of upright headstones and monuments.

"I was just thinking of some of the famous cemeteries, like in New Orleans and Paris, that are like little cities of the dead. If you'll pardon me for saying so, this is more like a golf course for the dead."

Darrell's sudden snort of laughter was so unexpected that Neva didn't realize for a moment that he was laughing. Alarmed by the choking sound of it, she studied him with concern, saw that his eyes were amused rather than angry, and smiled.

"Everyone uses those now," he said, turning serious again. "You'll hardly find a headstone, a real headstone, in a cemetery today. It's far too costly. We do everything we can to keep the burden on our customers light at this time of grieving—" He stopped and cocked his head as though listening to his own words, then said in an entirely different voice, matter-of-fact and a little impatient, "It's better for mowing, nothing to go around. I suppose you could play golf on it."

"If the plaques were holes."

This time he didn't laugh though his mouth twitched and he undid his collar button. "I'm not used to people joking about it."

"Thank you for taking it in good spirit. I really didn't mean to insult your cemetery. It's very well kept and attractive. I guess I'm surprised that people, some people at least, don't want something more than a name and dates."

Darrell replied with the earnest manner of a boy. "Most people don't know what they want, you see. We have to tell them. And not so many even come to the graveside anymore. They just watch the video."

"Video?"

"The video tribute to the deceased. They give the grieving families a memento worth a thousand headstones. They're professionally done, a movie that brings the dead back to life onscreen. And it's there forever. Any time family or friends wish to view it they can use the big screen in the chapel or simply put it into the DVD player at home. Most people prefer the chapel, where the formal setting"—Again he stopped and appeared to be listening to himself, and again changed gears. "The funeral business has changed. I guess that sums it up. Anyway, your old-fashioned graveside service is too depressing for most people. They don't want to see their loved ones go into the ground. Are you finished walking the dog?"

Glad for an excuse to end the exchange, Neva gathered Juju's rope up more snugly. "I think she's had enough. Nice talking with you."

She moved away but instead of saying goodbye, Darrell fell into step beside her. When they were just halfway to the sidewalk and he still had not said a word, she asked, "Is entomology a hobby?"

"I used to collect butterflies and beetles. That was before this." He waved around at the wide lawn. "I don't have time now. And I never did like to pin them."

She left him standing with his hands in his trouser pockets and a studious look on his face, as though they had enjoyed a philosophical discussion that required additional thought. Next time, should there be one, she would find the city park that was certain to be somewhere not too far away and walk Juju without strolling through that minimalist suburb of the dead where living guests, it seemed, were not particularly welcome.

Sheriff McCarty greeted her affably outside his office in the law enforcement building, but the instant she said she had come to visit Reese the jovial manner switched off. "I thought you only met him once."

"I'd like to reassure him about his dog."

"You'd be the first."

"To visit?"

"That's correct. Folks who've known him all his life haven't even bothered." There was silence for a moment, and then his manner relaxed somewhat. "Don't expect him to appreciate it."

Having never set foot in a jail before, Neva was prepared for a movie-style guarded visiting room with a long table divided by glass. Instead, she waited for Reese alone in an airy room furnished with upholstered chairs and a coffee table. There was nothing to read, and the longer she waited the more uncertain she felt. Just what was she doing here? What kind of arrogance had led her to be so sure of his innocence? There was at least a possibility that she was about to get cozy with a killer, and to confide in him that she had hidden his gold in her woodshed.

The door crashed open. She stood as Reese approached, walking tough and unfazed in stained jail pajamas that were too short for his arms and legs. The guard remained near the door with arms folded, looking at the ceiling.

"Well," growled Reese.

"Well, hi."

"Hi, yourself."

She sat back down but Reese remained defiantly on his feet. She said, "I would have brought your dog in but they don't allow them."

"You have Angie?" There was suspicion in his voice but he did settle in the chair opposite her.

"I call her Juju because she arrived late one night and scared me stiff banging around on the porch. She's pretty good company."

"She's a dumb shit. Won't even go after a stick."

"Does being nasty come naturally or do you have to work at it?"

He blinked, and then laughed with his head thrown back. "Shit, you should be a lawyer. They gave me a candyass kid right out of school. I might as well sign a confession and ask for the electric chair tomorrow. Or do they use injections now, the civilized way, I forget?"

"Maybe it would be better to talk about how to prove you didn't do it."

"You think I did it?"

"No, I don't."

"And how come is that?"

"Partly instinct and partly Henry Wadsworth Longfellow."

"Who? Sounds like a prick to me—a long one!"

"Reese, could you drop it? You didn't talk like this when we were looking for Lance."

"First tell me about this guy Henry Whatsis, then I have something to say." He glanced at the guard and edged his chair closer.

"Longfellow wrote the poem you quoted when you threw the whiskey bottle off the ridge."

For a moment he looked blank, then recited, "*The day is done, and the darkness, Falls from the wings of night, As a feather is wafted downward, From an eagle in his flight.* That one? That's

Longfellow, is it? I wouldn't know. I just had to write it a hundred times for swearing at my English teacher. I liked it okay. I also had to do, *A feeling of sadness and longing, That is not akin to pain, And resembles sorrow only, As the mist resembles rain.* I can tell you one thing, sadness and longing can go fuck themselves. This is pain." Again he looked at the guard, then lowered his voice. "I think I figured out where Lance went and it's driving me crazy. If he finds out about this he'll try to come here and I don't want him to. He needs to keep away or they might get some crazy idea to throw him in the clink too."

"Could I get a message to him?"

Reese sat back in the chair with his arms folded and a hard, gauging look on his face.

Leaning forward, she murmured, "I took the cigar box out of the cabin and put it somewhere safe until you get out." Expressions flitted over his mobile face faster than she could read them. Finding the sight oddly painful, she kept talking as a distraction for them both. "Gene told me, not where the nuggets were, but that you had some. I thought you might worry about it. The box is at the very back of my woodshed covered with firewood, easy to find if you know it's there. I wanted you to be able to get it even if I'm not around."

"Well, damn me. Just damn me. I don't know what to say except excuse me for being such a butt hole. I just keep wondering what you're up to. Even my own mother hasn't set foot in here. Not that I'd expect her but you get the point. I am not a nice guy, really, I told you I've been a bastard to Lance every day of his life." Again he leaned toward her, this time with his hands shielding his face at the sides like blinders, and spoke through them in a whisper. "Lance is hiding. He ran away because he was scared, I'm sure of it, and for good reason with what happened to Roy. I don't have an idea in hell what's up, but I don't want Lance in it."

At that moment the door opened and Sheriff McCarty looked in. Clearly surprised by the scene, he barked, "Wrap it up, time's about over."

"Almost done, thank you, Sheriff," Neva said as sweetly as though he had invited her to tea.

"Five minutes then."

When the sheriff was gone, Reese spoke fast. "It's going to be hard to find, but don't write this down because they might take it away from you. Just listen." There followed whispered directions for finding an old cowboy line cabin in the hills between Elkhorn and Billie Mountain, which she could approach to within half a mile by car. She tried to memorize the series of turns. Take the highway past the Dry River Valley turnoff to Angel Creek Road, then on to Little Spring Road, then Forest Service Road 3580, turn right on the 150 spur and go to a fork, take the left to a small quarry, leave the car there, take the path from the west side of the quarry up to a small meadow. The cabin was in the meadow.

"Take him some food and tell him not to come down until I'm out of here. Tell him that's an order. The dumb shit will just get into trouble."

The door opened and he stood up and walked away, but turned before he reached the sheriff and said, "Angie likes pancakes with syrup. Lots of syrup."

◇◇◇

Pork and beans, barbecued beans, frijoles—was she right or wrong to assume that young bachelor miners eat mainly beans from a can? Her hand hovered, moved down the shelf, selected, put back, and moved again. At this rate she wouldn't get to the line cabin until sundown. She knew better than to try to find such a place in the dark, but it seemed important to get the right supplies, food that would keep if she had to leave it on a porch.

It was midafternoon when she headed out of town. The sight of the big white federal building reminded her of the letter to Ethan she'd brought along to mail. She pulled into the parking lot, circled around to the front of the building, dropped the letter in the box and was approaching her car again when she noticed a blue Blazer with smoked windows parked at the end of the small lot. Surely, the same car, notable for its unusual star-pattern hubcaps, had been parked at the jail? McCarty, it seemed, was a determined man.

Slowing her step, she stretched before she got into her car, waited for an extra long break in the traffic to pull out, drove three blocks, turned right on a residential street and headed back toward the center of town, watching the rearview mirror. The blue car was behind her.

Back in the center again, she stopped at the bookstore and bought a slim paperback on techniques for gold panning that she had passed up the first time she was here. When she left the store the Blazer was pulled over at the end of the block. Again she started out of town, again turned off the main street, again returned downtown, and again went into Blue Mountain Books.

This time she bought a *New York Times Book Review* even though she had vowed to read nothing of the kind for the entire summer. When she came out the blue car was not in sight, but as she started out of town for a third time, she saw it three vehicles back. Again she turned off the main street, again headed back to town, but this time she returned to the law enforcement building, jumped out of the car, waved at the Blazer as it cruised past the parking lot, and went in for a word with Sheriff McCarty.

"Okay, okay," he said, holding up both hands. "You can't blame me for trying. I don't know what you and Reese Cotter are plotting, but whatever it is you'd better watch yourself. You two were thick as thieves in there. He hasn't said two words to anybody, lawyer included, so what's he got so much to tell you? Why don't you just tell me what you were chatting about and then we won't have to play these little games. It might even prove helpful to Reese."

"We talked about the dog, about where Lance might have got himself to, about the fact that Reese's mother hasn't visited, and I believe that's about it."

"There's what I mean. His mother died when he was a kid. You can't even believe him about his own mother. Now what do you have to say?"

"Maybe he meant stepmother, or maybe it was wishful thinking. I don't really care, but I would like your buddy to stop following me. It will be a long, boring trip for him out to the mine."

McCarty chuckled. "You're something else, aren't you? Do you promise you're not up to any harebrained scheme of Reese's?"

"I promise nothing other than that I will conduct myself like the free and guiltless citizen I am."

"Well, that's laying it on a bit thick, but I'll see what I can do."

If anyone tailed her this time, they did it from the air. Five miles out of town she pulled into a brushy side road and waited, but only a cattle truck and two minivans full of kids and camping gear passed going her direction. Nonetheless she continued to check the mirror every few minutes while she drove up the highway searching for Angel Creek Road, now and again checking the instructions she had scrawled as soon as she left the jail. The road wasn't where she had expected it to be. Hawley Road, Big Bend Road, Mountain View, Jorgerson, Slide Creek, and then she was heading up into the Elkhorn Mountains, which was all wrong. The sun was going down when she turned around, and retraced her course, but still she failed to see Angel Creek Road.

It was too late to continue the search today. More relieved than disappointed, she headed for the pass that would take her back to the mine. Her thoughts were confused, and for once instinct seemed to have abandoned her. She had misled an officer of the law in the cause of helping a rude miner who had lied about his mother. Her idea that Reese was a secret lover of poetry had proven absurd. No one seemed to have a good word to say about the Cotters apart from Reese's skill as a miner. What did she think she was up to?

Chapter Twenty

Neva woke up the next morning knowing that she would not carry out her promise to Reese. She would not look for the line shack, would not deliver food to Lance, would not entangle herself further in business she knew nothing about. This was the kind of situation she got herself into in town. Too often, needy subjects and sources confused her journalistic interest in them with something more personal, as though she were a priest or counselor, and they continued to seek her out long after the official purpose was served, the interview done, the column written. Her interest was genuine but most problems were beyond her ability to help, apart from lending a sympathetic ear. If she could not protect herself from such frustrating and wearing involvements in the simple world of an idle gold mine, there was no hope for her at all. She had been warned away from the Cotters by both the sheriff and Skipper, men who were not easily alarmed.

Relieved to have escaped entanglement, Neva split wood with particular pleasure, enjoying the hollow "pock" of the echo that came back across the creek. She used the stove only briefly in the mornings and evenings now, for cooking and heating water. This required very little wood but she kept up her morning routine for the fun of it, and stacked the split wood in the shed as though preparing for winter.

Her departure from the cabin was right on time this morning, and it was not yet noon when she reached the ridge top and wandered happily through bright rock gardens, where green and orange lichens were as colorful as flowers. The air was especially clear today, the shapes and colors of the land crisp, the smells rich. With her senses acutely alive, she managed to be mostly a feeling creature rather than a thinking creature until late afternoon, when she headed back down into the canyon. She was hungry, more so than usual during the day, and as she considered what she would eat when she arrived back at the cabin she thought of Lance. The sack of food she had chosen with care still sat in the car. Was the young man entirely without supplies?

"It's not my business," she said aloud.

Juju let out a yip at this sudden sound of a voice.

"Was that a yes or no?" Neva paused on the trail to look down at the dog, which remained Juju to her rather than Angie. She had come to enjoy this quiet company, this shadow at her feet that seemed to take in everything without asking for more than food, water, and an occasional pat. Her rare comments, as Neva thought of the subtle whines, yips and tail thumps, never seemed random. "You think I should stick to my promise? Do you want to see Lance?"

Juju looked up impassively, her impulse to communicate apparently satisfied for the moment by that single yip. Walking on again, uncertain and lost in thought, Neva arrived at the cabin, and as soon as she cleared the woodshed and started across the dooryard, she saw the note on the porch. Since the day of Andy Sylvester's eviction notice, she had developed a habit of bracing for further unwelcome communications each time she returned to the house, but this note was not from the mining technician. It was from Tony Briggs. Terse and to the point, it included no greeting.

"By rights this belongs to you. I don't want it anyhow. It works okay, like I said. T. Briggs."

A rifle stood propped against the porch post, and next to it sat a box of bullets. Neva took an elegantly tapered bullet into her hand. It was heavy and cool on her palm. She lifted the rifle, held it to her shoulder, sighted down the barrel. Was it really as simple as slipping a shell into the chamber, closing it, aiming and pulling the trigger? She should fire it at least once, for the experience, but she would wait for Skipper to show her how. She was so ignorant she didn't know what kind of rifle it was.

Had it been Briggs' idea to return the gun, or had his mother insisted? Whatever had prompted the restoration, Neva felt suddenly glad to own something significant that had been her uncle's. She carried it into the kitchen, and paused to consider where he might have kept the rifle. On the wall? In the pantry? No obvious spot struck her, so she leaned it in a kitchen corner where she would be able to see it as she went about her simple chores and dinner preparation.

Skipper did not come back to Billie Creek that night as promised. Neva stayed up late listening for the sound of his rig and writing in her journal. When she gave up and went to bed at last, she did not fall into her usual easy sleep, but was troubled by a persistent image of Lance—a younger version of Reese—hunkered in a remote shack, alone, hungry, and afraid. That Reese had decided to trust her was a surprising compliment, and to let him down seemed suddenly shameful, even cowardly. The worst she would suffer if she delivered the food was to lose a day at the mine, while, on the good side of the ledger, she would justify Reese's trust and bring comfort to a frightened and hungry young man. She would do this one additional thing for the Cotters and then withdraw from involvement.

Relieved to have made a decision, she fell asleep and woke up feeling energetic and even eager for the adventure. She recopied Reese's instructions in large block letters that could be read easily while driving, and headed down the canyon without taking time to split wood or fill the lamps. This time, instead of going halfway to Sumpter in search of the right road, she stopped at a ranch house in the general area where the first turnoff should be and waded through the usual dogs to a weathered front door.

"Angel Creek Road? That's it right across the highway there," said the man in a thermal shirt and red suspenders who answered her knock. "You won't see no sign sayin' Angel Creek, not if you paid to see it. It ain't there, that's why. And it ain't there on account of Whalen Hawley and his damn ego. That road's been Angel Creek Road since before I could button my own fly. Why wouldn't it be? That's Angel Creek itself flowin' right along it. But no, that wasn't okay with Whalen Hawley, no, Whalen Hawley had to have a road named after his own self, Hawley Road. Why? He don't need no why to do what he wants to do. Why? Because he owns half the county and don't care a rat's knuckle for you or me or Joe Blow either."

Nodding and smiling, Neva listened to the old man until it became clear that nothing other than her departure would stop the bitter recital. "Thank you, thank you so much," she said, backing away.

Angel Creek/Hawley Road traveled up through long, easy switchbacks spotted with seepages where the plant growth was lush and bright green. Whether or not she was doing the right thing, at least she was getting a close view of the foothills and canyons on the north side of Billie Mountain. As usual on the north side, it was wetter here, and more heavily treed, mainly with pines.

Little Spring Road was marked by a hand-painted wooden sign nailed to a fence post, and not far beyond it Forest Service roads took off in all directions. She turned onto 3580 and began to watch more carefully, stopping to look for small numbered posts wherever a spur road split off, no matter how rough or overgrown. The 150 was clearly marked, but when she reached the fork soon afterward, she stopped to consider. Reese had said to turn left, but that branch looked as though it had not been traveled for a long time, certainly not by gravel trucks. It was possible, however, that the quarry had been abandoned long ago along with the road, and if Reese had expert knowledge of anything besides mining, it was the back roads of Elkhorn County.

She turned left. Laboring in low gear, the car crawled around bends and over ruts for so long that she thought of turning around, but then the road leveled and soon ended at a half-circle of pale stone walls. Like the Barlow Mine Pit, the old quarry was silent, the air still and hot. It had clearly not been used for years, probably since the Forest Service last resurfaced the nearby logging and access roads. There was no view, nothing to be seen but rock, the line of trees across the road, and plain sky overhead. The quiet and trapped heat cast a soporific spell that made her long for coffee.

She splashed water on her face from the jug in the car, then settled on a large rock to consider the situation. Weeds grew tall and rank wherever there was a scrap of soil, including on ledges and in cracks in the rock walls. It didn't look as though anyone had come through here in a very long time, though if Reese was right that Lance had fled on foot from Billie Creek, he would have walked over the top and down to the line cabin rather than coming through the quarry. Estimating where the quarry lay in relation to Billie Mountain, she guessed the distance from the Barlow Mine to be about fifteen miles, less than a day's walk for a healthy young man—or even for her at this point.

Reese had said the trail was on the west side of the quarry, but she could see from here that trails led out of the half-bowl on both sides. The instructions had been correct so far, so she would stick with them until there was a good reason not to, and the trails very likely met on top in any case.

But when she hitched the canvas sack of food onto her shoulder and started toward the west-side trail, Juju barked and fixed her with an anxious look.

"What is it, little pal?"

The dog had explored while Neva sat reflecting on the rock, and now ran in the direction of the east-side trail and then returned to Neva. It was such a cartoon pantomime—*Follow me!*—that Neva again studied the zigzagging path leading steeply up through weeds and tumbled rocks. If Lance had been through here, and he might well have walked down to the quarry, Juju would pick up his scent. Whichever route she tried first, if it proved to be wrong she would backtrack and go the other way.

"Okay, pal, we'll give it a try," she said, and changed direction. The little dog took up her usual position at Neva's heel with no more fuss.

The route was difficult and slithery until it topped the quarry, where it turned to a pleasant path that wound through open pine forest. When it joined the other trail, as expected, Juju raced ahead. Neva called her back but when the dog dashed forward a few minutes later she let her go. Lance would see Juju before he saw Neva and realize that whoever followed must be a friend.

As Reese had described, the trail met a creek and followed it to a small meadow. On the other side of the creek the meadow grass was so clearly trodden into a path that Neva felt a surge of triumph, as though she had solved a tough puzzle, followed by a sense of relief when she saw the small cabin at the far side of the meadow. Reese had been right every step of the way, and her mission was not in vain.

She looked about for Juju but the little dog was not to be seen. "Lance," she called, starting along the meadow path. "Lance! Hello, I've brought food."

There was no sign of life at the cabin, no face in the window, no smoke from the roof pipe, no underwear drying on the porch rail. She reached the two planks that served for porch steps but instead of going right up them, she set the heavy bag of food on the porch, then moved back a little to study the rustic cabin. It must have served as a line shack for several generations of cowboys caught out overnight. Roughly built of weathered logs, poles and boards, it was about the right size to contain one set of bunk beds, a table and cook stove. Judging by the lone window next to the plank door, it must be dark inside as well as cramped. A stump hollowed into the shape of a seat stood in front of the window. On the plank floor below it were scattered wood shavings.

Avoiding the two rickety stairs, Neva stepped directly onto the porch, squatted by the stump, and felt the shavings. They were limber, slightly damp, and they smelled of sap. Someone had sat here whittling very recently.

Suddenly more alert, she held her breath to listen but heard only a faint stirring of air in the nearby trees. She knocked on the door, tried the handle, and pushed. It didn't give although there was no visible lock. Turning, she surveyed the meadow, which showed no signs of disturbance apart from the narrow path.

The small window was covered, and there were no others, as she discovered on circling the cabin. It must be very dark inside indeed. A sense of acute solitude made her call and whistle for Juju but the little dog did not appear.

From the back of the cabin a trail led into the woods. Uneasy, missing the dog, Neva followed the path a short distance until she spotted a plank set across two stumps above a hole in the ground. She didn't need to look any closer to know its purpose, and her nose told her that it had been used recently, most likely that very morning.

"Lance!" she shouted. "Juju! Angie!"

Impatient now rather than uneasy, she walked briskly back to the cabin, circled to the front, and discovered a young man sitting on the porch stump with Juju at his feet, both wearing an air of having been there for hours.

"Lance?"

"Yeah." He did not stop whittling.

He was very like Reese, but not like him in the least. In basic appearance the two were clearly brothers, but while Reese's every gesture and facial expression were aimed straight at the world, Lance's manner was passive and watchful. She might well have frightened him, even with Juju for an emissary. He must have watched through the window, trying to figure out what sort of intruder she was.

"Sorry if I startled you. Reese asked me to bring supplies." She indicated the bag.

"Why?"

"Because he thought you needed food," she said, wondering at the foolish question. Though he had been described as not very bright, she hadn't believed this could be literally true of anyone closely related to Reese.

"Why didn't he bring it himself?"

"Well, he couldn't, you know. He's in jail."

His surprise and confusion reminded her that he would have no way of knowing what had happened since he ran away from the mine. It was up to her to break the bad news. "I'm so sorry, Lance. Of course you wouldn't know. He was arrested for, well, in connection with a terrible thing that happened at your mine. I'm really sorry to have to tell you this, but Roy DeRoos died a few days after you left. They thought at first that it was an accident but he appears to have been killed deliberately and they've arrested Reese for it, without any evidence that I know of. I don't believe he did it, which is one reason I visited him in jail."

Placing the stick and knife on the porch boards by the pile of shavings, Lance sat up straight with one hand on each knee as he gazed out at the meadow for some time in silence. Then his gaze shifted to the bag of supplies.

"What's in there?"

"Mostly canned food, beans and stew. I was afraid fresh things wouldn't keep in the heat."

"You have an opener? I couldn't find an opener in this place. I had to use the axe."

"I put in an opener. And a couple of books."

He stood with the slow care of an older man or someone with an injury even though there was nothing visibly wrong with him. Crossing to where she had left the bag, he knelt on one knee and took out the books that lay on top. They were Westerns, from the small stock at the mine. Setting them aside, he removed cans and other items one by one until he came to a bag of dried apricots she had added from her own supplies. Wrenching open the heavy plastic, he put a handful of apricots in his mouth and said while chewing, "Looks okay. I about ran out. There's mostly soup."

Wishing she had brought more fruit, and vegetables as well, Neva felt a confusing mixture of sympathy and outrage. He had shown no concern about Roy's death or his brother's arrest, and no appreciation for Reese's effort to get him food despite his own problems. But the young man was starving, and might not be absorbing information very well. Once fed, he would no doubt think more clearly about her news. "Reese is in jail," she repeated. "He said to tell you not to worry about him, and he particularly stressed that you should stay away from town until this all settles down. Do you have any message for him in case I see him before you do?"

"Reese?" Lance considered her with a wondering expression, as though she'd mentioned someone barely known to him, then returned to stuffing apricots into his mouth. When he had emptied the bag, consuming them all apart from one he gave to Juju, he took a long, shuddering breath, looked up, and said with a sudden boyish smile, "Thanks. I was pretty hungry."

"You're very welcome. I'm sorry I didn't bring anything fresh, but I wasn't at all sure I'd find you here and thought I might have to leave the food on the porch. You probably know this, but I'm staying at the Billie Creek Mine for the summer. I have no idea when Reese will be out of jail, but I really do think they'll let him go." She looked at Juju, who lay with her nose inches from Lance's foot, and said with regret, "I suppose you want to keep the dog with you?"

"I guess so. She can have the soup."

"Well, then, I'll be off. Is there anything I should tell Reese?"

Lance bent his head and appeared to be studying the pile of books next to his knee. After lengthy thought, he said, "Tell him I'm okay. And thanks for the food."

"Fine, though you may end up seeing him before I do." She reached to pat the little dog's head. "Bye-bye, pal. You were very good company." She waited for a moment to let Lance say something more—to thank her—but his attention was on a can of beef stew. "Goodbye then. Take care of yourself and maybe I'll see you sometime back at the mine."

She walked briskly down the meadow. At the creek she turned to wave. Lance was standing now, watching her, the can in one hand, the opener in the other. Juju also had sat up. Lance lifted the can in response to her wave, then dropped the opener onto the porch at his feet and dug into the stew with his fingers.

Clearly, she had done the right thing in bringing the food, and now her involvement with the Cotter brothers was finished.

Chapter Twenty-one

The drive down from the quarry went faster than going up. Though she missed Juju already, she felt lighter in spirit than when she left the mine, and easily put Reese and Lance out of her thoughts. As she approached the turning that would take her back over the pass to the Dry River, she had a sudden idea and pulled onto the shoulder to consider it. If she continued straight on toward Elkhorn and I-84, she could be in Hatlee in less than two hours. The day was more than half gone already, and by the time she got home to Billie Creek there would be time only for a short walk. It made sense to take care of all her outside errands at once, including meeting Enid Gale.

An unexpected bypass took her around Elkhorn and she was soon driving south on the interstate through dry, rocky hills sparely dotted with junipers that stood above their spots of shade like gnomish umbrellas. She reached for the radio dial but withdrew her hand. Along with avoiding book reviews, newspapers and periodicals in general, she had resolved to avoid radio news for the summer, to give herself a complete break from the crazy outside world. The sound of warm wind through the window was sufficient.

The exit to Hatlee was clearly marked, though the road was so narrow and winding that she would have suspected a wrong turn had there been any choices. And when she reached Hatlee, she drove quickly through what she assumed were the outskirts, only to come out on the other side.

Hatlee, Oregon, was not quite a ghost town, but most of it was missing, its heyday long past. Houses and shops had disappeared from their lots like neglected teeth, leaving the few remaining buildings scattered higgledy-piggledy over the weedy ground. Such desolate Western towns were dotted all over the arid part of the state, some abandoned when the gold was gone, others when a promised highway or railroad failed to go through. A few, like Greenhorn and Granite, had been partly resettled in recent years by solitary souls looking for the cheap and picturesque, but Hatlee was not one of these. Although clearly only a fragment of its original self, it had never been fully deserted, judging by the good condition of the few remaining buildings.

Neva turned, drove all the way back through town, turned again, and cruised through a second time going just five miles an hour. First came scattered sheds and outbuildings, then about a dozen solid two-story frame houses with gaps where others had once stood. The Hatlee General Store and the small wood-frame post office appeared to be the only commercial and official enterprises, though there were benches and boxes full of bright flowers to mark this minute town center. Both store and post office were closed. Neva pulled up to the curb outside the post office and turned off the ignition. Having counted on the clerk to direct her to Enid Gale, she felt momentarily at a loss.

Not a soul appeared on the road or in the tidy yards of the houses within sight. The open car window let in the sound of birds, a distant lawnmower, and a rhythmic banging that suggested carpentry. Clearly there were people about. She would return to the edge of town, park the car, and walk along the road until she spotted someone.

On her slow drive through, Neva had taken the shacks for chicken coops and small barns, but as she passed them a third time she saw that these must be dwellings of some kind. Laundry hung outside one rakish little structure and window curtains showed in another. Rather than shacks, the buildings now struck her as imaginative playhouses, the sort of elaborate little dwelling that clever kids might build with help from a cooperative adult, or that a set-builder might construct for a film about Sixties communes. She stopped the car on the grassy edge near the outermost of these quirky structures, a small barn covered in colored tarpaper shingles arranged with a rainbow effect and randomly interrupted by small windows. A stovepipe rose jauntily from the patchwork roof.

It was charming, but what was it? As she wondered, the front door opened and out came a figure so perfectly suited to the structure that Neva felt an impulse to applaud and offer compliments. The old woman wore pink overalls over a turtleneck the same white as her hair, which was swept up into a loose topknot. The overalls were tucked into large rubber boots. Her arm was hooked through the handle of a bucket as gracefully as though through a purse strap. Nodding once at Neva without evident surprise or curiosity, she set off down the road.

Neva got right out of the car but the old woman's brisk stride had taken her nearly to the first of the big houses by the time she caught up.

"Excuse me. I'm looking for Enid Gale?"

The woman considered her for a moment with a canny, appraising gaze. "Enid Gale lives there," she said, nodding back up the road toward the house she had just left. "She'll be home in half an hour if you want to come back."

"I will. Thank you."

The woman went through a front gate while Neva walked on and soon reached the general store again. A sign in the window said the hours were nine to three, Monday through Saturday. That it was not yet three, according to the clock that showed on the inside wall, suggested that today might be Sunday, though she had been certain it was Saturday. Feeling vaguely disoriented, wishing she could settle on a bench with a cold drink, she went on to the railroad tracks at the far edge of town, where a historic marker informed her that Hatlee had begun as a Wells Fargo stage stop called Express Station. The name had been changed in 1883 when the railroad bought a right-of-way from the Hatlee family, and the town had become a shipping center for placer gold, farm products, and lumber.

A hundred years ago, there would have been a busy station here. Trains, wagons, miners, farmers, loggers, speculators, adventurers, children, horses, dogs…It was easy to picture but difficult to imagine as anything more than a picture, a static scene from a history text. Now only redwing blackbirds called from the cattails along an irrigation ditch. Fields of hay, or maybe it was grain, stretched west to the mountains. Turning, she saw mountains to the distant east as well, presumably in Idaho on the other side of the Snake River. The Seven Devils? The Sawtooth? She would have to check the atlas later.

She strolled back through town to the patchwork barn and was not really surprised when the woman in pink overalls answered her knock. Offering her hand, she drew Neva inside with a warm rush of words. "I'm Enid Gale. I'm so glad you came back. I was just on my way to pick raspberries for a neighbor with a broken ankle. I would have asked you along but I needed a little time to prepare myself."

"Prepare yourself?" Neva found it hard to focus on what Enid was saying because her attention was fixed on the extraordinary room, where every surface was decorated, patterned, or painted to the imaginable limit beyond which it would have been a mess rather than delightful.

"To talk about Orson," Enid said. "I thought maybe you'd brought his things. It is rather soon after the letter. I can't say I found his death shocking because we had expected it for years, but you're never really ready for such a thing. He was my only brother."

"Oh, dear," Neva said and closed her eyes.

It took some sorting out before they understood how things were: that Enid had received word a week ago that her brother had died and his few possessions would be delivered to her soon by a staff member who would be in the area on vacation, but that Neva was not this person. In fact, she had come to visit because of Enid's friendship with her uncle and had not known of Orson's death.

"It isn't so very sad," Enid said, pouring dark tea into hand-built pottery mugs. "When you really leave this world is when your mind goes, and his mind went years ago. He used to be such a bright, funny boy. When he lost Burtie he lost interest in most things."

"I barely knew my uncle," Neva said, the quick words propelled by a sense that here, at last, she could speak freely. "Since going out to Billie Creek, I've become so curious about him it's become a bit of an obsession. You knew him. You can tell me what kind of man he was, if anyone can."

"A lovely man, one of the nicest I ever knew. I was in love with him, you know." Enid's bright blue eyes were not in the least coy.

"He wasn't gay?"

The words, which had popped out in her surprise, were met by a merry laugh. "Not by half, young lady, not by half. Some thought so because of Orson. They did love each other but not in that way, although I always thought Orson had tendencies. People can't seem to help jumping to conclusions if you live with a really dear friend. My friend Adele and I lived together for years, until she died, and we knew what people thought. We just didn't care one way or the other."

"This is a bit awkward, but if my uncle wasn't gay, and you loved him—"

"Why didn't I marry him? Oh, dear me, I would have in a flash. But I couldn't. I mean he wouldn't." She paused, cocked an eyebrow at Neva as though considering whether to continue, then said firmly, "It seems you really are in the dark about Burtie. Your uncle was injured in Korea, between the legs. He didn't have everything a man's supposed to have, if you understand. I would have taken him anyway but he wasn't willing. He said I needed a normal man who could give me a family and he stuck to that view even though I waited for years. It was the injury that made him hide away in the mine in the first place, because he felt different. And he was different, wonderfully different. That's why I never did marry, I suppose. There was no one else, ever."

Surprise, sympathy, and a sense of precious new knowledge left Neva briefly without words. She sipped tea, then said with wonder, "I knew about Korea, that he was there, but I didn't know about the injury. No one ever mentioned it when I was growing up, but I'm beginning to think there was a lot that went unsaid in my supposedly open family. Do you think the people on Billie Creek knew?"

"Most likely not. He didn't talk about it. At first he was embarrassed and then after time went by it didn't matter."

"There's a photograph of a young Korean woman on the cabin wall. Was she my uncle's girlfriend?"

"That was a long, long time ago, Jeneva. He didn't talk about it."

"Enid, what happened to my uncle? Where did he go?"

"If I knew what happened, no matter how bad, the last fifteen years would have been easier. I thought I saw him again, years later, and I fainted dead away."

"At the art reception?"

"How could you know that?" Enid's large eyes opened wider with amazement, but she laughed with delight on hearing about the old news item that the librarian had sent to Neva. "I don't know why I said that about the glue, it just popped out, I suppose because I was flustered, and I certainly wasn't going to let on that I'd mistaken some unknown man for a lost love. But what a blunder that was. I got so many calls, from schools, from glue makers, everybody. Who would think such a little white lie could grow like that?" After a silence, she said, "One thing I can tell you, he'd never have walked away from Orson with no word, and if he'd left the mine he would have come to me. That doesn't leave us with very nice possibilities. I still can't think about it."

For the first time Enid looked like a truly old woman, the lines in her face deep, her eyes swimmy with unshed tears, but the moment passed. She poured more hot water into the teapot.

Neva said, "Did you know there was trouble between Uncle Matthew and my mother? They didn't communicate for the last ten years or so before he disappeared. She would never tell me what it was about, even when she was dying and obviously haunted by it."

Enid was stroking a large yellow cat that Neva had at first thought clashed with the dominant red, lavender, and pink color scheme of the house, but then decided was the perfect accent, a bit of vibrant decor on four legs. "Some things are best left to die with us," Enid said with a slow shake of the head.

Unsure of her meaning and unwilling to press too hard until she knew Enid better, Neva let silence stretch without finding it awkward. She could have sat with this rare woman all afternoon, talking or not talking, even though she had many more questions. The questions could wait. She would see Enid again, she was sure of it.

"This is a wonderful house. How did you come to live here?"

"Adele grew up in Hatlee, in a house that was destroyed by the big fire that wiped out most of the town in the Seventies. She left me the land and barn in her will. Of course, it was nothing like this, it was a wreck, full of chicken feathers and trash. I've had a time fixing it up. A lot of other folks have done the same, which you probably noticed. They're mostly summer places." After another quiet spell, she said, "I can't imagine Orson left much in the way of possessions, but if there are any pictures or letters of Burtie's I could let you know."

"That would be wonderful, thank you. You could send a note to the Angus post office and I'd come right over."

"Why don't you leave your email address?"

Neva must have shown her surprise because Enid said, "I don't like telephones. They always catch you in the wrong mood, or you catch the other person in the wrong mood. But I don't want to get isolated, either, which can happen out here, especially in winter. I still have a lot of friends in Kalispell, and I'm a great fan of the Internet. Have you ever checked for recipes? You can type in the main ingredient and all kinds of exotic dishes pop up."

"Why did you move here instead of staying in Kalispell?"

"I always loved this country over here. Did you know I stayed at the mine for several years? And then, I always wanted to live on ground of my own." Enid reflected for a moment before her merry laugh came again. "The real truth is, I've never been able to resist a fresh start. You always breathe easier for a few years. I may stop here. Or not."

Neva left Hatlee in late afternoon, richer on a number of counts, including a tub of fresh raspberries. She ate the berries one by one as she drove home thinking about growing old and wearing pink overalls.

Chapter Twenty-two

Evening was setting in when Neva arrived back in the Dry River Valley. Again, black Angus cattle were dotted over several of the narrow fields along the river and the song of meadowlarks came clearly through the open windows. In no hurry, she watched the light deepen on the hills while also watching for Darla's mailbox, but instead of turning up the lane when she came to it she pulled the car over to reflect on what to do. She wanted to sneak a peek at how a bachelorette ex-beauty-queen rancher lives, but to drop in seemed suddenly awkward. She barely knew Darla, and she had never suggested that Neva stop by. She needed an excuse, an errand to carry out, after which she could leave if the situation felt awkward. A moment's thought gave her what she needed. She would inform Darla that she had walked over to Jump Creek and had seen that the cows were still there, and further, that she had discovered none on Billie Creek since their trail ride. That Darla most likely knew this already didn't matter. It would do to smooth the first uneasy minutes, and then she could be on her way if need be.

The lane crossed the river, then wound to the base of the hills on the south side of the valley where it ended at a small ranch house with a large front porch that faced Billie Mountain. Two pickups were pulled up by the woodshed, one large and yellow, the other small and blue with a camper shell. Hay fields flowed right up to the porch and around the house so that it appeared to float like an ark on a sea of golden-green. Two wooden deck chairs sat facing the field and the distant line of willows marking the Dry River.

Darla opened the door and greeted her without surprise. She wore an apron over new-looking Levis and a blue work shirt with the sleeves rolled to the elbows. Her feet were in leather slippers. "Dishwasher broke. I'm washing up," she said. "Come on in."

Neva took off her shoes before crossing the expanse of cream carpet. The large, airy living room was simply but comfortably furnished with two leather armchairs and a Mission-style sofa. Photographs of horses hung on every wall. There was not a rustic object in the room, and nothing aside from the photos that suggested country life.

She followed Darla into the kitchen but stopped in the doorway to look with astonishment at a huge, bald, bespectacled man in a priest's collar, who would have seemed a striking figure in any setting but particularly so planted on a stool in this compact kitchen.

"Father Bernard Shore," Darla said. "This is Neva, the one staying up on Billie Creek."

"Gene Holland mentioned your name the other day," Neva said as Father Bernard engulfed her small cool hand in his warm mitt.

Darla pulled off the apron, poured Neva a small water glass full of red wine, refilled Father Bernard's glass with the same, and refilled her own with iced tea. They settled around the kitchen bar on stools as Darla repeated essentially what Gene had said, that Father Bernard was a Benedictine monk from St. Gabriel Monastery in Montana who took yearly turns as the circuit priest for the region's scattered Catholics. While he was out here, he worked on translating early church manuscripts.

"Sometimes there are only a handful of us at the service." The rancher's smile was apologetic.

Father Bernard chuckled and confided to Neva, "Poor girl. She thinks I come out here for her sake. In fact, this is my favorite country. Despite what outsiders think, it's not easy to find solitude among the cloisters. Thomas Merton said genuine solitude brings not separation but solidarity. I have to say that lack of solitude, even in a community of monks, can lead to peevishness. When I'm feeling peevish there's no better cure than a stint in the Dry River Valley."

The congregation out here numbered a dozen at most, he said, but every other weekend he traveled more than a hundred miles to perform services at even smaller communities where, on occasion, only a single worshiper showed up. "But one true soul is better than a crowd if their hearts aren't in it. To quote Merton again, 'Better just to smell a flower in the garden than to have an unauthentic experience of a much higher value.'"

His laugh was infectious and freely vented, as were his thoughts on the challenge of keeping repetitive ritual from becoming routine, how to deal with self-doubt as a priest, and other surprising topics, including the best method for cooking rattlesnake meat. He didn't appear in the least ruffled when the talk turned to faith and Neva confessed her lifelong atheism. And when, encouraged by his interest, she mentioned her mother's ashes it was Darla and not the monk who was shocked.

"I couldn't do that. I couldn't keep my mother's remains around in a box." Darla's expression was uneasy as she appealed to Father Bernard. "I never did like the idea of cremation. Isn't that blasphemous or something?"

The priest shook his large head. "As far as the church goes, it's fine. This wasn't always the case. When it was seen as thumbing your nose at resurrection, it wasn't approved, but now it's not an issue."

Despite her atheism, Neva said, she had sometimes found the idea of the monastic life appealing, particularly in earlier centuries. "But when I imagine myself in an order, it's always as a monk, never in an abbey. My impression is that men got to live more scholarly and interesting lives than the women who took vows."

"Well, yes, this has appeared to be the case but our knowledge of history is opening up. I've been reading about a monastery in Switzerland, Engelberg Monastery. It was a dual community, shared by men and women for about three hundred years. It's been well known that the men left a rich legacy, but now it seems that both men and women had their periods of flowering. The women of Engelberg put out magnificent books. They left the monastery in the 1600s, and even they seemed to have forgotten their own history until recently. Now we're learning of more women scribes, copyists and illuminators all the time. Don't forget that Anonymous was a woman."

"Thank you," Neva said. "Now I can fantasize about being a medieval scholar without having to change gender." She waited for the priest's chuckle, then said, "Did you know my uncle, Matthew Burt?"

"Not well, I'm afraid," he replied with regret. "I had just begun coming out here when he left the mine, but I feel that I know him in a different sort of way. You see, his portrait hangs on the wall of my small sitting room. It was taken by my predecessor and nicely framed. You haven't seen it I gather. I offered it to Orson but he said it would only make him sadder."

"Oh, dear, I'm afraid I've just been reminded of some bad news." Feeling ashamed at having forgotten about the death of the old miner, Neva related what she had learned from Enid. "She said he died in his sleep last week. She received a letter."

"Orson Gale dead?" There was wonder as well as unhappy surprise in Darla's voice.

"Enid said he really died when he lost his wits. She didn't put it quite like that but that's what she meant."

"The soul has little to do with wits," Father Bernard said gravely. "I was fond of Orson myself. He looked fine when I saw him in April. My habit was to see him twice a year, once in spring and once in fall. I don't know that he had any idea who I was, but his spirit remained the spirit of my old friend. I'll have to see about a service."

There was silence for a time. Darla turned on a light that hung low over the table and refilled glasses. Neva noted that she now also drank wine. The talk did not really get going again, and soon the priest got to his feet. Taking Neva's hand in both of his, he said, "Come for a visit. The sooner the better. You'll want to see the picture."

They left at the same time, Father Bernard going ahead in the dusty blue pickup. The sky was heavy with stars as Neva turned up the road to the mine and instantly she felt her heart lift despite the late hour and the long day full of surprises, both delightful and sad. Had it really been only this morning that she found Lance at the line shack? Deep in thought, she barely noted the dark road down into the Barlow Mine pit and even the sight of a light in Reese's cabin window didn't fully register as wrong in the first moment. Then her foot hit the brake, the car skidded, fishtailed, and came to a stop sitting sideways in the road. Without repositioning the car, she shut off the engine and listened, straining for clues on the still night air. Could Sheriff McCarty have let Reese out of jail already? Surely Darla would have known this and would have mentioned it. Could Lance have walked home over Billie Mountain? If he had set out soon after she left and walked steadily through the afternoon and evening, he might have covered the steep miles.

The car door clicked softly as she opened it. The thump of her sandals was light on the packed-earth road as she approached the cabin. An unfamiliar car parked next to the lone remaining pickup settled her speculation about Lance's possible return, and it was definitely not a law enforcement vehicle. Taking one careful step at a time, she eased her way onto the porch and crossed to the curtained window. Stooping, she peered through the gap between the sill and the bottom of the curtain. A propane lamp blazed so brightly within that she blinked and couldn't at first see anything but light. Then she saw that the room was no longer just untidy from the habits of young bachelors. It was a chaotic wreck, with drawers pulled open, boxes spilled, bedding tumbled onto the floor and the thin mattresses pulled askew. Someone had searched the cabin—for Reese's gold? Yes, and they'd been terribly thorough about it.

The whole interior of the cabin was visible, and whoever had made this mess was no longer inside. Neva felt the skin on her back and neck tighten. She had seen no one in the car when she glanced through the window, and no light had shone in the other cabin, which left just one possibility. The intruder was outdoors, most likely behind her, possibly watching at this moment.

Slowly she straightened and turned to face the darkness, listening so hard she felt a headache start up. There was not a sound, not even the usual night stirrings of wind and creatures. Why had she left her car down the road? Surely any sane person would have driven right to the cabin and remained in the car while sizing up the situation, possibly even honking to bring out whoever was inside. But it was too late to berate herself, too late to wish she'd gone straight home before dark rather than stopping at Darla's. The object now was to move, to cross the porch, descend the steps, get back to her car…she was on her way. Soon she was on the ground and as she passed between the car and pickup truck, the usual quiet voice of reason spoke inside her head. Whoever had searched the cabin was looking for something specific, surely Reese's stash, and would not be interested in her. She was an outsider on Billie Creek, with no connection to the mine or gold or the violence of young men—

"Are you looking for someone?"

The voice out of the darkness punched her heart into a gallop like a slapped horse. "Who is it?" she managed, clutching her shoulders.

"That should be my question," returned the same male voice.

Now she could make out a tall figure leaning against the tailgate of the pickup, a familiar figure, she thought. "Is that you, Andy? I was looking for Reese."

"He's in jail as far as I know," replied the voice in an offhand tone. "Sorry if I scared you but you gave me a turn too. I didn't think there was anybody out here except me. Who's Andy?"

"Andy Sylvester, with the Forest Service. I'm Jeneva Leopold, from the mine up the road. Who are you? I really can't see."

"Boris Dietering." He paused as though for a response and when none came, he added, "I own this mine. I flew out when I heard what happened."

"Flew out from where?"

"Baltimore. Let's go inside where we can talk."

Still unable to see him as more than a silhouette, Neva did not reply immediately. She didn't want to return to Reese's devastated cabin, and she was not interested in the mine owner from Baltimore, who, it seemed, had ransacked his own property. She said firmly, "I'd rather wait until morning. I've been gone all day and I'm really beat. You could come up to the mine for breakfast."

"I have to catch a flight early. This won't take long."

Unable to think of a good reason to refuse, she followed him without speaking again until they were inside the cabin. He turned as soon as she was through the door and she found herself facing a figure that could not have looked more out of place in the smelly, chaotic little room. Tall, slim, neatly formed in every feature, brown hair softly waved to the side like a young boy's, eyes very blue in a lightly tanned face, his fine cotton pants and shirt fitted enough to show a tidy build but loose enough to appear debonair, casual—all in all, a mine owner was the last thing he would be taken for.

Glancing around at the wreckage, he said, "Looks like they should have locked the door."

"You didn't do this?"

"Mess up my own cabin?" His laugh was easy and melodious. "Any idea what they were looking for?"

"Gold bullion, no doubt."

"You make it sound like a joke but Reese was getting gold, you know." He shook his head thoughtfully. "The theory seems to be that gold was the reason he killed Roy but I don't buy it. What do you think?"

"I don't think Reese did kill Roy, but I've got no real reason. And if his temper did get away from him so violently, I really couldn't see him trying to make it look like an accident. He's too straightforward."

"Sounds good to me. What about Lance? Where is he, anyway? I thought I had three employees here. One dead, one in jail on suspicion. Where's the third?"

"He left the mine without telling anyone where he was going."

"Is that so? Before or after Roy died?"

"Before. Several days before. I'm sure he'll come back when he's ready, probably when Reese gets out of jail."

"Well, I guess I wouldn't blame anyone for disappearing from this place, even if I do own it." At ease with his hands in his pockets, he surveyed the mercilessly illuminated mess that surrounded them. "That is a terrible light. Propane is it?"

"I believe so."

"Not a very comfortable spot to spend a night. The other cabin's just as bad." His eyes settled on Neva with sudden, confident warmth. "Maybe you would have someplace more comfortable?"

"I do, but I'm afraid it's fully occupied," she said, and though uncertain whether it was true, she added for good measure, "Skipper's at the mine and probably wondering what's taking me so long to get up the mountain. If you change your mind about breakfast you're welcome to come up. Just watch for where the car tracks veer right toward the creek about four miles up."

Chapter Twenty-three

The sight of Skipper's camper in its old spot by the creek took away the uneasiness of the meeting with the suave mine owner. Neva wanted to talk with him, but the windows were dark, and she turned the car back up the road to the cabin without disturbing him.

In the morning, he was pounding on her kitchen door while the coffee was still dripping. "You gave me the slip yesterday," he accused. "I was back by suppertime and waited for you all evening. How can I look out for you when I don't know where you've gone off to?"

"Look after me? Skipper, all I do is walk or sit around, although yesterday was different, it's true. I went over to Hatlee. You were supposed to be back two days ago, you know. I waited up for *you.*"

"Sorry about that, but I got held up," he said, accepting a mug without appearing to notice it. "I've got some news for you. I did a little checking while I was out. That squimp Sylvester was right. Orson's not the only owner of the Billie Creek Mine. The other owner—are you ready for this?—the other name on the claim is Mr. Gene Conrad Holland. That's right, folks, Gene Sufferin' Smith himself. He's been registered as a partner since just after your uncle disappeared."

Neva had been leading the way out the screen door, but turned to look at Skipper with astonishment and consternation.

"It's true, as sure as I'm standing here," he asserted.

"Well, for God's sake, that's just plain bizarre. Why didn't he say so? He had plenty of opportunity and I even asked him about the mine ownership. It's outrageous."

"Beats me. I could hardly believe it myself."

Neva continued out to the porch, sat down, and waited until Skipper was settled on the settee before saying, "And you know what? This means that Gene's the sole owner of the claim now. I found out yesterday that Orson died. I went to see his sister in Hatlee and she told me that he died a week ago. This is all very strange."

"Isn't it just." Skipper nodded thoughtfully. "That's too bad about Orson, but I don't imagine he had much in the way of quality of life. Still, it's life."

After reflecting for several minutes, Neva said, "I feel like going straight down there and asking for the whole story. In fact, that's just what I'm going to do when I finish this nice cup of coffee."

"Sorry, no can do. When I came in yesterday Gene was just pulling out for Pocatello. He said he'd be gone a few days, maybe until next week."

"Did you tell him you'd found out he owns the mine?"

"Well, as it happens, I did say that. I hope it's okay."

"Why wouldn't it be okay?"

"I was thinking maybe you'd want to talk to him yourself, without him knowing you know the truth, if you see what I mean."

Neva regarded the old artifact hunter quizzically. "I don't quite see, I'm afraid. It's a bit odd that he didn't tell me, but when you think about it, he's the most logical person to own the mine. He's been mining this creek since he was a boy, and I'm sure he has his own good reasons for keeping quiet. Mining's a funny business, remember. At least that explains why he came into the cabin one day when I wasn't here."

"Maybe you don't think it's screwy, W.T., but I do. I think there's something rotten in Denmark and I don't mean fish. You know what's wrong with you? You're too goddamned nice. You go through life thinking everything's going to come up roses. Well, I'm here to tell you from experience that it's more likely to come up weeds. And I don't mean marijuana."

Two hours later, lying on her back on a hot rock halfway up the ridge, Neva had to admit to herself that she felt more perplexed about Gene's behavior than she had let Skipper believe. She could think of no good reason for him to keep her in the dark about the true ownership of the mining rights, and the more she thought about him the odder he seemed. Since he owned Billie Creek Mine, why wasn't he working it instead of the Sufferin' Smith Mine, which was said to be difficult and unproductive? Billie Creek Mine hadn't been worked in so long there was no sign of mining apart from bits of pipe and other such debris, along with overgrown gravel heaps by the creek, but surely it would be easier to excavate than the ridge top. And when she told him about the eviction notice, why had he not done something to help? He could have told Sylvester that she was the caretaker, or that she was cleaning up the site in preparation for his mining efforts later in the season. On the other hand, maybe he was the one who had alerted the Forest Service in the first place, hoping that she would be evicted.

For some time her thoughts swirled like silt disturbed in a pond, but at last, gazing into the endless blue sky, she felt her mind settle and clear. Surely there was nothing to be uneasy about. With Orson gone, who better than Gene Holland to own the mine? Had he intended to make dramatic changes—for instance, to turn it into a pit like the Barlow Mine—he would have done it long ago. He must believe that the claim had been mined out already. It had been the first mine on Billie Creek, after all, and had been worked for nearly a century. Maybe he was attached to the mine for sentimental reasons. He had seemed fond of Uncle Matthew and Orson, and very interested in the mine's history. Whatever his reason for hanging onto the claim, it had to be better than having it fall into the hands of someone like Boris Dietering, a man with no apparent relationship to the land or local history. If she did decide to leave her mother's ashes here, she would feel comfortable knowing that Gene had control of the mine for at least the foreseeable future.

And the longer she stayed in the canyon, the more inclined she felt to bury the ashes here. She was healing spectacularly with the help of the hills and the desert sun, and feeling closer to her lost uncle than she'd ever expected to, and what better connections could there be than these? For as long as she lived, she could return here whenever she chose, to renew her own strength and to come closer to…to what? Her mother's spirit? Her uncle's legacy? She didn't care, she realized with a sudden sense of release, it didn't matter how the situation was defined in words. What mattered was that she had found physical and emotional bedrock here.

Neva wandered until late afternoon, paying little attention to where her feet led her. The sun dropped below the ridge but the hard ground radiated comfortable heat. Picking her way down a rocky slope, she realized that she was below the outcrop where she and Reese had shared the whiskey. Thinking of the bottle he had sailed out into space, she watched for glass fragments as she zigzagged across the steep slope, stepping with more care than usual. Four buzzards circled overhead. If she were to trip and break a leg, forcing her to crawl, would they spiral closer and land nearby to wait? Had her uncle's bones been picked clean by ancestors of these birds?

The ground grew less steep and was dotted with knee-high bunchgrass growing out of shale gravel rather than soil. She crossed this patch and entered a stand of unusually tall sagebrush, some standing higher than her head. Following the path of least resistance through prickly shrubbery she rounded a shoulder of the hill and stepped into a narrow clearing that felt like a courtyard even before she saw the tunnel.

About twenty feet in front of her, an irregular, arched hole opened into the hillside. It had to be the old Calypso Mine, but just to be sure she turned to look across at the opposite ridge. Yes, the position appeared right, and so was the packrat smell that Darla had described. With a hand over her nose and mouth, she approached the dark tunnel, which was topped by a large lichen-crusted rock that stuck out horizontally like a door lintel. The packrat nest was too far inside to see, and there was no sign of the cave-in. The tunnel roof was higher than her head by several feet and supported at intervals by rough timbers that looked perfectly sound, but the stench was stronger than her curiosity and she turned away without going inside. Plunging again into the fragrant sagebrush as though into a cleansing pool, she breathed deeply of the delicious evening air. She could never be a miner—at least, not the tunneling variety—even if she felt the lure of gold. She was far too claustrophobic, and would not have gone more than a few feet into the Calypso Mine had it smelled like roses.

Busy with starting a dinner fire and putting on water to heat, Neva didn't notice the note at first. Not until she lit a lamp and carried it into the big room did she see the scrap of paper next to the ashes. On it was a scrawled message.

> *Thanks for the food, it was good. Why do they think Reese done it? Put the answer at that cabin with the front fell out in that little can on the tree. You can put it in there and I will get it. I took my knife and hat. See you, LC.*

The thought that Lance had been in her house was disturbing. Andy and even Tony Briggs had been satisfied with leaving notes on the porch—but, of course, Lance would have had to come inside to find paper and a pen. He had used her special pen, the only one that had not dried out, and he had not bothered to cap it or replace it on the desk. She turned in a slow circle examining the room but found nothing else out of order. It was fine that he had noticed the hat and knife on the kitchen table. She had meant to take them to him along with the supplies, but had forgotten in her rush to get an early start in her search for the line shack. That he knew about the tobacco can on the tree suggested the answer to at least one small mystery. Lance must have left the nugget there for some reason of his own.

After dinner she wrote a reply explaining that she had no idea why McCarty had arrested Reese except that there wasn't anyone else to arrest and Reese had a bad record. As she finished writing, Skipper's quad roared up to the door, and she went eagerly out to meet him. Cayuse jumped off the seat as soon as the scooter stopped and charged around with his nose to the ground, barking.

"God damn it, get back here!" Skipper roared, then addressed Neva in a normal tone. "Well, he's picked up some sort of scent. Did you have company today, or what? I hope it wasn't that squimp from the Forest Service again." He swung one leg over to sit sideways on the seat and crossed his arms over his chest with a satisfied air. "I've been all over the territory today, and did I ever get an earful. I'm beginning to see why you like being a snoopy journalist."

"Who said I'm a snoopy journalist?"

"It's a compliment, W.T., so don't get fussed. You want to hear this or not?"

"Do you want tea or something first?"

"No thanks, I don't want to pee all night. Now listen up. I saw your pal, Darla."

"She's hardly a pal."

"Are you going to argue with everything I say?"

"Okay, okay, go ahead, I'm all ears."

"Well, then, here's the deal." Waiting until Neva sat down on the chopping block, he continued, "Darla told me that the fellow that owns the Barlow Mine has turned up and was telling everybody down at Angus this morning that he found you snooping around the mine late last night, and that the place had been torn up pretty bad and some things stolen. He didn't say what was missing, but everybody figures it's Reese's stash, and this guy wants it for himself. Now why would he be trying to pin it on you?"

"Because I was there last night just as he says."

"It's true?"

"Not that I searched the place but I was there. When I was driving up late from Darla's I saw a light in the house and thought maybe Reese or Lance had come back. I looked in the window."

"And he caught you?"

"He about scared me to death. I assumed he did the ransacking but he said he didn't."

Skipper regarded her in silence. It was now so dark she could barely make out his unhappy expression. "If you'd told me about it this morning I wouldn't have made a fool of myself telling everybody the guy's a shyster. You aren't being square with old Skipper, Walkie-Talkie."

"I'm truly sorry, but I didn't think of it this morning. I was so interested in what you found out about Gene, it drove everything else out of my mind."

"So who searched the place?"

"I have no idea. I don't know why everyone's making such a big deal out of Reese's stash. It doesn't amount to much."

"So you have seen it. And just when and where might that have been?"

"A few days ago, after Reese was arrested. I got to thinking about it, and it occurred to me that once word got out about the arrest somebody might decide to search for the gold." She described finding the box and hiding it in the woodshed. "It was probably silly. It can't be worth much. Reese just seems to like the so-called jewelry nuggets."

"Thank you for telling me," Skipper said with dignity. "I guess I'll be getting home. Good night."

"It didn't seem important," she began but was cut off by the revving of the engine. Skipper sped away, his back straight, with Cayuse dashing along behind rather than riding.

Even after the camper door banged shut, Neva didn't go inside right away, but sat as Skipper had left her, feeling deeply unhappy. He had managed to get inside her heart, and he clearly felt some real regard for her—or had before tonight. He had rearranged his summer plans out of concern for her, and had put time and energy into getting information about the mine and her uncle, and had even defended her against local gossip. Now she had clumsily let him see that he was not fully in her confidence.

What would he say if he knew that she was keeping other secrets? She had not told him about taking food to Lance at the line shack or about being followed by the sheriff's minion in Elkhorn. She hadn't meant to be secretive but had simply not thought of telling Skipper. Even accidental secrets nearly always cause more trouble than they're worth, and now clearly it was time to tell all.

First, however, she must prepare a peace offering. For the next hour she worked fast. The pantry yielded a dented cake pan. In a drawer she found a vintage rotary eggbeater with the lovely name Dazey on it, which nicely whipped the whites of her last two eggs. Lacking powdered sugar she puzzled over what to do for icing, but then remembered caramel glazing and put plain white sugar in a saucepan to melt. Now and again she went to the porch to listen for activity at Skipper's camp and was reassured when she heard Cayuse bark, followed by the usual, "Shut up out there!"

The oven failed to get truly hot despite the kindling she fed into the firebox, and she was not surprised that the cake rose only about half as high as it should have done. Still, it was enough. The sugar syrup was bubbling but hadn't thickened so she let it simmer while the cake cooled, then she poured the dark, melted sugar over it in a thin stream. When she had seen this done the syrup had formed a delicious, chewy coating, but her syrup hardened instantly into something more like fiberglass than food. She tapped it with a spoon, whacked harder, and giggled. It was the gesture that mattered, and the inside should be edible enough.

Relieved to see a square of dim light through the trees as she approached the camp, she tried to think of something funny to say when Skipper opened the door, but seeing the cake, he said instantly, "Well, shit, you didn't have to do that. It's not my birthday."

"Lucky thing or I'd have had to drive into Elkhorn for candles. If you break a tooth on the caramel you can sue me. Am I forgiven?"

Skipper's face was flushed and on the table behind him she could see the glass and bottle. "Only if you tell me the rest."

"Could I come in and put the cake down first?"

"No way. You're too damn tricksy for Ol' Skipper. Just spill the beans."

"Number one. When I visited Reese in jail he asked me to take food to Lance and told me where to find him over on the other side of Billie Mountain. I found him there yesterday morning."

"That's only number one?" Skipper's bloodshot eyes regarded her coldly. "I know I'm an ignorant, dumbshit longshoreman but I had the funny idea we were paddling the same boat. Looks like I was fooled. I never did like cake anyway."

Standing motionless in front of the closed door, Neva could not quite believe what had happened. Had she completely lost her diplomatic touch, or was Skipper being ridiculously unreasonable? The light went out in the camper. Turning, she rushed up the road still carrying the cake like a trophy before her. Naturally she stumbled, and naturally the cake went flying, and naturally she said, "The hell with it."

In the dim kitchen where the smell of cake lingered deliciously, she stood with her back to the stove even though the evening was not cold. Should she put a note on Skipper's door to be found in the morning, or simply forget about him? Her gaze, moving randomly around the room, fixed on the corner by the built-in shelves where she had leaned her uncle's rifle. It was gone and so was the box of bullets. Lance, it appeared, had taken more than his hat and knife.

"Damn him," she raged aloud. "Damn Skipper. Damn them all."

Chapter Twenty-four

First thing in the morning, before making coffee, Neva went down to the camp and looked at the empty spot where Skipper's camper had been. Nothing remained apart from the stacked eight-by-eight timbers he used as supports for the camper when it was not on the pickup. The ground was clean of everything but twigs and pinecones. Even the cake had left no trace.

Her anger had given way entirely to regret. That she had failed to hear him pull out deepened the sense of loss, which stayed with her through breakfast and chores. She had enjoyed Skipper's company despite their great differences in age, education, interests, life experience—everything—and that she very likely would not see him again and would never have the chance to explain or apologize filled her with sadness and self-blame. It did no good to tell herself that he was just a cranky old artifact hunter with no importance in her life. Something that had felt like real friendship had developed between them with remarkable speed and she had destroyed it. She had no permanent address or phone number for him, not even the name of a hometown where she could check directories.

Exercise would have to be her salvation yet again, exercise and the high desert air. Striding up the trail with forced energy, swinging her arms like a soldier, she headed first for the collapsed cabin. In her pocket she carried a new note for Lance, one that demanded the rifle back immediately. She rolled it up, pushed it into the tobacco can along with paper and a pen, and walked briskly on, cutting through the woods to reach the next creek over. Here she turned left, aiming for the upper bowl and the steepest route she knew to the top. She would not stop for a breather or a drink until she arrived at the highest point on Billie Mountain.

Pushing hard, she reached a massive, sloping limestone outcrop near the top of the ridge in record time. Her entire body throbbed with heat and the force of pounding blood, and a rest now seemed like a pleasant choice after all. Contouring along the base of the pale limestone, she found a hollow sheltered from the wind that always blew up here. Her back fit into the hollow, and her outstretched legs rested comfortably on the coarse white sand at the base of the rock.

Yellow flowers grew close by and on the flowers bees worked as though the world would end by nightfall. Those eternal turkey vultures floated above the canyon in lazy, hypnotic circles. Her blood slowed, her face cooled, the sweat dried. Cradled by the warm rock, soothed by the low hum of insect life, she fell into a doze that lasted until she was tickled by a line of ants running over her ankle.

Refreshed and calm again, she gazed out over the creek canyon and thought about the last few days. There was no ignoring the fact that her quiet retreat at Billie Creek had become complicated in ways she didn't understand—and did not want to understand, she realized with satisfaction. What mattered was the richness of natural form and color spread out at her feet, the vast panorama of shifting light, the smell of sagebrush, pine and hot rocks, the silence, the views that reached all the way to Idaho in the east and the Wallowa Mountains to the north. What she cared about was this monumental landscape where no sign of human activity showed except for a distant, narrow strip of cultivated green in the Dry River Valley…Her gaze fixed on a tiny figure far down the slope on the west side of the canyon.

Keeping her eyes on the spot, she felt for the binoculars, focused, and let out a disappointed, "Damn." She had hoped to see Skipper returned to patch things up, but instead this man appeared to be a stranger, though a billed cap hid his face so she couldn't be sure. The lanky build was right, but it could also be Andy Sylvester or Gene Holland. He wore long pants and a long-sleeve shirt, with a knapsack over one shoulder. As she watched, he seated himself on a rock, felt for something in the pack, and lifted it to his face.

Neva almost laughed. He was looking through binoculars. He was scanning the territory just as she was doing, but looking up rather than down. Imagining the cartoon moment when they would aim the binoculars at each other in mutual scrutiny, her amusement turned to discomfort. She had always felt gloriously solitary on the ridge, invisible to the human world as she strode along with the sun on her bare back and chest. Had she been watched from afar without knowing it?

She stuffed the glasses back into their case, scrambled to her feet, and half-ran along the base of the outcropping to where she could duck out of sight. Keeping the limestone between her and the canyon, she continued to climb. Soon on top of the ridge, she stood behind a twisted juniper and studied the lower slope through the glasses. The man was gone from the rock and she found no sign of him on nearby slopes, where sagebrush would have provided no real cover. Next she studied the Sufferin' Smith Mine far down toward the valley. As usual, there was no sign of life, only scattered mining debris and the small winking eye of the pond, but she hadn't really expected to find activity with Gene away in Idaho.

Again she searched the area where the stranger had been, then checked the slopes above the spot until she felt satisfied that he had gone down rather than up. Certain that she was alone on the ridge, she walked on, but did not take off her shirt.

◇◇◇

It was late afternoon when Neva returned to the cabin. Father Bernard was seated on the large quartz boulder near the door with a book in his hand. He waited until she was close before saying, "The fifteenth-century Benedictine writer John Trithemius said that, in the midst of the multiple activities of the day, you should stay free of multiplicity and preserve oneness of spirit within yourself. This strikes me as a mighty fine spot for preserving oneness of spirit."

Delighted, Neva laughed and extended her hand. "Have you been here preserving your spirit for long?"

He shook his large head. "Not even long enough to shed the multiplicities of Angus gossip."

"You mean the story that I ransacked Reese's house? Sensible people aren't believing that are they?"

"There are no sensible people when it comes to good gossip." Father Bernard pushed himself to his feet and strode to his car as though setting off for an all-day walk up the ridge. Despite his age and size, he moved with the vigor of a young, active man. From the backseat he pulled a flat package tied up in brown paper. Following Neva inside, he placed the package on the table and looked around the cabin with interest. "Very unusual furnishings for a mine. I haven't been here before, you know. The few times I saw Orson and your uncle it was in church."

"Church? No one in my family went to church."

"Nonetheless, church is where I met Burtie. It's possible he came for Orson's sake."

Neva heard paper crackle as Father Bernard unwrapped the package but she waited until he was done before turning from her coffee preparations to look, knowing what it was but not how she would react. She went closer, studying the man in the photograph. Slim and young, he stood with his hand on a weathered fence post and one foot resting on a low rock, gazing into the distance with a half smile and a listening look. Rather than mining clothes, as she had expected, he wore a suit complete with waistcoat, tie, and looped watch chain, with a fedora held gracefully in the hand that hung at his side. He reminded her powerfully of her son, not only in features but in his thoughtful expression, as though he'd just been asked an interesting question.

"According to the date on the back it must have been taken when he first moved out here, in 1951," the priest said. "I don't know how it came to be on my wall. I offered it to him but he said no, he'd rather look at a picture of a turnip than himself every day."

The words, like the image, struck Neva as intensely, even painfully, familiar. It was just the sort of quirky, self-deprecating comment her mother would have made. She said, "I'd be happy to look at him every day."

"Good. He's all yours. I've enjoyed his company but he obviously belongs with you. I'm glad I had him for an excuse to come up. I always find it hard to settle into work the first few days out here, where there's beauty in every direction. I just like to be here with my eyes open. But I believe you understand about that."

Father Bernard's talk as they sat on the porch with coffee was as witty and well-informed as before, and Neva was particularly interested in the description of his current writing project, but still she found herself wishing to be alone with her uncle's portrait. She didn't speak during a long silence that ended when he said, "I see you're deeply affected. I hope that's a good thing and not painful. To be honest, I'll miss the picture. It's been sweet company to me off and on for fifteen years. I hope you'll forgive the fancy, but I've always had the feeling that he wanted to tell me something. Maybe he'll tell you."

As the priest was leaving his eye fell on the box containing her mother's ashes. His quick glance at her was so clearly questioning that she nodded. "My mother. I'm thinking of leaving her at the mine, as I said. How did you know what it was?"

"Perhaps you forget that my work deals with death as much as life. I've blessed such packages before." And so saying he made a quick sign with his right hand in the direction of the box as he murmured something unintelligible.

Startled but unable to disapprove of anything this extraordinary man did, Neva said, "That's the first time she's ever been blessed, as far as I know."

"It's about time then."

She almost confessed that, had anyone but him made this gesture, she would have found it intrusive. Instead, she said, "I talked to one of the funeral home owners in Elkhorn the other day when I was walking in the cemetery. He told me that graveside services are too depressing for most people so they've begun making videos about the life of the dead person. I don't see anything wrong with the video, but what's the point of a ritualized burial if there's no one there? You might think it's strange for an atheist to be bothered about this, but I've been giving a lot of thought to human remains because of Mom's ashes. I hope this doesn't strike you as a foolish concern. I'm kind of surprised myself, that I care, that is."

The priest thought for a moment before saying in a reflecting tone, as though feeling his way as he spoke, "Very little that truly concerns people is foolish, especially when it has to do with those we love. As for the funeral business, it's bound to change with the culture, and it has generally been aimed at the living rather than the dead. Personally, I think a good graveside service helps people let go."

"Does the cemetery at St. Mary's go back very far? I enjoy the old sections of graveyards."

"The oldest grave is 1899, a Steadman as it happens, Darla's great-great something or other. There aren't many of those, but there are a few very original headstones if you'd like to take a look sometime. Be sure to stop by the house if you're over that way."

When the priest had gone Neva stood the photograph on the sewing machine next to the ashes, turned the white platform rocker so it faced the picture, and sat into the twilight looking at this precious image from the irretrievable past.

Chapter Twenty-five

Neva was on the trail early again in the morning, and reached the collapsed cabin as the direct rays of the sun reached the canyon bottom. Her hope of finding the rifle by the ponderosa was disappointed, and though her note to Lance was gone, he had left no reply. She put the pen and paper in her pocket and walked briskly on. When Reese got out of jail, he would see to it that she got her uncle's rifle back, and until then, she would waste no regret on it.

Today she had no walking plan beyond checking for the rifle, and headed up the canyon out of habit. As she was crossing Billie Creek Road, she heard a vehicle and thought instantly of the night truck, which she had now heard for certain three times, but this was no diesel approaching. She waited by the side of the road. Soon a yellow pickup came into sight with dogs peering out from behind the cab on both sides.

"You weren't home," Darla said through the open window as she pulled up, her face shadowed by a billed cap rather than the usual cowboy hat. "I'm going over to Jump Creek to check salt blocks and thought you might be interested in coming along." Not waiting for an answer she leaned to open the passenger's side door.

"Why don't I see salt blocks on Billie Creek?" Neva asked as she settled on the worn fleece that covered the seat. Her feet found a place among the machine parts, gloves, rags, and tools on the floor.

"I don't put out many salt blocks on this side." Darla drove slowly in second gear, easing across deep ruts and around large rocks without appearing to notice the obstacles, including the trench that had stopped Reese's mad dash. "They don't need a whole lot of supplement out in this country with all the natural minerals. It's more of a backup."

After a silence, she said, "How's life at the mine?"

"Just fine, as long as I don't think too much about Roy. Father Bernard brought me the photograph of Uncle Matthew. He's dressed up in a suit with a watch chain and everything."

"If I remember correctly, he always wore a watch with a chain, even with his coveralls."

They topped the low pass that divided the two drainages and dropped steeply toward Jump Creek, the truck roaring in first gear down a track that Neva would not have called a road but that at least was not as steep as what they'd ridden down on horseback. Once in the creek bottom they followed the road downstream, stopping now and again to check salt blocks. Most needed replacing, a simple matter of lifting a block from the pickup bed and setting it on the ground within sight of the road.

They had set out the last salt block and were heading back up the canyon, when Darla turned onto an overgrown track that angled up the east side. "You'll like this," she said.

The track leveled out, crossed a flat dotted with ponderosas, and ended at a path through mixed shrubs and trees. Darla led the way up the path, walking with the same ease she showed in the saddle, as though she owned the ground underfoot, the sky overhead, and everything in between. After about ten minutes, she stepped aside to let Neva come up beside her. Before them lay a small, sloping meadow with a stream running through it, that reminded her of the site of Lance's line shack. But rather than a shack, there was a proper little house standing at the top of the meadow. That Neva regarded it as a house rather than a cabin didn't strike her until later, when, recalling the scene in detail, she realized it was because the door and window trim were painted the same dark green as the roof shingles, giving a finished look. The porch railing, also painted green, enclosed a small sitting area where two rocking chairs stood. A path wound from where they stood through grass and flowers to the cabin. It was lined with chunks of white quartz.

"It's a fairy tale," Neva marveled.

"It was Gran's. After you." Darla waved for her to go first across the plank laid over the creek and up the path.

From the front porch, they looked out at a wide view of meadow, distant ridges, and sky. "No one lives here?"

"Not since Gran died. Sometimes I stay a night when I want to get away. It's the only piece I own on Jump Creek."

Darla pulled a small plug of wood out of one of the logs a few inches from the doorframe, retrieved a key, and unlocked the door. When Neva followed her in after a few moments, she was lighting a fire in a small Wedgwood stove in the corner that served as a kitchen. The inside of the cabin was as perfect as the outside, from the diamond-shaped windows in the front door to the firewood basket with braided fiber handles. That such a hideaway existed just over the ridge from Billie Creek seemed so unlikely that Neva asked again, "Your Gran lived here?" She sat down in a small armchair with a view out the front window. "Tell me about her, please."

"There's not much to tell." Darla opened a tin, spooned tea into a blue ceramic pot, and unhooked two white cups from a rack made of naturally twisted wood. "She married Gramps when she was hardly more than a kid, had three boys before she was twenty-five, then a long time later when the boys were about grown she had a girl, Lindsey Ann. I guess she loved Lindsey more than anything in the world, everybody did. Those are her watercolors there on the wall. When Lindsey died in a riding accident Gran went kind of strange and never was the same after." Darla was silent for a moment, her head bowed, before she concluded, "Gran thought I would be another Lindsey Ann. When I left for New York she moved up here and hardly came down for the rest of her life. They found her sitting in that chair looking peaceful as a baby."

"She died in this chair?"

"Does that bother you?"

"Not at all. It would be hard to think of a better place. When was that?"

"Fifteen years ago."

"But that's when my uncle disappeared."

"It was about a year later. They were real good friends. He used to walk over here and back in a day. I believe she would have lived a lot longer if he was still around."

When the tea was ready Darla set it on a wooden table with an inlaid top, the small pieces of colored wood forming a simple picture of the ridge that could be seen from the chair. "Gran's work," she said. "Talk about patience. Sometimes I wish I inherited that instead of the ranch."

"You don't strike me as impatient."

"She taught me that if you couldn't be patient or decent or generous, the next best thing was to act like it. She said, 'It's better to feed a beggar with orneriness in your heart than not feed him at all.' If it wasn't for Gran, I'd just tell beggars and everybody else to go fuck themselves. Sorry, I'm not much of a lady."

Darla dropped Neva at the turnoff to the mine in the early twilight. Again she refused to stay for dinner, and again blamed the stock. "If I'm late they're as cranky as old goats," she said.

"Thank you for taking me to the cabin. It's a magical place."

Neva did not add that the image of her uncle and Gran drinking tea there together had been deeply moving, but as soon as she reached home she went straight to her uncle's photograph to see if she could discover something different in it. She had left the picture on the table with her mother's ashes, and now stared, dumbfounded. The picture was there but the ashes were gone.

Where they had sat for weeks there was only a clean rectangle of wood that stood out on the otherwise dusty surface.

Lighting the lamp with shaking hands, she carried it through both rooms, searching frantically but knowing she would not find the ashes. They were gone and she knew why. Someone from the valley who had heard Dietering's story had come up to scour her cabin in turn, had mistaken the heavy box for Reese's gold, and had hurried away with it before looking inside or having to ransack her cabin. At least she could be grateful for not coming home to chaos, with her papers, books and clothing flung across the floor.

Despite the faint nausea that sent her to the porch to take deep, slow breaths, Neva felt laughter rising inside. What a joke. What a colossal, crazy joke. Her mother would have loved it and so would Ethan. If only Darla had come for dinner she would have had someone to tell, but even as she imagined relating the tale to friends her amusement gave way to a crushing sense of loss. The rifle would come back, but the ashes were gone for good.

Hunger at last drove her to heat a bowl of beans, but every few minutes she went into the big room to look again at the empty spot on the table. At last she got out what remained in the bottle of wine that Gene had brought, carried it to the porch, and drank as she listened to coyotes cry. A year ago, the loss of the ashes would not have meant much. Now it felt as though she had lost her mother all over again.

Chapter Twenty-six

"We've been talking it over at the office and we've decided you should leave Billie Creek." Andy Sylvester half sat against the porch railing holding a cup of coffee and looking down at Neva on the settee. He had taken off his green Forest Service cap and appeared even younger than usual with pale hair sticking out randomly from a pointed head. "Just until this business is cleared up. Then you can come back. As long as you camp, of course."

"Leave Billie Creek? Andy, this is nonsense. I'm spending the summer here. Period. I'll leave the cabin if I'm forced to, but not the mine. Even if I wanted to leave, my house in town is rented out for the summer. I have nowhere to live in town until September."

"There's been a murder," the young man said with ill-disguised impatience. "Murder. As in, someone was killed just four miles down the road. Nobody knows who did it or why. Everyone says McCarty has the wrong man. In fact, I think he knows he has the wrong man and is up to some plot of his own, but that's got nothing to do with your safety."

"Come on, Andy. Murders aren't random. Roy DeRoos was killed for a specific reason that has nothing to do with me. Remember, this is the Old West. We are in gold mine country, land of the natural outlaw."

"You seem to know a lot about it."

"Oh, for Heaven's sake." Neva shook her head but managed not to laugh. "Thanks for your concern, but I'm far more interested in talking about how you came to be working out here."

"All right, then, be that way. Nobody can say I didn't try. As for your curiosity, I followed in my dad's footsteps. An old story."

"He also worked for the Forest Service?"

"Not only that, but for this same district. I got the job when he retired. Not very original, is it? I just like it out here."

Disregarding the note of self-disparagement, Neva said without forethought, "Do you ever wish you'd taken up mining instead?"

"God no! I couldn't do that, tear up the streams and rivers. Do you have any idea how long it takes for this kind of dry country to heal? One day there's a creek flowing happily along, minding its own business like it did for hundreds of years, and the next day there's devastation. And now that gold is back up above six hundred dollars an ounce, it's bound to get worse."

Neva found herself beginning to like him a little but she couldn't help teasing. "Reese said they can't dig a test hole without filling in ten forms in triplicate."

"And a damn good thing, too! You have eyes. Can't you see what was done to this creek? It was assaulted and left for dead."

"Bravo! Well said."

Blinking in confusion, Andy flushed like a thirteen-year-old. "I don't know how you do it but you make me mad every time I come up here."

"Sorry, I was just teasing this time. To be honest, I'm finding it pretty confusing out here myself. My sympathies are with the environmentalists and always have been but listening to people talk, particularly ranchers like Darla, I can't help sympathizing with their problems too. If the ranchers, loggers, and miners are driven out there won't be anyone left but the recreationists, retired stockbrokers, and enforcers, people like you and me, in other words. Pretty boring, if you'll excuse my saying so. We have no roots here, no survival stake in the land. And now I need to ask if you'll do me a favor."

Enjoying the look of pained amazement that grew on his face as she talked, Neva explained about the stolen funeral ashes. "I'd like you to mention it to everyone you see on the chance that rumor will reach the thief and he'll realize how important the ashes are and get them back to me, no questions asked. By now, at least, whoever did it knows it's not gold."

"You are beyond weird," Sylvester said with a real smile at last. "You're so crazy you probably are safe. They say insane people and drunks survive things that would kill anybody else. Sure, I'll tell people but they aren't going to believe it."

The dust of the Forest Service pickup still hung in the air when Neva got into her car and also headed down the canyon. It was too true, what she'd said to the mining technician—whoever had taken the box knew by now that they had carried away ashes, and every hour that passed made the chances of getting them back slimmer. They would throw them on the ground or into a stove, and the ashes would be gone forever.

She must get the word out herself, now, by going to Angus.

Bumping past the Barlow Mine she did not allow herself more than a glance at the closed cabins with the lone truck still sitting out front and, as had become her habit, she did not look at the road down into the pit. When she reached Gene's she was glad to see his truck, which was parked right up against the small porch rather than in the usual spot to the side of the cabin. He must have returned early from Pocatello. She knocked on the weathered plank doors of both the cabin and the lab shack but got no response. Where had Gene gone without his truck? The road up to the mine site was steep and at least a mile long.

On a scrap of paper from her purse she wrote: "Sorry to miss you. How about coming up for dinner sometime this week? Tonight would be fine. Something kind of crazy has happened and I've had to go out to Angus. I'll be back by afternoon. Hope to see you soon."

The next disappointment was the locked post office door. It could not be the weekend again already, so Bernice must have got sick or decided to go fishing, so to speak. Neva slid her letter to Ethan through the mail slot, and then, before her courage could fail, she marched across the stark gravel lot to the café. Three men sat at the bar staring in silence at nothing, not even the T.V., which was off. Al Fleck stood at the grill with his back to the room.

No one looked at her or greeted her as she slid onto a stool at the end of the bar. Al took his time but at last approached wiping his hands on the stained once-white apron.

"What can I do for you?" he said as though they'd never met.

The rumors about her had done their evil work, as she feared. Drawing a deep, slow breath, she said, "You can give me a cup of coffee and kindly tell everyone who comes in that I did not ransack Reese's house for any reason whatever. I'm far too tidy to make such a mess, even for a pot of gold. It's just a stupid rumor."

After a startled moment he guffawed, winked, and reached for a sturdy white mug. "How about some fries? The grill is just right."

"Sounds great, thanks. And a nice fat steak, on the rare side."

She had not got a clear look at the men at the bar. The one on the end farthest from her now stood, stretched audibly, slapped a bill onto the table, said something low to the man next to him, and walked out. It was Tony Briggs. He let the screen door slam behind him.

Al brought the ketchup squeeze bottle and winked again. "So much for Smiley. He was just telling us he saw you in Elkhorn coming out of Archie's Gold and Silver."

"Nobody believes him, I hope?"

"Some people don't have enough to think about. Of course, we all know Briggs, too. Wouldn't surprise me if he took the gold."

"You know," Neva said, "it strikes me that everyone seems more worked up about Reese's little stash than about Roy being dead."

"Whoa, now. That's not fair, not a bit. What can anybody do about it? The kid's dead but the gold's still there somewhere. It's a shame about Reese, too."

"Do you think he's guilty?"

"I don't know word one about this whole thing. That's McCarty's job." He went to the grill, flipped the steak, and shook the basket of potato chunks. He didn't return to her end of the bar until he brought the food on a large, hot plate.

Neva whistled. "That's not a steak, it's a side of cow." Encouraged by his smile she continued, "I have a favor to ask, if you wouldn't mind."

"What's that?"

The two heads at the other end of the bar turned toward her at last as she explained about the ashes. "They were sitting on a table in a little box. Yesterday they disappeared while I was out of the cabin. What I think is that someone who heard the rumor that I had Reese's gold took the ashes thinking they were his stash. Doesn't that make sense? The point is, I want them back. I want everyone in the valley to know that that's my mother and I'd like her back, no questions asked."

Al was shaking his head just as Andy Sylvester had done, and the other two men, both strangers to her, began talking in low voices but stopped to listen when Al said, "I'd love to have seen their face when they opened that box. Damn me, that's rich. Tough luck about your mom, though. I never have had to make any decision like what to do with mortal remains and I hope I don't any time soon. I'm not much on fancy funerals myself."

"You mean you're not shocked or horrified that I had my mother's ashes?"

"Each to his own I always say."

Relieved and grateful, Neva bit into a fat fry with sudden greed for grease and salt.

The café door opened. For no logical reason, she assumed it was Tony Briggs again, but it was Darla Steadman who slid onto the stool next to Neva, and said before she was fully seated,

"Hey Buster, give me what she's got, only more fries. And a lemonade."

"Will do, Miss Pendleton Round-up."

Neva's jaw would have dropped had her mouth not been full of fries. What had come over Darla? The usually cool rancher had turned playful, and rather than scowling at the reference to her beauty contest days, she was happily pulling napkins from the dispenser. When she had a good wad she dipped it in her water glass and wiped the dust from her face and hands.

"In case you're wondering," she said, "I'm allergic to the soap in the washroom. I should just bring in my own and leave it here, but I never remember until I'm already in the door." She examined the grimy paper and wrinkled her nose. "You'd think I work outdoors or something. Ever since Al found that old newspaper article about me being the rodeo queen, he brings it up some way every time, so I figure the least I can do is eat his food with a clean face." Darla wadded the dirty napkins tighter and pitched the ball in Al's direction. It landed with a sizzle in the grease vat, but Al had turned to the cooler and didn't appear to notice.

Darla shrugged. "They're my fries, anyway."

"I bet you were a holy terror in high school."

"Nothing holy about it. But don't tell Father Bernard."

"Where is the high school?"

"Over in Charity."

"You grew up on the ranch?"

"I did, my dad did, his dad did. Before that, they ran the stage over the pass to Elkhorn."

"What happens next, I mean, who takes over from you?"

"Nobody. I mean it. Everybody but me was smart enough to kick the bucket before things got too bad. I'll never have any kids"—here a micro-glance in Al's direction put a new idea into Neva's mind—"but you can't leave your ranch to your kids anyway because the taxes will kill them. The land might be worth millions on paper but you have most of your ranch families in debt. I know some that figured out ways to give it to their kids piece by piece so they can keep the operation going, but most don't figure that out. And this life is about over anyway. You can't make a living like it used to be. Used to be you could count on good enough prices every few years to get mostly out of debt, but now you have all this South American beef coming in. The price is flat. This never was the best range, not like over in the Willamette Valley, or even John Day."

Al had drifted close and chimed in with, "That's why these rich boys from California can buy up the ranches so cheap."

The man sitting closest to Darla said, "They can afford to ranch just for the hell of it, for a goddamn hobby. You have your old ranch families going broke, and some jackass investor from Modesto comes in and buys three ranches just for play."

"I'd rather see them ranch for play or any way at all than opening private hunting lodges," Darla said. "The first thing you know you have a hundred 'Keep Out' signs. Next comes a campaign to keep cows from eating the deer food or elk food, like there's not enough to go around."

"You see what they did over at Salt Springs?" said the man who hadn't yet spoken. "That's no house he's building on the hill, it's a goddamn castle for dudes. But that Owen fellow isn't so bad. He hired Mitch to be his foreman."

"Big deal," said the other man. "How'd you like to be hired foreman on a ranch your family owned since before they invented white bread?"

"He's better off foreman than owning the place, if you want my opinion," said Al. "If anybody loses their shirt it won't be him. And they're building him a better house than he ever hoped to live in this side of the grave."

"It isn't just prices," said Darla. "Every time you turn around there are new rules. We have to keep the cows out of the creeks, which I understand, but it means more fences. I have to ride up three times a year and measure the grass along each creek. They used to have somebody that did it, but now it's the ranchers that have to do it. Just one more thing to keep track of. Not that I want to hurt the creeks, but sometimes it just doesn't make sense. Last year this fish biologist told me I couldn't irrigate my alfalfa by pumping the water out of the river and letting it run back down through the fields, even where they slope good. He said they figured out that trout need 65 degrees. Well, I said there wasn't even any water in the river in August before they built the dam, so how could there be 65 degrees for the trout? In other words, there never was a year-round trout population in the Dry River.

"He said irrigating made the water warmer. I said the irrigation water soaked into the ground and stayed there until it got back to the river, which should make it cooler, not warmer. I said, 'Did you measure the temperature upriver from my place and then downriver to see if it got warmer?' He said no, he hadn't thought of that."

She paused long enough for Al to prompt, "So they measured it, right?"

"They did. Like I said, the water got cooler by irrigating. They mean well, I guess. He wasn't a bad kid, he just had an idea that worked in the laboratory, but that doesn't mean it works on the ground. I don't know what to say about the trout, but it wasn't the farmers that killed the salmon in this river, it was the dam. They built it in the 1930s without any fish ladder. My dad said the Chinook beat themselves against it for a couple of years and that was the end of the run."

"It's not that the environmentalists' ideas are so bad," said Al. "Nobody wants to see the land wrecked. But you have these people in Washington making the rules, people that've never been out here, so what do you expect? Why don't you write about that in your newspaper."

"Maybe I will," Neva said.

"Send me a copy. I'll frame it," Al said, setting a plate down in front of Darla. The steak was decorated with the deep-fried paper wad on top of a spray of parsley, like a weird rose on a stem. The two exchanged a look, no words, but it was enough to confirm Neva's guess. Al appeared to be in his fifties, older than Darla and a bit on the short side, but height wouldn't make any difference in the saddle. The Steadman ranch might yet see some heirs, taxes or no taxes.

Al winked at Neva. "How about telling Darla here about your recent loss. I think she'd find that very interesting."

Darla not only found it interesting, she was sufficiently outraged about the stolen ashes to head straight for Father Bernard's when she finished eating, to get him to mention it to the congregation on Sunday. The two men, a rancher and a logger, also promised to spread the word, and of course Al would tell the tale to everyone who stopped for a drink or a meal.

As Neva drove back up the Dry River Valley, she felt satisfied that she had done what she could about the ashes. Rounding the final bend before the Billie Creek turnoff, she saw a small red car parked at the bottom of the road. Her first thought was that whoever had taken the box had already heard the story and come to meet her, to return the ashes with apologies. In the next moment she saw that the person standing next to the car was Enid Gale. She was wearing a sky-blue dress.

"Funny thing about time," Enid said when Neva pulled up beside her. "I don't remember any road sign here, and it seems to me the road used to go in at a different angle. I had to get my feet on the ground just to be sure it's the right ground. The air, though, is just right, hot and heavy with the smell of cooked sagebrush. But now to business. It's just as well we met because that will save me going all the way up, and to be honest, I'd get sad seeing the place. I have something for you." She opened the back door of her car and half disappeared inside as she rummaged, then emerged with a shoebox. "Letters and papers. They were in Orson's stuff but I could see they were your uncle's. I don't know why they didn't go to your mother at the time but they finally made it to where they belong."

Neva looked at the older woman rather than down at the box hugged to her chest. "That's a long drive, Enid, too long to turn around and go right back again. I wish you'd come up to the mine. I'd love to talk."

"Oh, dear me, kiddo, I'm most certainly not headed straight back home." Enid laughed gaily. "I'm on my way to John Day for a workshop. Fused glass. I didn't show you my studio but I've been working with glass for a year now. I never thought I could love glass, so brittle and rather nasty to work with but, oh, my, the magic grows on you. I really did enjoy your visit the other day." Enid offered Neva the shoebox, then held her by the shoulders, kissed her lightly on each cheek, looked into her eyes for a moment, and said, "I don't think I mentioned how much you're like him. He could have had such a rich life, and I don't mean gold."

"You would have been a lovely aunt."

"It's funny you should say that. All my life I've felt like an aunt. Only thing missing were the nieces and nephews."

Chapter Twenty-seven

Neva watched with regret as Enid drove away. What fun it would have been to spend the afternoon with this sensible, humorous woman so tantalizingly linked to her own past. Standing with the shoebox cradled in her arms, she felt suddenly bereft and lonely, and this led her thoughts to Reese in his solitary jail cell. Could it be true, as McCarty had said, that she was the only one to visit him? How many days had it been since her trip to the jail? Four? Five? She couldn't remember for sure but it felt like a long time. He must be half crazy by now, pent up like that. And he would have no way of knowing that she had found Lance and delivered the food.

She was out of fruit and vegetables, and had begun to crave oranges. It would take an hour to get to Elkhorn, a half hour to visit with Reese, another half hour in the grocery store, an hour to get home. This would still leave her time for a late walk and a long evening in which to read Uncle Matthew's papers.

Tenderly, as though it were alive, she set the shoebox on the passenger's seat and headed up the empty highway toward the pass. It was about two when she reached Elkhorn and pulled into a spot near the door of the law enforcement building. Recalling the long wait last time she visited Reese, and the lack of even outdated magazines to read, she took the top few papers from the box and put them in her bag.

The young officer on duty at the reception window smiled happily, pleased to be able to deliver good news. "Reese Cotter?

He was released this morning, first thing. Did you want to talk to anybody else?"

Too surprised to say more than a mumbled no thank you, Neva returned to the parking lot and stood squinting in the hot July glare. Of course it was good that Reese was free, but still her sense of disappointment was acute, and it struck her suddenly that she had not been on a mission of kindness. She had wanted to see the young miner. Like Skipper, he had managed to get tangled somewhere in her affections, even if only on the edge, and she had anticipated some lively talk about jail life and the useless twit lawyer, and she in turn would relate the quarry adventure, the meeting with Boris Dietering, and even the loss of the ashes. It was a pleasure just to imagine his explosive reaction to that one. How odd that she felt comfortable talking to this man whose life was so far removed from her own. She could say anything to him, she realized with surprise. Was it his bluntness, or not really caring what he thought, or a result of spending their only evening together spilling out "whiskey truth," as Skipper would call it?

At a loss for what to do next, she felt a rare flush of self-pity. She was hot and dusty, and not one person in the whole town knew or cared she was here.

"Hey, there, Ms. Leopold," a hearty voice called. For an instant Neva didn't recognize its owner, then saw it was Sheriff McCarty in street clothes.

"I hardly know you out of costume," she teased, genuinely glad to see his robust and beaming figure.

"Costume! Somebody should teach you a little respect for the law, young lady. You've been inside, I take it."

"You let him go."

"You know any reason why I shouldn't?"

"I didn't know any reason why you should arrest him in the first place."

"You really want to know?"

"I do."

"Good. I'll tell you all about it on one condition—you join me for that beer. The Grand's nice and quiet this time of day. Best brew around. It's only a couple of blocks but we'll drive over, if you don't mind. Arthritis in my hip, a goddamn nuisance. It's best to park on the side street there right past the hotel. I'll just run inside here a moment and be right behind you."

Neva parked, as directed, just beyond the Grand Hotel and had finished a quick hair brushing when the sheriff pulled up behind her. Watching in the rearview mirror as he got nimbly out of his car, she wondered about the extent of his arthritis. He could not be sixty yet, and he moved with energetic pleasure in his own body like a fit young man. Escorting her into the elegant, restored bar, he cupped her elbow, and she found herself regretting her shorts and visibly scratched legs.

"It was the finest bar in the territory a hundred years ago," he said with an air of personal pride. "Probably still is, come to think of it."

The elaborate Victorian lights were unlit and not a soul sat at the carved wood bar, but McCarty strode into the deserted room as though bellying through crowds. A diminutive bartender appeared, smiling and half bowing.

"How you doing, Marvin?" the sheriff said. "Two pints of Billie Creek Brown." Pulling out a chair for Neva, he said, "Most women don't care for stout but seeing as how you're so stuck on Billie Creek you have to try it."

"Sounds great to me. Where is everyone?"

"The bar doesn't open for an hour yet, but they like to keep me happy."

Looking around with pleasure, Neva said, "I heard that Elkhorn was so rich the banks used to mint their own money."

"True enough. They say about twenty million dollars in gold came out of the area in one year. One of my few regrets in life is that I wasn't around to see it."

Launching into stories about growing up on a nearby ranch, McCarty kept her laughing until they were on their second round of stout and the bar had begun to fill, when he turned serious.

"Now that I've got you warmed up I'm going to order us some Cajun fries with Ranch dressing and we're going to talk about your pals on Billie Creek. I didn't have enough evidence to justify holding onto Reese, but there's something funny going on over there and if the Cotter brothers aren't mixed up in it somehow, I'll trade in my badge for a bongo drum. Where's Lance been hiding out, anyway?"

"How should I know?"

"You'd have to know where he is to take him food."

Neva had lifted her glass and now held it to her lips as though taking a long sip, but she would drink no more this evening. Two stouts had not diminished the sheriff's gamesmanship, and she had better keep sharp or he would pick her clean of secrets rather than telling his own. That he was using her own favorite method with sources—talk about yourself to make them think it's a conversation rather than an interview—amused her even as it sounded a warning bell. And yet, why not admit taking food to Lance? He was no longer at the line shack, as far as she knew, and she might well be wrong about the Cotter brothers' innocence in Roy's murder. Who more logical than his partners?

McCarty was studying her more unguardedly than before, and suddenly she felt his physical presence as distinctly as though he had reached out and touched her bare arm. The dark blue cotton shirt suited him better than sheriff's drabs, and accentuated his look of easy strength. Under the scrutiny of his canny eyes she felt that unpredictable female animal rise up inside her and reach for the controls. Oh no you don't, Woman, she protested. You are out of order. This is business thinly disguised as a jolly drinking date. McCarty has no personal interest in you. He wants information and he's accustomed to getting what he wants. She set down the glass.

"What do you really know about the Cotters, about their background?" he pressed.

Neva drew a slow breath and said as though reciting, "Their grandfather was the mayor of Elkhorn and he lost everything in a poker game, including that fancy funeral parlor that was their house, and since then it's been more or less hard knocks for the family."

"That's so. A bad deal for them, but plenty of folks have worse luck. Lance got something out of it, anyway, working for Lloyd Guptill like he did till Reese dragged him off to the mine."

"Guptill—is that an East Indian name?"

"Not that I ever knew. Lloyd's as white as they come and so's his boy, Darrell."

"I've met Darrell. I got the impression that his heart isn't really in the funeral business."

"I'd say you got that right. It's really the old man's show, though he's getting pretty long in the tooth. I wouldn't be surprised if Darrell sells out and leaves the territory when Lloyd packs it in. Now, what about your pal, Skipper Dooley? What do you know about him?"

Neva looked steadily at the sheriff. As far as she could recall, she had not mentioned Skipper in their previous meetings. How did he know about her friendship, her ex-friendship, that is, with the old artifact hunter? Had he succeeded in having her watched after all? Thinking of the stranger on the ridge with binoculars, she felt anger flare even as good sense told her that the suspicion was absurd. She was not worth that kind of surveillance…though he also had discovered somehow about the supplies she delivered to Lance. Glancing around, she saw that they were now entirely hemmed in by broad backs and cowboy hats. Laughter and the crash of glassware made a din she hadn't noticed while they were talking. She was one of only a few women in the bar, and the only person wearing shorts. The sudden sense of being transparent and conspicuous sent a chill through her. She wrapped her arms around her shoulders and shifted on the chair to hide her bare legs under the table, bumping McCarty's knees. "Excuse me."

"My pleasure. Looks like you wrestle bears for fun, but in case you missed my point I'll say it straight out. Bears might be better company than some of the folks you've taken up with on Billie Creek."

"Now that's too much, Sheriff. I haven't 'taken up' with anyone. I spend ninety-nine percent of the time alone. I'm friendly by nature and interested in just about everyone. That's the way I am. That's why I'm sitting here drinking with you. I'm interested in people. I don't think they're all angels but at the same time I tend to assume the best until I see otherwise. Kind of like innocent until proven guilty."

"Hey, now, easy does it. I didn't mean to get your back up. I didn't really mean anything except you have to be careful about people. It's my job to look a little deeper. Take Skipper now. He claims to be an artifact hunter, but did you ever see him with any artifacts? No, I didn't think so. And that miner fellow, Gene Holland. As near as I've been able to find out, he hasn't got any profit out of his mine for a good ten years, only enough to pay for the operation. What's that all about? You may see the best in folks but don't forget I see the worst, and maybe that's what I come to expect, right or wrong. And I notice when people suddenly change their ways, like Lance Cotter, who used to hang around this very bar every night. He disappeared like a rock in water. I was beginning to wonder if he was dead, too, but then I heard Reese on the phone before he left the jail, that he was going to meet Lance."

"Don't tell me you didn't have him followed? What's got into you, Sheriff?"

"Damn straight he was followed. But the tricky bugger went to his mother's house and left out the back way while my deputy cooled his butt out front."

"His mother? You said his mother was dead."

"Did I? I must have been thinking of someone else."

Neva remained silent until the sheriff said, "Well, hell, it's my job."

"Sheriff McCarty, you are not the man I thought you were. You're up to some strange tricks that truly surprise me in a law enforcement officer."

Neva stood up as she spoke, bringing McCarty to his feet as well. Forced together by the crowd, they stood face to face in tense mutual scrutiny until a sudden buzzing made him reach for his cell phone. He listened for a moment, said "Bingo," and returned the phone to his pocket. "This is a complicated business, Neva, and I can see I'm going to have to play it straight with you. But not here. There's a new restaurant close by where we can get a table in a private room. I'll just give them a call. You don't want to drive home hungry anyway."

The thought of being closeted for the rest of the evening with the sheriff while he was intent on playing games made Neva feel impatient and tired. The sheriff had eaten most of the Cajun fries, and lunch at the Angus Café was no more than a delicious memory, but a meal wasn't worth more of this cat and mouse routine. She said, "I can't go to a restaurant in shorts."

"Lady, in this town you could go to church naked as long as you were with me."

Neva's sudden laughter brought a more injured look to McCarty's broad face than her disapproval had done. "I'm sorry, Sheriff. But I don't want to drive back to Billie Creek late after a big meal that will make me sleepy."

"Stay the night then. Here at the Grand Hotel. On me. When you go back home you can write a newspaper piece about Elkhorn's historic hotel and do us a little publicity."

Why was he being so insistent? The interest wasn't personal, she felt sure of this despite their intimate proximity in the crowded room. Almost pinning her against the low room divider at her back, he looked so closely into her face she could feel his warm beery breath. Didn't he have a family to get home to?

She shook her head. "I'd love to talk with you some more but not tonight. I don't sleep well in hotel rooms, and I really want to get home. It's been a long day. Why don't you stop at the mine sometime soon?" She moved to go around him but he seemed to swell to block her path and grasped her upper arms in his large hands. The shock of his touch on her skin went through them both, making her stiffen and him forget for a moment what he was going to say.

"I don't know what you're up to," she said at length, "but I suggest you be a good boy and let me go right now."

They stood like a single carved figure for perhaps half a minute longer while McCarty went through a visible inward struggle that Neva could not begin to decode, then he let his hands slide down her arms until he gripped her right hand in his. He led her like a child through the crowd, which parted and greeted him familiarly. She intended to wrench her hand free as soon as they were outside, but they had no more stepped from the air-conditioned bar into the warm night than his cell phone rang again. To answer he had to release her, which he did without hesitation.

"McCarty. That so? Very good."

Uncertain what he would do on ringing off, Neva hooked her arm around a light pole, but rather than try to take hold of her again, he said, "Sorry if I alarmed you. I'm not used to uncooperation."

"Especially from women?"

"Especially from anybody. And I have to say you're not quite like the folks I usually deal with. The dinner invitation still stands, by the way, any day. I wouldn't mind seeing you in a dress, if you own such a thing. Have a nice evening."

Watching him walk jauntily away Neva didn't know whether to laugh or be angry. If anyone were to recount such an incident to her, she might not believe it. Sheriffs don't behave like this, even when off duty and out of uniform. Was she under suspicion for Roy DeRoos' death? Impossible. Then why the silly shenanigans? At least she had not allowed him to buffalo her into dinner and a night at the hotel.

Neva could see the back end of the sheriff's car, and waited until he pulled away before letting go of the light pole and half-running to her own car. Watching the rearview mirror to be sure she wasn't followed, she headed for a taqueria that was on the road out of town. She found a parking spot, collected her bag, and got out, but then remembered the shoebox with joy and relief. She would begin going through the papers while she waited to be served. She leaned over the driver's seat and reached for the box, but the passenger's seat was empty. In the dim light from a lamp pole halfway down the parking lot, she could see that there was nothing on the floor. Still, she went around to the other side, searched the floor, felt under the seat, and at last checked the backseat and floor even though she knew that the box could not have slid through.

The box of letters was gone as though it had never existed. It was too much, really too much. First her mother's ashes and now the precious papers. What kind of insane business had she wandered into? The shoebox had been in the car when she drove from the jail to the bar so it had to have been taken while she was with the sheriff. No real thief would take a stained old shoebox full of papers and leave a pair of binoculars and her CD player behind. Therefore, it must be another instance of the sheriff's high-handed investigation style, carried out under the weird notion that she was holding useful evidence about the murder. But was it really possible that law enforcement officers would break into her car? A week ago she would have said no. Now it seemed all too likely, and it would help explain McCarty's weird behavior. To spring the door locks and remove the papers would have required no time at all for an expert, so they must have taken the precaution of getting a search warrant. McCarty had to keep her with him until he got the call saying the job was done.

Well, he would not get away with it. Not only would he be sorry, very sorry indeed, but she was getting those papers back right now. Striding into the restaurant, she yanked open the door of the old-fashioned phone booth in the entryway and flipped angrily through the directory until she came to the M's. She checked every possible spelling of McCarty but without finding a single entry. She dialed information, which told her there was no such listing, then called the jail and got a recording. Full of rage, her face hot, she wanted to rip the receiver off its cord and beat it on the wall.

Willing herself to breathe slowly, she returned the phone to its hook and stood with her eyes closed. She would drive to the jail and demand McCarty's address. No, they would never tell her how to find the sheriff. She would go back to the bar and chat up some drunks. They all knew him, it was a small town, someone would tell her where McCarty lived, maybe the little bartender…No, no, it would never work, and she was far too tired to try outwitting anyone, even a drunk. She must make a plan tonight and return to Elkhorn in the morning, but first she needed food.

She found the bathroom, splashed cold water on her face, settled at a corner table and ordered chicken tamales. Waiting with nothing but a glass of ice water, she could think only of the papers. If the sheriff really had got a search warrant he would be unable to deny taking them and would have to return them eventually, but if her theory about McCarty's involvement was wrong, then the papers were most likely lost for good. Were the Fates really so determined to keep her from having any material mementos from her family past? If only she hadn't met the sheriff as she was leaving the law enforcement building.

With an exclamation, she snatched up her bag and pulled out the handful of papers she had taken into the jail. She kissed the small bundle, and hugged it to her.

When her emotions calmed down enough to let her read, she saw that the note on top was from Enid and was addressed to her.

Dear niece of my only real love,

Included here with other papers are some of my letters to Burtie, which I almost decided to keep but they might have ended up with you anyway had things gone differently in his life. And they'll help show you, I hope, that he was a complex, warm man because you can bet that his letters to me were in the same mode—sorry, I'm keeping those forever! I only glanced at the other things but saw enough to know they'll mean something to you. Let's do keep in touch.

Affectionately,
Your (almost) Aunt Enid

The tears Neva had struggled to control poured down her cheeks. So much loss, so much sadness…Her hands fell into her lap along with the papers while she gave in to mourning. When the tears were spent, she wiped her eyes with thin napkins from the dispenser and laid her few treasures out on the table. There were five letters from Enid, two letters from what seemed to be a military buddy, her uncle's birth certificate, and an envelope containing a handwritten note to Orson. The note was brief.

Orson, I heard it again last night and I'm almost certain my suspicion is right, as horrible as it is. It's late, so I expect you won't be back tonight as planned. I'm going up to get a closer look. If anything happens to me don't go to the law because it will just make things worse for you without helping me. You know you're sick of the mine anyway. Take what we've got, though it's little enough, thanks to me, and go make a different life for yourself. We've had some good times, haven't we? My love to Enid and her best brother, B

What affected her more than anything else was the simple letter *B* as a signature. It was her habit to sign notes to friends with a plain *N*, just as her mother had signed with a simple *F*. Orson must have found the note when he returned to the mine and discovered that Burtie was gone, but what did it mean? *I heard it again last night and I'm almost certain my suspicion is right, as horrible as it is.*

Could her uncle have heard the night truck fifteen years ago? Goose bumps rose on Neva's arms and suddenly she was aware of the overhead fans spinning too fast, washing her skin with clammy air.

The waitress set down the tamales.

"Thank you," Neva said, shivering, "but I'm feeling sick all of a sudden. Could I please have them to go?"

Chapter Twenty-eight

Gene's windows were dark when Neva arrived back on Billie Creek. She felt calmer after the long drive and the tamales, but the lack of visible life at the little cabin was disappointing. She had convinced herself that Gene would be awake, and had counted on his sympathetic ear. He had said he usually went to bed around nightfall after working in the sun all day, and while she could not see herself waking him up to cry on his shoulder, she could not immediately give up the prospect of his company. Acutely aware of the empty eight-mile road ahead, she sat in the idling car looking at the cabin and the pickup truck.

The truck was pulled in with the front bumper nearly touching the tiny porch, just as it had been when she left the note this morning. Gene must have pulled in hastily, and not moved the truck all day. Could he be ill? Injured?

Neva turned off the ignition and got out of the car. The air was warm from heat stored in the rocky ground, and the creek murmured pleasantly. She crossed the plank bridge, approached the porch, and saw her note lying undisturbed under the stone. Either Gene was inside and had simply not answered her knock this morning and not come out all day, or he had left the mine sometime before this morning without his truck. She picked up the note, stuffed it into her pocket, and stepped onto the porch. The hasp was over the staple and the padlock was secured. Had it been locked earlier? She could not remember, but at least this meant that Gene was not lying unconscious inside.

Relieved, she turned to go, but the sight of the truck stopped her again. Gene had no motorbike or other means of getting around apart from walking. Someone must have picked him up, possibly a fellow miner from some other part of the territory, or he had walked somewhere. That he might have gone up to her mine on foot in response to the dinner invitation and be waiting there at this moment struck her suddenly as the most likely explanation. On seeing her note, he had set off walking—assuming she would drive him home—and might even have prepared dinner to surprise her when she returned. It was, after all, his cabin she lived in.

The prospect of arriving home to find the lamp burning and Gene ready to hear all about her wretched day in Elkhorn lightened the drive up the canyon. As expected, her kitchen window glowed invitingly. She hurried across the dooryard but hesitated at the porch steps, struck suddenly by the improbability of finding Gene inside. He would not work all day at his mine and then walk eight miles uphill to join her for dinner.

Could it be Lance who waited inside? Or Reese?

Neva eased up the steps and across the porch to the window. The curtain was open, as she always kept it, and a lamp burned low on the table. The tableau it revealed was surprising, even beautiful. The rocking chair from the back porch had been brought in and placed by the table, and in the chair, sleeping with her mouth open and her hands in her lap, was Tillie Briggs. She looked so at home in the old-fashioned kitchen that Neva stood for some time observing her, wondering at the affection she felt for this near stranger. How could such a woman have produced a son like Tony?

Neva went into the kitchen, knelt by the chair on one knee, and said softly, "Tillie. Tillie, wake up, it's Jeneva, I'm home."

Tillie stirred, whimpered, sighed and opened her eyes. Regarding Neva without surprise, she said, "I know you're not a ghost because there's food on your cheek. Tomato, it looks like."

Raising a hand to feel for the offending salsa, Neva resisted laughing. She must think of something wonderful to send this surprising woman when she went home to the Willamette Valley, maybe a subscription to a magazine full of opulent pictures, or better yet, she would renew her subscription to that agricultural newspaper Tillie had said she could no longer afford.

"You look so peaceful I hate to wake you up."

"Must be late. I didn't mean to sleep, usually I can't sleep, but here I couldn't keep awake. It's so quiet and away from it all. I thought I heard you coming before but it must have been a varmint on the porch." Letting her head lie against the chair back and her eyes close, Tillie became again the personification of Rest Well Earned. But her eyes soon opened and were filled with distress. She sat up, turned to the table, grasped a worn burlap sack, and handed it to Neva with an effort that clearly was emotional as well as physical.

Beyond surprise by now, Neva accepted the sack, looked inside, and hugged it to her as she had held the letters scant hours ago. "Was it Tony?" she said. Tillie nodded, then shook her head in a gesture of such evident parental pain that Neva set the sack back on the table and took the old woman's hand in her own, urging, "Don't let it bother you, Tillie. The ashes are home again, that's the main thing. Thank you so very, very much. It was amazing to look in and find you here. I didn't see your car."

"I went too far. It's down the hill past the woodshed. You know, he thought it was Reese's gold. Really, I don't know what comes over men sometimes. He's been worried about losing the ranch. He's not really a bad boy, just never thought things through since he was little and was always left behind by his brothers. We taped the paper and everything back up. Nothing spilled, at least not much. I think it's a real nice idea to bury her up here in her brother's home place. You're a good daughter. I always did want a girl."

◇◇◇

"McCarty hath murdered sleep." The words slipped round and round inside Neva's head as she lay in bed exhausted but unable to turn off her thoughts. Immediately after Tillie's old pickup had climbed out of sight up the lane, she had placed the battered box of ashes back on the table, and stretched out wearily to sleep. But sleep did not come. Instead, the incidents of this disturbing day clamored in her mind for attention. Lunch with Darla seemed a very long time ago. The gift and almost immediate loss of her uncle's papers, the sheriff's game playing, the calm of Tillie Briggs waiting in her kitchen, the return of the ashes, even the departure of Gene Holland without his truck—everything was off balance and strange. Most unsettling of all was Matthew's note to Orson. What had her uncle heard on the last day or night when he was known to be alive?

Maybe Andy Sylvester was right that she should leave the mine.

Neva's face set in stubborn lines. She was not going home until she was ready. All of this was a mistake, a colossal error that would soon straighten out if she remained steady and continued to pursue her own business on Billie Creek. The immediate problem, the only problem to worry about right now, was sleep. Insomnia was an old demon that she thought she had vanquished in coming to the mine, but she might just as well be back in her house in town counting the hours until dawn, her heart pounding harder than it ever seemed to in daylight.

With an exasperated twitch, she threw off the covers, sat up on the edge of the bed, and considered what to do. Reading sometimes worked but she would not be able to focus on a book tonight. She needed to let her thoughts run on for a while yet, outdoors where the cool night would gradually chill her through. Then the warm bed would feel welcome and soothing rather than like a trap.

Without dressing or lighting a lamp, she got a cup of water from the kitchen and took it to the wicker settee. The night was particularly fine, the darkness rich and star-heavy, but she didn't feel the beauty in her usual way, as physical sensation. Struggling to remain in the present, to listen and smell and feel with the kind of acute sensory delight she had rediscovered at the mine, she only grew more frustrated. Her thoughts would not be controlled, but continued to track back time and again over recent events on the creek. What did it all mean?

At last, resignedly, she returned inside, pulled on the shorts and sleeveless shirt she had worn during the day, exchanged flip-flops for walking shoes, and set off up the lane. The quiet was so complete when she stopped at Billie Creek Road to listen that it was as though she had lost her sense of hearing. Her sense of smell, however, remained sharp. Turning up the road, she detected scent pockets of pine, cooling dust, the sweetly musty breath of night flowers. Walking with a long stride to stretch her leg muscles, she felt the weight of the day's strangeness slip away, and it seemed exactly right that she should have been pulled from her bed to experience this other face of the canyon, this night world of simplified shapes and secretive smells.

Some distance up the road she rounded a bend and walked into a different smell, a smell that made her stop to test the air with sharpened attention. Surely it was diesel exhaust. Moving ahead slowly, placing her feet with care on the rocky road, she continued for about a hundred yards without seeing anything unusual, but then the faint but distinct ring of metal striking metal made her stop again. The sound had come from the left, where a sidetrack led off the main road. Because it appeared to end within sight she had never bothered following the spur, but now, letting her feet find the way, she entered the denser darkness created by pines on one side and the canyon wall on the other. Her heart was beating harder than usual but she was not afraid. Everything has an explanation if you just possess the facts, and now, it seemed, she would at last get the facts about the mysterious truck, which must have arrived tonight before her own return to the canyon.

Rather than ending, the lane made a right turn to run parallel to Billie Creek Road, and as soon as she rounded the corner she saw the large blocky shape of the truck box. The engine wasn't running and the headlights were off. The back end was toward her, and one half of the double doors hung open to reveal a dense black interior. No longer moving, barely breathing, she listened to silence. Before reading her uncle's note, she would have assumed that whatever was going on here did not concern her beyond plain curiosity. Now she felt driven to find out what the truck was doing in the canyon at night, and whether it could have had anything to do with his disappearance.

The driver, it seemed, had gone elsewhere, no doubt to take care of whatever business it was that brought him here. Neva crept closer to the open cargo door, and stopped again to listen and test the air with her nose. It carried a musty smell, like a shut-up attic in an old house. A few more steps would take her to the door, though the interior of the truck box was so black she would have to feel with her hands to find out what, if anything, was in there.

A stone rolled on the hillside nearby, followed by the soft crunching of gravel.

Neva darted across the road and slipped over the bank, easing one leg after the other onto a rock about three feet down. Hunched out of sight below the roadbed, she listened and waited. Just enough air moved through the trees to make it impossible to tell whether there was also a stealthy movement of a different sort. After several long minutes, she half stood and peered toward the wooded hillside beyond the truck. A light flickered, vanished, flickered again. It was moving down the hillside, and soon a figure emerged from the trees.

She ducked below the bank, shrinking into a tight squat on the rock with her head on her knees and her eyes shut. Footsteps circled to the back of the truck, easy and confident, without stealth. Metal clicked against metal, there was a rummaging sound, and then came a thin whistling of the sort triggered by dull or routine jobs.

It was a normal, even friendly, sound in the dark. Neva raised her head. The random notes formed into a tune, something familiar, something ceremonious...*Here Comes the Bride*? No, no, it was something she'd heard more recently, in the last few years—*Pomp and Circumstance*! She had looked it up after Ethan's graduation. A march by Elgar, surprisingly, first played at a U.S. graduation ceremony in 1905—light flared and she drew in a breath, then pressed her hand over her mouth and stared. She had stood up again, intrigued by the whistling, and now watched in fascination as though looking at a big screen in the dark. The truck box was full of light, and silhouetted against it was the featureless shape of a man bent forward over what appeared to be a carpet roll. He dragged the roll toward him until it was half out of the truck, then grasped it by the middle.

A sudden image of her uncle filled Neva's mind. She saw him standing just as she was doing, watching a strange midnight ritual, and then, and then? Vanishing from the known world. Wrapped up in a carpet and stashed in a hole?

She sank to her heels.

"Who's there?"

Neva's foot slipped off the edge of the rock, sending smaller rocks rolling down the bank. Light stabbed overhead. She leaped down the slope, throwing up her hands to protect her face as her feet slithered and stumbled. There were trees all around. Branches caught at her hair and clothing but she did not slow down. Directly ahead was the main road, a pale line striped by dark trunks. She burst into the open, stumbled, caught her balance, and began to run. Within seconds a powerful beam of light cut the darkness to her right, and then her own shadow sprang out ahead, and again she heard a shout. The light bounced crazily as footsteps pounded the road behind her.

Neva tore through the night, her elbows and knees pumping. She had never been a runner but now she felt a strange new lightness. The breasts that used to bounce and weigh her down were gone, and the weeks of hiking had left the rest of her equally streamlined and hardened. Unhampered by extra flesh, her arms and legs bare, she sped up the road like a trained racer.

Up the road? She was running the wrong direction!

Shocked, she slowed down, but sprang ahead instantly as the light beam caught her again. She was headed up the creek toward Billie Mountain. There was no shelter, no protection, no savior ahead. There was only the empty road.

She ran along the edge, away from the ruts and potholes, feeling the shape of the canyon change as she climbed. Her mind was clear, her perspective oddly removed as though part of her floated overhead watching. Her best hope, this watching intelligence said, was that she was fit enough to outlast her pursuer, to keep out of reach until he had to stop, and then to make her way back to the cabin through the woods.

Rounding a bend, she slowed down to ease her breath, but footsteps pounded close behind and she spurted ahead again. Soon they would reach the high point of the canyon where the road curved to head back down. She couldn't run downhill in the dark, she'd trip and fall.

Her breath was raking now, and a rock had got into her left shoe.

The road turned to cross the creek and without forethought, as though driven by some external force, she pivoted sharp right and jumped into black space, aiming for the trail. Her feet sank into powdery dust. Relief swept through her, but the next instant her leg struck something hard with a violent blow. As her body catapulted forward, she flung up her arms to protect her head, crashed through branches, and fell.

For a long time she lay without moving, conscious but dazed. She thought she heard the thud of footfalls, and possibly voices. Was there more than one devil out here? Curled into a ball with her arms around her knees, she waited, her senses taking in information from the night. Trickling water, wet earth, leaves, a stone pressing into her hip, an owl, cold.

She had no idea whether ten minutes passed or two hours, but when she was ready to sit up, she moved slowly, expecting broken bones. Her left eye recognized stars, though the right eye was stuck shut, evidently with blood from a cut on her forehead. Tree shapes stood black against the sky. At her back was a high bank. She must have landed at the very edge of the trail, tripped against a rock or branch, and been hurled into the creek channel.

Scooting forward on her bottom, she shifted into a kneeling position, bent over the stream, and scooped icy water over her eye until it opened. Her fingers found the cut, which didn't seem serious. It could wait for cleaning until she found soap and warm water. Slowly she stood up, wiggled her shoulders, lifted her right foot, her left foot, tried a few steps. Everything worked as it should, and no broken ends of bones stuck out anywhere that she could feel. Her head and leg hurt in a dull, throbbing way that felt like a warning of worse to come.

The inclination to return to her cabin and bed was so powerful that she started walking downstream, but stopped after a few steps and said aloud, "No, Neva. You can't." Her pursuer couldn't know her identity but it would take no brain at all to figure out that she had come from nearby. The only safe place to go was Gran's cabin but it seemed a thousand miles away. Nonetheless, she turned in that direction and began to plod uphill. She could rest there, eat the canned food Darla kept stocked, and when she was ready, walk out to the main road and get herself to Elkhorn.

The cabin was no more than five or six miles distant, but a high, narrow ridge lay between the two creek canyons, and once she had struggled to the top her legs were so weak that going down the other side was even slower. She arrived at the cabin in late afternoon, thirsty, exhausted, her head throbbing. She fumbled for the key, dropped it, and almost fell over when she bent to pick it up. Never had a room appeared more beautiful or homelike as she stepped inside with the low sun shining in around her. Half a can of cold ravioli was all she could get down before crawling into bed with mental apologies to Gran for not cleaning up her cuts and scrapes first. Sleep came instantly, but after a while she woke up, and for the rest of the night she drifted in and out of awareness, her thoughts stumbling among the events of the past week. The only clear fact was that something strange and terrible was going on at Billie Creek and had been for years. This strong land that had given her back her own strength was being used for something secret and dreadful. The night truck was at the center of it. The truck was hauling something away from the creek that must be kept secret. Gold, it must be gold…but it could not be gold. Mining makes a terrific noise and mess, and no such operation was underway in the upper canyon.

But maybe it was not newly mined gold. Maybe an old stash had been uncovered. Her uncle's stash? But no stash would require more than fifteen years to haul away, and if the hauling had been going on in her uncle's lifetime as well, it could not have been his gold. A precious mineral other than gold? Andy Sylvester had said there was copper ore in the canyon, but this would not require a secretive operation, and he'd claimed it wasn't worth the cost of mining. On the other hand, could Sylvester be trusted? The urgency of his demands that she leave Billie Creek had made no sense from the beginning. It would make very good sense if he were involved in something that had to be kept secret…But maybe she was thinking in the wrong direction altogether. Maybe something was being brought to the creek rather than taken away. The truck had been parked roughly below the Calypso Mine. Maybe smugglers were storing illegal goods in the tunnel, though no one would go to such lengths unless it was highly profitable, and she could think of nothing that would be worth it except, maybe, toxic waste. It wouldn't be the first time a contractor had dumped poison chemicals or radioactive material in a ditch or old well to avoid the bother and expense of proper disposal.

Neva shook her head on the pillow and flinched away from the touch of a wool blanket against the cut above her eye. It did not make sense. There was no dangerous industry in Elkhorn County, and to haul waste a great distance would save no money or time. The whole idea was ludicrous.

Well, then, how about a drug operation? Methamphetamine manufacture was a big problem in Oregon, but this was exactly why it would make no sense to hide such activities in a remote and foul-smelling tunnel. All you needed was a kitchen.

Just after dawn, Neva got up purely from habit, but soon returned to bed and continued to doze until late afternoon. When at last she felt ready to be moving around, she stood out on the porch in her underwear and looked at the view that had seemed so perfect when she visited with Darla. It was still beautiful to her eyes, but not to her heart, and the sense of loss, of having been robbed of something more precious even than her uncle's papers, raised tears in her eyes. She hadn't cried from fear or from the cuts and bruises, and these tears didn't last. Before they were heavy enough to fall they were stopped by anger. She would not allow anyone to ruin her love for this high desert world, no matter what they were up to, and she would not allow fear into her life. She had to pull herself together, walk out to the road, and get help, either from Darla or Father Bernard, for she certainly would not go to the sheriff, not on her own.

Washing was the first order of business. She found a bucket under the sink, dipped water from the creek, and filled the kettle. Before building a fire in the stove she considered the likelihood that her pursuer would still be looking, and decided that it was extremely unlikely, and he certainly would not be searching Jump Creek Canyon. While the water heated, she found soap, rags, towel and washbasin, and was soon set up for a warm sponge bath on the porch. Gently, she scrubbed away the blood crusted above her eye, on her left shin where she had been struck by whatever tripped her, and on various minor scratches and scrapes. Nothing was serious, though her forehead was puffy and bruised, and her shin would be purple and yellow for many days.

Dry and clean, she searched for something to wear instead of the shorts and tank top, which were stiff with dried mud, the shorts ripped up one leg. In a cupboard that served for a closet, she found a rain jacket, two flannel shirts, a soft print dress and a bulky blue sweater. First she tried a shirt but it wasn't long enough to be of use without pants. With a second silent apology to Gran as well as Darla this time, she slipped the dress over her head. The thin old cloth was light on her skin, and mildly scented with jasmine or rose despite hanging unworn for fifteen years.

Darla, she was certain, would never put on such a garment, and must have kept it in memory of her grandmother. Buttoned up the front, with her braided leather belt around the baggy middle, it hung to just below her knees. The sweater smelled faintly of wood smoke. She draped it around her shoulders despite the warmth of the evening, and soon was sitting on the porch with sweet tea, feeling fully human again.

Had she overreacted? Had she startled her pursuer in the middle of an innocent, legitimate activity? She had turned up without warning in the night where anyone would expect to be alone, and might have been chased simply because she ran. But it wouldn't do. Even without her uncle's note she would have rejected this explanation. In any case, the next step was up to someone else. Her sole concern was to get to Angus or Elkhorn, tell the tale, and let others sort out what to do, if anything.

It was full dark when she returned inside, locked the door, drew the curtains, lit the lamp and heated stew. Glutinous and heavy, the stew tasted more like can than beef, but she dug out every scrap of it, and topped the meal off with half a stale chocolate bar. As she ate, she examined the cabin. Darla had kept it in perfect condition, and most important, she had managed to foil the packrats, which would have made short work of the two shelves of books in decorative editions and the tidy dish towels folded and ready for use by the sink. There were few knick-knacks about, and no photographs, though three faded watercolors of flowers hung near the door. They were by Gran's daughter who had died, she recalled as she studied them to see whether she could recognize the plants. One was blue penstemon, one a lily of some sort, and the other a yellow blossom she didn't know.

Below the clothes closet was a drawer that stuck at first pull. The next tug opened it enough to reveal stacked composition notebooks, the kind with pebbled covers that Neva had used years ago in school. On the third try the drawer jerked open all the way. She picked up the top notebook, opened it at random and read: *"June 18, Tuesday. Burtie brought a bouquet of the dark blue flowers I've always known as Oregon lupine but he said it's not a lupine at all. Well, live and learn."*

Without moving from her spot on the floor, Neva turned to the beginning and read the entire notebook, then opened another, and a third. She looked up with unseeing eyes, stunned and disbelieving, and yet it was most certainly true—these were journals kept by Darla's grandmother, and they were full of references to her uncle.

Simply but literately written, the diaries detailed Gran's daily life at the cabin, which had not been as solitary as Neva had understood from Darla's account. In addition to frequent references to animals, plants, weather and her own thoughts, Gran described many visits from family members, and her good friend and neighbor Burtie. Uncle Matthew, it appeared, had been expected at the cabin on specific days for lunch, which generally also involved a walk and a great deal of conversation that was summarized in the diaries.

It was like getting her stolen papers back many times over. Why had Darla not told her about the journals? Was it possible that she'd never read them?

Neva transferred a stack of the notebooks to the table by the chair and settled in to read, her own situation forgotten. The script was firm and clear, and she read until the lamp ran out of kerosene. As she lay again in the soft, old bed, she felt deep gratitude toward the woman who had lived for so many years in this cabin, who had been fond of her uncle and had prepared this extraordinary gift for a younger woman she would never know, an outsider who shared her love for the rocks, flowers, birds and wide sky. What a pleasure it would have been to join her uncle and Gran for lunch and a walk. To think that she might never have discovered the journals…She could almost feel grateful toward the night truck driver for sending her here. The ludicrous thought made her smile.

In the morning, Neva felt strong enough to leave the cabin but she wasn't ready to leave the journals. She continued to read, the stick figure that had been her uncle growing more solid and real in her mind. Every hour or so she made herself put down the notebooks and walk, never going far from the cabin but moving her body vigorously, stretching and bending. She would leave in the morning at first light, and carry only water, a lone stick of jerky she'd found in a coffee can, the rest of the chocolate bar, toilet paper and matches. And, as soon as possible, she would come back for the journals and have them copied in Elkhorn.

Having failed to find more kerosene, she settled on the porch to read after a dinner of canned chili, skimming fast to beat the fading light. She was on the final journal now, and the entry she had been bracing herself to read came sooner than expected. It was about halfway through the notebook: *"Burtie was here for lunch. I could see he was upset which really shows on him because it hardly ever happens. I made corn bread and potato soup, which he likes particularly. He was so quiet, I kept bothering him with questions until he left early, saying he had found something he couldn't figure out and he would tell me about it when he did. Now I'm as curious as the proverbial cat—I hope he hurries up!"*

Skimming the neat paragraphs, Neva hurried on through half a dozen brief entries about the weather and what was blooming in the meadow, followed by a gap of several blank pages and then: *"I haven't written in this book for weeks. I've been too sad to think or know what to write. We have lost Burtie. Just like that. Gone. Some people say he went away because he was tired of mining, but I don't believe it. He would have said goodbye. It happened when Orson was in town overnight. He came home to the mine and Burtie wasn't there and he hasn't been seen anywhere. Orson's as close-mouthed as ever. He won't tell me anything. When I asked if he knew what Burtie was so bothered about, he got upset and told me I was imagining things, just like a woman. 'Just like my sister, Enid,' he said. 'Everything set her off when we were kids. Burtie didn't like fuss.'*

"No, Burtie didn't like fuss, but he didn't like rudeness either. Going away without telling anyone would be a great rudeness. I don't know why the sheriff isn't looking harder for information. He was just about as bad as Orson when I talked to him. He acted

like I was being hysterical. Hysterical! I know some people think I'm
the crazy old lady of Billie Mountain, but I never was hysterical in
my life, maybe even when I should have been. Something terrible
has happened to Burtie, I just know it, and I can hardly sleep for
thinking he might need help."

Though many pages remained in the notebook, only a few
half-hearted entries followed. They offered no answers or hints
of answers.

The sun was not yet above the ridge when Neva left the cabin.
Soon arrived at the road that followed Jump Creek Canyon, she
paused to listen from the shelter of the trees. She was unlikely to
meet a vehicle here, where only Darla drove, as far as she knew,
but she meant to be cautious even so. The sandy road curved
out of sight in both directions. The highway lay to the left,
though how many miles distant she didn't know. She did know
that Jump Creek meandered more than Billie Creek, and flowed
about fifteen miles from the upper spring to the river. Given that
she was less than halfway down the canyon, she faced a walk of
at least eight miles by road, more if she stuck to the creek.

Clearly, she must take the road. In the unlikely event of there
being a vehicle in the canyon, she would hear it in plenty of time
to hide. She stepped out into the open and soon settled into the
familiar trail rhythm that had carried her over so many miles
in the past weeks. It was good to be walking again despite the
bruised leg, and she felt calmer and more confident with each
hour that passed. When the sun was overhead she sat on a log a
little way from the road, ate half the jerky stick and two squares
of chocolate, and sipped water from the jam jar.

Neva was tying up the jar in her sweater again when she
heard a distant hum. It sounded at first like an airplane, but the
sound swelled rapidly into the rumble of a truck. She pushed the
sweater and jar behind the log and stretched out on the ground
beside them, her heart beating against matted pine needles. The
truck soon passed by, heading downstream. In the next moment

she was on her feet and running toward the road, furious with herself for being a fool. It had to be Darla checking cows. Right now she could be sitting in safety and comfort on the way to the ranch house instead of facing hours of walking in the heat with a bruised shin and head.

The truck was out of sight by the time she reached the road. She hurried after it, thinking Darla might stop to check salt licks or fences, and sure enough the engine sound changed. She stood still to listen, and with a rush of joy realized that the vehicle had turned and was heading back up the canyon. This time, she waited in plain sight.

The truck that soon appeared was not yellow, and it was not Darla who leaned from the open side window to gape at her. It was Lance.

"Your head's bloody," he blurted.

She lifted a hand to the cut, which felt sticky. She must have scraped it again when she dropped down behind the log, though she was not aware of pain. "I had a bit of an accident, but it's nothing serious. Do you know if anyone's been looking for me?"

"What?"

"Have you noticed anyone looking for me? No, never mind. It's complicated. Have you been to the cabin? My cabin, I mean."

He nodded, shook his head, and shrugged like a small boy unsure of the meaning of the question. He smelled like sweat and wood smoke, and his gaze roved nervously, resting on her for a moment, sliding away, dropping to the ground, fixing on her again.

"Where's Reese?" she said, trying a different tack. Is he back at the mine?"

Lance nodded, this time without hesitation.

"Good." If she could get to her cabin with Lance for protection she could change her clothes, pack a few things, head out in her own car, and if necessary enlist Reese's assistance on the way. "I need some help, Lance. Could you give me a ride home and then follow me down Billie Creek Road?" At his blank look she added, "My car's acting funny. I'm not sure it will make it.

I need to pick up a few things at the cabin, then take the car to be fixed."

Car trouble was clearly within his realm of experience. He nodded and leaned to open the passenger's side door. She climbed in with a grateful smile, though marveling at how different he was from his brother. Had Reese met her on the road like this, he would have rushed up shouting, "Where the hell have you been anyway? You look like you tried to die and gave it up for a bad job." Then he would have whooped with laughter. But it wasn't important, nothing was important aside from the fact that she was in a truck in the company of a strong young man who owed her at least a small debt for the food and dog care.

"How's the pup?" she said.

"Okay."

Lance navigated through the rocks and pits with skill equal to Darla's, and with far more patience than his brother had shown. Though he gripped the wheel hard, his young profile appeared focused rather than tense. Maybe, if he could get out from under Reese's shadow, he would turn out to be interesting in his own right, with unsuspected skills and opinions about the world. Rather than attempt more conversation with him at the moment, however, Neva sank back against the warm upholstery with her eyes shut, and must have slept because in no time they were pulling into her dooryard. The sight of the familiar cabin brought such relief and delight that she said without forethought, "Thanks, Lance. But I've changed my mind. There's no need for you to wait. It's going to take me a while to get ready to leave and I'm sure the car will make it out to the highway. It is downhill all the way."

"I can wait. Nothing better to do."

"No, really. I need to eat something, and to wash properly, and then pack a few things. It could take hours. The ride was a great help."

He turned then to look at her directly. "Are you leaving? For good?"

"I don't know about for good." Had she said she was leaving the creek? She thought she'd said only that she needed to get the car fixed, but she was too tired to recall clearly. "I should probably get my cut head looked at in town, too, so I may spend the night."

"Why did you want to come out here for? What are you looking for all the time?"

"I'm not looking for anything, Lance. I just like to walk. It's been very good for my health. It must sound funny since you grew up around here, but the dry desert air and exercise are great for healing when you're sick. I was quite sick when I got here and now I'm not. It's kind of a miracle, really. Thanks again for the ride." She closed the door with a smile and waved to get him moving. He continued to look at her for a long moment before hunching forward, shoving the truck into gear, and speeding up the lane.

Neva raised a hand to touch the sticky cut on her forehead as she watched the truck vanish over the rise in a tornado of dust, and then she turned to examine her car. It appeared to be just as she'd left it, including the usual sprinkling of pine needles on the roof and hood. She fetched her keys from the bag that was hanging on the kitchen wall, started the car, and pulled up to within a few feet of the kitchen porch for easier loading. As she was passing the washbowl on the porch shelf, she glanced at the small mirror she'd hung above it and stopped in surprise. Her forehead was a worse color than her shin, bright purple right around the cut and then yellow farther out, with new blood trickling toward her eye again. No wonder Lance had looked at her strangely. She dabbed at the blood with the towel, but proper cleaning and dressing would have to wait.

Inside the cabin, she discovered nothing out of order. The comfort and familiarity of it all was deeply soothing, and as she arranged her books and papers in a duffel bag she felt more regret than urgency. How lovely it would be to build a fire, stir fry whatever vegetables remained in the cooler along with heaps of ginger and garlic, and settle in for an afternoon of writing, mainly notes about Gran and Uncle Matthew. But there was no time, and the cabin was not the sanctuary she had believed it to be.

Working fast, she wrapped the portrait in a towel and set it with Frances' ashes on the backseat of the car, then packed enough clothing for a week. She got out the one-burner camp stove, barely heated a can of curry, and ate it from the pot. Her clean clothing was laid out on the bed and she was about to pull the old dress off over her head when the screen door in the kitchen scraped open and slammed shut.

"Hello? Lance, is that you?"

The only reply was the sound of footsteps crossing the kitchen. A man appeared, a stranger—no, not a stranger. It was Darrell Guptill from the funeral home.

Her astonishment was no greater than his, and for a long moment they stared at each other without making a sound.

"You—" she said.

"What—" he said.

Again they were silent. Darrell was dressed exactly as he had been the other day when they met at the cemetery, his shirt buttoned to the collar and wrists, his chino slacks as smooth as though just pressed. His expression, however, was unrecognizable. Rather than bland, remote interest, he now registered extreme shock, far more so than she felt despite her genuine surprise.

"Darrell, hello," she said. "Now we meet on my territory. If you're collecting butterflies, the best ones are up on top, but I'm sure you know that already."

Rather than reply, he put out a hand to steady himself against the doorframe, looked at the floor, at the ceiling, anywhere but at Neva, and blew out a long breath through such narrowly parted lips that the sound was just short of a whistle.

"Are you all right?" It was hot out, and he might have walked a long way looking for butterflies. "Would you like a drink of water? I guess you couldn't know this, but I've been staying here all summer. This was my uncle's cabin years ago."

He undid the top two buttons of his shirt, took out a large white handkerchief, wiped his face, and said, "I didn't know it was you. What happened to your head?"

"I had a little accident, nothing serious."

"Where have you been?"

"Been?"

"Since you hit your head?"

Apart from extreme thinness, Darrell Guptill was of average size for a man. Thinking about the implications of his question, Neva pictured a dark silhouette against the light inside a truck box. Narrow shoulders, a stoop, and then later, a hoarse shout. A funeral home, a lumpy canvas roll, a mining tunnel—and a cemetery standing on solid rock. She sat down on the edge of the bed, clasped her hands in her lap, and said, "You chased me."

He nodded.

"Would you like to sit down?" She gestured toward the platform rocker.

He crossed to the chair and seated himself on the edge with his knees together, both feet on the floor, his head bowed.

She shifted on the bed to face him squarely. "Could we talk about it?"

He did not look up or reply.

"Would you like some coffee? I could really use a cup."

"It hurts my stomach." A slight pause, and then, raising his head to observe her with distressed eyes, he said, "Thanks anyway. What are you doing out here? People die from sun. You should wear a hat."

"I do wear a hat, sometimes at least. I came out here partly because I craved sunlight. But please explain why you chased me."

"I didn't know it was you," he said again, but this time the words came out in a mournful wail.

"It's all right. I didn't know it was you either, or I wouldn't have run. It really doesn't matter. I'm fine, and I want you to know that my time here at the mine is finished. I'm leaving for the Willamette Valley today and I won't be back. Truly. I have no particular interest in anything out here apart from the land itself, which I find very beautiful."

"Beautiful?"

"Very. It's one of the few places that's not an actual desert where you can see the bones of the earth."

"Bones!"

Neva looked away, aghast, saw no way to fix the blunder, and said with at least an appearance of calm, "Rocks, you know. Ridgelines against the sky, wonderful light. Now I really do have to get going as it's a very long drive back to Willamette."

She stood up and instantly he was on his feet as well. "You can't go."

"Ah, I see." She sat again just as before, and observed him in silence until he, too, resumed his seat. She said, "Well, here we are. You may as well tell me about the funeral business. It must be difficult in Elkhorn, with that stony ground."

He nodded.

"Is that how it all started?"

Another nod.

Neva studied Darrell's face but found little she could read there. He hadn't shaved lately, but the pale stubble was nearly invisible against his white skin. He couldn't be fifty yet, and probably not much over forty, but he had the stooped, discouraged bearing of an older man suffering hard luck. He didn't look strong enough to carry a body across a room, let alone up a rocky hill to a mine tunnel. She said with a musing air, "Is that why you started making videos, so people would be less interested in going to the cemetery and seeing the coffin go into the ground? They'd wonder why there was no actual hole."

"People don't like to see a hole," he said with sudden interest. "They used to faint sometimes. This is better for everybody. I didn't see you in a dress before."

"It's not mine, it, well, someone left it behind. The sweater, too."

"I like blue," he said as though testing a new thought.

"So do I, especially blue flowers." Wondering at her own calm, she added, "The campanula around here is the bluest I've ever seen in a flower. You must know Billie Creek pretty well, coming out here for so many years. Darrell, what happened to my uncle, Matthew Burt? You must know."

"It wasn't me that did it. I never did want to do any of it, but there wasn't anybody else to help out. You have to help your family."

"Did my uncle surprise your father the way I surprised you the other night?"

"He didn't know who it was. He never took anything off him. He left him just like he was. The others are dead already so it doesn't make any difference."

Mystified, Neva didn't know what to say. They sat in silence for some time, Darrell casting anxious glances her way in between studying the floor, while she tried to make sense of his words. An idea formed—but surely Darrell and his father didn't go that far with their appalling business?

"We're finished here," he said almost dreamily. "We're moving the operation. It's a real long drive over the pass. I've been working on it, getting ready."

"It must be hard work. Lots of heavy carrying."

"Not so heavy. We have a dryer, and sometimes it's only parts. It's been a secret my whole life, you know. I never could tell anybody. I couldn't even get married."

"That's really too bad. Secrets are rarely worth the trouble they cause, in my experience."

"I'm good at keeping secrets. I didn't tell Dad, not a word. He doesn't have to know everything."

"Didn't tell him what?"

"About you. Being out here and all over the place all the time. It would have been all right if you didn't see the truck. That's a problem."

"I didn't know it was your truck. Not until today. And I could easily forget it. I came to Billie Creek to get well and I got well and that's the whole story, as far as I'm concerned."

Darrell shook his head with a regretful air as he gazed around the room. "You made it nice here. Nobody lived here for a long time."

"Not since my uncle."

"Not since your uncle."

Again they sat in silence. It was late afternoon, and soon it would be the golden hour when the canyon was suffused with apricot light. She should be preparing dinner, writing in her journal, moving around the cabin barefoot and at ease after the day's walking.

"Are you hungry? I just ate some canned curry but it wasn't much of a dinner. I have the ingredients for a vegetable stir fry, if the vegetables haven't gone bad by now."

Darrell shook his head.

"Something to drink then? Mint tea? Hot chocolate? I really do need coffee. I'll put on water to heat while you think about what you want."

He had sat back in the chair and was rocking slightly, and this time he did not get up when she went into the kitchen. She clattered pots and talked aloud, speculating about where she might have put the sugar. There was no reaction from the other room. The rocking continued. She felt for her keys, which were still in the sweater pocket where she had dropped them after moving the car. A glance out the kitchen window told her that Darrell had parked somewhere other than the dooryard, giving her a clear shot at least as far as the rise above the house. Beyond that she could most likely drive around any vehicle parked on the lane.

Humming wordlessly, she assembled filter, drip cone, and large mug, and dropped a tea bag into a second mug. The camp stove sat on the kitchen table. She placed the pot of water on the single burner and struck a match, but did not light the gas. "I want to ride through the West where there ain't no fences," she sang. "Gaze at the moon till I lose my senses…"

She opened the screen door with one hard pull, jerking it past the sticking spot, then dashed across the porch and yanked the car door open. He was right behind her. His hand landed on her shoulder. She slipped out from under it and ran but he caught her before she was halfway to the woodshed. Struggling to break away, she felt the sweater slide down her arms. He spun her around to face him, ripping the thin dress, which split down the front.

"Oh, Jesus," he cried, dropping both hands and staring at her exposed chest with its two horizontal scars like closed eyes.

She backed away, allowing the top of her dress to gape open. Watching him, she miscalculated the distance to the chopping block, rammed her heel into it, and lost her balance. He caught her before she fell, cradling her almost gently, then pressed a cloth over her face, a nasty, acrid cloth that made her gag. She clawed at his hand, got hold of the cloth, pulled with all her strength, straining for air, for air, for air…

Chapter Twenty-nine

Déjà vu all over again…The laughter was buried and would not come up but she felt it there in the depths, prowling around like a shy fish. What a kettle of fish. It stank of fish. No, not fish. Nasty old blankets. Some people never open the windows. Someday she would build her dream house, all windows, all of them open all the time. She would fly in and out like a swallow, a pigeon, Peter Pan…*Ha*, she said, and the deck tilted violently under her—the ship was going down!

With a convulsive heave, she got up on her elbow and vomited. Damned fool. She knew better than to sail. It made her sick every time. She raised a shaky hand, wiped the spit off her chin, and snatched her hand away. It was flaming hot, it had scalded her skin. And now she smelled smoke. My God, the room was on fire with invisible flames and suffocating smoke. She had to get out. Struggling to lift her giant head, she fought against gravity, digging her fingers into the sand…But someone had cut her strings. She couldn't move her legs. Not much of a puppet show. You had to have strings to move the arms and legs, two strings each, to the knees and ankles, elbows and wrists. Working the hand strings, she found a leg, pulled it up, found another, pulled it up, felt for the blanket that had slipped off her shoulders, got it over her knees, let her head fall forward and buried her nose in it, away from the musty, suffocating air.

Her face was pressed into the blanket, the little smoky blanket. She breathed deeply. Wood smoke, sweeter than pine, most likely alder. If the fire were going she could make coffee…but there was no fire, only terrible cold and darkness. She lifted her head and looked for stars. There were no stars. She was in a vacuum, vacuum-packed like a sardine. *Ha.* She didn't even like sardines.

Time passed, time like a dripping faucet, time like a fripping daucet, time like a dipping raucet—what was wrong with her brain?

Slowly her thoughts cleared and coalesced into an idea, a terrible idea but the only one that made sense. She was not outdoors, though she was sitting on sand in the cold dark. She was in the mining tunnel. Darrell Guptill had knocked her out with something nasty and left her in the old Calypso Mine. And somewhere close by were stacks of bodies that belonged in a cemetery. She had been left deep under the earth, a living corpse among the dead.

Huddled into a ball, she buried her face in the blanket. More time passed, formless and cold, but after a bit she recognized that the small cover was not a blanket, it was Gran's smoky sweater, though there was no Gran's cabin to shelter her. There was blackness stretching endlessly, and there were bottomless holes, and bodies and pieces of bodies stacked all around. Her face was on fire, her head pounded, her stomach wanted to turn inside out. Better to have died of breast cancer out in the light and air. What if she had been offered a choice, to die two years ago or end up in a tunnel stuffed with the dead?

Roy must be here, and her uncle.

She raised her head, listening for her uncle's bones to speak. She heard no bones, but she did hear something, a small movement, a whisper, a rasp. Breathing. Something was breathing nearby.

Her own breath caught and her arms tightened around her knees. Rigid, she waited, and again heard the whisper of air, regular now, moving in and out. Some creature was sleeping not far away in the blackness. Claws, teeth, venom, what would it be that got her? Maybe it was a bat, or a whole colony of bats breathing in unison…ridiculous. A bear? Packrats to go along with the stench?

Could one of the bodies have come back to life?

A violent shudder shook her even as an internal voice commanded, Stop! Pull yourself together.

If only she had matches. She did have matches. Her hand found the sweater pocket and closed on the small box, but still she continued to sit, unable to find the courage to look at what she faced, or to expose herself in the flare of light.

And yet there was no choice. As long as she was alive and able, she would have to act. It was not possible to sit waiting for nothing while she could still breathe and think. She struck a match. It flared and died. The second burned long enough to reveal tunnel walls. With the third she lit a scrap of toilet paper and saw a sandy floor littered with sticks, that stretched about ten feet to the opposite wall. And for an instant before the weak flame died, she saw a figure curled up at the base of the wall.

Blackness returned, but the dark was different now. She knew that form. Gene Holland was here—and he was breathing. She was not alone with the corpses.

"Gene?" she said, and then, "Gene! Gene! Wake up, please, wake up, it's Neva."

She listened but heard only the regular slip of breathing, which now struck her as very weak. Her mind began to issue orders. Cross the tunnel, help him, protect the matches. The nausea and headache were tolerable now, and though her arms and legs felt rubbery they responded to commands. She slipped her arms into the sweater sleeves and fastened the buttons over the torn dress front. Hitching the skirt up, she tucked it into her underwear so it wouldn't catch under her knees, and began to crawl, her right hand curled around the matches.

Stones on the floor jabbed into her knees. She crawled and crawled. Could she have veered up or down the tunnel in her confusion?

Her hand struck something yielding. It was cloth, coarse like canvas. Crouched on her heels, she tried to open the matchbox, but her hands shook. She must not spill the matches. Willing her body to calm down, thinking of blue sky, flowering ridge tops, clear creek water, she waited in the dark. Her heartbeat slowed and the roaring in her ears ceased. A tiny snore, as though from a baby, came from just ahead.

It was Gene she had touched, not a wrapped corpse, and the light of the first match showed that his upturned cheek was darkly bruised. His upper body moved as he breathed but he did not respond when she touched his arm and spoke his name. How long had he been lying here injured, without food or water? Two days? Three? It seemed a very long time since she first noticed the pickup truck parked in the wrong spot.

Working in the dark, she took off the sweater, curled up against his back, and stretched the heavy old wool over them. The close touch of another living person, even unconscious, was such a comfort that she shuddered again, this time from relief. "Gene," she tried again. She breathed on his neck, rubbed his limp hand, and talked, intensely at first and then with quiet determination. When she ran out of real talk, she began to count, saying his name in every ten's place. Eight, nine, Gene, eleven, twelve…nineteen, Gene…At four hundred and sixty-three he stirred.

"Gene! Wake up, for God's sake, wake up," she pleaded.

He coughed, groaned, muttered wordlessly.

"Gene, you have to wake up. Come on, just do it, you can do it, you're a tough miner, we have to get out of here, come on, come on."

"Water," he whispered.

To get him upright and seated against the wall was a long, slow job but at last they huddled like lost children with the sweater over their shoulders. Through dry, swollen lips, he rasped, "Neva, there are old bodies in here."

"I know, Gene. I know. Don't talk. Save your energy."

But he could not keep silent, and with pauses between words, he said he had begun to put bits and pieces together for himself after she told him about the mystery truck. Over the years, he, too, had heard vehicles in the night, though never so often as now. He had assumed they belonged to the Barlow Mine, but with all three young miners absent, who was driving up Billie

Creek in the small hours? One night he had waited up, and followed the truck in his pickup with the lights off. He saw it turn onto the spur road, and had left his own truck to continue on foot, knowing the road ended below the Calypso Mine.

"The light was on in the back and I could see that man that did Roy's funeral. He pulled a carpet roll thing out of the truck and went away. I went to look in the truck. There was a body, an ancient woman, all shriveled up and dry."

"They dehydrate them," Neva said matter-of-factly. "Not only bodies but pieces of bodies, for easier carrying. They've been doing it for years. They can't bury them in the cemetery because it's solid rock. They're in the body parts business."

"Body parts? What in hell?"

"They can get a lot more per body if they break it up into useful bits, kind of like selling the working parts out of an old car. My newspaper ran a story last year about some funeral homes in the South that were getting thousands of dollars for every corpse."

"Jesus."

"There's a market for almost everything, even hair I think. They're called body brokers."

"Stop," he rasped, and gagged.

"Sorry. We shouldn't talk about it now."

"Right," Gene said, but after a brief silence, he mused in an almost normal voice apart from the hoarseness, "If this is true, they must've made a hell of a lot more money putting bodies into a mine than I ever made taking gold out."

"That's very funny, Gene. I'd laugh if I didn't feel so sick."

They didn't speak for some time. Neva listened to his breathing and felt the heat in his arm and leg that were pressed against her own. They were both very much alive, but without food and water, Gene might not be capable of walking, and she wouldn't last long either. Her mouth was drier than it had ever been in her life, even on the longest hikes when her water ran out early. They had no idea which direction to go, or how far away the mouth of the tunnel was, or whether it would be possible to get out through the supposed cave-in once they got there. That Darrell wouldn't have left them alive if there was a possibility they could get out was a thought that she shoved sharply away as soon as it surfaced, but Gene was thinking along the same lines.

"I don't understand why he didn't kill us," he whispered. "He must have figured there's no way out."

"I don't think he's up to actual murder. The people, bodies, he usually brings in here are already dead, and believe it or not, he's squeamish." She was recalling the look on his face when her dress ripped open. And hadn't he said he quit collecting insects because he couldn't stand pinning them?

"Squeamish! You have to be kidding. That wasn't any love tap he gave me. What about you?"

"Chloroform, I think, some nasty rag over my face. My eyes sting, my face burns, my head hurts. But I almost think I could have talked him into letting me go if I hadn't tried to run for it. I don't think he cares for the business at all. But we are getting out of here, Gene. That's a fact. And it's time we got started. We just have to figure out which way to go."

"Go? I can't even crawl."

"Well, I'm going and I'm not going alone. Do you have anything that might burn, a handkerchief or paper? All I have is a little toilet paper."

Gene twisted to reach into his back pocket, and groaned. "He must have run over me with the truck. Ah. I knew there was a reason to fool around with old engines."

He pressed an oily rag into her hand.

"I'm going for a stick," she said, and got onto her hands and knees. Working by touch, she wrapped the rag around one end of a sturdy bit of wood, just as she had done as a kid when making torches to go along with a game of make-believe. In those days the rags had been soaked in melted paraffin. Uncertain whether the oil would burn, she was triumphant when it caught on the first try, but rather than blaze it smoldered. This was enough to reveal mummy-like shapes piled up the tunnel to their right.

"Decent of him to wrap them," Gene said grimly.

"We're going that way." Neva pointed in the other direction.

Gene took several deep breaths and attempted to stand but his legs refused to hold.

"It's probably best to save your energy anyway," Neva said, trying for a reassuring tone despite her horror at going alone. "I'll explore and come back. I won't be gone long, I promise."

"That's what they all say," he lamented.

Her giggle brought a satisfied look to his swollen face, and when she said gently, "I'll be back for tea," he managed a one-sided smile.

She walked with care, watching for the pits that Darla had described, but the tunnel floor remained level and not too rocky. Each time she rounded a bend she expected to see the wall of tumbled stone and each time she was disappointed. The light from the rag had been feeble from the start and now turned so dim that she stumbled on the shadowed floor. Panicking again, thinking of the long trip back to Gene alone through solid blackness, she was about to retreat when she saw something on the ground ahead and went toward it automatically. By the time she realized it was a skeleton, a human skeleton, she was also close enough to see the shreds of clothing that clung to the bones, and a dull glint of metal. A fine chain lay draped over the arched ribs and at its end, dangling inside the ribcage, was a watch.

She dropped to her knees next to the bones, bowed her head and whispered, "Uncle Matthew. It's Jeneva."

She knelt for a long time, still and silent. The rag faded out but she didn't move. To leave her uncle now that she had found him at last was unthinkable—for fifteen years he had lain here alone in darkness—and yet to remain was impossible. She was miles under the heavy earth, miles from daylight and breezes, miles from the creeks of Billie Canyon. She must get back to Gene and go the other direction, for she now felt certain the cave-in was beyond the pile of bodies. There was no choice, she had to go, but she had lost the will.

A cry reached her, and another, the sound echoing thinly as though from miles away. Gene was alone, without matches, and now he must think she had fallen down a hole.

"I'll be back, Uncle Matthew," she whispered. "Next time I'll take you with me."

The return trip was easier than expected. She felt the way, letting her fingers slide along the wall to keep from bumping into it or becoming disoriented, and now and then she called Gene's name. When a faint response came, she shouted, "Stay there. I'm coming."

"Here, I'm here."

When she sank down next to him, he rasped, "I thought you were lost. I tried to follow."

"I'm so sorry, Gene. I found my uncle. And then the torch went out and I couldn't leave him. He's not wrapped. He's lying on the floor of the tunnel, just bones and bits of cloth. And the watch chain draped on his ribs. I'm coming back for him."

"Of course." Gene's arm went around her shoulders.

"And now we know which way to go."

"We're going together this time, Neva. If I have to crawl."

She didn't argue. Another dark foray alone was more than she could bear, and the sooner he made the trip to the entrance the better. Once on his feet with her help, he managed to walk with a hand on the wall, just as she had done, while she supported him with her left arm. In her right hand she held a stick for probing the ground ahead. Though they said nothing about it, both were braced to run into more stacks of bodies, and this made their progress all the more slow and uncertain. The pile of canvas shapes they'd seen before was now hidden by the dark, on the opposite side of the tunnel.

They rounded a bend and were hit with an acrid current of packrat stench so foul that Neva could taste it, like breathing contaminated fog that seeps into every pore and cell in the body. The musty odor of canvas-wrapped corpses seemed sweet by comparison.

"We might step in it, Gene. We'll have to look."

The pinprick of flame blinded them for an instant, and then no more than twenty feet ahead they saw tumbled stone and timbers blocking the tunnel.

"Eureka?"

"Let's hope."

They went closer. A second match revealed a rough door and trampled ground. The door was made of stone and old mine timbers cemented together, like something out of a troll's palace. Without having to discuss it, they settled Gene against the wall to conserve his strength, and then Neva felt her way to the door. Again working by touch to save matches, she pushed, pulled and tried to slide any bit of wood, stone or metal that stuck out from the surface on or near the door. Nothing moved. The whole jumbled wall might have been one solid piece forged in hell.

Focused on the search, Neva paid no attention to the scrabbling sounds coming from Gene's direction. When light suddenly flickered and then blazed, she turned to look dumbly at a fire that leaped through dry sticks.

"I guess I'm good for something," Gene said from his seat on a rock by the fire. "There's plenty of fuel in here."

"You're a genius."

Looking almost cheerful in the uneven light he managed to join her at the wall and they went over it together with minute care, concentrating on the door. It had to open, but they could find no chink, latch, device, or any indication of moving parts. More and more sticks went onto the fire, until they had cleared the tunnel floor for some distance. Gene's brief resurgence of strength was soon spent and he sank down by the fire.

"It must be locked on the other side," Neva said.

"No wonder he left us alive."

Neva soon joined him by the low flames, first sitting cross-legged and then sagging over onto her side with her head propped on her hand as she studied the tumbled stones, the heavy boards, the carelessly blobbed-on cement, every shape and shadow exaggerated by shifting shadows. The clean air of Billie Creek Canyon was no more than thirty feet distant but it had become unimaginable. The fire burned down and neither of them moved to collect more sticks. Neva's eyes slid shut and she let her heavy head sink onto her outstretched arm.

A long or short time later, she woke up but was not consciously aware of the fact, or of noticing a change. Then the word *daylight* struck her like a sound or smell. She sat up and looked at a bright streak on the tunnel wall. It was definitely daylight, a long, pale stripe of it, beaming in through a crack in the stone overhead. Her thoughts began to clear as she mentally traced the beam back up the crack to the sky that must be above, and the morning that must have dawned while they slept, casting light into their prison.

Gene lay snoring on his back. Rather than wake him, Neva got to her feet, stiffly like an old woman, and went to stand below the source of the light, resting her hand directly in the glow as though in water. The slit in the ceiling was about three feet above her head and two feet wide, and rather than sky, she saw a chute of illuminated rock that angled enough to hide the hole or fissure at the upper end. She looked down at her shadowed body, back up at the slit, and down again. She might fit.

Gene was against it at first. Still groggy, peering up like a blinking badger, he croaked, "It's way too small, Neva. I could get you up there, I think, but it's way too small. What if you got stuck?"

"I used to do this kind of thing with Ethan," she said with a fair imitation of confidence. "It's called chimneying. If I can get into the crack I can inch my way up, I'm sure."

Without another word, Gene half-squatted with his back against the tunnel wall and patted his slanting thighs, then offered his hands. She stepped onto his legs, wobbled, and grabbed for the lip of the opening. Her right fingers curled over a ridge of rock, her left found a crack in the chimney wall.

"Now step on my shoulder."

"I don't want to hurt your head." Her hands did not want to grip the rock and her arms felt like string. She could not possibly pull herself into the opening, even with Gene lifting from below.

Disregarding her protest, he said, "I'm going to push you up by the legs and then let them go one at a time. Have you got a hand-hold?"

Recalling those long-ago sessions at Smith Rock with Ethan, when his love of geology first surfaced as a passion for rock climbing, she jammed her hand harder into the crack, tearing the skin. Gene's arms went around her legs, he heaved, her head rose into the fissure followed by her shoulders. He released her left leg and she flailed wildly for an instant before her foot found the tunnel wall below the opening.

"Reach!" he barked.

Her right hand shot up the chute and scrabbled for a hold as she was shoved upward. Her right leg swung free and without thinking, she bent it, jamming her knee and foot against opposite sides of the chimney. Her hand gripped stone, her left forearm slammed flat against the vertical wall at her back—and there she was, lodged in the crack, her knee screaming, blood trickling down her wrist from her right hand. Pain, adrenaline, and then strange elation. She was not going to fall. She was strong, she had walked the ridges, swung an axe, packed water, swum every day. The rocks had hardened her and now she would use that hardness to conquer the rock.

Gene's voice came from below, but it was too weak to make out the words.

She called down, "Try to rest but don't lie in front of the door. I'm going to be opening it in a few minutes and you want to be out of the way."

Her bravado brought no response.

Above her the fissure rose for about five feet without narrowing much, but then it bent out of sight. Just in front of her eyes a two-inch crack ran up the wall to the bend. She repositioned her right leg so her foot was where her knee had been, wedged the toe of her left foot into the crack, reached as high as she could overhead and jammed her left hand into the crack as well, and straightened her legs while she pulled from above. Her back hitched up the wall. Resting between moves, she crept up the fissure until she was just below the angle, and here she stopped for a longer rest.

Sweat streaked her face and soaked what was left of the dress. How could her body continue to produce sweat when she'd had no water since yesterday? She could not afford to sweat.

When she was ready to face what lay beyond the bend, she hitched upward again until she could see. The crack sloped gently for about twenty feet to a rectangle that framed glowing white rock and a slice of bright blue sky. Warm air touched her face, and with it came the exquisite smell of sagebrush.

With new energy she pushed herself up and around the bend until she half lay on her stomach, her chin on one hand as she studied the stretch of rock that lay between her and freedom. The crack narrowed close to the top, no question about that, though it appeared to widen again above a sort of bottleneck. Even here, where she lay, the crack was smaller than in the stretch below the bend behind her. She wriggled ahead, half climbing and half scooting along on her belly, the walls closing in. Soon, unable to bend her arms or legs, or put her head back far enough to see what was coming, she lay stretched out at full length with her hands reaching ahead, feeling the way.

Her right hand gripped a rim of rock. She had reached the narrow bit. Her left hand also took hold. She pulled until her elbows hit stone, then got her elbows through, followed by her head and armpits, her torso, her waist.

Her upper half was in a narrow funnel. Ahead, almost within reach, lay the bright outdoors, though she could see little apart from an overhanging rock. Resting with her eyes closed, she breathed in the smell of sun-baked stone. Then, moving slowly as though to sneak through, she pressed her hands against the funnel sides and drew her body up. Stone encircled her hips, hugging intimately like a familiar belt. She dropped her tailbone, tilted her pelvis, lifted her left hip and then the right. The left was above the rim but the right would not follow. She strained against the grip of stone, twisting, pulling with her arms and pushing upward with the one foot she could jam against the wall below.

She could not be stuck within sight and smell of freedom— stuck like a fishbone in the stone throat of the earth. Life doesn't work this way. For several long minutes she lay still again, no longer struggling, willing her mind to be calm, to think about the shape of the stone and the shape of her body. Why couldn't she have lost her hips rather than her breasts? A nice, neat hipectomy. Darla would slide right through, and so would Gene. An inch would do it.

The rock would not change, her hips would not change, but she could get rid of the dress and cotton underwear. She should have thought of this the first time through. Reversing direction, she pushed up against the stone walls now rather than down, wiggling and shifting until her hips broke free. She backed down all the way until she was below the hole, then tilted her head back and studied the irregular barrier of stone that would not let her pass. It looked large enough. She would have bet she could get through.

Her arms were still stuck overhead but by shifting around she was able to bend them, leaving the elbows pointing up and her hands down by her shoulders. Taking hold of the dress fabric with her fingertips, she pulled first on the front and then on the back while adjusting her body to free the cloth. Slowly, it gathered into two handfuls and cleared her hips, then made a thick roll just under her armpits. Twisting like a contortionist, she got the roll up over one arm and shoulder, then the other. She was about to pull it over her head and let it drop when she pictured herself arriving back at Gene's side wearing nothing but shoes and socks. She let the dress hang from her neck like a big, rumpled bib.

The underwear was not so easy. With no way to get her hands down, she would have to use the abrasive surface of the wall to snag the elastic and drag it over her hipbones. Again and again she tried this, flattening one side of her waist against the rock and then the other, but the strong elastic refused to catch securely enough to roll over her hips. Her scraped skin burned but she barely noticed. Intent on the job, she retreated down the crack toward the bend where the rock was more irregular. Recalling one particularly sharp bit that had scraped her front, she felt for it with her foot, then lowered her body until her hips were below the protruding rock. She was just able to roll over onto her back. This made returning up the slope even slower and more difficult, but as she hoped, the elastic caught on the rock and stayed there while she inched her way up again. The material stretched down below her buttocks but the top edge remained trapped in the hollows above her hipbones, strained tight across her belly.

She lay still, afraid that any more stress on the elastic would tear it loose from the rock. After a bit, barely breathing, she edged her hips toward the left wall of the crack, tilted her pelvis slightly to get her side flat against stone, and slid upward half an inch. The elastic caught on the rough surface. Another half inch. And another.

The material cleared her left hipbone and slid several inches down toward her leg. She shifted to the right side of the chute, repeated the maneuver, and the underwear snapped down around her thighs, and slid down her legs. She kicked them off, furiously, hating them, and already turning onto her belly to wriggle back up the crack.

Again her arms, head, and torso cleared the stone lip, again her hips touched on all sides. She turned, twisted, and pulled while shoving upward from below. One hipbone scraped through and then the other, but the wide fleshy part below the bones would not clear. Resting her forehead against rock, she breathed slowly, and thought about buttocks. Skin, fat, blood vessels, muscle. The muscle she had worked so hard to strengthen was knotted with tension. Stone won't give, bone won't give, but flesh is malleable, flesh and muscle can relax, soften, change shape, and move. She was sitting on the cabin porch reading, at peace with the universe, no tension anywhere, every muscle in her body at ease, face, neck, shoulders, arms, belly, butt, a butt of Jell-O, soft, formless, yielding…she slipped through the hole, amoeba-like, boneless and flowing.

Neva lay flat with the sun on her back, her feet still in the shadow of the boulder that overhung the hole. Her body was heavy and unresponsive, but after a few minutes' rest, she struggled into a sitting position, put her arms through the sleeves of the dress, and knotted it again across her bloody chest. Was there a square inch anywhere without scrapes and cuts? All she wanted was to find water, to drink as she had never drunk before and then get in. She would swim across the pond without a second's thought.

How long had she been in the crack? Hours or minutes? She had no idea, but there was no time to spare now. Gene was still down there, alone in the dark, starving and dehydrated. She turned back to the hole to call down to him, and saw something she had missed as she heaved herself out into freedom. Sitting back a few feet from the opening, half-hidden by a large rock, was a wooden crate. There wasn't room under the overhanging boulder to stand up, and it was too painful to crawl, so she managed to scoot on her feet while crouching until she could read the label.

Dynamite?

Dynamite!

Her heart beat with sudden violence, and adrenaline worked on her system like coffee. Her thoughts cleared as she backed away and looked more carefully at the escape hole. Rocks, sticks, and sand were heaped and scattered around it. Someone had dug it out recently, had cleared the accumulated debris from the mouth of the crack. Someone was preparing it for their own purposes and without these efforts, she would not have seen daylight shining in, would not have known the crack was there.

Darrell had said they were preparing to move to a new mine closer to Elkhorn. He was getting the tunnel ready to blow up. He was going to blow it up with her and Gene inside.

"Gene!" she called down the hole, her voice hard with fury. "Gene! I'm out, I'm coming to get you."

There was no answer but she had expected none.

The dress hung on her like a tattered sarong as she set off walking downhill, her steps stiff but as rapid as she could manage. It was late morning, very still apart from the buzzards that circled overhead, and it struck her that they were directly above the fissure into the tunnel, lazing in the updraft. Horrible—but death and vultures go together. It was no fault of the birds.

The mine entrance looked just as it had the day she found it. Filling her lungs with sweet air, she wrapped her arms around her shoulders and walked in without allowing time for fear or revulsion. The cave-in was around the first bend, and enough light reached it to show the reeking mound of a packrat nest against one end of the tumbled stone wall. At the other end stood a second crate of dynamite, and above it was a line of freshly drilled holes.

She took these in with a glance, then set to work. The supposed cave-in was a masterful assemblage of tunnel debris, including rock, rusted iron spikes, roof poles, and random chunks of old metal, all fused into a solid mass with cement that she saw only because she knew it was there. The door, on the end opposite the packrat nest, was disguised as a wooden pallet embedded in a section of rubble. Timbers along both sides served as a rough doorframe, and two depressions along the left side could indicate recessed hinges. There was no evident latch, but it had to be well hidden or any wandering kid or miner might find it.

Concentrating on the right side of the door, away from the probable hinges, Neva repeated the same probing, twisting and pulling they'd attempted on the inside. Again nothing moved, even when she beat on the protrusions with a rock. At last she sank down onto her heels and fixed an angry and despairing look on the impenetrable barrier that separated her from Gene Holland, a man she barely knew but who was now the most important person on earth. She had hoped to hear some answering knocks in response to her pounding, but there was not a sound.

But there were sounds. An agitated scrabbling and squeaking came from the nest. She had stirred up the natives, it seemed—but how did the packrat stink penetrate so powerfully to the other side of the wall? Though there had been no nest over there, there were signs of rats. Rats would not come and go by way of the ceiling crack.

Neva stretched out on her belly and began feeling her way along the bottom of the wall. A foot to the right of the door a round stone protruded about six inches beyond anything else, and under it her hand discovered an opening. Without pausing for thought, she thrust her hand in and struck something hard, but even as her face tensed with pain she grasped the metal ring and pulled. There was a simple click and the door moved.

Gene lay curled on his side by the charred remains of the fire, his eyes closed. She knelt and touched his shoulder.

"Hey," he whispered.

"Sorry it took so long, but that story can wait. Can you get up?"

"No."

"Will you try?"

"No point."

"I might be able to pull you out into the fresh air."

"Just leave it open. Bring water."

"Yes, water and food. It shouldn't take long to get to the cabin and back. I'll bring the car as far as I can. You just have to hang on a little longer."

"Sure."

She kissed his bruised cheek, got to her feet, checked the stone that held the door open, and left the tunnel.

Later, she could not recall the trip back to the cabin. It was a blank, an empty spot in her mind, but she would never forget the first drink of water from the bucket on the counter. Tepid from sitting for days in the warm cabin, it was sweet syrup on her throat. She ladled water over her face and arms, letting it run onto the floor, then drank again. She stuffed raisins into her mouth by the handful. Stale crackers were next, but they stuck in her throat. She seized a can of V-8 juice, ripped off the tab and chugged it.

The cabin must be safe for the moment since she was trapped in the tunnel as far as Darrell and his father knew, but nowhere on the creek felt safe, and she was aware of every outdoor sound as she took off the dress for the last time and pulled on jeans and a T-shirt. To be properly dressed again should have been a relief, but her scratched, unwashed body shrank from the rough cloth. Had Gene not been waiting in the tunnel, nothing could have kept her out of the pond.

She put a bottle of water in a bag, added juice, prunes, and two cans of sardines, cast a regretful look around the cabin, and went out to the car. The road to the spur and the spur itself were rutted but easily passable with the wheels on the high spots. She turned around at the far end of the spur and parked facing the way out before heading uphill on foot. The mining tunnel was less than a hundred yards through the sagebrush along a well worn trail. As she climbed, her dread returned full force, but when she caught sight of the tunnel entrance she cried out with joy. "Gene!"

The miner sat propped against a rock in the sun. He lifted his right hand and splayed the first two fingers in the shape of a V.

◇◇◇

They didn't have the energy to talk much on the trip back to the cabin, though they did decide on a simple plan. They would load Neva's car with basic gear in case they had to camp, and then head for the top of the drainage and try to get the Honda down the other side of the creek to the Dry River Valley. There was no danger of meeting Darrell over there, and not much chance of meeting one of the Cotters.

"They have to be involved," Neva said. "They must work for the Guptills. When Lance left me at the cabin, he obviously knew where to find Darrell to tell him I was there. It makes me sick to say it, but I think Reese must have killed Roy. Darrell isn't up to straight murder, and Lance, well, no one would trust him with such a job."

"It's really too bad," Gene said with a mournful shake of the head. "I've always liked Reese Cotter. He's one of the few good miners under forty."

"I don't understand why they left Roy in the pit."

"Less suspicious. You can't have everybody disappearing out here. What I can't figure is why they risked putting us in the tunnel, especially you. It would have brought out the blood-hounds for sure."

"I don't understand why they bothered with me at all. I was no threat."

"They couldn't know that. The way you wandered around and asked so many questions. And you did stumble on the truck."

"It seems a long way to haul bodies."

"There aren't many good tunnels around anymore. A Guptill uncle or cousin owns a place down past Angus, so they would have known the canyon. I must be a complete idiot. It's been under my nose all these years."

Neva again pulled up as close to the cabin door as she could. Gene rested on the chopping block, keeping watch while she went inside to throw the gear together. The first thing she saw was the pot of water she'd placed on the camp stove while pretending to make coffee for Darrell. She had been too intent on food and water to notice it earlier, but now the thought of coffee made her go weak in the knees. Coffee would keep her going for hours, even if they had to leave the car and continue on foot. Moving fast, she poured more water into the pot from the jug on the counter, lit the single propane burner, and spooned grounds into the filter that was already waiting in the cone. While the water heated, she stuffed food and bedding into two boxes and set them on the kitchen porch with a wave at Gene to indicate that they were ready to load.

Her hands shook as she opened a can of milk. The smell of coffee made her stomach cramp. She should eat something solid but there was no time. Instead, she drank half the can of milk, then divided the rest between two large mugs, added plenty of sugar for energy even though she usually detested sweet coffee, and poured in the lovely, steaming brew. She drank and caffeine power spread through her like magic.

It was nearly as pleasurable watching Gene's expression when she handed him a cup. Despite the heat, he gulped half the coffee down without stopping, and then looked at her with wide-open eyes. "Damn me. I'll never take it black again."

Neva transferred two bottles of water from the porch to the car, then went back inside for a last look around. She would return, but only to collect the rest of her things. The summer at Billie Creek Mine was little more than half over but it was finished for her.

She was securing the padlock on the kitchen door when she heard a vehicle on the lane, and turned to run to Gene. As she pulled him toward the car a large pickup bounced down the road and skidded to a stop next to the woodshed. Reese was the first out, though Lance was right behind.

Striding toward them, Reese called out, "For Jesus sake, woman, where've you been? What in hell's the matter with you two? You look like the walking dead."

Speechless with shock and revulsion, Neva clutched Gene's arm. She had liked Reese in an almost maternal way, and had believed that there was some current of sympathy between them. Now he was not only a killer, he was making jokes about the horrors in the tunnel.

"What's got into you?" He sounded almost angry. "I haven't seen you since I got out. I've been up here three or four times now. You look like you've had a run-in with a cougar. What happened to his head? And your head, for that matter."

"We were just heading for the doctor in Elkhorn," Neva said in little more than a whisper. Reese was not making sense, but nothing had made sense for days.

"Well, shit, why didn't you say so. I'll move the truck."

Reese turned and that's when they saw Lance. He stood near the truck gripping a rifle, his feet planted wide, his face expressionless under the Wallowa Tractor and Irrigation cap.

"What the fuck," said Reese.

"They can't go."

"Says who?"

Lance's reply was to lower the barrel so it pointed at Neva.

"Put that thing up, you dumb shit!" Reese barked, then added in a quieter voice, "Anyway, it's her gun. What's the deal, Lance?"

"We just have to wait is all."

Speaking for the first time, Gene said, "It appears your brother is mixed up in a very bad business, Reese. We thought you were in it, too, but I'm not so sure now."

"What bad business? What have you been up to? Put that stupid rifle down and tell me what's going on here."

Lance looked at them in silence, holding the rifle steady, and when Reese started toward him, he said, "Don't."

"You're going to shoot me, are you?" Reese sounded amused. He continued to walk slowly toward his brother, talking in a low voice. Lance stepped back and shifted the rifle barrel to point at his brother's stomach.

"Don't, Lance," Neva cried. "He's your brother."

"Lance," Gene said. "Lance, I'm alive and so's Neva. Roy's dead, but the others were already dead when they went into the mine. That's nothing like shooting your own brother."

"What are you talking about? What do you mean about Roy? Lance didn't have nothing to do with that." Reese stopped and turned to look back at Gene, then faced his brother again. "Did you, Lance? Well, did you?"

Lance opened his mouth, shut it, and said nothing.

Reese, also, was silent. Neva saw the smooth brown skin of his bare shoulder and upper arm tense. He started forward again, walking with determined steps toward the level rifle barrel. Her eyes shut. She would not be able to bear this.

"Jesus," Gene said under his breath. And then, "He did it."

Neva opened her eyes. Reese and Lance stood face-to-face about a foot apart, the rifle dangling at the end of Lance's arm with the barrel down. Reese set a hand on Lance's shoulder and bowed his head.

Chapter Thirty

From the *Elkhorn Times-Standard*
July 23, 2006

Illegal Trade in Bodies
Horrifies Loved Ones

Grisly Practice Highly Lucrative,
Potential Health Threat

--When Josephine Lord died at 68 after a long bout with skin cancer, her children were advised against an open coffin because of the disfigurement.

"They said, 'You know your mother wouldn't want anyone to see her looking like that,'" recalled Agnes Lord, wiping away angry tears. "I'll never forget the disappointment. But we didn't feel we could argue with the professionals."

The "professionals" were long-time Elkhorn residents and funeral owners Lloyd and Darrell Guptill. The Lord family was just one of hundreds in the area that suffered shock and grief at the recent exposure of the truth: their loved ones were not in the graves that family members visited and graced with flowers. They had been dismembered and sold piece by piece, and what was left was dehydrated and hidden in a mining tunnel in the Blue Mountains east of Angus.

As this newspaper has reported in a series of stories over the past week, the Guptills, father and son, have for decades supplied knees, elbows, heads, toes, skin, and bone to a medical parts distributor based in San Francisco, often at a profit of thousands of dollars per body. For the first few years, the Guptills ran a proper funeral business, but when the ground under the new cemetery addition turned out to be solid bedrock, they looked for other ways to dispose of the remains.

The revelations have shaken this small community to its roots, but Elkhorn is not alone in its pain. Trafficking in body parts illegally harvested from the dead is a lucrative, underground business driven by growing demand for human bones and tissue. Over the past 19 years, more than 16,800 families have been represented in lawsuits claiming loved ones' body parts were stolen for profit. During that period, profits from the sales of thousands of suspected stolen bodies are believed to have topped $6 million (a figure based on estimates from federal and local investigators, lawsuits and public organizations such as medical universities).

Funeral home employees, crematorium operators and others with access to the recently deceased have secretly dismembered corpses, taking non-organ body parts such as knees, spines, bone and skin without the knowledge or consent of family members.

While federal law prohibits most sales of body parts, it is legal to charge fees for handling, procuring, storing and processing human tissue. Thus an entire body, parceled out and delivered to the highest bidder, can fetch from $5,000 to tens of thousands of dollars in so-called processing fees, creating a powerful incentive for illegal sales.

Tissue banks or others that "buy" material such as skin and bones from these body brokers often don't know the parts are stolen. They then provide the purloined tissue for research—or for implantation in living patients. But it's a risky business: Stolen body parts that are implanted in humans can potentially expose recipients to HIV, hepatitis and syphilis, according to the FDA, although the risk of a recipient contracting these diseases is small.

To hide the thefts from families, perpetrators may replace bones with PVC piping and sew up the bodies before funerals. The Guptill operation was unusual in that they made no attempt to restore the bodies, relying, instead, on avoiding open coffins during funeral services.

"Folks around here trusted Lloyd," Sheriff Tug McCarty said during an interview immediately following the arrests of the funeral home operators. "If he advised against viewing, few folks would argue. And if they did, there was still enough room in the old cemetery to do a proper burial. Like everybody else around here, I'm in shock. There are some things in this life that you just don't want to believe."

Agnes Lord and other members of her family want only to put the nightmare behind them. The parts of their mother that were not sold have been identified through DNA testing, along with the identities of about half of the other remains in the old Calypso Mine.

"Bodies of loved ones are important," said Lord. "This has been worse than I could ever imagine. I am a nurse and accustomed to death and bodies, even amputated limbs, but this is different. This is desecration. I just hope my family and everyone else can reach a place where we can let it go."

Chapter Thirty-one

"Reunited in death," Father Bernard intoned. "Brother and sister laid to rest at last in the land he loved…"

The words slipped through Neva's conscious mind, continuous and unsegmented, full of meaning that had little to do with language. It all felt right. Uncle Matthew's bones had been retrieved from the tunnel and there had been no question that they should be reburied at the mine. It had been just as clear that her mother's ashes should be buried with them. The brother and sister belonged here, together again at last, in the spot that Matthew had loved for thirty years and that had given Neva new energy to live.

The decision was the easy part. Making it legal had taken a lot more doing.

Skipper had urged her to bury the bones and ashes quietly, with no permission from anyone. He had returned to the creek when he heard the news story, gruffly apologetic for his fit of temper and subsequent desertion, and tried to make up for it by helping with all that followed. "You could bury them anywhere you want out here," he argued. "Nobody cares, and nobody has to know."

But she had wanted certain important people to be present, and such an event could not be kept secret. She had begun her search for the proper procedure with a visit to the Forest Service office in Elkhorn, where the desk clerk had appeared intrigued by the question.

"Well, I don't know," she said. "Let's check our list of frequently asked questions." Turning to her computer keyboard she pulled up a screen, scrolled down and read, "*The disposal of human ashes in national forests is not regulated in any way, but the disposal of human remains is prohibited.*"

Surprised that the answer had been found so easily—was it now trendy to scatter ashes in the national forest?—Neva had asked the clerk to read the rule again. After a moment's reflection, she said, "So I could scatter ashes but not bury bones?"

"That's correct, according to what it says here."

"What about very old bones?"

"No difference, I mean bones are bones, don't you think?"

"How about private property? Is it the same rule there?"

"I expect the laws for private property are different, but you'll have to check with the state on that."

Neva had called the state health and forestry departments with no success, but a funeral home assistant in La Grande had the answers as ready as though the question came up every day: "In Oregon you can bury human remains on private land but only if you go through the proper procedure to have the land declared a cemetery."

Relating this to Darla in the kitchen over lemonade, Neva had been ready to give up.

"How do you get to be a cemetery?" the rancher had asked, and on hearing that it was a matter of filing the right papers with the right offices, she had said without hesitation, "Then that's what we'll do. Maybe I'll be buried there myself someday. We didn't go through any such fuss for Gran, but then we didn't ask anybody for permission."

After considering various possible sites, they had chosen a grassy flat that Darla owned upstream from the mine. At this point the sheriff had weighed in, pulling strings to whisk Darla's cemetery request through in record time. He had already returned Neva's shoebox with apologies, not only for the "borrowing of it," as he put it, but for shanghaiing her in the bar. "I was so damn sure you'd been sucked into something and were headed for trouble," he said. "I told the boys to collect anything that might tell us what you and the Cotters were up to. When I saw what was actually in the box, well, I felt bad, let's just say that."

The hole that Neva and Gene had spent half a day digging with pick and shovel was smaller than a normal grave, just big enough for the simple wood box that held both her mother's ashes and her uncle's clustered bones. The funeral gathering, like the grave, was small but the right people were here—Enid, Darla, Gene, Skipper, McCarty, and Reese Cotter. Al Fleck also had joined them, at Darla's offhand request. "He wants to be part of the community, you know. Good for business, I guess." Neva had not been fooled, and wasn't surprised when the rancher and café owner arrived together.

She hadn't been sure Reese would show up but he had pulled in at the last minute, snatching off the blue cap and tucking in his wrinkled white shirt as he climbed out of the pickup, with Angie bounding along behind. Neva had moved over to stand next to him as Father Bernard started the service.

The service was Catholic enough for Uncle Matthew but simple and poetic enough for her atheist mother. The priest put in understanding words even for Lance and the Guptills, suggesting that clemency was to be hoped for. "As the holy Father Pachomius said, 'For it happens when good is done to a bad man he may come to some perception of the good. This is God's love, to have compassion for each other.'"

When it was done Reese faced her with a grim look that turned sad as he spoke. "That was all very nice and everything but it won't keep Lance out of prison. Or worse. The dumbshit kid. We could have quit mining in a few years and started something better with the gold."

"In the cigar box?" The incredulous words popped out before she could think.

The pain cleared from Reese's face and he said with satisfaction, "Hell, that box was just my play pieces. I've been putting gold away for years in safe deposit. You think we're all dumb shits in my family? Whatever happens, he'll get his share when he gets out. If he gets out. I guess this is as good a time as any to tell you I've decided to go traveling for a while, and that gets me to a big favor I want to ask."

His glance down at the dog was enough of a prompt for Neva. She said, "I'd be glad to keep Angie while you're gone."

"I'll be back before long. I can't stay away from working. Now I don't know about you, but I'm ready for a beer or three."

He sauntered toward the plank table spread with food and drink and fell instantly into conversation with Sheriff McCarty, all anger and suspicion between the two men apparently forgotten. Al was just beyond them helping himself to a roasted vegetable kabob. Gene and Enid sat on a log happily renewing old acquaintance, Enid in her pink overalls as Neva had requested and Gene with a bald spot around his stitches. Darla and Skipper were deep into a conversation that made Darla laugh heartily while Skipper nodded as though to say, "It's as true as I'm standing here." The rancher had honored the occasion with a new cowboy hat and crisp red bandanna. Skipper's hair was tied in a ponytail with blue cord and he wore a dark blue cotton blazer over the usual white T-shirt.

Beyond Darla and Skipper, Father Bernard stood holding a heaped plate and listening to Ethan, who gestured so broadly as he spoke that Neva expected to see the contents of his plate go flying. She had overheard them before the ceremony discussing medieval cartography—Ethan lamenting that individually crafted maps were a thing of the past, and speculating that he might have been a cartographer in an earlier era rather than a geologist—and was tempted to join them now, to stand next to her earnest son.

She was not ready to talk with anyone yet, however, and continued to watch the others. Finding her uncle's remains had at last brought doubt to an end, though it had also finished her small hope that a living ancestor survived somewhere on earth. As a family, their survival rate was not impressive.

But I have risen from the dead.

She had beaten cancer, depression, and a midnight plummet off a creek bank that could have broken her neck, but these paled next to escaping an actual grave. Buried deep in the earth and left for dead, she had refused the offer. Now here she was among friends in the sunlight, the vital blood coursing through her, the high ridges calling her to an evening hike. Resurrection, a near escape, a reprieve from Fate, whatever it might be called, it added up to something beyond mere survival.

Maybe I've turned the family luck. Maybe Ethan will live to be ninety and I'll have twelve grandchildren.

Tears arrived so suddenly that Neva ducked her head and turned away. She walked downstream a short distance and stood next to a small pool while the tears ran their course. When they were done, she wiped her eyes on her shirt. Not far away a frog sat on a limb half sunk in the water. A kingfisher swooped off a branch and streaked away toward the pond. Yellow quartz gleamed, gemlike, in the shallows. It was all gold, everything out here at Billie Creek was gold…but it was best not to describe it like this to anyone else. The funeral home scandal and her part in its conclusion had been reported all over the country, and she had already received several urgent letters from her editor demanding a personal account for the *Willamette Current*—ASAP! There was no getting out of writing an eye-witness story, but one thing she would not do is use gold as a metaphor. The mine had given her personal riches beyond all hope or expectations, but this aspect of the story was her own private stash. She would keep it tucked in her cigar box.

A shadow fell across the frog, which leaped into the water with a musical plop as Skipper came up beside her. "Well, W.T., you know how to throw a good funeral, I will say that. You should go into the body business. I hear there's a real good opening over at Elkhorn. I never knew there was so much money in not burying folks."

"Didn't you tell me one time that your former wives would like to see your skin nailed up on the wall? Looks like they'd do a lot better to sell it."

Skipper chuckled, but his amusement turned to indignation as he went on, "And think of the bucks they made on coffins, selling them over and over again. What a shitty thing to do to people. Think of the families, visiting graves and putting flowers on and so forth, and there weren't even any remains. And those poor folks that ended up getting eyes and what have you that might have been contaminated with AIDS or syphilis. What kind of person would do that? I heard there was hardly anything left of Roy. He went for $18,000 total because he was so young—sorry. I shouldn't have brought it up, but it makes me sick and there isn't much in this old world that really bothers me any more."

They watched the stream in silence until Neva said, "Did Darla tell you about her cousin who died a few years back? She said they tried to talk her out of viewing and graveside services but she insisted, so they buried him in the old part of the cemetery."

"You know, I thought you were more than a little nuts carrying your mother's ashes around, but it looks like you were on the right track."

"If the Portland funeral home actually gave me her ashes. There's no way to know. The only thing I can be certain about is my uncle's bones."

"Well, my bones tell me those are your mother's ashes we just put in the ground and you should know by now that my bones are about as smart as your nose. No, what I'm wondering about is how they thought they were going to get away with putting you and Gene in the tunnel. It's not like an old miner disappearing. This canyon would have been torn apart."

"They wouldn't have found us, not under a ton of rock. The tunnel was almost ready to blow up when he put us in there. Darrell had been working on it, to make it look natural, which is why he was out here during the day a couple of times. He watched me through binoculars, you know."

Skipper's look of disgust made her laugh. Unfazed, he said, "One good thing, you'll be a lot more careful from now on."

"What do you mean? The bad guys are all gone."

"I didn't hear that. You may think everything's hunky-dory, W.T., but I'm still more than a little griped about a couple of things. Take Gene, for instance. Why didn't he tell us he owns Billie Creek Mine? He could have told Sylvester you were working for him and saved everybody a lot of trouble."

"That was just it, he didn't want any trouble. He's already pushing the rules by never actually mining up here, and he was afraid Sylvester would get tougher with him if he made an issue out of me. You know what the rascal said? 'Anyway, it looked to me like you were enjoying the whole situation.'"

Skipper nodded, though his look remained serious despite her teasing tone. "Sounds about right. You know, I've been trying to feel sorry for Lance but it isn't easy. What I don't figure is how he sneaked out without Reese knowing about it."

"Reese told me he sleeps like road-kill, but Roy noticed. Lance told the sheriff that's why they got into a fight by the water trough. He tried to convince Roy that he was working a night job to earn extra money so he and Reese could mine for themselves, and it was a surprise for Reese. He offered to pay, but Roy said he didn't want any money, and he wasn't going to tell anyway. Lance didn't believe him. He got scared and ran off to the line shack."

"Why didn't Roy say something about that when everybody was looking for Lance?"

"McCarty thinks the poor kid believed Lance's story and didn't want to ruin the surprise."

Skipper only grunted but his meaning was clear: So the poor sucker died for being nice. See what I mean about this world?

"Lance didn't want to do it, you know. The old man came up with the bulldozer scheme."

"The world has two kinds of people, W.T. The kind that you put a gun in their hand and they stick it in a drawer and forget it's there, and the kind that shoots somebody. If you ask me, that kid was looking for trouble to get into all his life long. And by the sounds of it, doing something that was a secret from Reese would have been reason enough."

The frog had climbed out on the branch again. They watched it for a bit, and then Neva said wistfully, "It may sound ridiculous but I keep thinking how sad it is that Orson missed it all by only a few weeks. He probably wouldn't have understood that we'd found Uncle Matthew, but after all those years it seems colossally unfair."

"Sometimes life is about as fair as a rigged cockfight. It just can't be helped so I wouldn't lose any sleep over it. Anyway, I can't help thinking he knew something about the truck. I mean, there was your uncle's note, and anyway, it looks like he'd had to be deaf and stupid to miss it."

"Enid says he was nearly deaf, from the blasting they did in the early days." Neva felt a sudden urge to tell Skipper about Enid's revelations, but hesitated. She had not fully absorbed them yet herself. The two women had spent many hours together since Enid arrived two days ago to help with preparations and, as she put it, "Just be here for you and dear Burtie. And your mother, too, since I failed her once already."

"You failed my mother?"

"Now that we know what happened to Burtie, I feel free to let go of his secrets. I just wish I'd done it in time to give your mother some comfort. Your uncle had a child."

"Uncle Matthew! A child? I thought you said he was injured, he couldn't have children."

"It happened before the injury."

"Are you saying I have a cousin?"

"Had a cousin. She died years ago."

Enid had told the tale quickly and simply. The child, Su-wan, had been conceived with his local sweetheart during Burtie's service in Korea. Burtie married her as soon as they learned about the pregnancy, but she refused to leave her Korean family.

"The picture on the cabin wall?"

"Yes. I'm afraid I don't remember her name, only the child's. She was born breech and suffered brain damage. That's where Burtie's money went for years, to pay for medical treatments and care, whatever was needed. I think he really loved them both, and I'm sure he would have stayed in Korea if it hadn't been for the injury. He was in hospital here for months, you know."

"Do you know what came between him and my mother?"

"Your mother needed money for something, some emergency, and asked him for help. But he didn't have the money because of Su-wan. He should have told her why he couldn't help, but that would have been hurtful in itself because she would have found out that he had kept his marriage secret for all those years. I never did understand the secrecy, but there were areas in your uncle's life that were off limits, even to me. There was a long period after he got out of the hospital when he saw hardly anyone. He shut himself up at the mine. That was before Orson came into his life. I don't know if he told Orson everything."

"You don't know why my mother needed money so badly?"

"I hope this doesn't upset you," Enid had said gently, "but I've always assumed it had something to do with you. I don't have children, but it's the only thing I can think of that would hurt enough to cause such a break between people who clearly loved each other. Thinking someone is slighting your child could stick inside you and keep hurting for years. And it would have been all the harder for your mother to accept since as far as she knew, you were the only child. She must have thought Burtie wanted to keep his gold for himself, which is just plain sad. He never really cared about gold. It was a way to make a living quietly, out where he wasn't bothered by the world. I'm truly sorry to be the bearer of so much difficult news."

"Oh, no, Enid," she had said. "It's a relief, really. It's so much better to know. I'm just trying to think what it was that happened. It was probably when I almost died of a bacterial infection I picked up from crawling around under a rabbit coop. Dad was between jobs and we didn't have health insurance. I was in the hospital for a long time."

"We'll never know that part," Enid had said, putting an arm around Neva's shoulder. "But they're together now."

Recalling the gentle hug, Neva smiled fondly. She had gained and lost a cousin in the space of minutes, but she would have

Enid Gale in her life for a long time to come. And Skipper as well, she hoped.

"So you'll be back next year?" he said, suddenly gruff and businesslike.

"Not on Billie Creek. I'll be over in Gran's cabin. You could get the camper in as far as the trail."

"Well, I don't know, I'm pretty fond of this creek, and I expect you'll be over here to pay respects to your relations often enough."

"I expect I will. And now it's time to settle a more immediate question. When are you going to give me back my gold from the tobacco can?"

Skipper bent, picked up a stone, and examined it with an air of deep concentration.

"Well?"

He dropped the stone, put his hand in his pocket and pulled out a familiar jewelry-grade nugget. "I thought I'd make a little puzzle to liven up your stay at Billie Creek. Looks a bit stupid now, considering. Did Enid tell you?"

"Of course. She said you confessed when you two were setting up the lunch table yesterday."

A slow flush deepened the color in Skipper's weathered face. "Well, I should have known the ladies would stick together. She's some kind of gal."

As they turned back to the party, Neva said, "I swam all the way across the pond this morning."

"I thought you did that every morning."

"Not across, just around the edges. I've always been afraid of murky water where you can't see what's down there. But this morning I went early and swam right across. I may never do it again now that I'm just about ready to rejoin the world, but once felt good."

"Well, I'm glad to hear you're afraid of something, Walkie-Talkie. Even a drunk chicken shows more sense than you do sometimes. Maybe now you'll believe me that it's not a nice world."

"What do you mean? Darrell could have killed me straight out but he didn't. That's rather nice."

"I give up. But if you promise to do me a nice party like this when I get my ticket to eternity I'll leave you my camper. Then you can stay wherever you want."

"Any particular burial instructions?"

"You know, W.T., I've been thinking about that. Like I said before, I've had three wives, and any one of them would be happy to see me skinned, dead or alive, especially if they could sell the hide. But I'd just as soon pass. When you come right down to it, a body means something. Since we've got us such a nice little cemetery right here, I wouldn't mind joining the company. Who knows, maybe you'll be one of the party some-day. You wouldn't be a boring neighbor anyway. And you could make me another cake."

"Angel food?"

"Don't I wish, but I'm afraid it's way too late for that, W.T."

"Devil's food it is then."

The old artifact hunter chuckled, shook his head, started to speak, and instead bent to scratch Cayuse behind the ears.

Acknowledgments

This story is set in a real place and draws largely on actual experiences that changed my life, though not because of a murder. The power and beauty of the land healed me after a long illness just as it heals Jeneva Leopold. When I began to crave the high desert light one gray Oregon winter, I called my friend, Allen Throop, a retired expert on mined lands reclamation, and he suggested a cabin at an idle gold mine he'd visited years before near the Oregon/Idaho border. Not only did the mine heal me, it led to this mystery, so my debt to Allen is huge. Bob Kroeger, a retired longshoreman and artifact hunter, was a surprising visitor to the mine, and served as the model for Skipper Dooley. Allen and Bob have since died, though not before they read an early draft of the story. Certain ranchers and miners also were important, notably Eleanor Sullivan, who gave me her own horse to ride on the cattle drive. At first uncertain about my intentions, the local people became generous storytellers and guides.

The first to hear the mystery were Duncan Thomas and my daughter Laurel, who listened as I read the manuscript by a campfire on a later visit to the mine. They came up with the title as well as smart editorial guidance, and Duncan continued to read drafts until I became embarrassed to ask yet again. His fine ear tuned the whole manuscript. Other helpful and supportive readers include Jane McCauley Thomas, Sorche Fairbank, my agent, and my brother Scott Gilroy, who proved an indefatigable cheering section in Canada. My son Kurt, an astute reader, has remained overall encouraging for this and other writing projects.

The steadfast reassurance and sweetness of Monty Montee, a member of the Poisoned Pen Press Editorial Board, made the months of manuscript evaluation and revision not just easier but a pleasure. I also am grateful to the press' insightful editorial readers, including editor Barbara Peters; though I resisted certain suggestions at first, they turned out to be very right indeed! Thank you all. Maybe you'd like to visit me at the mine someday and pan a bit of gold? There won't be any more murders…well, one never knows for certain in gold country.

To receive a free catalog of Poisoned Pen Press titles, please contact us in one of the following ways:

Phone: 1-800-421-3976
Facsimile: 1-480-949-1707
Email: info@poisonedpenpress.com
Website: www.poisonedpenpress.com

Poisoned Pen Press
6962 E. First Ave. Ste. 103
Scottsdale, AZ 85251